Grace Before the Fall

a novel

Geri Lipschultz

Grace Before the Fall

Copyright © 2025 by Geri Lipschultz

Cover image *Carmine Street* © by Philip Henry Allen

Cover Design by Jeff Wong

First Printing: September 2025

Published by **DarkWinter Press**: www.darkwinterlit.com

ISBN: 978-1-998441-30-3

For David & Eliza
& for Felix

Advance Praise for
Grace Before the Fall

"Voices dance above a terrestrial balloon of ruin. Yet dancing voices may save the world! Gracie is a Rose in Bloom in search of love and holiness. What does it mean, what does it take, asks Geri Lipschultz's novel *Grace Before the Fall*, to live in full sincerity yet stay within the absurd, ambiguous contours of language and world–to turn the skin of the mind inside out as it learns to speak? This is a novel in bloom. In her search for salvation and meaning, Gracie Rosinbloom is an illustrious great-niece of Salinger's Holden Caulfield and Pynchon's Oedipa Maas. In short, this is an intriguing and impressive book."

James Berger is author of *The Meaning of Poems: Selected Poems (as) Poetics* and other books of poetry and scholarship.

"To read *Grace Before the Fall* is to travel through time. Geri Lipschultz has captured not only the pivotal events of the 1970s, she's also created an amazing heroine, Grace Rosinbloom, whose life and dreams magically merge to recreate what it was like to be a thirty-something-year-old woman living in New York City at that unusual time. I am reminded of Neil Young's "After the Gold Rush": "Look at mother nature on the run in the nineteen seventies." Grace is a person led by her dreams, pondering where reality ends and begins—and whether it matters. She senses the importance of what she is experiencing, yet is unsure what to do with the advice she hears from her unusual guides: "So, save the world if you can find anything worth saving." Grace knows. Everything. Everyone. Every moment."

Cornelia Guest, poet and professor.

"Geri Lipschultz is a real writer. She writes beautifully. She's a real storyteller. She leads you to water and you are very, very happy to drink there. It's hard to decide what's more compelling in her novel, its flights of imagination or its concrete grounding. The tale takes place in New York City in the seventies. You may want to slow down, word by word, in order to savor the insight and incisiveness. At any rate, you will want to read this book."

Diane Stevenson, poet

Table of Contents

FOREWORD

By John Irving

It's New York in the '80s, the summer solstice. Grace Rosinbloom is 30; a woman on a spiritual quest, seeking romance, she stumbles on activism. A civil servant, Grace has a part-time life as an underground actress; she also hides out in a serial dream, which resembles the psychedelic '60s. When her waking life begins to mirror her dream, a feminist tale turns into a nonbinary Cinderella story. Just imagine a messianic meeting of a nonbinary Cinderella with Joan D'Arc.

There's a character called PreHistory who speaks in warnings—he hints "if you knew the past like I know the past," and so on. Grace's best friend is a mime named Em. ("As she walks, Em imagines herself injected into a large needle that is shot into her lover like a serum.") When she's not miming, Em's dialogue with Grace counts as some of the most convincing dialogue among best friends I've ever read. Their closeness is so perfectly captured that what Em perceives as Grace's betrayal is among the saddest parts of the story.

Theirs is a world of men, drugs, guns, and each other—a world Grace tries to wrest herself from, only to be pulled in. Her unwitting exposure to a government file leads to a more treacherous undertaking—one she must conceal. At the same time, she finds the love of her life—a man Em has already claimed for herself. Despite the danger, it's the pursuit that drives Grace. Persistent dream entities break through Grace's fourth wall, which she perceives as proof of the importance of the efficacy of her mission.

Geri Lipschultz was my student in the fiction workshop at Iowa in 1974; she was 23, I was 32. In that workshop, I remember her reading aloud to the class—a strange, obsessive-compulsive story titled "The Mouse." A woman is afraid of being molested—by a mouse, as the story turns out. Geri does weirdness well. That was a great fiction workshop; Jane Smiley and Allan Gurganus were students in that same class.

In 1982, I read Geri's first novel in manuscript. That was this novel—the same storyline, the same characters—with a different title. I wrote Geri about her novel at the time; I recommended some agents. This was when I first met the character named Em, a mime in a New York club. Geri's mime named Em must have gotten into my head, because—40 years later—I created a very different character in *The Last Chairlift* (2022), but my Em (a nonspeaking pantomimist) owes a big debt to Geri, whose mime named Em came first and never went away. (Thank you, Geri.)

Geri is a former writing student who's become a good friend. We've been reading each other's writing, and sending each other photos of our children, for a very long time. It's a mystery to me why *Grace Before the Fall* hasn't been published before now. Geri's characters will get into your head, like her Em got into mine. Just imagine magical realism meets *Alice in Wonderland,* and have a good time.

John Irving's sixteenth novel, *Queen Esther,* will be published by Simon & Schuster on Nov. 4, 2025.

"And God prepared a worm..."
Bk of *Jonah*

Chapter 1

There must be a sign she will recognize. Like a nut from a tree, something edible if bitter. Palpable as an acorn, splayed open and bitten up after the business of a squirrel. Or even a worm, the smell of worms after rain, their desiccated bodies offered up on the streets of her New Jersey childhood, poor worms, poor acorns.

She is on a mission for love. Through dreams he is calling her. She saw his face. Not necessarily handsome but marked. A sign sufficient to sting her into sudden recognition.

You will know you wi—wi-will know.

That buzzing again, and her hands again sliding down her hair, again finding no bug.

Andrew was the first and so almost the one. Andrew who once ate a worm. And she—she ate an acorn. She'd confessed. Couples do that, share their private histories, their private scorns. But Andrew was not the right somebody because all he wanted was babies, and it isn't that she didn't want babies, but she didn't want *just* babies. There has to be more than a nice house with kitchen cabinets and sofas and televisions till your eyelids cracked. Such old thoughts going round and round in the window of a washing machine.

Late night newspapers, she's caught their headlines. "Hostages," it says. "Khomeini," it says. Should she hate him, the Ayatollah? His sad face draped in robes, his beard long. Is he a grandfather? Does he touch women? Do his fingers press to feel the pulse? Someone should soften him up. We don't even know him, but we hate him. *Not good to huh-huh-huh-hate.* Of course. Too much is dangerous.

1

On the television, she has seen them paraded about, walking in a line, to prove they are alive and well. The hostages. But do they have enough food and water? Don't they miss their beloveds? A failed attempt, eight people killed trying, helicopters. But what about talking? President Carter—he tells the truth, but people call him weak for it. She voted for him, and he won. But he may not win next time. Carter, his face so serious, his eyes hooded. These men making all the decisions for a planet. Something they know and won't tell. This thought, war. Makes for longer strides. Hers are cross country legs, muscled, tight, and long, good for a track team, for the long haul, not for short spurts. These shoes are not for running.

Grace walks. A large circle it will be, her heels sticking in between large, wooden, gray, weathered slabs. Now she's turning back, leaving couples kissing on the pier, returning to the more commercial part of town where, if you go far enough, you will find the bars.

On Bleecker, crossing Seventh, she acknowledges her own building—a smile, her eyes taking in the half-light of evening, and looking up at etchings, remnants of pink strewn across the sky like jacks flung onto a sidewalk.

Lay-lay-later.

Her eyes rest upon fruit stands with gourds overflowing. It is almost the entrance of summer. Her thoughts waterfall, about Jonah and the gourd plant and the inevitable crimson worm. Jonah stopped a war, although he didn't want to. He stopped it, and it never happened. A war. She can feel it. The whole city can. It's there, this feeling. A feeling of before. Hard to spot, but easy to feel. Stem, too. They've talked. Em—she can't really talk to Em about it. Nor Breanda, her officemate, either. Breanda always thinking about her baby, her baby-to-be. And Em thinking about darkness, her love-affair with darkness. And why oh why did she sleep with Em's prince of darkness? For love? What was she thinking? No. But nevermore. Promised.

I promise you, street, my beloved street taking me from west to east.

2

Now passing the closed-up bakery and the closed-up cheese store and the darkened church on Carmine Street. You could make love in a pew or under a pew or on the altar with all that velvet. All so elaborately dark with that cross, with that blood dripping down. But never again with the wrong somebody.

Can't recall how it happened, cannot let it happen again.

Nevermore.

Crossing the wide Avenue of Americas, heading uptown, north, and toward MacDougal. Hearing the acoustic licks from one musical cave after another, turning her head to the opened door of *Sound City*, and walking on past the brick facades and the beckoning of the Park with its arch, that grand copy of the one in Paris, which itself was a copy of the one in Rome—there before Dylan gave it a branding. Now she makes her turn to go south again. And looks up into the fire escapes where others like her are sitting, taking in the night with its crescent moon.

Grace passes closed-up jewelry shops, restaurants with spice and enticing oils and espresso shops, with odors escaping from windows and door jambs, with the tinny riffs of radio, and something live, as well, and then she turns the corner to go east once more. The desire for something liquid, because what if the love she is looking for is harbored in one of the many ships sailing on Bleecker Street.

Un-li-li-likely.

She stands, a silhouette of considerable height, before the huge door of *Meows* that appears cider-colored in the mix of moonlight and man's light. The steps she takes weave her through a measured darkness, from the brass and wood of the bar to a cushioned perching place. She negotiates, then imbibes quickly, enjoying, if just for a fraction of a second, the sensation on her lips.

A sign you must look for, or does a sign find you?

A no man's land.

And she's back on the street looking up at a blank sky, just that crescent with its laughter.

At her own threshold, Grace looks down at shoes that will never recover. Not to mention her feet. She turns the brass knob with her right hand, opening the large glass door to her entryway. With the bulge of keys already in her left hand, she clicks that lock, pulls off the shoes, and runs barefoot up three flights to undo her own door. First, she dumps the shoes down the incinerator.

And then sleep. In her own house, her own bed. And night-time. The time to sleep.

Night-time. Perchance to dream.

"Just Grace?"
"Yes."
"First name Grace?"
"Yes."
"Last name Grace?"
"Yes."
"Grace Grace?"
"No."
"Just Grace."
"Yes."
"What kind of a name is that?"
"Pardon?"
"What nationality are you?"
"American."
"Before that?"
"I can't swear on my former lives."
"Your parents?"
"Of Russian and Polish extraction—Jews."
"Are they alive?"
"My mother lives."

4

"Age?"

"Gee, I don't know my mother's—"

"Your age."

"Thirty."

"Sisters, brothers?"

"Yes."

"Aunts, uncles, grandparents, cousins, etc.?"

"Naturally, some no longer in life."

"I'm sorry."

"They're not."

"Have you ever been married?"

"Not in this life."

"Do you engage in normal sexual play?"

"Normally."

"Presently?"

"Not at this precise moment."

"Do you engage in any of the deviations upon which if you'd like I shall be glad to elaborate?"

"No comment."

"Fine. With steady boyfriend?"

"Only in my mind."

A nondescript white-jacketed, panted, shirted, socked, shoed, and hatted man in her dream. His face falls, and he says, "In this case, we might consider sending you on to the fantasy expert promiscuity ward."

Grace asks, "Have I lost my chance?"

"Not entirely. Let's see. Another question, delicate."

"Fire."

"Have you ever experienced, ah—?"

"Orgasm? I have never not, sir."

"Wonderful." Glee dances in his little eyes, and beads of sweat hang over them. "My dear, all is not yet lost."

5

"Terrific."

"I take it you've indulged in the art of self-manipulation?"

"I've mastered it." She cooperates with appendages and tentacles of a vast monitoring machine. Its electrode flowers on her forehead, back of neck, tits, arms, wrists, hands, underarms, up her spine and down to some secret hiding places between her toes and lower lips.

"Now begins my recitation," the man in white continues. He points to the sprawling metal and plastic humming mass. "You or Dickie-Doo will stop me if you have any 'Yes' responses. First, I'll tell you since no doubt a thought looms in your mind, frames the question, 'how does my body know yes from no?' Suffice it to say, my dear girl, it does. It does, indeed it does, although, thank the Lord, you shall tell no one of my gratitude, which they say is unprofessional. You see, I can swear you to secrecy in the presence of Dickie-Doo. I can confess my very own bizarre self. I like you Grace-just-Grace. So now tell me true: do you hate Mom in thought, word or deed? Did you in mind or body sleep with Dad, sodomize with Sis, castrate or in any way fondle or otherwise conjoin with brothers, dogs, tigers, pigs, sheep or other animal, vegetable, mineral. On the lighter dry side, have you, again, in meditation or action, performed the act of murder, theft, gross lying, cheating, either malicious or benign, any and all counts, for reasons religious and temporal? Any leanings extreme, atheistic, anarchistic? Have you perchance seriously contemplated and/or attempted the foolish, cowardly sin, or shall we say act of suicide? Have you entertained the notion of, or actually attempted, engaged in the art of… drugs—shot, snorted, swallowed, smoked—Ah ha! Naturally, no one of your generation escapes. Let me guess, and we might let this go. Has your curiosity for marijuana exceeded the limits of experimentation? Fine. Your alcohol intake—oh, even before the question is asked. Do we have here a sixties alcoholic, Dickie-Doo? No. Wonderful, but you are advised to consider the matter. Return return return all bottles.

Bottles? Ah, we are fading fading fading—*ah chooo*! Soon to recover and here I am again," the man in white says. His face in sneeze has surely undergone a marked color change, from salmon to green to gray, to white, and now up he perks, back in the pink again. "OK," he resumes, picking up a scribbled page. "Just a few more routine considerations: says here you are a Ph.D. from a league of ivy; interdisciplinary humanities; thesis incomplete—subject: 'salvation of man in his technology suit'; floundering presently in civil service; desired position in life—revolutionary, comedian, saint, spy, ranger, courtesan; conflicts normal—seeks love, profuse pleasure, hope, lucid meaning; finds humor saving grace, in addition to fleeting glimpses of great Other, notably in Spring and Fall, melting mountain gushes, dying spectral burst of maple leaves, horizons, a grain of sand and accompanying ocean break of shore, animal kingdom in flight and roar, rush of still light in the Milky Way, smell of rain, glisten of dew, all things of nature's divine and lovely ilk save you. Next."

Like an item on the factory line, she is dollied along. The next stage of her examination is entirely physical. Although de-frocked, she tries to remain poised, while prone as a mummy, with only a sheet between her fair, slim, supple self and the herd of men in white, who are in terrible juxtaposition, dressed to the gills. Only their eyeballs can be seen. Drugged with all kinds of wonders, she is, to provide her with a certain immobility and apparent numbness, actually a failure of the brain to discriminate between pleasure and pain. Grace, free to register sensation, sans physical judgment.

"A spanking beaut." One specialist gives a rapid pull of the sheet.

"I'd have to agree, Fred." A second specialist.

"Say, Charley,"—a third, "haven't seen such firm ones in the last hundred or so."

"I don't know, Bud." Fourth.

"You never do, Jooper." The fifth chuckles.

7

"Not too big, not too small." Fred.

"Nice 'n tight." Charley.

"Same down at this end." It is the one not identified, not named by his associates. "Don't you agree, Joop?"

"Plenty of room as far as I'm concerned."

"Speaking of room," says Fred. "Do you think I could bring a few more friends tonight? It's at your house tonight, right Rog?"

"Yes." Rog's head within centimeters of Grace's poor vulva. "'Tis."

"Don't forget the gin." Joop.

"Who brings the chips?" Fred.

Rog raises his head, "Forgot to tell you. I've got all the equipment."

"How many decks?" Charley is worried.

Rog assures him he's got cards. "Just make sure you all bring the food and drink. Bring as many friends as you'd like."

"Nice guy," says Bud. "You know, she's got a strange face."

It's Joop who comes to her defense. "I think she's sweet."

"Well, as I said to begin with," says Fred. "She's a fine specimen and one of the finest. I vote to call in the big guy."

Even in the dream, she knows what this means. The big guy—voted in. Perhaps later she will ponder why it is that this occurs just as her alarm goes off, which it does at the precise moment that he arrives, this long white-robed beast. And his eyes, even behind the white mask, reveal a light that rings like a bell.

This light in his eyes—it's the sign. The sign that it's him.

Her roused lungs and vocal cords offer a series of shrieks and moans in varying decibels as she drags herself through her morning ritual.

*

8

Confronting Grace Rosinbloom—a large sky, brilliant with sun. Nor does she lack for words to offer the equally bewildered, but for the most part reciprocal, world at large.

"Hey yourself." The moody Breanda mumbling in the cubicle, her watchful ear attending the clicker ring of approaching bicycle spoke wheels and sneaker steps.

"Hello," Grace says, following the "Hey," she first offered.

"You're late, Grace." Breanda's eyes knit, forming a wrinkly bulge, dividing her brow in two.

"Not only do I acknowledge, but I warmly welcome your existence. And you pronounce cruel, harsh judgment upon me—on the basis of circumstantial evidence." Grace angling the bike into its parking location between file cabinets, behind a door, fiddling.

"I'm a first-hand witness." Breanda persists, the conflict sudden, at odds with the smile in her eye, that relaxes the pucker on her brow. "On the basis of fact, a thing we presently have in abundance." She points to the ever-increasing folds of printout as a terminal quacks silently away into anything but oblivion.

"OK, I'm game, lotsa work," Grace says. "But one day before I die, remind me to tell you what I think of fact."

"It's a fact that I'm pregnant, right?"

"Facts, too, are inventions," Grace says, still puttering with her bike. "It's a long argument. It's like a geometric proof. It takes time."

"You don't agree?" Breanda patting her very big tummy.

"I'd say it was a fact you've got a bug up your butt."

"It must be contagious."

Grace joins her, as they sort out the coded data for computer entry. "I had a hard night last night."

"Me, too."

A fresh breeze brings Walford in seersucker cotton and bearing gifts of coffee. He smiles with news that he and Tina will be moving

9

their desks so that the windowless room might be reserved entirely for the team of researchers and terminals.

The two girls eye each other.

"Oh great." The words come from Breanda.

"A place of our own." It's Grace, this time, slouching toward diplomacy, for the express benefit of Tina who is standing two steps back from the door.

Tina's cue. "We hardly need you to help us move, so you girls can keep going updating the new building list."

"Oh, terrific." Breanda does not budge from her self-made lounge, complete with trashcan hassock and reclining swivel chair. "When is the eviction slated to take place?"

"Lunchtime," Walford says, with the kind of grin that rings false. "So, feel free to take a long one."

"Meanwhile, we're at meetings." Tina's eyes the dullest blue on or off the planet. "So have fun."

"I wonder," Breanda says. "Wonder what's up."

"Think I'll have a talk with Walpho after five," Grace says. "Definitely seems as though the regime has spoken. So, tell me why you had a bad night."

"Money, what else?"

"What about big Richie big lawyer big money?"

"Forget big money. We had a huge fight, and I know it's my fault. Just that baby is going to be reality in less than a month, and we don't have the bread."

"Wait a few days till we see what this regime's up to, and then we'll ask for raises, you know—substantial. Also, when I talk to Walpho—"

"Yeah, yeah, yeah," Breanda says, having finished dialing up for connection and hearing the telephone siren indicating time to plug receiver into the terminal and jump into their favorite system.

"I will."

Breanda nods, and they began tapping and speaking. For a time, it is Grace who reads the changes and Breanda types them in. Then they reverse.

"So, did you dream the dream?"

"Yup."

"Summarize it if you can." Breanda takes a swift glance at her watch.

"Last night they tested my sexual, ethical, and physical. Probably next is intellectual, maybe spiritual."

"How'd you fare?"

"I'm a perfect specimen. They said so."

"Don't forget who's doing the dreaming."

"Well, at least I've got a good self-image."

"Wait till your belly starts growing." Breanda's chuckle does not belie her earnestness.

"Anyway," Grace continues. "I woke up screaming, some kind of torture, and man, these doctors with their powers. I mean everything was incredibly vivid, in such detail. Parts of it were funny, but parts of it were terrifying, when I think about it."

"I hesitated to say this at first," Breanda begins, "but maybe you should go tell this to a shrink."

"A shrink! Breanda, this is a message from the gods!"

"But really, if it's, you know, an obsession..."

"This dream points to my purpose. A contribution I can make."

"Well, of course you can have a baby. I mean if I can have a baby, why can't you?"

"I mean it's something I should do in the world, you know! But, what can we do?"

"What exactly are you saying?"

"I mean should we just learn to cope and ignore the horror? I mean milk it for our own little ends, while the whole world falls relentlessly down."

"How do you go from the dream to an idea like this?"

"If you take it symbolically, this is what my dream predicts," Grace says.

"Symbolically?" Breanda looks down at her belly—and then she looks up and smiles. "This is not a symbol. This is what I call a fact."

"In my case, it's a symbol."

"You mean motherhood itself isn't sufficient for you?"

"Not saying that."

"What are you saying, then?"

"The dream signals hope for me, Breanda, don't you see? It's like my future, like prophecy!"

"But you can't live in a dream world."

"Better to live in the real nightmare?"

"But what can we do?"

"Our work."

The managers who have been strolling in and out of meetings now appear at the doorway, their manner of announcing lunchtime.

"Take at least two hours," Tina says. "Unless you want to help."

"Oh, is it that time?" Grace says, speeding up, squaring off piles of pre- and post- input and then signing off.

"Oh, is it that time," Breanda says. "Such innocence."

They make their rounds, from the women's room to the elevator, exchanging grunts and groans and giggles, and finally silence as they reach the sweltering sidewalks already humming with passengers and vendors and those grabbing a bite enroute to secret caves of pleasure.

Like a magnet drawing out insensible filaments, a mournful trumpeter delivers up the blues, heralding that time when lunch hour strikes the southern tip of Manhattan Island. There they are, Grace and Breanda, making a steady path through crowds, past beckoning storefronts displaying their gaudy wares, stuffs spun out of petroleum into orange food, purple clothing, and self-activating gadgets. They walk by newspaper headlines proclaiming "Horror Story Slasher Strikes Again". Wafting through almost as palpable as kites, the smells of shish kabob and leather mixed with the rising stench of grime vapor, cigarette smoke from walkers, coffee breath, not morning yawning, but a breath already wakened into talk. The air is saturated with an orchestra of human burbling, an emotion garbled in adult fashion, for they are free, set free, a free-for-all, the great hour recess from work.

Breanda bites her tongue on a certain desire to pause, the thing for which Grace lacks all patience. With just a stop at Fulton Mart for health-food sandwich, juice and cookie, onward they walk, to their destination—the pier.

"It's going to be hot." Breanda grumbling again as her sandaled feet touch upon the wooden walk.

"I'm sure you're right."

"It's already hot."

"That's true."

"You think we'll get a seat?"

"I'll get you one." Grace makes a dash to the very edge, by the milky river where there are actual rows of connected metal seats nailed to the wood, along with logs and a wooden platform, where people find a place to settle. Grace turns toward the general expanse of the pier, her eye on Breanda plodding, making her way past a thousand daydreaming men in business suits who are consuming roast beef, or obsessively stirring their fruited yogurt, or just soaking up the sun, watching the sky, the water, each other. She turns once more, facing

13

the East Riverbed of ships, cruisers, and row, motor, and tugboats making passing distinction between Breanda's Brooklyn and Grace's Manhattan.

Chomping on tuna and egg-salad, while sitting on the log and chair respectively, Grace and Breanda gaze outward and inward. Perhaps their silent thoughts join those of all the other members of the financial district, hovering at least fifty stories up like the gulls perched on masts of ancient boats.

Suddenly Breanda points out the famous couple, the mousy assistant-commissioner Kreitz, and his gorgeous administrative assistant, Zabrina Roos, with her long dark glossy body and Rapunzel hair. Breanda notes that here is a woman unafraid to display in public what she can do in private. But it is apparent that Kreitz does not like to be seen clinging.

"Makes you just wonder," she says.

"I bet there's a way that floors and desks and swivel chairs can be pretty sexy."

"With whom is the question?"

"Well," Grace says, with a nod at a lone fellow staring blankly into the waves. "Take that young banker, certainly International creases, adorned in all cotton and leather; surely his breath is sweet and his armpits dry."

"No thank you," Breanda says, turning her mouth down.

"Take that man with the red beard," she says. "His eyes spark, his thoughts perhaps not so lofty as the man who thinks of money—but perhaps within the penumbra of his mind, he sees where we're going." Grace walks up to him, hands him half of her tuna sandwich.

"Nice of you," Breanda says.

"His is the face of hunger," Grace says. "It is a face I know."

Breanda offers Grace the half of her egg salad.

"Ah, my hunger is of a different sort," she says, refusing.

"This is not much of a choice," Breanda says.

14

"When I find him," Grace says, "I'll know."

"I suppose."

"And yes," Grace says. "He, too, may be a metaphor."

"For what, dear Grace?" Breanda says.

"Purpose," Grace says.

"I don't like either of these choices," Breanda says. "But I suppose over the red-beard, I'd take the banker."

"Yes, here we have the Renaissance man, but I wish to be the Renaissance woman."

"You are, Grace. You are."

"Not yet. For a woman to be a Renaissance woman, she has to either have her man—or be dead. You say I should take the banker...."

"I was joking—neither is right. One is too slimy, the other too dirty."

"But, my dear, the pickings are so slim. Everyone who is anyone serves the city, money, or the sea. Now, we take this docile-appearing, though certainly corrupted random sample of humanity, and imagine his oh-so-straights quivering at the database of his feet, flowing like cash over his investment shoes and stockings. His clean pressed white Carter's or pinstriped boxer shorts down at his shins, as his tiny dawning pink jack sprouts giant, greeting you in the middle of a computer run."

"Disgusting." Breanda is laughing so hard that the world can both see and smell the mayonnaise between her teeth.

"You don't like him?"

"You like him?"

"Who, my green pinkie?" Grace says. "Actually, I do," and she fixes her eyes into the distance at the blond banker whose face seems abandoned to the water. "Sure, why not?"

"You know him?"

"I'm sure I've seen him here before. Shall I go ask him which way is Brooklyn?"

15

"Think he'd know?"

"Yup. I think he'd know every significant line of history, a Renaissance man he'd be, with a way with words and nature, possessing knowledge of every sort of music, science, or art. He chooses banking because of its innate goodness—power to feed and clothe the world, to heal the sick and make peace between nations. An economist, social reformer, just playing the game in order to be there when the world changes hands, when it's taken away from those who wish to destroy all beauty, spread hate and terror, control all information, making every little Tom, Dick, and Harriet despise their rotten lives. Listen—this little mortal—you wait and see—we've gotta make this world safe for your baby. There must be a secret password between those of like minds, you know. Maybe it's, 'Do you know the way to Brooklyn?' I mean, why not?"

"Anything is possible."

"Precisely. Like the way we get into the computer, the secret nonsense password. Piece of pie. If I could just think of the perfect thing to say, I would approach anyone under the sun, you know?"

"I bet he would know the way to Brooklyn," Breanda says. "But the question is, would he know a city from a non-city building?"

"Even a rat knows that, speaking of which—" as one scurries out of sight. "Oh Lord," Grace exclaims. "What a world. So rich in life. Tell you what. If he passes, I'll say hello."

Which she does, as the passing gentleman smiles, walks.

"Do you know the way to Brooklyn?" she asks.

He walks faster.

She follows him. "And might you be the Renaissance man?" she asks.

He keeps walking.

"Rasputin in disguise, then?" she says, following.

He turns a corner, and so does she.

16

"Your aspirations, sir," she says, "I need to know—will you share, please sir."

He's running, and she's turning back.

"I know the way to Brooklyn," the red beard says, having taken an interest. "And I aspire to feed, but I fear instead," the red beard says.

"You fear?" Grace says.

"I fear that we shall all be taken hostage."

"I will save you," Grace says.

"And who will save you?" he says, bowing.

She is without an answer.

"What I know," the red beard says as they part ways, "is that you might need saving more than I."

"Many thanks, sir," she says, returning to Breanda, and they sit there eating, drinking, without speech.

"Red beard passed the test," Grace says, after a while.

"What were you two talking about.?"

"Peace," Grace says. "He had a light around him, it seemed."

"A light. And the banker? Did he have no twinkle?"

"Just the sun." Grace looks off into the gothic gateways of the Brooklyn Bridge.

"You mean he failed the test?"

"He didn't stop, did he?" They sigh, collect the remains, scavenge for a garbage can.

"You want to go?" Breanda says. "It's too hot for me."

"Sure, why not?"

"Seems like Kreitz and Zabrina left awfully fast."

"Maybe they were hot, too."

Upon their return to the department, the duo are directed to the conference room to code up some more changes for inputting, while Walford and Tina complete finishing touches on their new little home away from home across the hall.

Grace stands at the windows, shut to preserve the effect of the air conditioning. She opens a window and peers out in the various directions.

"What'cha looking at?"

"You know?" On Grace's face, a pale glimmer of revelation. "You can only jump out a window once."

"Astute."

"Maybe I should be a saint."

"You can't be a saint." By this time, Breanda is herself quite comfortable at work at the conference table, and, except for the look in her friend's eye, would—and rather disagreeably, at that—announce that she wants the window shut.

"Why not?" Grace says, her full chest, neck, and head extended out into Maiden Lane, so she can see the masts and sitting gulls and Brooklyn, too, not to mention the fellows with their binoculars in the building directly across.

"You always have to be thinking about other people," Breanda says. "It could be a drag."

"So, I don't mind. I could save them."

"Well," Breanda muses. "It could be nice…"

"Because you could have visions?"

"For the one being saved," Breanda says.

Grace sees a fly flitting about, watches it grow—not into a seagull but a crow.

"Seems like you already have visions," Breanda says, watching Grace.

"And think of the miracles," Grace says, her eyes on that very sliver of a moon she had prayed to as it turns into the smile of a man, and not just any man but the man with the red beard.

"True," Breanda says. "Whose patron would you want to be?"

"I think the spots are all taken up." It's that smile, how it's growing into a man, a moving image, by way of the filaments of the clouds. She's both mesmerized and wondering if she's lost her mind.

"Something modern," Breanda says.

"Yes."

"Like outer space?"

"Yes."

"You could be the patron saint of space."

"Spacepeace," Grace says, closing all the windows, and then with a meek look, she throws her arms around Breanda for putting up with open window violation and everything else.

"Pretty funny you are."

"Actually," Grace says, now leafing through some coded sheets. "I'm not really the type that takes a leap from cliffs, bridges, window ledges, rooftops, treetops, steeples, ladders and all that."

"Sounds like you've given it some thought."

"I'm the type that goes down with the rocket ship," Grace says. "Which type are you?"

"Neither," Breanda says. "Martyrdom doesn't interest me in the least."

Grace says, "That's probably why we make such a great team."

But why think of martyrdom, why that feeling of doom always so close. Maybe pregnancy is a cushion to such thoughts. Terror not a happy bedfellow with impending motherhood.

"Okay," Grace says. "I'm going back to the cubicles. I'm going to help them."

"See if you can get us raises," Breanda says.

"Just consider me an extension of this here terminal," Grace announces to Walford and Tina, who are frolicking like bees in a hive transfer. "Pay no attention to me."

And to be sure, they aren't.

But there is Walford with his rolled-up sleeves, knee-deep in Tina's computer packs, while Tina arranges little piles of pencils, clips of two sizes, a stapler, refills, a staple remover, pens of various colors, envelopes of several sizes.

Something about Tina's possessions makes Grace cringe. Utility, is it?

But she must work, and now she's repulsed by the gentle waves displayed on Tina's poster still tacked to the old plaster wall. That sun shines its not-so-hidden symbol of Tina's religious affiliation. Now looking at the cliché tacked on at the bottom of the poster: "Love is the work of mankind."

Sinister it all is because of hypocrisy. They say it, but they don't do it. Hypocrisy and juxtaposition—of ocean with crucifix, and crucifix with love, and love with work, and work with Tina.

Staring absently into the heart of instructions she has on principle refused to memorize, Grace dials up the mystery phone number and blindly completes the three-stepped process of getting into the system. She glances at the crucifix flashing of sunlight that reflects into the ripples of the ocean, and she sees Tina taking a letter opener to the thumbtack, prying loose the offending love-object. Tina catches the tack in her fingertips and carries off the poster into her room across the hall, where she begins searching for a new spot to tack it back up.

Grace looks down at the sudden outpouring of data, and a startle blooms in her throat. Silently, she scrutinizes the instruction sheet that is so completely unfamiliar, that she must have so hastily followed that she hadn't even noticed. How did she not notice that the ink was red? How could she have not seen? She tears off the printout, which reads "Central Intelligence Agency Report of Loans by Country." A small gasp, but apparently she has sufficient oxygen to think fast. With trembling fingers, she flicks up the little sheet of instructions to find underneath, the set of familiar instructions dashed off in Breanda's quick manner.

Upon hearing the voices of Tina and Wally growing nearer, Grace quickly switches the two sets, so that the one presently showing is not the set she followed which gave her the data that was burning her fingers and is now burning the seat of her pants.

"Oh Jesus," she says repeatedly to herself, words mouthed, nothing uttered. She is stunned, yet supremely alert, surprisingly aware, considering her consistent lack of sleep, but then again, registering a profound satisfaction at having her suspicions of snakes and moles in her midst confirmed. She finds herself smiling when both Walpho and Tina enter the room.

"How goes it?" Walpho says, in the middle of whose strawberry blond curly locks, Grace now spots horns.

"Wonderful," Grace says. "Let's see, take off the forty Brooklyn buildings, plus those hundred marked for redemption, uh." Hoping all attempts prove futile, Grace spins around to witness both Tina and Walpho uncharacteristically sitting atop their completely emptied desks, as if assistance might possibly descend from the clouds.

"I hope you are deleting all forty with one command," Tina suggests, her polished lips in a superior smile.

"Naturally." Grace bites the insides of her cheeks. "Say, you look as though you're ready to move some desks."

"How did you guess?" Tina leaps off the desk, followed by Walpho, who adds, "Just let us know, soon as you can." And they are back in their new room.

With a newfound sense of curiosity, Grace fiddles with the keys.

"What" is the computer's response to Grace's command of "Print".

"No such command," the computer prints out, in response to her command of "Write." Followed by: "Consult Manual, Page 379 lvz."

Immediately after the command to "List," the pitter-pat of printing produces a series of loans in dollars and foreign currencies, from Abu-Dhabi, Afghanistan, Ajman, Albania, Al-Fujairah, Algeria, and so on, with recent outstandings and a whole host of data in columns under abbreviated headings.

"Sounds good," Tina hollers from the other side. "You think you can help us move the desks now?"

Failing in her desperate struggle to disengage the machine, using commands like "End, Final, Detach," Grace lifts the receiver, and the connection goes dead, just as Tina and Walpho come through the door. Grace tears off the printout.

"Be back in a jiff. Breanda really needs this." She turns back, remembering the printout she was sitting on as well, makes a run for the conference room trailing the treasonous tails behind her.

"Breanda, Breanda, Breanda." Grace rolls up the heated sheets, begs her friend to hide them in her pocketbook, instructs her not to look at it until she returns.

"What."

"I tell you this for your own protection," Grace says, a dull voice, absent of expression.

"What?"

"Please, just wait till I come back," Grace says, her eyes directly into Breanda's, with that same expressionless tone. "Pretend it's the deletion of the forty buildings if anyone asks. But don't show it to anyone. Promise you won't."

Grace takes several breaths to steady herself, then walks slowly back murmuring to herself, "I don't believe it," but she is ready to move a hundred steel trap desks if need be.

After some minutes of intense physical labor and some inconspicuous but nevertheless pointed scrutiny of the now-exposed set of instructions, Grace returns to the conference room.

"Did you look?"

Breanda's lips are in a serious pout.

"Well, did you?"

Breanda shakes her head.

"Good, I'll be back soon as I finish the inputting." When she returns this time, however, there is but one very familiar set of instructions, which she follows and whose dreary system she updates and signs off, tearing the page and hurling it off to Breanda in much the same manner as before, saying loudly, so that it could be distinctly heard in the room across the hall, "I think I've got it right now, Breanda."

"That was fast."

"I did all the deletions in one shot." Grace quickly removes the hot scrolls from Breanda's purse, folds them up into two sets of squares, stuffs them in her bra.

"Will you please tell me what the hell is going on?" Breanda's hands are raised. "I mean this is my purse."

"I'm sorry," Grace says. "I mean to protect you."

"Protect me against what?"

"I'll tell you."

"Tell me now," Breanda says, about to sit down, about to listen to a long story. "I promise I'll listen."

"Tomorrow I will," Grace says.

"Tomorrow?"

"Please say nothing to anyone of all that you know."

"Not anyone?"

"No," Grace says, her hands still in her bra, still trying to find room for the printout. "No one but Richie. Tell Richie, please tell him.

You've got your own personal lawyer. Yes, tell Richie what you know, and tell me what he says."

"What do I know? I know nothing."

"Good," Grace says, looking for something to touch, looking to rid herself of an itchy feeling of filth from having touched the paper, with all its dirty information, the paper now at her breasts that suddenly become itchy. Her fingers rolling pencils, picking them up, pencils and thumbtacks, removing them from one end of the table and placing them at the other end. And then pacing, walking around the conference room like a twist-up toy.

"Just tell me," Breanda says. "And please stop moving! You're making me dizzy."

"OK," Grace says and sits down, swiveling.

"What I want to know is," Breanda says, "—does it have anything to do with our getting raises?"

"I didn't think of that, but it just might, although not immediately."

"Have you said anything to Walpho?"

"God, no," Grace says, raising her voice, and standing up, pacing again. "And don't you."

"What could I say?" Breanda says this looking at her computer. "There's so much work to be done, Grace."

"Right," Grace says. "Right."

*

On her bike now. Nausea and curiosity. Fear and malaise. So palpable. How they mix with exhaustion. Not to mention steering a hand-me-down bike. Going forward with a fire in your breast. The feeling of slick crumpled rolls of printout. Informative filth. An oxymoron. This series of loans. Countries you've never heard of. New ones sprouting every day. Others changing their names. New owners, or are they breaking free? South Africa still fighting the damn apartheid. Are there loans for apartheid? How can it be? This world of hatred. The idea of holding hostages. Carter's failed attempt. Operation Eagle Claw. More killed doing it. How they cannot negotiate frightens her. The idea of so many unhappy people in the city. She sees them. These boys who make her coffee, she feels them. The red-bearded man. And the men dying. In her own apartment building. Some of them are not old, these men.

And what else will she find on that printout. More sadness to investigate?

And why can't she find her love?

She could be the patron saint of love—so what if redundant. If she were in charge, she would free Mandela and rescue the hostages. She would heal all the dying New York men. Find just one for herself. Just one. But where's all this money coming from? Money to be begged and borrowed. Do they just go ahead and print print print? But guessing there's more than money. Oh, what a dirty girl she is! Not a saint but a thief. Saint Genet. Right. Knowing too much is like stealing. How she felt while researching for her dissertation. What to do about what you know. Funny this feeling again. When you lack, you sweat. When you have, you sweat. Like finding stolen treasure. Stepping on a mine. Like burglary. Like finding your father's letters in your mother's drawer and reading them. Like sleeping with your best friend's boyfriend. Her secret, but whose secrets are these? Certainly not Breanda's. Walford's or Tina's or both. Steady, steady. Wheels going forward, mind thinking back. How they parted friendly ways, she and Breanda. Fear not. A sky radiant, the eyeball of a goddess.

This is what life should be—a gift of the gods, the goddesses. More about the women. Women are the deliverers. Women know things these men don't know. That's why so many angels are depicted as women. Angels and saints—they should all be women. Or gay men.

And there is the sound of one, too. Is that a harp she hears? Or bells? There's a sound curling the air. The waves of sound drawing her near, so soothing. Strings or bells? Piano? Is it a hammering, this sound—a resounding sound, like waves going through a prism. Like music of the spheres. Transported by waves, lessening as she descends from the West Side Highway, as she pedals down Morton Street, pausing at the small square gardens, little plots guarding big tree trunks, with impatiens and baby roses and tiny gated paradises, and stopping at the triangular island before crossing Seventh, and looking up as if the sound could splash into the street, but now—gone those bells. Gone. And how the sound has not only intoxicated her but drenched her—in tears as she approaches her own building, among the flocks of people always on the sidewalks, for this and that, cheese and bread, the heavenly smells. That sound ringing out from her own building. From high up, the roof? A scrambling sound now—piano, then? How could it be? And now so suddenly gone. The mailman entering her building. She sees him, with his stacks of letters. Like a stack of chords. Through the glass, she sees the mailman separating the letters, the magazines. Like a series of bells—but now nothing, no sound. And here, now she is, at the door, pulling it open as he is coming out, holding the door for her, a greeting, a smile as she is sliding her bike in, and look who is also stepping down the stairs on the inside, about to get his mail?

"Stem!" she says. "And in a suit—to boot."

"No boots! But yes, a suit. Some business to attend to," he says, his eyes right on the printout where her cleavage should be. "Fancy seeing you when you're not wasted."

"Oh," she says. "But I am."

"It's too early," he says. "Although I see your eyes are full."

And now both of them with their own stack of mail.

"I've got trouble," she says, her voice low. "And I think I'm hearing bells."

26

He starts singing and snapping his fingers, "I've got rhythm, I've got music…"

"I thought you were classical," she says.

"I consider Gershwin classical," he says.

"Right," she says.

"Come up, now," he says. "I'll play you some Gershwin. It's next on my list."

In the elevator now. "Next?"

"Yes, I am crazily practicing. A series of Preludes."

"Preludes," she says. "I love that word."

Leaving the bike just outside his door, a quick leafing through the mail and a quicker dumping down the incinerator.

And he opens the door, while doing his own leafing.

The equivalent of mail in her bra.

It impresses her that he practices in formal attire. His entire domain impresses her, so filled it is with items she would like to touch, whose history she would like to explore, but Stem is at the piano pressing his slender, well-muscled fingers onto the keys.

"Grace," he says, looking up, still playing. "A few things," he says. "One is a warning—as always, be careful." These are arpeggios that he enhances, that he can play without looking at his fingers, with his eyes closed. He can play them and speak at the same time, although his voice changes, and the drawl slows. "You are looking for yourself in others, you know."

She knows not to interrupt. Messages come through Stem. Others, though, she's thinking. Which others?

"Males," he says. "Not the females. You look to men—maybe because of your father. You looked to your father. Your father knew you. The others were perplexed by you, fearful for what you might encounter. Your very name means charisma, darling, Grace and *charis*. The sound so similar. Well, this is the one half of your name—there is more, more to come, but for now—this." He opens his eyes with a

27

smile, but no, he makes no eye contact, and instead of arpeggios, he moves to a series of trills—it sounds perhaps like maybe it's a run from a longer piece, from the Liszt—she heard him play the *Liebestraum*, that run up and down the keyboard, that he's surely using to warm up his fingers. Once again, his eyes close, and he speaks. "Grace—here the meaning is in the sound, something that can be heard—something that can be seen and felt, but no word contains this thing. Nor can you be contained, my dear. It literally spills from the word. And yet the word itself holds multiple worlds. One of the worlds is you, Grace. The word is from the Greek. You know this? You are this—what you see in me, what you will see in him."

Although Grace sits ten feet from him, from the man who is as beautiful and elegant as the eight-foot piano, she feels herself propelled into the runs of Liszt. Her own mind is elevated, but she does not fail to hear this, Stem's very words forming the prophecy of her dream.

And the *Liebestraum*, those very words—love and dream, offering her something, something to counteract that idea of being careful—and what to be careful of—a love that she can at least dream of.

"So, yes," he continues. "Your name also means more, the mercy, the Hebrew *chesed*, of mercy and loving-kindness. And also charity—from charisma to charity through love. You see, Grace—all this is in your name—all this that you will grow into, and yes, the men will help you. They will help you more than the women, and this you instinctively know."

"But what," she says—it just comes from her, as though she cannot keep the words, the thought from erupting from her lips. "What must I be careful of, Stem?"

And the moment ends, crushed, as his eyes open.

"Did you say something, Grace?" he asks, as if there had been no conversation at all.

"Your windows are open," she says, walking over, looking out at that sky, once again on this day, extending her head and chest out, this time charting the path of her bicycle, not to mention the imagined trail of the bells, the journey of the wave. That path she took—all there before her, and she smiles, knowing that what she heard came from directly, unmistakably from this window.

"It's bad for the piano, I know," he says.

"It's good for the city," she says. "You may think this odd, but I think I heard bells coming from the roof," she says. "They were calling me home."

"Did they sound like this?" he says.

His playing delights her, the speed and the recognition.

"Yes, yes."

"This is by Olivier Messiaen," he says. "*Les sons impalpables du rêve*," or "The Impalpable Sound of a Dream."

"Keep playing," she says. "Please."

"It's one of his preludes," he says, and then shifts into the preludes of Gershwin. Somewhere in the middle, he says, "Leave when you wish—I must practice."

Everyone knows about Gershwin, the tumor in his brain. The *Rhapsody* with the drunken clarinet—her father's instrument. Preludes, the beginnings—the befores. A feeling of drunkenness in these notes, too. A lilt, the syncopation. A promise of knowledge, an event to come. The mystery of time. Einstein it makes her think of. She played the piano once upon a time. Those runs from the Liszt had been in her own fingers. And there he is, Stem, his grand heart in his fingers. True elegance—restraint and then leap. The music like water. His face impassive. She's looking there at his lips as if a god had sculpted them. Not a hint of sorrow. Grace imagines his lover, his one man gone. Stem doesn't like to talk about himself, his life. She finds herself in tears, recalls him saying she would find hers.

"I'll hold you to this," she'd said.

His real name Stephan, but everyone called him Stem. She'd gone to hear him play the Prokofiev alone, and then Brahms in a trio.

In her mind, his piano, that big Bosendorfer, all eighty-eight keys of the monster, rising up past her windows. Preternaturally startling her, and she, going straight to Frank the super, begging to know who was the pianist, then introducing herself right then, insistent, when Stem answered the door and invited her in, to watch the operation of a monstrous beauty thrust through a window.

And Stem, everything about him, beauty.

She could stay there forever even as his entire body was swaying with the word "don't."

And then, later, when the piano was grounded, and she was back up there, when she'd just said it, "I could fall in love with you right now—and that would be it."

"Now that would be a bad idea," Stem had said. "Next—or perhaps a former life. Yes, probably the life we had in Paris, when you were the boy. One of us lost their heads. Or maybe not," he said, his hands going for her back. "Maybe you were the girl there. Maybe we were both girls."

He'd pulled her hair and then sat down to practice.

"Come by anytime, sweetheart."

Behind the piercingly intoned arpeggios, all she'd heard was his drawl his drawl his drawl.

Her long hair, so good for pulling. Ragged now, dry as strings, but his touch. How she loved him. How unattainable he was. Was love, too, completely and utterly unattainable?

Down two flights, she parks her bike, removes the slick, crumpled rolls of paper from her breasts, pushes them into a drawer filled with tools, whereupon she flops down on her bed and sinks into the mattress, pulls up a sheet with its tiny yellow fleur du lis.

*

30

Large hall with men in suits, women in hats and in heels, the music of Tin Pan Alley and Busby Berkley high-heeled glittery shoes on marble, a clattering of crinoline and crepe du chine dresses draped around them like shrouds. It is cocktail hour, and Grace herself is dressed likewise, her own long, thin frame wrapped sassy and smart, but with the back left open, flattering pastels that bleed into darker colors as they reach the very edge of the long dress and become black. She wears a flouncy white hat with feathers, and her own thick, golden hair a waterfall down the back of the backless dress. She draws a part of her hair around her ear and then forward to cover the cleavage.

Before her, a kind pink-faced, grey-suited gentleman.

"Care for a drink?"

"What do you suggest?"

"A Tanqueray I always say."

"Your name?"

"Best to think of me as an anthropologist." He returns within seconds, bearing two shots and a toast: "To peace—and courage?"

"Courage?" Grace, nearly choking on the gin.

"Yes, my dear girl. I might just as well be quite blunt about the matter. Your brain scan and I.Q. have put you well into the 99th percentile. Indeed, there are a number, well, maybe several, well perhaps another candidate of your caliber—but, in fact there is not, and so you have selected and been selected. And, I have chosen and been chosen, no matter the passive/active interchange, to be your escort, to escort you to the insemination ball. Therefore 'courage' best sums up my grand, fatherly advice. Now the questions to which you will—or ought to, in my estimation—apply yourself, are those that require an intellectual maturity, a root system of scope that encompasses even the most spiritual of realms—and please do not repeat this; I use spiritual for lack of a better word. It seems as though the world is now in your hands, my dear woman, and your courage must spread from the very core of your being to the call for action,

31

which perhaps sounds pedantic, simplistic, or merely enigmatic. You will no doubt soon begin to understand. Soon all that has seemed merely excessive supplementary goose-drippings, the stuff of mud-pie and frolic, the luxurious waste of a doomed civilization, all this and more will soon slowly, irrevocably unfold its mystery—a matter of light before your very eyes."

"I am ready."

"For what, my child."

"Another drink—this time a highball."

The kindly old man goes to and fro for drinks, while Grace contemplates her speech.

"To love!"

The toast consummated, the two join arms and walk down a long, double two-way mirrored hall behind which Grace spies the white and silvery crowd of laboratory experts, machines, and humans measuring their every move.

"I have one question."

"Speak," says the gentleman of Anthropology.

"May I choose the sperm to be...?"

"My dear, to the extent that you can, you already have."

Further they walk down the straightway to a closed door, whereupon the gentleman raises his hand. "Now I shall hand you over to nursemaids who will prepare you for the brave event, which I promise shall prove to be more than you dreamed, but in comparison to all that which is sure to follow, will seem wondrous, easy as pie. Such is the woe and joy of a first step."

"Shall we knock?" Grace makes a fist.

"If you wish, although I should warn you that Impatience is unnatural."

"To whom?" She retracts her clenched paw.

"To all of nature, of course," explains the endearing fellow with a smile, and with his shiny shoe, gives the door a brush that pushes it

32

open, revealing a glisteningly white arena with sparkles of chrome and kind blue and brown eyes, and several tables and test tubes galore, cabinets, refrigerators, machines for every occasion—a not altogether unfriendly atmosphere at all, thinks Grace, as she turns her face toward Sir Anthro, his right soft, soft cheek in particular that she kisses in a gesture of sad gratitude and fond farewell.

As angel-nuns go, Grace thinks nursemaids seem pleasant enough hosts, as they remove her pastel sheathe and bathe her, wrapping her up in white, trimming nails and hair in all places. They douse her in a deep spell of alcohol.

They nod and gurgle like doves. One rather small young nursemaid holds up a mirror to her face, and another props up a pillow for her, though she is quite prone on the narrow wheeled table and talking a blue streak about a myriad of things, including her own reflection. "Well, I look rather like a nun myself," she says with a gurgle, "and this gauze tight against my face makes me rather dramatic looking, pitiful, a ridiculous, if tragic movie star heroine about to be thrown to the coals."

"Shhhhh," says a nurse with a calming voice. "Don't be frightened."

"The doctor is quite gentle," says another. They seem to nod to each other in secret agreement about rather something else, Grace decides.

"And handsome, we all think," says the one with calm.

Now they want her to relax, so relax she does as they wheel her into the great auditorium of the laboratory. Grace begins to imagine her role in history, as muffled voices speak in grand tones about all the prized inventions in fields of physics, chemistry, medicine, literature, great Peace, and the relatively new economics. She hears talk of the illustrious and noble contributions of humankind, ranging from making a sweet end to war to finding ways to blow up the family of subatomic parts. Around words she doesn't understand are enveloped phrases she does, such as the discoveries of Radium, Argon, radioactivity in general, hormones, vitamins, X- and Gamma Rays, and theories galore. There is a quantum theory, a money theory, an actual wireless, theories about allergies, nerves, enzymes, the great brain, cells, molecules, atoms and so on. There are theories consequential in lasers, computers, copy machines, bombs, light, and human rights. Oh, she thinks, to rekindle, mother, nurture, the sperm of Einstein, Galileo, Socrates, Michelangelo, Leonardo, Bach, Beethoven, Rembrandt, Jesus, Buddha, Shakespeare—but even with her eyes closed, Grace realizes there is no insurance. The sins and rewards of creation are not necessarily visited upon the daughters and sons of the gifted parent. She is about to abandon everything, when she hears a gentle voice speaking very close to her.

"It's time for you to open your eyes, Gracie."

And open them she does, only to see the dream man, the light of his eyes piercing, this doctor, his eyes—their color hazel, a mix of everything—and so directly upon her as to melt all fear, to atomize ambivalence. So, once again, Grace, cleaving to her destiny, smiles and says, "Who are you?"

"Just a person." The fellow points to the curtains that ripple as they open.

"Ohhhhh."

"Not so loud. They have us greatly amplified."

"Ohhhhh."

"Nothing to be afraid of. It's just the impalpable sound of a dream." He gestures toward the ten-tiered well of sterilized spectators—special guests, workers, residents, members, donors and sponsors of the bank. "We have the whole world watching us now."

"I would rather this part were done in private," she whispers. "I don't mind about the delivery, but really, this could be embarrassing."

34

"Hmmmmmmm," says the doctor, celestial, his light, like that moon sparking clean borders. "Might be tricky, but we'll see what we can do." She watches his face, as he lifts the mask in order to speak, and that crescent moon, its smile, comes into her mind. She watches as he grasps the microphone that is attached to a wire suspended from the ceiling and hangs loosely above the lower third of Grace. The young shining doctor introduces Grace to the multitudes and dreamily rehashes the entire Nobel project, once again, beginning from the very beginning, with the invention of dynamite, and just how it came to be that this and no other specimen lay presently before them. He speaks of what else remains for Grace, the weekly checkups, her regimen of diet, exercise, study, and her need to keep abreast of all fields until the great, grand delivery, approximately nine months from this date, when they will all meet again. The doctor lifts a rod and points to the number-changing, ticking time machine. "You may mark that on your clock, wrists, and calendars my dear sirs and madams, when the mating of Father Science with our choicest mother will bear such fruit as the first Nobel Child—with all due respect to Nature herself."

A trickle of applause prompts the doctor to wait and then to resume.

"And so, on behalf of science, and with eternity as our guide, I thank you all for coming."

A great sound of clapping fills the hall as the doctor gestures for the curtains to be drawn.

"That was terrific," Grace says, as the curtain closes. "Do you think you'll get away with it?"

"Yes, although certainly not on paper," he says, this doctor. "But now I must be very quick, before they have second thoughts. Are you quite relaxed?"

"Oh yes." Grace watches the doctor as he makes his way with the bottles of this, and tubes of that, and the great glass syringe that sits atop the highest glistening shelf. He walks to the sink and nearly washes the pink flesh off his poor hands, and then he returns, stretching his fingers into plastic gloves. He retrieves the mask with which to cover his mouth.

"I have another request."

"And yet another wish you have? Only this, then, and no more!" Under his mask, the doctor is humming something that sounds, Grace thinks, like something that would surely pass as a prelude.

"Take off your mask for a second, please."

"Just for a second."

"I would like a kiss."

"Just a kiss?" He removes one glove and faintly touches the inside of her wrist with unearthly soft fingers not feeling for pulse. Their lips meet with more than a slight charge, and so transpires in the grand, sterile compartment of the Nobel auditorium a monumental act of coupling. Grace's gauze headdress unrolls and unrolls and unrolls, following her from the table to the floor to the toilet to the sink, where she receives the noble sperm of her dream, along with a terrific ringing of light throughout her entire body. And from this whirlwind, Grace's arm reaches for the telephone, at which point the ringing stops.

Chapter 2

"Hello—"

"Hey, honey." It is a low, feathery masculine voice. "Did I wake you?"

"Go sit on an umbrella."

Her heart pounds, and her eyes open. A pink sky waves at her from the windows, and she falls back on the mattress, feeling a cresting river at her back. An explosion of dandelion seedlings. A spindle full of anguish for her bedraggled psyche. She is swimming with her eyes closed.

The phone rings again, and she groans. She picks up the receiver and exhales like a grizzly bear.

"Gracie?" It is the voice of Em.

"'Tis none other."

"What ails thee?"

"I am in shock."

"Par for the course. And do you hunger?"

"Assuredly."

"For what, my dear."

"For peace."

"A piece of what?"

"Yellow," says Grace. "Soothing starlight, pine needles, wands of onion grass perking up meadow, moon, frog blurps on lily pond, waterfalls. Oh, even the evening dew would do."

"I'll be there. But not directly. Wait for me."

You can be roused, but waiting for Em can be a protracted trial of endurance, and so Grace has her windows open, her bikini on, for the heat, which even after a shower is prolific, and she is reading her beloved Goethe, her beloved Werther, a perennial lover. Reading while

37

perched on a towel on the fire escape, the sizzling black-painted steel coated with sunset and grime. Small folds of belly and breast flesh slipping out, warm and damp but at least not coated with printout. She rises up like a sailor and looks out at the sky graying, pinking. Some tears on her face, more of the same that came earlier, those bells and syncopations coming from the hands of a real man, but not hers, but man enough to admit it. Why read this, so mournfully beautiful, and Bleecker Street beginning to cool down. She curls up through the half-opened window, now barefoot on the warm wood of her room, that masterpiece of chaos.

Will she stay in? To ponder this moment of insemination? This list of numbers, of countries, of something started? Or that impalpable dream?

She pulls in the drenched towel. A fly comes in with her. Missing him, she slaps the paperback on the flattened edge of the highboy—what Frank the super called the dark mahogany dresser, shiny except for where water spilled with its white stain.

Grace fancies seeing fairies flying in, pinned there, her fairy godmother; or her long-dead grandmother; or her slightly-less-long-dead father.

Someone watching her always.

Instead of wings, hers were horse legs. Andrew called them that; "elegant" not a word in his vocabulary, but that didn't mean his eyes couldn't be drawn to beauty. He would grab her legs just above the knee, and his thumb would be touching his fingers.

The first time he said it was like eating olives. And when would be the last time?

And now it was no time because she wasn't going to unless it was with *him,* her man of the impalpable dream.

Rummaging now for something to wear.

Em's arrival looming.

"Dress for success," she hears that voice issuing through her belongings and through their histories. Most were someone else's before hers, and that would include the books, clothing, dishware, as well as the furniture—the highboy, the hutch, and the endless shelving—dedicated to their storage. Even the self-annihilated Werther belonged to a dead man.

Of course, Stem had told her to think nothing of it.

Stem knew them. He lived here for years, having first come to New York City from far west, then Midwest, but long enough in Texas to cull that lovely drawl—to make a new home way uptown where Juilliard was harbored, before it and he slipped downtown, although Juilliard stopped midway, landing in Lincoln Center, and Stephan Von Stemeroff found his home here in the Village. However long it has been she's forgotten, but certainly long enough for him to know those whose belongings have now made themselves home in her room.

No, nothing to concern yourself with, but you won't see him coming to visit her, coming to see those belongings without their people. And now his thoughts, the thoughts of flies or friends of hers, thoughts winding their way into her consciousness, of this she thinks nothing. The thoughts of flies or friends different from the thoughts of the departed stranger.

It isn't as if she hasn't heard voices all her life. Voices of her grandparents, of her father within the first hour after he'd passed. Even from her animals, so many, and the voices of the children coming into the world, as well.

A lively imagination—is what they said. So now, what's to be made of a dream or two, or lives lived in the dream world, who was to say whether they were more real than this one, this one with people you think you know and then find out they're narcs, or her dear, crazy Em, who makes an art of it, or like Bruce, corrupt and sad and so hard to fathom. In the end, everyone was unfathomable, dead or alive.

39

Grace wrestled with strings of words of dead writers for almost a decade while going for the doctorate. But when voices come blasting in the dead of the night, it feels like a knife. That voice from the telephone, a knife wielded by Bruce, asking for more.

Testing her.

Nevermore.

And Stem found his man, then lost him, and now searching, his research, his own hidden universe. But never would he resort to her. He'd said that. That first meeting—how he'd known everything about her.

She was still adjusting to the acquisitions, as she was accumulating things to bring into her flat. Working madly on her dissertation with her books and then her growing list of books, and Stem warned her about getting too many books. He was thick into his lover then, and when she'd see him, she'd see them together.

Stem's predictions that came true.

"You'll start reading and reading, and you'll stop writing."

"What makes you think that?"

"It's what happens when I start listening—too much listening."

Yes, she had stopped. Confusion came between the reading and writing.

"For doing," Stem had said, "you need courage."

Yes, courage in her dream, too.

She'd heard Stem's voice even before she'd seen the piano rising. The drawl. It was a voice that came from above, rather than the voices of the dead from below. And even now, when she'd opened and closed the drawers of the highboy, she imagined them admonishing her for all her sloppiness, thick clusters of nylon and cotton bunched in the overflow of every drawer. When she was younger and druggy, the voices came with visions, and when she was still younger and sick, they came with delirium, but now, they just came, and there were times she couldn't help but wonder if this building was crawling with dysfunctional invisibles, and where did they live, in the grime, or in the bricks themselves, or were they also coming up from sad ones living in the IRT directly underground, or from the dead enslaved ones buried not far, or were they her own dead trailing her, watching her every move, her every thought, or were they from the behemoths trying to sleep in the earth's core, and how did they know all they spoke of— did they read the newspapers or the best sellers? Or did she just have a good imagination?

Or was she just reading too much, thinking too much, listening too much?

The imbalance of the world living in her.

And couldn't she find a boy to save the world with?

Werther! She would take him in a heartbeat.

Where was her Werther!

And would he show up, for gods sakes! Or would she have to constantly go a-looking!

You will-will know. You will just-just know.

Like this voice. This invader. Or was it a self-comforting reflex, what these voices amounted to, what Em said they were, what Em's therapists told her.

This one came with a buzzing.

She is willing to use the Goethe on this fly, if only she could find him.

But no, now making herself tea. Might as well. "Coming," Em said. "Not now, though."

Calling her now.

"Yes, still planning to come," Em says.

"But *when* is the question!"

"It's a good question, Grace."

"Tonight? In time to eat?"

"Yes!"

41

"An hour?"

"Less."

An executive decision it is to rise, chances it, there, with her herb tea and the tea-cozy (a gift from Stem), and sitting there, now inside, a wooden chair and the small round table (a gift from a dead man), and the cup and saucer as well, with their pink fleur de lis. A few sips with the cup in her hand, then down—rising up to rescue the printout from the drawer with her tool case (the tool case also a gift—from her father, also a dead man). Her father was in his sixth decade, not in his third or fourth or fifth.

Some of these dying men were not old, Stem said.

One in particular, he said.

And now she unrolls this, like the blueprint of an architect, and she examines the data, so much money there is in the world, and more countries than you can shake a stick at.

So, they lend money, the U.S. does.

Lots of it.

Is this anything to worry about?

Lots of money.

Buh buh burn the evidence.

What evidence.

There is oh so much-much-much more-more horrible than before.

And then the buzzer announcing Em's arrival. Grace returns the "evidence" to the tool drawer, and buzzes Em in.

"Here I am." And there she is, Em, at the threshold of Grace's door. It was already opened.

Grace, having now exchanged her bikini for the equivalent in underwear, peers deeply into the dull well of Em's eyes, as her own eyes fill up with water.

"What?"

"Just oh."

42

"Sounds exciting." Em, nonchalant, takes a seat on the armchair. She rests her head on her elbow, crosses her legs, and all the little joints relax as her body collapses like a collection of spare parts— a gesture dependable for reversing the direction of almost everything. Em watches her friend fall into a spell of laughter, bending over double and then somersaulting into all of the valuable debris on the floor. Em pretends to give the doggie a bone if she does what she is told. "Speak," Em says.

"I can't—I must be cautious," Grace says, half to herself.

"With me?" Em says, her eyes wide with incredulity.

"You forget."

"What."

"The sensory apparatus of inanimate objects," says Grace, eyeing the walls, furniture, windows, telephone, fixtures. "The walls have eyes, they say."

"Oh, I get it," says Em. "You want to sublet my room at Bellevue?"

"I don't want to implicate you."

"I'm innocent," Em says.

"Right. And I don't want you to lose that property."

"Thanks, pal."

"Anyway, maybe it's nothing."

"In which case..."

"I'll tell you when I'm sure."

"It's a deal. Meanwhile, do you have eating plans?"

It's as if something in her mood has just turned a corner, and suddenly Grace is in motion, gathering herself, and says, "What I have...," and then she snatches up from the tower of clothes on her bed a shirt, and then a pair of jeans, marching to the bathroom sink, splashing some water on her face. "What I have...," she repeats the phrase, peeling off the one pair and slapping on the retrieved pair of pants, and then doing the same with the shirts. "What I have...," she roars now, returning to her beloved main room, adding the crumpled-up clothing to the collection on the floor, which is somewhere underneath the indistinguishable pools of clean and dirty, paper and material, items and furniture. It is—all of it, in total disarray, a chaotic chamber if there ever was one, and she fishes in the cottony waters of the chaos for something solid, dredges up the octagonal bottle of her favorite spray. She perfumes her upper and lower centers, and offers a squirt to Em, who raises up her thin, well-scarred wrists. They are standing in the hallway of the room, when Grace hugs Em, says, "What we have...," then slips on her sandals. Grace repeats, "What *we* have......," as she locks the door behind them. They hurl themselves down the steps and are on the road headed to the nearest bar. Grace feels in herself the great lightness in her toes of someone having relieved herself of a gallon of water on the salty brain. "What we have are drinking plans."

"To love." Em clicks her glass into Grace's.

"Peace," Grace says, a printout in her mind.

"Dignity."

"Courage. To the death," Grace says, now with the word "evidence."

"I beg your pardon?"

"Bear with me, friend," Grace says. "I will tell you strange things."

"You are a tease, angel."

"To our friendship. Let's drink."

And they do.

"So, how's work?" Em asks.

"Jesus Christmas."

"I know what you need."

"What might that be?" Grace says.

"Some naughty interaction."

"Out of the question."

44

"Not with Ben?"

Grace shakes her troubled head.

"Nor Raymond nor Zack? Not Marcus, Simon, Mr. Henneley? Your old Economics professor? Not with that cousin of your sister's husband? Not that poet-comedian? Never again with that cabbie in Jersey? The cop in the Midwest? That Greek philosopher? Not with the mounted police or the dying swan or the unknown stud on the white charger?"

"No."

"Not with that mechanic you lived with for three years, what's his name, Angelo? Not with Angelo?"

"Not with Angelo."

"Not with the one who deflowered you?"

"You don't forget, do you?"

"What was his name...?"

"Andrew, he was," Grace says, "and...no."

"Nothing pleases you, madam," Em says, with the reserved and offended air of a lady waiting upon her queen who, one by one, has been introduced to, and refused hats, dresses, creampuffs, tarts, and soda-pop.

"Oh silly, it's not that. Of course they please me."

"So, you want them all at once, then. I wouldn't have a one."

"It's true, they're all too bland and nice, next to Bruce—"

"Bruce has blood."

"But apparently not as much as he needs," Grace says. "Why don't you join me in celibacy, Muriel Lyons?"

"I probably could for the week that it is going to last."

"I have something to tell you," Grace says.

"No walls here?" Em says.

"Something else," Grace says. "I'm done with the nonsense."

"Spare me," Em says. "Please spare me."

"I'm done with it all," Grace says.

45

"Right," Em says.

"You'll see," Grace says, with the fire in her eyes of strong feeling mixed with strong drink. "Never again except in love."

"I'll be surprised if you last the night."

"Oh Em," Grace says, eyeing the elders, stooped men who've limped to the neighborhood bar, hung their work hats on sweet hooks, and now sit, so thinks Grace, as though umbilically wrapped up in the extended news program blasts. Some Mesmer physician of the world giving his prognosis of the tensions, from the totalitarians vs. the barbarians in the next hemisphere to the clash in our very own backyard. The men, the hostages, the dying men, the men she won't sleep with anymore, and the one man she wants, whoever and wherever he is, and what if she will never find him—what, then?

"All this loneliness," she says aloud. "And such little time left for all our selfish pain."

"Oh no. I disagree," Em says. "There's always time for pain."

"You think so?" Grace rising to pay the bartender a tipsy bill. They stumble out the door into a fresh hot slimy green night. The baked buildings steaming, puncturing the air with their mute cries. The two walk in silence, the sound of sandals gently abrasive against sidewalks, their eyes grown accustomed to the sights. A young fellow holds a tight fist around the neck of a lean tree, an older fellow thumbs through a garbage can overflowing with rot. A still older man whose face is a pink blossom, the drink shouting through him. So much heartache and despair and still so early, with a long nightlife ahead in this part of the world.

They open the door to *Sound City* where five men on stage are glowing, reflecting light off hungry listeners, whose eyes are pinned on their eyes, hips, arms, and fingers that caress metal strings. Their very souls enter the catatonia of the lovely drummer, the riveting lips of the vocalist who croons a violent lullaby to some nameless woman whom he loves and hates, and so reconciles his ambivalence by sundering:

46

Sleep love sleep
The world is tumbling down
& I have broken my crown
That by your side I did keep
Goodnight and sweet dreams oh
Love leave me or let me go.

This verse is rather peaceful, Grace decides, with its rippling passionate chords of love, followed by a refrain that switches ironically to the tune of "Ain't she sweet":

Now I ask you very confidentially
Ain't this ---------sick?
     and
Now. . .
Doesn't this suck?

Upon which the lights flash on the dark satin and glittered T-shirts of the performers. Their expressions show not only teeth, but tonsils, nostril hair, as well as the whites both above and underneath their pupils. Grace turns to the bartending woman with a dark thrill in her own eyes and orders her fifth mix of sweetened Tequila.

"I think they're great," Em says.

"Do you?"

"Yes," Em says. "They make me feel alive and kicking, and my heart beating like a fetus. I want to shout, Yes yes yes yes. I'm here, Ma."

"They make me numb."

"Why?" asks the woman tending bar who, in her unassuming way, will oversee everything. "Why numb?"

"Operated upon," Grace says, smiles. "I forget…"

"Loo," she says.

Grace introduces herself and Em.

"I actually know you two quite well," Loo says, going off to an anxious customer down at the other end of the black marble counter.

"But not with less than ten shots swimming in our bloodstreams."

"And I hardly know myself," Em says, that unearthly gray look of distance in her eyes now, as she smiles at a private non-existent onlooker, who approves.

"They're celebrating death," Grace says.

"They're reflecting our lives," Em says.

"Humans addicted to slaughter," Grace says.

"It's the drug of choice," Em says.

Whores of Waterfall it says on the band of the largest drum, black on the flashing steel, with its driving beat against tonal dissonance. As if something were colliding without meeting, like a mathematical equation, postmodern, or postmortem. But it is clearly self-adoring in its adulation of pain, its embrace of terror. The milk of destruction, Grace sees it on everyone's face, above the lip, that milk.

Sleep love sleep
They go on without us
Hear the jungle noise clash in the night
Steel against steel
Of automobile

Now I ask very confidentially…
Don't I suck?

Imagine someday me and you
Our blood will pump up worms oh
Sleep love sleep
Just kiss me once before your lipstick dries

48

And we say goodbye
Now I ask you very confidentially…
Doesn't this suck?

Oh Hiroshima Nagasaki
Glorious Auschwitz
Fanciful Dachau
All possibilities if you stay with me
Just imagine World War Three

Instead sleep love sleep
Now I ask you very confidentially
Ain't this sick sick sick?

Grace whispering to Em: "This makes me cold, and you make me sick for liking it."

"I'm fading, Grace. I'm almost used up. But Grace," Em says, "they have a right to sing this. I have a right to like it. Anyway, I'm only trying to see the softest of demons dancing before me."

"There's logic in your thoughts, Em," she says, "but they're hard to swallow. Hard to live by. Hard for me."

"Not for them, Gracie-pie," Em says. "Take a look."

The audience cries for more, abundant applause filling the air, while the fellows in the band bow graciously, begin something entirely instrumental, their sounds like snakes. Meanwhile, Bruce approaches Grace with a furtive look of something up his sleeve.

"Hi doll." He is dressed in jeans, a silk shirt, and his eyes are dark crystals pointing at her, his elbow grazes the bar, his tall, slim figure at a slightly crouched angle. Their eyes meet directly despite the dimness of the light, and he slices through the gleam, gives her a soft kiss on the lips.

"You here on business or pleasure?"

"Both." He turns toward Em, only one seat apart but worlds away, her head in her hands, her focus somewhere in an internal labyrinth behind the closed door of her thoughts.

"What is your pleasure?"

"Want to perform?"

"Gee, I thought I said 'pleasure'."

"Tonight, here, now."

Grace is good-natured with her show of laughter, but then she roughly seizes Bruce's elbow, drags him out, beyond the swinging doors, where she feels free to ask him if he is out of his mind.

"This is for Em," he says, "not for me."

"I don't know. What about that audience…"

"Leave the audience to me."

"Which piece?"

"What about 'The Respirator'?"

Grace slides her finger on the dusty sweaty body of a parked car, while the drone of metal music leaks out into the night. "Beats listening to that."

"It's been a while. You sure you can do it?"

"What's to it? All I have to do is think with a microphone."

She rubs the sooty finger on her jeans and goes through the doorway. She walks directly to Em and whispers in her ear, whereupon the pink-and-blue-haired mime star pops right up, muttering, "OK." Em stares into the mirror across the bar, winks at Grace, then turns to face her.

"Are you ready for catharsis, Muriel Lyons?"

"If you think you can get it for me," Em says. They scurry down to the cellar where they preen before the larger mirror. Em stretches her legs, and Grace clears her throat. Upstairs, Bruce Steen sets up the first part of the show, a silent film. He makes the introductions with a silver glow in his eye and polished tongue. He steadies the audience, which springs to attention like an oversized puppy. How easy it is to convince them to attend the play of light flashing upon the back wall with its holes and what-not, crying out for spackle, inadvertently providing the surreal effect of three dimensions.

The Respirator opens with a girl (Em) confiding to a blank wall as if it were a father figure. She mimes a wish for true love, and there flashes a couple kissing in a valentine. For the first time, Bruce is in one of his sequences, the camera shooting his prone body as a still. Em mouths the sweet nothings he had once said, and she points to their implication, a white veil with flowing brown hair, outlined by her watery fingers, her soft face responding to the redolence of flowers, and her legs abandoned to the gaiety of near flight. Images appear of calendar pages flipping backwards, newspaper headlines going out of date, photographs of a time gone by, then a flash of the pulsing couple locked in the heat of a deadly embrace. The screen then floods with seasonal changes upon a natural landscape, icebergs crackling on the shores, trees stricken with barrenness, and the great soil gone from lush brown to grey, the color of Em's eyes, which become the focus of the camera's eye. Cut to Em watching the back of Bruce as he recedes into the distance. In that one facial statement, Em conjures the magnitude of her longing, the curse of poor Eve recognizable on any woman. As she walks, Em imagines herself injected into a large needle that is shot into her lover like a serum.

So powerful is the mime that both chuckles and gasps can be heard from the very attentive audience. Suddenly, so it seems, as a result of this manipulation, he turns back, and together they walk through a graveyard, past brushfires and a charred church. The sound of steps is audible against shots of pink morning haze, a windy rain, sprouts of grungy green grass in sidewalk cracks, a sweet-smelling garbage bin stacked with sticky soda cans and apple cores, above which hovers a family of bees, and in the background Central Park. Gradually lifting the focus, the camera finds pigeons perched everywhere, and finally pans the plain blue sky. There is the sound of inhale/exhale and

51

a cut to the face of closed-eyed Bruce, who is yet prone. A last flash to Em down on her knees, as the film ends, followed by a moment of darkness, while she and Grace scramble onto the stage in their street clothes.

Em stands still in the center, while Grace, seated on the floor far right, begins her narration.

"*The Respirator*, Part 2," says Grace. "A living epilogue."

With most profound concentration and, in the fashion of a superb mime, boxing herself in with hands, feet, torso, neck, Em creates a multi-shaped form that she puts into motion. For a while, as her gestures indicate, the thing remains in this motion, but gradually, it slows down, seems to stop entirely, and even begins to shrink.

"How to keep things alive," Grace says. "There are rules."

Em begins to press the thing into being once more.

"First rule is dedication."

However, Em now seems to have lost her touch. The thing begins to shrink further, and she panics.

"But a rule is not necessarily a guarantee. Rule Two is knowledge and conviction of purpose."

Em, in the manner of a young soldier, collects herself but betrays a worried eye at the further demise of her thing.

"Third, perfect action."

Constricted by the notion of "perfect," Em's movements, very natural and flowing at the outset, become mechanical and abrupt. A certain faltering, a quivering, is detectable, despite the absolute clarity of her form. The thing exists, but it does not accept motion, and for this reason, Em despairs.

"Fourth, perfect timing."

Em's actions become more clock-like and rhythmical, yet she is unable to conceal her dismay at the thing's inability to take off on its own momentum.

"Fifth is constancy, resignation to one's role in the above relationship forever…"

While maintaining the thing with her arm and one leg, Em manages to make a gesture indicating that she is disturbed by that last statement.

"…Or be responsible for its death."

Em looks lovingly at the thing she is nurturing.

"Which may not be such a terrible thing."

Soon Em begins to show signs of weariness.

"Hey! No sleeping on the job."

Boredom and ennui suddenly strike poor Em, who looks resentfully at the thing she is all the while maintaining.

"Remember, this is your life," says Grace to Em, who instantly lets the thing go and watches it flit around the room like a balloon losing all its air. She giggles, which is a sign for the audience to breathe. Then Grace giggles, and they both giggle and join hands and bow to a cheering, howling audience. They giggle all the way down the stairs.

"You liked this one?"

Em giggles more.

"You were great."

Em is too giddy to speak. Then she suddenly changes, as her face turns suddenly serious, suddenly angry. Eyes wide open, the blues cold and glaring, she says to Grace, "You're telling my story." She is screaming. "That talk about keeping me alive! You are one hell of a manipulator, friend! You think I'll die if you let me go? You think I'll die without you?"

Grace is nodding. "I wasn't talking about you, Em. I was talking about life—my life, anyone's life. I thought it was properly depressing. I thought this crowd would just love it."

Em starts giggling again, her hand cupped over her mouth in an attempt to stop herself from laughing. They are going down the stairs now, and when Em reaches the bottom of the never-ending flight of cement steps, still laughing, she falls softly in a slow, forward motion against the cinderblock. She flaps her hands flat against the wall while Grace sits on the steps, both of them steeped in clouds of inexpressible feeling. Em's malleable body, never losing its contact with the wall, turns, and she slides down in a heap, trying to look up. Now tears are falling in her lap. The sound issuing from her depths is nothing funny, Grace thinks.

"It is so funny." Em's eyes fill up with tears again, her face swollen and red.

"You look like you're drowning, Em. It's not funny at all."

Suddenly, the electrons in Grace's brain jump into emergency room gear.

"Oh yes!" Em moans, now holding her face in her hands, as if it were a cut flower that has been disengaged from its stem. Still laughing, Em slams the back of her head violently against the bricks, and Grace screams.

Meanwhile the cellar door opens, revealing Bruce, who stands there without looking, his mouth open. "They're still clapping," he says, his voice trailing as he swallows the sight. "Oh shit. I'll be back in a minute." Upstairs, Bruce shifts his manner to pacifying, and the audience begins to gurgle in its disappointment. Even as he coos to them, he wonders how—with the least amount of splash and splatter—to effect the delicate transition from cellar to cab without exposing the lovely cheering sinless crowd to the shocking pink spectacle of his lover-mime and her antediluvian cry.

It is always Grace to the rescue, which—to the audience— appears to be the encore, after all. With a slightly reddening towel around Em's head, Grace holds the laughing girl pieta style, dragging her right past Bruce and his three-ring-circus mind, and all heads veer in the direction of the last act. Grace feigns her own hysteria. "Alas," she cries, "the deaf must lead the blind. Else, who will? Brucie, baby," she continues. "Tell them the story about the woman who swallowed

54

too many hyenas. Sleep tight, friends, and don't let the dream bugs bite." She throws a kiss to Loo as her biceps and triceps and quadriceps blossom and roar with the relative lightweight of Em in her luminous distress. As soon as the beast of two heads arrives on the street, there appears the cab Loo has called. It travels far east and less than a mile north to the stately, if fallen, empire of Bellevue Hospital and environs.

"Hi. Oh, my." They are friendly pink and white and bronze and golden faces of all ages, bearing wheelchairs and walking in a brisk manner. They relieve Grace of her responsibility, and she kisses Em goodbye on the lips.

A world is exchanged in that glance.

"Gracie, it *is* funny."

"You mean ultimately?"

"I mean catharsis. It's painful and funny."

"True, true."

"Gracie, I haven't forgotten about your strange secret."

"Nor have I."

"Do us all a favor?"

"What's that?"

"Fuck Bruce again tonight."

"Nevermore."

"This time for me."

"I'm sorry, Em."

"Me, too," Em says.

"Nevermore," Grace says.

"All betrayals forgiven," Em says, "if you do this for me."

"No."

"This time for me," she says.

"I'm done," Grace says.

"As best friends," Em says, "what you do for me you do for you."

"I'm not doing this for you," Grace says.

55

"We're one," Em says.

"We're individuated," Grace says.

"We're all the same."

"I have a self, and you have a self," Grace says.

"I am self-less," Em says. "Please—for me."

"Nevermore."

Grace throws one last kiss to Em and waves goodbye, as the nurses wheel around the chair, and off goes Em. Grace turns on her heels, only to face, and in near collision, to meet up with a fellow, who by pierce of eye resembles the man of her dreams. He is all in white, from head to toe, a sensational sight that Grace ingests in passing, especially the message on the little pin. She smothers her gasps, yelps, and sighs, for what is he—some kind of pornographic material? By the time she braves the turning back, the sweet name inscribed on the pin—"D. Starlinsky"—now forming on her lips, the fellow has vanished, and the hall is bereft of both Starlinsky and Lyons and all other human activity as well.

"Wait," she cries, with only an echo for answer.

*

It feels like no-woman's land, as Grace loiters on First Avenue waiting for a cab to take her back to her own little spot of turf, three flights in the air. A sorry number of yellow cabs spin by going north, and soon enough comes one with its starry blinker that stops and unloads a passenger, namely trim Bruce Steen with his golf hat, bow tie, and arrow eyes.

"Hello Grace."

"Goodbye."

Bruce holds the taxi door open for Grace, and then follows her in.

"I thought you were getting out."

56

"I was being a gentleman."

"If you really want to be a gentleman, I'm rather hungry and you could take me out to dinner."

"Now?"

Grace nods.

"I hope you don't have health food or anything exotic in mind."

"Take me to the fanciest place you know."

Bruce leans over and whispers to the cabbie. Within a few minutes, they arrive at the gold and crimson palace of the sesame bun and patty of ground cow.

"I'd say we are a brutish species."

"Look at it this way. We're just a bad idea. Nothing to go hang yourself for. Anyway, the sky's the limit. Have any and as many burgers as you wish. I'll have two quarter-pounders."

The expressionless gal sprouts nonchalant out of her brown-striped uniform.

"And that and that and that." He points to French fries and milkshake and coffee. His face creases with humor as he watches Grace consider her options.

"I wish I could eat the smell and be done with it."

"Give yourself a few incarnations. I thought you were hungry."

"I'll take five cheeseburgers. And ten large coffees. Four apple turnovers. Two French fries. One fish sandwich. Cole slaw. Three chocolate milkshakes with extra preservative. I guess that's it. Oh, ten glasses of water and—wait a minute." She turns to the one lady and handful of gentlemen gathered, their momentary home in the eating parlor with unguent delicacies, mingling smoke with liquor and coffee and beef, not to mention onions and mustard-mayo smells and those of ketchup and cleaning fluid. Cry of chair leg on floor, occasional groan of words, a flow of yawns. "Poor old humanity," Grace mutters, not quite under her breath. With nine heads, the entire flock facing her, she asks, "Anybody hungry? I guess that's it."

The waitress waits as those heads turn back to their own wonders, Bruce paying up now. Bruce and Grace knee-deep in Em and art and politics and money, when a fellow shows up, stands there, with his red gristly beard, earthen and bloodied face, street slept-in rags of terrific weight and odor, and a brilliance in his eyes bespeaking humor, madness, or both.

"And so we meet again," Grace says.

"Again?" Bruce says. "With *him?*"

"It is a pleasure to eat at your table," Grace says.

"I'm given to understand that you might have some extras," the red beard says.

"Always," she says, gesturing at the remaining cheeseburgers, coffees, turnovers, and shakes.

"Thanks, doll. Bless you, baby." He takes a share and departs out the door.

Bruce allows a moment for transition, then says, "She's running herself dry."

"Why did you think doing this little gig would help?"

"She needs the contact." He bites into his second burger, dangling the fries and opening wide for milkshake. Then he rises, wending his way to the room for all things that come to pass.

Grace, meanwhile, nurses water number eight, nibbles alternately at burger and turnover, the red beard still there even though he's out now, enveloped in the blue gold that's releasing a sunrise, unfolding Wednesday.

Bruce's cheeks still bulging on his return. His brow wavers, but his eyes are unchanging. "Was a great show, anyway. Juxtaposition, I mean. I wrote it down. The things you said. Too bad you're working today. I'd like to check it out with you."

"I don't remember a word."

58

"Oh, you would when I started bringing it all back again. You'll see, maybe I should take—"

"Forget it, Bruce." Grace, rising. "It's time to—"

"You know you told me to sit on an umbrella this afternoon."

"You should have taken my advice."

"Gracie, can I come with—"

"No."

"We don't have to—"

"No."

"No one would know."

"No."

"Who'd know?"

"Everyone would know. God and Buddha. An angel would know."

"Never heard of 'em."

"Nevermore. Good night, Brucie." There, now, just a small, pert kiss on a select spot at an angle from his ear, so red, a little dank. Don't remember, just kiss, the small, hairless spot imbued with memory, as if one could ever forget what one has kissed, as the nose and lips have a mind of their own, indelibly so, to the delight of microbes, but so be it.

"I'll find my way home from here alone. I mean, good morning, sweet Bruce." A giggle betrays the guilt. And now her great adroit and lanky legs will cover the twenty-block distance in no time flat, her adrenaline making her heart squeeze out lumps.

She walks now, the last block. The smell of bread already mixing with the warmth of the night.

Holiness. This city of darkness, those cries for violence. Em's cry. Bruce's desire. This passion for love that turns in the gathering. Em's beauty and talent, wild with a fury like the horse that pulls the cart, but driverless, except for when Bruce is the driver. Better driverless than driven by Bruce. Where does a woman stand? High up in liberty, high up with the law, holding the scales, is a woman. The woman on the streets, however, the mortal, always in danger, which is why she was running. And why now, with the smell of bread, the knowledge that there are others present, she may walk. She may take in her thoughts. And press her eyes to find a star, to remember they are there. Galaxies. Along with the smells and sounds of the street. The other nocturnal ones, bats and rats and flies and bugs and viruses and humans of all ilk.

The streets and sidewalks not empty but there he is. She sees Stem, walking, the bounce.

In a suit, no less.

"Performing?" she says aloud.

"A little something," he says. "And you?"

"Same," she says.

"Be careful," he says.

"Like you?" she says.

"No," he says. "Unlike me."

"No?"

"And remember courage," he says. "That's like me."

They hug, and she looks at him—feels a large sorrow, but there is no way to penetrate that country of his.

"You'll talk to me someday," she says.

"Might," he says.

"I certainly know what you mean by courage," she says, "but tell me what it means when you say 'unlike' you."

"No promises," he says. "But come visit me soon."

And they part like that. Opening doors, walking the stairs. And now she's at her own door. Quickly into bed, but not before reckoning with the window and the moon, and a thought to red beard out there among the serenading insects, and then setting the alarm, an appeal to her father, noting that he has been coming to her more often as of late, visualizations of holiness, namely for ocean, sky, sun, breeze, great smell, peace to Stem and Em, peace to everyone as well as them, soon work, computer sheets, whatever work, the thing to be done tomorrow, work, don't think about it now, need courage, courage and sleep, and oh, Starlinsky, oh.

Chapter 3

It is a fly that maneuvers its flight in spirals, returning from a visit to a thumbnail moon, a fly that once played in the filaments of Grace's hair before its spiraling flight to the prayer mounds upon the moon—that fly returning to carry Grace upon its back. She is indeed riding upon the back of this fly, returning—in what rare ether form, in what fabulous timeless manner of flight—to Bellevue. Her carriage takes her right through marble walls, through planes of plaster and glass, into and out of the chambers of many a sleeping sufferer, and she lands, releasing herself from the frame of the glorious insect only to find herself in a room where Em stands draped in a translucent salmon negligee, one milky white breast falling out, the other thinly veiled, her face pink, vacant and yet radiant, her eyes blue with morning light.

The fly itself recedes into a darkness, careful to elude the webs of spiders and then he takes off, disappears.

Grace is moved to embrace her half-angel friend and foe. Wordlessly they wrestle until some overwhelming feeling of repulsion or awe overtakes poor Grace. She looks through a large hospital window to where a huge spire stands alone, beyond which lies a full landscape of castle ruins and grey boulders nestled in rolling greens, with shimmering animals grazing freely. There are zebras, lions, snakes, turtles, as well as cats, dogs, eagles, and dinotheriums, too—all striped, winged, spotted, plain, and hairy four-footed ones—and the footless reptile, as well—with and sans trunk, horns, tail and cry: one grand whispering hush of beauty.

"Where in heaven's name am I?"

In response, a four-lane highway suddenly appears, engulfed by two- and four-wheeled vehicles.

"Must be the late twentieth century."

But alas, and without a flash, the scene changes, much like the picture on the television, with its myriad of visions offered simultaneously. And here she sees a graveyard, stones with the names of men on them.

Grace instantly relocates, now standing barefoot on the wood floor of her own studio, when she hears the voice of a man. "I am here to fix your tube," says the grey-eyed TV repairman, whom she lets in, opening the door to him. The man is dressed in grey-green overalls with matching cap. He carries a strangely-shaped toolbox that he sets down upon a carpet. The tools themselves are metal and wood, probers and pryers and pummelers.

"You are a famous man," she manages to say, watching him at work. She is otherwise paralyzed until she notices his companion—a worm. Rather small and inconspicuous, the worm is nevertheless golden, a series of balls comprising its body that is centipede-like, about the size of a newborn's forefinger curled slightly. It sits by the man's side and tells him what to do.

"Cerebrum's connected to the contrast. The contrast's connected to the eyeball. The eyeball's connected to the brightness. The brightness is connected to the finger. The finger's connected to the nostril. The nostril's connected to the vertical. The vertical's connected to the otiological. The ear is connected to the volume. The volume's connected to aesthetics, your sense of taste. Now take the Phillip's and turn three times to your right and leave the screw by your side. And then, unplug the television and take it up to your roof and dump it."

"That will be $640.00," says the man with the cap to Grace—however, in the voice of the worm.

"It's too much," she cries. "I hadn't anticipated that."

"That's okay," says the man, who in departing has left the worm. "You can pay me later."

"I'm yours." It's the worm (who resembles a golden centipede) with the same voice as the man's. Grace takes the worm into her hands, examines his golden balls.

"What a wonderful worm you are!"

She finds herself on a bus to the Library of Congress where the worm has apparently been requisitioned for inspection by the authorities.

Telepathically, they discuss truth, beauty, philosophy, commodification, and god.

"I understand that you're concerned about the self."

"Yes," she says. "I'm not sure whether this is a good thing, whether it is better to develop yourself or to lose yourself."

"In a certain sense," the worm implies. "You create yourself. But in the larger sense, you *are* pure creation with the seed within. The trick is multiplying by dividing." Grace envisions amoebas with unearthly colors, themselves long-lost cousins in the ocean, springing from the same source. Arriving at the Library of Congress, they marvel at the sheer numbers of books. It's very formal, with people in suits and long dresses making speeches, but the worm continues his teaching: "Multiplying by dividing," he says. "It's just making distinctions. There are levels, stages, distillations, evaporations, transmutations, but nothing is lost, and everything matters. You must love everything. You'll see."

And then the worm is as if vaporized—gone.

Grace, fearing he's been abducted, taken for dissection by the powers that be, attempts to locate him among the stacks. She crawls, her hands and feet on the floor, among the shoes and stockings of great men and women. She climbs the ladders suspended from the ceiling, ladders with little wheels, frantic in her search; she rifles through periodicals, reference, fiction, poetry, science, art, philosophy—but finds nothing. It is while standing tiptoe on a ladder, reaching for tall thin books, the annals of local history, that Grace has a macro-epiphany: namely, that the worm has chosen not to be found. In her mind, she hears a distinctly male voice, saying: "You will not save the worm, but perhaps the worm will save you."

Instead of music, it is the thought of worms that awakens Grace. And then the business of salvation: whom shall she save?

Like a cat, she stretches in her bed. She extends those horse legs, those willowy arms, all the little and great appendages, whereupon her great toe collides with a desk drawer. She hooks her toe onto a rung, pulls gently, extracting one printout and then the other from the inside, and by complementary action of toe two and toe one, as well as fingers one, two, and three, she hands them over for perusal by eyes and otherwise.

"A worm that will save me."

Instead of its listings of loans or its names of countries, its alphabetizing genius, no—she's looking to see if she can replicate the code itself, if there is more to be found. Standing now and breathing, aware of her dry, malodorous mouth, she holds up the waxy thermal paper to the window light to read through blacked-out secret codes to see the delicate three-tiered password that had gotten her onto the system. She flashes on tier one: "Cornflaker?"

Mumbling, still trying to focus, squinting no less, due to her eyes' unreadiness to see the light, she agrees with herself. "Cornflaker, that's it."

The second comes to her memory letter by letter. They are letters she speaks aloud to the non-entities who are nevertheless, listening: "G...R...I...P...S. Yes." A thrill runs through her. "What's the last, oh yes," she says, somehow recalling the superimposed cue, "GALERIES. Leave it to the government to disguise by misspelling. Or are they being French?" It becomes her spoken mantra as she pees, brushes teeth, runs shower, applies soap, scrubs, purges pores. "CORNFLAKER GRIPS GALERIES," she says, emerging drippingly with towel, which she flings to the floor, as the music alarm sends

65

sounds of golden threads, the double cellos of Schubert's glorious Quintet. Grace is now galloping through dresses, skirts, pants, and shirts, attacked by the what-to-wear syndrome. Lastly, she selects— this time from her closet, a sleeveless dress, black and white checkered, with a full dirndl skirt. No socks, nor stockings, but sandals alone will do. She manages to look at a banana, but further than that, alas, she cannot, will not go.

She saddles her steadfast cycle, bunching the excesses of the skirt up under her seat. She squirms, what with the delicate juncture of clustered cotton lumps against her delicates, and she makes her winding way through a gaggle of trucks, a pod of buses, a few litters of vans, an exaltation of cars, all breathers under one heaven mother, she thinks, all of them doing a tamp, tamp, tamp on the asphalt smothering earth. All making their way to work, today no different from all other days. Just more tired, so much harder to resist the gravitational pull. Resist, she thinks, we all do. She creates such a fine friction that she is at the City offices in no time, on time, with time to spare. Early she is, riding alone on the elevator, saying hello to none, admitting her bike and self into the room with terminal, closing the door, parking the bike, sitting her seat in the swivel, dialing the line to GE, hearing the pierce, rooting the receiver into the well and turning the terminal to ON.

"egup gu tximkur," says the computer for no reason.

"CORNFLAKER GRIPS GALLERIES," Grace types.

"Validation Error #1," replies the computer.

"CORNFLAKER GRIP GALLERIES," Grace types.

"Validation Error #2," responds the computer to muttering typist (expletive deleted).

"CORNFLAKER GRIPS GALERIES," she types, smiling, remembering with satisfaction the French.

"ID:," demands the computer.

"TW," suggests Grace.

"Good morning, Tina Wand," writes the computer.

66

"List All," requests Grace.

"What?" inquires the computer.

"Print," orders Grace.

"Invalid Command," contests the computer.

"Print, shithead," retorts Miss Grace.

"No such file," proposes the computer.

"Print All," commands Grace.

"Ready," the computer indicates.

"Top Secrets," says Grace out of the blue.

"No such file," says the computer.

On they bicker for an hour, until Grace lands on some profound goods, and out pours a bundle of Dangerous People listed in four columns in order of alphabet, danger, age, social security number, respectively. Grace scans the list for a familiar face, so to speak. Among the masses of names, she observes a smattering of heroes, but then pushes the interrupt button, honoring the developments taking place in her third ear, namely the slow step-plops of her favorite octopus mother in sneakers. Breanda's gasps become presences as the door opens, and she exudes with penitence, many apologies for her extreme tardiness, all the while nosing in on the printout that is trying to make its graceful exit.

Grace fails to take the look of horror off her face.

"Really sorry about it," Breanda says.

"It's nothing," Grace says.

"I know you think otherwise," Breanda says. "It's written all over your face."

"No, no," Grace says.

"It's a fact," Breanda says.

"I excuse you for being late," Grace says. "Please excuse the look on my face."

"I won't ask what you're doing." Breanda is finding the limits of her neck.

"Tiddily, click, clack, smack a talaposhtitatatapooo," sounds the computer signing off, whereupon Grace makes a flourishing attempt to shred the paper, stuffing its remains in her little bicycle pouch.

"But I won't stay mum for long." Breanda's tone is threatening.

"Do you think they'd let me take the portable terminal home for a day or so?"

"Sounds like espionage." Breanda giggles, a nervous giggle. "Or are you trying to print up false checks?"

"What, me a crook?"

"Yeah, Saint Crook, sounds catchy. The patron saint of thieves."

"Let's go get a cup of coffee."

"They're all here, you know," Breanda says. "I mean it isn't like they wouldn't notice our disappearance."

"Hell," Grace says. "We'll skip lunch. Who needs to be escorted by ten million mobs of bankers, city workers, stockbrokers, and secretaries anyway? Just say it's an early lunch."

"A late breakfast?"

"I'll take care of it. They owe me a favor. I moved great loads for them yesterday. So, it's settled." Grace trundles off to the office of her superiors, and Breanda nods in that sort of all-encompassing manner perceived by the outside world as prescient glow.

"So." Grace announces herself, her arrival in the new icy room of Tina and Walph, whose backs face each other with desks against opposite walls. But theirs are windows with southern exposure, and Grace can't help but to look out, mesmerized by more than the metaphor of light, those tiny licking threads, tongues of light, moving and zooming and zapping, filaments of the firmament shooting in from above and through cracks in buildings behind buildings and bouncing off every conceivable reflector in the history of encounters.

"Good morning, Grace!" Tina's mouth barely moves, with her pulled-tight smile and matching suit, under which a shiny print bodice prevails. "Did you mention anything to the girls, Walford?"

"Uh, no," Walford, too, is smiling, what with his excellent breeding, while awaiting his turn to speak.

"Walpho," Grace says. "Tell me on the way to the water fountain. I'm absolutely parched."

"Uh, okay." Rising, it would seem that Walford is consciously sending blood to his flanks as they extend, so tall he is, a near seven-foot blonde rugged specimen of an androgen mixture of the most upright species. He makes his way through corridors, and despite it being her request to gather at the waterhole, she is following, but this is fine, as she is working up her nerve to ask for a raise from a narc, and it's nice to know that she is not being followed.

"I know what it is, Walpho, and it's just as well." Grace begins in a voice that is just for Walpho's ears as they wend their way, "Since I was going to ask you. I mean both Breanda and I have worked for nearly a year here, and you must admit we're geniuses of a sort and cooperative at least, and certainly upstanding contributors to the business and affairs of the City. We've manned the computers and conserved energy and trampled through the field, surveyed the inner and outer sore spots owned by the City, and we emerged sweet without corruption. We've shaken hands with slime-and-bile politicians and pacified the outraged poor. We've kept track of rents and fees, and we've mastered the mountains of files upon files. And we've kept our mouths closed to the press regarding dirty laundry, so I quite agree it's about time we got a raise."

"A raise?" Walpho is near spitting. His mouth, by this time has filled with water in addition to the pre-existing oxygen, and now it is all splattered down and around his chin into the stainless steel but surprisingly rusty drain. But Walpho collects himself, puts hand to nose and mouth and eyelids, rises from his humbly hunched pose and says, "One moment please," lowering his head to imbibe once more.

"I mean, even if it could come in time for the baby," Grace says, in an attempt to be toneless and tenuous, more slight but with innuendo to spare.

"The baby?" Walpho's glance is in the direction of Grace's flat tummy.

"Breanda's." Grace, reddening, nearly stutters, as they move to change places.

"Right," Walpho says. "When's Breanda's baby due?"

"Any day now this baby is due to be born," Grace says. "You never know about a baby. I mean first it's just a matter of ectoplasm, and then it's protoplasm, but soon you know that baby is a thing of needs. It will be a child, a person. Well, you'd better ask her, but certainly within the year, this will be a child of needs!" Grace is stooping, drinking with an unquenchable thirst, requiring streams and streams of transported mountain gurgle.

"Welp. A, uh, raise isn't exactly what I was going to talk to you about, no indeed, not exactly a raise at all, but in fact—"

"Are you looking to demote us?"

"Nor that." Walpho manages a smile, beating water out of his stone face.

They are nearing the terminal room door. "Out with it, Walpho."

"Just a matter of putting in extra time."

"Overtime?" Breanda has risen to open the door and let them in. "You mean with extra pay, twice or time-and-a-half? That sort of overtime?"

"That might be arranged." Walpho is now in the room, seating himself in Gracie's swivel, noting the vast change his ex-room has truly undergone, sending a wave, no doubt, down deep in his biosphere with its ocean and umbilical mass of memory and desire.

70

"On project new or old?" Grace is curious.

"New. Well, new to all of us." Walpho speaks with something that amounts to excitement, a spark igniting in his fine blue eyes.

"Something creative?"

"Of a sort, Grace. We have been given the okay to start tearing down buildings, and we've got to determine which ones will stay and which ones will go."

"And what about the people?"

"And what's to be done with the people?" Walph continues, nodding to them both. "In other words, we shall decide which shall go and which shall stay and where we shall relocate the tenants."

"Bus the homeless?" Grace, again and again.

"We have to determine which buildings can accommodate the extra load, and you see there's lots and lots to do. We're thinking of hiring a new researcher, maybe a temp, unless you want to work overtime."

"Can some of this be done at home?" Grace asks.

"I don't see why not. So long as you're organized and we all know what's going on."

"When do you need this information?" Again Grace.

"We want to start sealing up for demolition by the weekend."

"Why suddenly?" Grace asks.

"Orders from Kreitz and higher than that."

"But why?" Grace asks.

"A few elections coming up," Breanda mutters.

"That's neither here nor there."

"Nor is anything else," Grace says, "but—"

"We'll do it," Breanda says. "Right?" She and Grace, both nodding.

"So long as we can have an early lunch," Grace says, quickly, sighting a telling smile on her friend's face, more stiff than soft.

"Shake." Walph holds out a large hand, large fingers, all with a slight quiver, the sign of someone not to trust.

"And an eventual raise." Grace observes the sudden stillness of Breanda's head, her lips drawn together, a small sigh escaping.

"Shake." Walph, his hand out there, with no takers, but then they do shake, the ghostly trio.

"Has everything been arranged?" There is a shadow just outside the partially-closed door.

"Looks good, Tina," Walph says. "I think we'll start this afternoon, okay mates?"

A chorus of "fine," as both Breanda and Grace grab their respective pocketbooks and pouches and tramp out through the Vatican-like series of halls and doors to sweet morning sun.

"So, you going to tell me?"

"What I'm going to tell you," Grace says, "is. That. This. What I'm doing. Going to do. I don't know. But. No matter. I will. It's. I think—honestly, it's treason."

"You mean lying, cheating, stealing, spying, dishonoring—killing? Grace?"

"Might," Grace says. "Don't know."

"God," Breanda says. "Didn't think you had it in you."

"So, that's all I want to say."

"I wish you hadn't."

"Sorry."

"It's okay. I'll get over it."

"Good."

"I thought I was incapable of being shocked."

"So, you learned something."

"So, how's the Peace Mother?" Breanda says as she settles on her breakfast of choice.

"I was planning to be the Love Saint, actually."

"I think it's impossible to be a saint and a mother at once," Breanda says.

"Because…"

"Something about virginity."

"Virginity is overrated," Grace says. "Sex with love is saintly."

"In whose religion?"

"Last night I dreamed about a worm." Grace runs her fingers down the black and red lettered plastic menu seeing nothing but grease.

"Hmmmmmmmm."

A white-smocked, black hair-netted, stockinged, high-heeled, cheeky, orange-lipped, blue-lidded female arrives with pen and green pad in hand, ready to capture their orders. They change their voices for ordering, and Breanda requests the special with bacon, and Grace follows suit.

"And you?" Grace finds a far-away place for the menu, which the waitress neglects to remove. "Any news with you?"

"Just the same old monetary squeeze pleas. Bicker, bicker, bicker. It's a good thing we're already married and not trying to impress each other with kindness. He can be such a pig, and really I'm no better. Sometimes I hardly recognize myself."

"The earth must break a little to make room for sprouting seeds."

"Yeah. It's reaching the breaking point, what with heartburn, hemorrhoids, backaches, nausea, peeing every other minute, and the great spread of nose. According to his mother, that means it's a girl."

"Ah ha—a girl!" Grace says. "Grace, Gracie or Gracia?"

"I'm beginning to think I'll name her Tina."

"Please, not while we are eating."

Meanwhile the waitress has intervened with steaming dishware, and one by one sets down eggs, bacon, juice, toast, coffee, and a rack of jams. She bids them joyful eating and continues her rounds.

Breanda applies grape jelly to her eggs. "I have inordinate cravings, which also means girl—and she can't sit still."

"Guess it gets pretty tight in there."

"Yeah. I feel like a water balloon."

"A gyroscope?"

"A hippo."

"With octuplets?"

"Please. One is plenty."

"So, whaddaya think about this extra work?"

"Not on our time, please."

"Right."

"Did you go out last night?"

"Yes, but I came home quite alone."

"Too bad."

"Actually, I'm beginning to think it might be my saving grace, for a change."

"That is a change," Breanda says, as they gobble up eggs and things, breathing and making eye contact, while the waitress clears the table and refills the half-filled coffee cups.

Breanda pushes away her three-quarters-finished egg plate and turns her head in the direction of the bathroom.

"You done?"

"Yes." Breanda rises and disappears.

Grace ponders the fries on Breanda's plate, snatches a few, then motions to the obliging waitress.

"Check, love?"

Grace looks into the waitress's shiny dark eyes. That idea, the idea of love. Loving *everything*. Especially that worm.

"Check, love?"

"Sure," Grace says.

Still smiling, the waitress places the already completed account of the now partially-digested goods into Grace's hand, then sidles past Breanda, which is no mean feat.

"I guess it's a hard thing to do," Grace says as they scramble to split the check and tip and fumble between tables and chairs and out the door to face the full blossom of summer heat.

"What's a hard thing to do?" Breanda says, walking slowly but slightly ahead of Grace.

"Well, it's certainly an admirable thing."

"What's hard, what's admirable?"

"Love everything."

They stroll along, catching the glares of truckers in bandanas unloading their wares to delis and bookstores. Approaching the great Maiden Lane, they pause to allow a few galloping mail trucks and semis to pass.

They cross the street.

Before entering the buildings run by the brothers Klang, something just out of Kafka, Grace takes one last peek at the sky. "Must mean to incorporate everything," she says.

"Incorporate what, pray tell?"

"Though one might suppose love is anathema to certain things."

"Anathema—a nice ring."

"Except that it largely means a curse."

"I like three syllables for a girl."

"Gracia, too, has three syllables."

"So it does," Breanda says.

"Welcome, Anathema," Grace says, under her breath but loud enough for Breanda alone to hear, as they march past the posts of fellow employees to the teeming terminal room itself.

"Here we go," Breanda says, as they settle into the room thick with registers.

Grace says, "Give me books of buildings rated A, B, C, and D for demolition."

To the computer they go, taking first the thick list of all current "D" buildings that have yet to achieve their fates. These are buildings in the South Bronx, predominantly, but some in Brooklyn, Queens, Manhattan, and Staten Island. They consult one register in particular, the Landovitz list it has been called somewhere along the line. This one contains the collection of soon-to-be-extinct beasts, dinosaurs, shrines of another era inhabited by the conquering race of rats, and hungry beings of the human species. They are marked, so it reads, by bugs, bombed-out furnaces, missing windows, cracked beams, no running water, and the criteria continue. They are noted by great four- to six-digit numbers on streets named Clinton, Rivington, Bergen, Grand Concourse. Dark caves, they are, hideouts for the poor whose names range from Argez to Zigowski, and include Gotzcha, Loxquisto, Qarrator, Slomber, Tetracottio, and whose landlords sport first names like Rosa-Sue, Jemima, Roy-Louis, Francesca. Some are inhabited by squatters, others sealed up and running wild with rats, cats, raccoons, lizards, and droppings of all kinds, not to mention, Grace imagines, the thorny green milkweed and other such summerish intruders as dandelions and purple crabgrass and sunshine itself.

"What are the criteria for demolition, anyway?"

"Let's take every 50th one," Breanda shouts, "as it's all so arbitrary.

"Let's tear down Wall Street, all the towers of Babel," Grace says. "Tear it all down."

"And replace it with??"

"Igloos?"

"Tipis?"

"Treehouses!"

"Wombs!" Breanda says.

"Light. Just light!" Grace says.

Breanda stands up next to seated Grace, as both watched the printout zingle and zam, slapping down its thermal ink of letters and numbers from its secret storage of darkness. "Anybody watching us would think we are—"

"What we are!"

"Nuts."

"Fruits."

"Crackpots."

"Weirdos."

"Goof-offs."

"But not squares."

"Not clones."

"Spacey, it's true," Grace says.

"Cool, hip, neat, groovy, far-out," Breanda says.

"Not nice. We're not nice."

"Who'd wanna be nice?"

"No one wants to be—"

"Walph probably does—"

"You'd probably want to be nice too if you shared a room with Tina Meana."

"True—nice and scared."

"So," Grace says, tearing off the sheet. "Here 'tis. Now what?"

"Take it to our leader!" With exaggerated cheerfulness, they carry off their achievements to the terribly bright room across the hall.

"Wonderful!" Tina's arm reaches out to cradle the goods, as she and Walph and the two girls confer at her blotter over the randomly chosen list of the doomed.

"Ok, bye bye." Grace and Breanda whisper these words in departing, and they track down the terminal in order to start step two, namely listing out each selection in terms of occupants, apartments, all pertinent criteria for determining the buildings most accessible, those at the tippy-top of the list for demolition.

Puttering around, slave to the manipulations of Breanda's spongy fingers, the computer offers up its hoard. Grace watches as it tuts its tats and frizzles its dazzles and produces its clusters of historical facts, its names, dates, places, at any given point in time to be shifted or obliterated at the whim of an operator, or by some erring forefinger and thumb unaware of its own treachery.

Arbitrary it seems. Unreal city. Against this backdrop, this Landovitz list of impossible data, how easy it is to forget that names came paired with human beings, even for the humanists in the very room, who are, truth be told, *more than* witnesses. How unusual it is, in such a milieu as this for Grace to spot the surname "Starlinsky" dancing before her eyes. The shriek that comes from her mouth startles her fellow perpetrator.

"What in hell are you wailing about?" Breanda's lips are jarred out of a working purse.

Grace cries, "Jesus." Her adrenal glands are surely aglow. "You would not believe this."

"Oh, try me!" Breanda's expression, so heartfully simple.

"You remember writing these ridiculous proposals—you know, buildings to be destroyed, those with no occupants except rodents and insects? Well, we have selected for demolition one that's inhabited by a star. Just look, won't you?"

"What do you mean, my pretty?"

"I wish I could tell you!"

"Do tell. Do tell."

"Where to begin?"

"In the beginning was…"

"Yes," Grace says. "What exactly was in the beginning?"

"I do not know."

"Why not? Weren't you there?"

"I do not think so."

"Then, where were you?"

"Who knows?"

"You know."

"I know?"

"Yes."

"Well," Breanda says, sighing, her good nature beginning to ebb. "Where were you?"

"I was there, of course."

"So, what happened?"

"You would not believe it."

"You are not to be believed!" Breanda rises up and waddles out the door, presumably to pee.

With a quick lift and twist of her wrists, Grace flips up the terminal lid and tears yet another toxic document, scanning the list for Starlinsky. When she finds the name, she stares for a moment, then makes a few copies of the document upon which is emblazoned the address of Starlinsky's Lower East Side loft. She scribbles a "delete" symbol next to this entry, and places one of the copies in her bicycle pouch. When Breanda appears, teetering on the horizon, Grace sees her own exhaustion mirrored on her colleague's face.

Breanda mumbles something of her discontent and stretches high up in the swivel chair, frowning at the face of the upturned watch that sits on the terminal—her very own piece of frill. "Three more hours," she says, taking a tissue to burst her bubbles of perspiration.

"So, what we gonna do? Madam You-Know-Who wants us to kill ourselves for the sake of this fair city," Grace says, fretting and sweating as well.

"You have my permission to leave."

"Yes, I have only to finish my work. That is all they ask of any civil slave."

"As you wish, my servant."

"Remind me to leave my neck at the door before I go," Grace says.

*

In this room, it is an unlikely thing for the telephone to actually ring with a call from the outside world. And when it rings at all, it is usually Richard, and Breanda typically picks up the receiver. So Breanda is understandably jarred by the sobbing and abrasive female party on the other end of the flashing dial, who, after hearing Breanda's identification, requests to speak with Grace: "Who cares who you are or what you think!"

"I believe this call is for you," Breanda says, handing over the receiver, and whispering, "she's very loud—warning."

Grace holds the phone at a short distance from her ears. "Hi, Gracie, pal, friend for all seasons of laughter and tears."

Breanda is watching Grace, and Grace is watching Breanda, both of their faces in a warp mode.

"Grace, Grace, Grace!" These words are gongs coming from the receiver. Grace can see that Breanda can hear them and tries to muffle the receiver with her hand and lowers her own voice as she speaks.

"Ah," Grace says. "The chirp of the watery Muriel Lyons! Hello Em, my dearest, saddest cheerio. What soup is on? What wonder attends you? How can I be of service?"

"It sounds, my friend," Breanda says quietly to the room at large, "as if you are speaking a different language."

Grace pulls the receiver about a foot away from her ear. "This friend of mine—her voice is magnified, gratis her illness."

"Oh, what is not new," Em says, "is that I must stay here till the clock drips stop. Who knows when that will be? Some brilliance attends me, but still I cannot cope with sweet life. Pea soup today, pumpkin tomorrow, and pie in the face, right? Storybook, right?"

"Right, my Em gem. You will soon find a great wonder to give you peace of heart, okay?"

80

"I knew Gracie would be a treat for the right trick. Thanks. Now I'll be off. Come soon to say hi. Bye!"

And then Grace hears the click of the receiver. She notes the sour expression on Breanda's face. "She is not in good shape, my friend, Em, but for all I know, you could be in worse shape, and I wonder what shape I, myself, am in."

"I believe you've got some nutso friends," Breanda says, and then, noting the quizzical, virtually unreadable expression on Grace's face, she falls silent.

"We are all," Grace says, "so desperately sad."

"We are?"

"Drowning in a melancholy borne of frustration," Grace says, a sudden thought of Werther, paired with Em.

"Not me," Breanda says. "I'm going to have a baby!"

"This is true," Grace says. "And there it is. The hope that will keep us all willing to breathe."

"Yes," Breanda says. "We're breathing!"

"We have no choice," Grace says. "We lack gills!"

They work for a time without many words, both of them taking a turn to go to the bathroom, and more often than not, Breanda's eyes rolling, her eyebrows raised. But Grace is fast at work. Until she looks up, and it is with silence and astonishment that Grace takes in the sight of Breanda as she lowers herself to the floor.

"Should I ask what you are doing?"

"I found a grey hair when I was in the bathroom," Breanda confesses tearfully. "I wanted to show it to you. But I lost it, and now I can't get up. I feel like a mammoth monster."

"A mammoth monster of heaven you are!" Grace says this in the sweetest of tones, as she helps Breanda up off the floor.

And when the time to depart finally approaches, Grace helps herself to an extra load of cargo, namely the pretty portable that she manages to balance on her handlebars, along with a phone-cradle, in addition to a great roll of thermal paper that she deposits in her pouch. She delivers one of the dabbled-with copies to the commander in charge and gives one to her trusty, but unwitting squire.

"I don't like you sometimes, Grace. You have too many secrets."

*

One hand is gripping the portable. The other grips the handlebars of her bicycle. When the doors to the tiny elevator in her building open, Grace wheels the bicycle quickly toward the door of her studio. Placing the portable on the tiled floor, she unlocks said door, beyond which lies her favorite country, a slum of sorts, and of sorts a slumberland, where sooner rather than later, she finds herself in a telepathic dialogue with her friendly worm who she thought had deserted her for another woman. Indicating by precious thought rather than gruesome speech, the worm informs her that he will never be without her, although he might lack the present body of his identity.

A conversation, such as it is, follows:

"Is it possible for you to appear to me in the body of Starlinsky?"

"Not only possible, but definitive," the worm answers in his own inimitable fashion.

"So why don't you appear so presently?"

"That's a very particular point you just made," says, for lack of a better word, the worm.

"Now you are teasing me, I hope you know."

"You are making matters extremely personal."

"Sometimes that happens."

"So, I'll tell you that you have some say, so to speak, in the matter."

"That's news to me."

"If I may be the first to say so myself, there is something new on the Rialto."

"What, *Romeo and Juliet?*"

"No, Grace, the Prince of Peace."

"But—I thought I was going to bear a girlchild."

"That's a thought for pretty minds."

"Yes, and you know I was selected and found suitable, but really the truth is that I've been seeded by Prince Starlinsky himself. This is my confession to you, most noble worm. I've been had, but I'm not complaining."

"Why not?"

"Because it was precisely what I wished for, with no extenuating circumstances, if you know what I mean."

"That is pretty par for princes." The worm serenely brushes off one of his shimmering balls.

"The wonder is, Señor Worm, laboratory atoms have been sent up the garden gate for the sake of my baby."

"I believe you will further all stuff of science, pretty maid, so please don't faint when you hear that there was a worm around during that fallout. The truth is people run from most truths, which causes the spread of lies, naturally. To be sure the live lie is the fastest and healthiest growing thing. Gracie, my precious darling bunny, why not invite Mr. Starlinsky—"

"Doctor, my worthy worm."

"Dr. Starlinsky, then, to my place, tonight at eight for dinner and drinks."

Grace, without words, is stammering.

"Grace, Grace, please prove true to me." The worm cries, with sound, mimicking actual human speech, a vibration not entirely superior to silence, but distinct in the matter of its residue, namely the echo, which can be reverberating upon the drum of an ear for almost an eternity. With just that and no address left by the aside, the worm takes his leave, and Grace is free to wonder what she might.

But not for long, for the fact of a ringing, which proves too violent a tremor, due perhaps to the distresses felt by the party on the other end of the still raging phone.

Chapter 4

From the sublime and preferred communication of the spheres, Grace extends her arm, her fingers reaching for the handset.

"Hello," she says.

"You don't know me," he says, "from a great piece of excrement, but I have been watching you for many moons and I would like to rope you into a good time. What say ye?"

"From my point of view," she shouts, "you have found yourself the perfect end to the story, so please eat it, Bruce." A piece of creamy advice, and now returning the receiver to its hook, but steaming when she sinks back into her still-warm musty old sheets, pondering a greeting if Bruce should try again. "You don't know me, fuck-ears, but I would love to rend you to pieces" is the one that finally satisfies her.

Lying on her right, she picks up a hand-mirror about the size of a giant's fist to peruse her billboard to the world. With only the slant light of a setting sun, she surveys the shadowed geography of her face, now less a facial billboard than a map to her soul, with its minor and major roadways, lesser and greater landings, oil spills, craters from small meteors, bits of stardust. Ah, tears they are. She examines locations for energies gone dry, wonders what else might be fading from her briar patch. What she cannot see, but that is nevertheless germinating, is bravery, not the most translatable quality, but among the most troublesome.

The phone rings again, and into the receiver she shrieks, "Suck, rat!" Her voice, a contralto if there ever was one, is also marked by an occasional predilection for taut consonants, which generally prick up the ears of those who might not necessarily be taken by what she has to offer visually. In this case, the plosives themselves release a bit of a poison dart. With a fury some reserve for their walls, or a punching bag, or their enemies or, God help us all, their mates, Grace rises to disconnect the telephone. Then she blows her nose and, prancing into the alcove that calls itself her kitchen, begins to attack the vegetables in the refrigerator, seeing only carrots. She removes two, selects some grapes and a pear, pours herself some orange juice, puts all the above on a tray, and grabs the plastic-wrapped leftovers, cold and miniscule as they are, including: chicken dumplings, ragout stew from Grandma Gristedes, rennet custard from Santa Sloans, Ma Daitch's cheesecake, Pa KMart's chips, and more—all piled high, now. She teeters back to bed, preparing for a picnic. "Be it ever so humble." She is singing now. "There's no place like bed."

She is grazing as she re-connects herself to the world, and within seconds, the phone rings, and she gingerly slides off the bed, girds up her loins, and greets the caller with her own encompassing roar of all colors.

"Grace Rosinbloom—for gods' sakes, what happened to you? Well, was thinking about you anyway, and where have you been for seven years—in the loony-bin? You'd never believe who called me, your friend Em. Said you were missin' me, and Gracie I'm always missin' you. Just let me know, Gracie. Just let me know. I mean, really, how the hell are you? Do you know who this is?"

"Hi, Angelo. Can you call me back? I'm sorry, but I've got to get some sleep."

"Sure, toots. It's only natural you'd be sleeping at dinnertime. I'll try ya later. Take care of yourself—dig?"

Now, without any rancor, she disconnects, anticipating the continuation of her heady excursion and the mitigating comfort of sleep itself. Having completed her nibbling, she stuffs her face into the pillow, wraps her arm around the collected contents of her refrigerator. She meditates, suspended in the down and polyester mix, eyes closed, bypassing the acknowledgement that this is the very bed she had once shared with Angelo when life was supposed to be all roses. Yes, of course she knows that all sentient beings must abide by principles, that it is ill-advised to allow oneself to suffer devastation simply for the loss of her worm. How to focus her thoughts, to summon him once again? Could it be that he is jealous of Starlinsky? Should she urge him to remember that she lacked dialogue with Starlinsky? For this is a worm she can talk to, well, not exactly *talk*. Communicate, then, and how she needs his communication! She lies there, her fingernails clicking on the tray upon which sit remnants of her repast, little carrot turds, a salty odor of chicken still hovering above her face, and in the distance the last few wisps of a setting sun. Her eyes closed, she breathes, releasing herself, body part by body part, catching sight of the murky dark circle of blue bobbing behind the lids of her eyes. Ah, the indigo light, her sign that some kind of healing is at hand. Before she knows it, she has slipped back, returned seamlessly, so it would seem, to that unseemly state beyond all boundaries, and she is in fact greeting a frowning worm that does not say, or in any other way indicate, "Hello."

"How can you ignore me, friend, when we have locked horns, so to speak. Rise, rare adder that you are, and be a bright grail. You are just where reason is concerned, but when it boils down to your heart, you lose it all, righteous though you may be. Why round up your baskets on just one egg?"

She tries other, softer, more sensual methods of rousing the worm, but once again he has disappeared from view.

But like life, dreams have a mind of their own.

"Look up," a voice in her mind commands. What does she behold but some kind of tower of Babel, in the grim outreaches of what she, in her own provincial way, determines must be New York State. Oh, it is a behemoth, a huge silver stem rising up like an elephant's trunk, like Jack's beanstalk, and oh, shall she be instructed to climb? "Ah," she thinks. "Can this be what a nuclear reactor looks like?" Fumes of smoke curling, snarling, circling about this almost iridescent test-tube of mammoth proportions. How slippery, how hot, and the smell, how putrid. Yet, she pursues, one step, then another, upon an instantly appearing spiraling stairway. She trods on, a tiny path it is, for feet the size of Cinderella's alone. And there she is at the top. Now, another voice, an anthem of voices: "Look down." A grown girl, she is, in Alice's shoes. She looks and then slides, wondering which bug is the sound coming from? Ah, are they all dead, then?

She selects one little dry body that sits quite still in the cradle of her open palm. "Hello bug," she whispers, but the bug does not in any way respond. She gropes like a fisherman at the ground, grappling with scorched carcasses of grasshoppers and gills of grouper, rose of the shore. Grace sets her eyes upon what she thinks are mountains but instead are masses of wildlife rotting at the horizon's edge. Vast landscapes of death before her: skeletons and exoskeletons, crumbled and crumpled-up beasts, not landforms at all, and what are they waiting for? Is resurrection possible? Her worm all but forgotten, she begins to cry, "Why, when there's this great crystalline sunlight right here all along?"

It is not the phone that startles her this time, nor the clock, but a vibration, a wave just the same, namely a profound ray of sadness, a spray of wetness on her cheeks, and it must be reported that other waters need to flow. Upsetting the precarious balance of her mattress, she stands, having the net effect of tumbling foodstuffs and a crash. Oh, she is upset with the contents of her mind. True tears they are, she observes in the bathroom mirror. She wonders about that Nobel baby, *her* baby, with its miraculous start. Whether metaphorical or not—it did not matter. No longer, then? Gone with the worm? At this thought fresh trickles spring from her eyes, sorrows for a world brought to an ordinary death. Once seated, she whispers an incantation for instant salvation, whether by way of angelic hosts or honorable aliens, both for self and world, and then she releases all of the hazardous waste from her body. Removing what has not yet been removed of her clothing, she enters the shower to draw out what meanness has remained upon her skin.

She returns to her room proper, dripping dew drops all over, and begins to sort out the teeming world of clothes and food, not to mention tomes, that have more than peppered the plain wood floor. It would not be an exaggeration to suggest that she is a young woman of extremes, Grace Rosinbloom, who stands there not unlike Aphrodite herself, or the biblical Eve, with her hair in similar strings, though not so long as to take the place of a fig leaf.

Her own little patch the color of Aphrodite's tresses, but her actual mane more auburn than red and golden in summer. Naked she stands, ankle-deep in perhaps three weeks' worth of possessions, a boundless endless world of things. Little nuisances, copulating with each other, are they? In her mind, she sees, remembers for just how long this very floor was bare.

And then it was no longer bare.

Six days to fill up a world with things.

Time and things.

Thoughts themselves, the creators of time, perhaps then, and not just the creation of time?

She stretches her toes; they are long and thin, as are her feet and almost every other appendage jutting out from her torso, which itself is slender, attenuated, pulsing with a longing, something insatiable that she can barely name.

And now, she is trying to feel the sensation of the wood, and somehow this provokes her to clean, to make order. She takes to the act like a racehorse, organizing, shuttling shoes, clothing, trinkets, foodstuffs, books, all off to their destinations—passionately, now, as though with sudden blinders. After all, she does love this floor that she herself had sanded.

This room, a studio with a history, with *her* history. Like a cloistered nun, she'd written her never-to-be-finished dissertation in this very room, with little but the small desk she'd sprung for, thanks to a scholarship. For a year, she'd slept in a sleeping bag. And one day, it was a day in the summer, when the pristine quality of her space was shattered. It was as if civilization had discovered Grace Rosinbloom. The furnishings and even the bulk of the books themselves—oh, she now had books galore—were, in effect gifts, gratis of her super Frank, whom she kept putting off. Prior to that, she was the library's best friend. "Listen lassie," he said. "If you wait any longer, I'll be dead." Every week or so, he'd just show up at her door. Finally, he just grabbed her by the elbow, like a child, and kept pulling. He'd held the elevator for her. A frail man with rheumy eyes, he was all bone and opinion. "Just come on, now," he said. "You're a stubborn one." Once he'd pinned her in the small elevator, he just stared ahead, giving nothing away. Together they rode down to the very basement, where he'd stored the contents of more than one apartment.

"Abandoned," he said. What he didn't say, and what she'd found out later, was that these were the belongings of men who died mysteriously. So many men, so beautiful, so well-educated, and so many books. "Whatever you don't take is going to the dumps tomorrow," he said. She hauled them upstairs. Again, he held the elevator for her. He begged her to consider shelves, bureaus, the armchair, coffee table, bedframes, even their beds. "You can't live in a room with nothing but a sleeping bag!"

She took it all, gratefully so, except for the beds. When it was all loaded into her small room, she motioned for him to wait, snapped open a small change purse, where she kept a wad of bills. She was struggling, trying to pull them out, but he put her off. "Don't be stupid. Just seeing you settled finally is all I need. Now get yourself a bed," he said. "And someday I want to see you with a boyfriend." He let himself out, and she could hear his laughter echoing in the hallway. And how it took months to find out that he died, her angel, and another super took over, someone who bought the building, who when you called, sent over people from a company, but Grace never calls. If something were to come up, she'd go to Stem's place. One time, going up there when she heard strange sounds, the smell of incense and cigarette smoke, and then later, when she went up again, piles of people pouring out, looking as if they'd seen a ghost. She'd mentioned something about that, and he'd told her not to worry but she should come up and see for herself.

"Next time, knock harder, and get yourself a seat in there," he'd said, pinching her cheek. "When you're ready," he said. "You'll come."

"Ready?"

"You'll know," he'd said.

No, she isn't ready, wasn't and isn't. But she'd like to think she will be.

Almost four years and still not feeling that feeling of "this is my life," as if you're following a stream that you hope will lead to the door of your future, and she is still rock-hopping, still within the stream. And how long she was with the sleeping bag, and then with the futon, and then the bed which was thanks to Angelo, and too many boyfriends later. And still a dissertation incomplete.

Things. The acquisition. As if they are what gives you equanimity, as if that is what makes you an adult. All those things that the dead owned! Now in her home. Things don't give you permanence. They are not the congratulatory sign of adulthood. She'd made use of the books—the psychology especially, and the art books—there were hundreds of them—and on shelves, stacks of them now, opened to the beloved pages of Caravaggio, Botticelli, Picasso, Vermeer, those men, real men, and where were the real men of this world? Certainly not on her floor but in her dreams, and she certainly took more than her share.

91

Yes, there are angels about her. If they could just manifest for her a certain man.

Well, there was Stem. Stem again. And with the thought, the desire to sit and drink tea, as she did when he finally did come to see her, and they sat there, like post-coital lovers, even though they were not and never would be.

Does everybody in NYC just sit there on a bed staring for an hour, sometimes more?

And now, as if before a lake. But the city exhausting. Each day a lifetime. The vibrations coming at you. So that now all she's fit to do is to just sit there with the tea, a self reminiscing. Trying to remember another time. All the moments with Stem, as if they could be placed consecutively in a book. And she could use it for her dissertation. And she could read it again and again like a poem. The words like music. A vibration. A prayer. It could be like one of those snow globes, and she could turn it around and watch the snow fall over something hallowed.

Life with the beloved—whether or not you slept with the beloved—was hallowed.

It wasn't too long after Frank parted with the information that she knocked on Stem's door a second time, and he invited her in. It wasn't too long after that when they had met outside—the time he actually came inside. He didn't come directly into her apartment, did he? She was trying to reconstruct a timeline. Like a narrative, a timeline was comforting. It offered sequence. It lulled you into thinking there was such a thing as order.

She recalled walking up Seventh, and that almost forested spot with the copy center, big-leafed trees, catalpa, and she spotted Stem like one long human pod standing next to that tree with those long pods like flute bodies. She couldn't help herself, taken by the heart-like form of his face, the legato of his vowels, and the warmth of his eyes. And then just to get him to speak—to hear his voice.

And yes, he'd love some tea.

And when he came up there, seeing all the books—how he'd floated around, taking out this book and that, saying little, but "Ah, yes", and "Right", and "Oh"—just exclamations like that.

She wondered if he were matching the book with the man, and the extent of his friendship, whether he was friends or lovers with the others in the building who'd died, whose books these once were.

And how tactile she was, he'd noticed that—he, too was tactile, he said, and it was an understatement to say how she noticed his fingers. As if they were antennae. And now she is fingering the Werther on the table with the tea, her fingers on the pages, though in no mood to read. A sadness now. That feeling, of passing through things, this thought, namely that we are *not* the "champions" but the *temporary ones*, so hard to fathom.

As if all that will remain are the snow globes.

And how glad she was that Stem asked for an hour first to practice, giving her time to tidy up, in one clean swoop, gathering the clothes—and yes, it was Beethoven that she was cleaning to, that she could hear, a cassette, that kept her on track—the clothes that had littered the floor for weeks, from the time of sweaters. She'd thrown them into one of the closets. She had time to make her bed and close the drawers of the highboy and flush the toilet and wash the dishes with wilted salad nibs, not to mention the bacteria-laden sponge that she quickly splattered with bleach, and then he came up, and she'd sat him down on the bed as she prepared the tea, then carried this very pot with its stained cozy, which he said he'd have to replace—and he did.

Everything then and now on the small round table, currently home to the portable, now placed underneath, on the floor, there with its cover. So as not to remind her, not to upset the peace offered by a pot of tea, upon this little all-purpose table. Five herbs brewing and simmering next to a jar of Egyptian honey…still that same brand from Murrays down her street. These pleasures, the small pleasures.

93

The day full of sun and promise, but also sadness—a day like today when she'd caught him just standing there.

And staring at his fingers and the sinewy arms of a pianist, and the florid clean smell even on the linen jacket he held that she would later totally associate with his apartment, but that he did not bring with him when they had the tea, no. But he told her about the day they lifted the eight-foot grand—up with ropes and pulleys and then dropped it— and she found what she was looking for: a glazing in the eye as he described the horrific sound as beastly, and of course they had to replace it—which was the piano she had seen rising, never realizing it was the second such piano.

And how he made it painfully clear using words like boyfriend and lover, not suggesting for a minute that he might be bi, never bi but only men and only one man, and yet she should hear him come to the church and play Prokofiev and she did that.

She, who might be carrying a metaphorical child, for having loved a metaphorical worm, a metaphorical man.

How close you can be—and that Dr. Starlinsky—so close as well.

And still it's a no!

The sadness comes with seeing the closeness but feeling the distance. And so Stem so clearly is not the one, but he inspired the one, and so she thinks this one she is waiting for must also be from the Midwest or Texas. She would listen for him, for his vowels, for the lilt, and she would wonder about the smell, as well.

And now thinking about this Starlinsky. Is he Midwestern? Tall and sinewy, yes, and he looked at her, in that way. But—.

"You will find your man," Stem told her that day. "You are a beauty, rare for the incongruity, if you don't mind me saying. I know you are looking, and believe me, I am not the one. It took me eons to find mine. I know your pain."

94

This man Stem had found was gone. Come and gone. Stem was and still is looking again. Many men, now. She figures.

"You have found your true home," he said, the medium of music and more.

"People are dying in this building," she'd said.

"We're all dying until we're dead," he said. That smile—a goof and sadness both there.

"Semantics," she said. She knew about semantics.

"Yes," he said. "I know, but you mustn't linger there. You have work to be done, and I have music to practice," and he was off, and yet she heard those voices now and again, voices coming from above and far off, voices or sounds, and she knew that he knew this.

"Rare for the incongruity," those words reminding her of the way Andrew praised her neck or knees or the iridescent shit color—he said this, shit, yes—of her eyes, the soft little ripple of skin at her belly as compared with the fine-tuned muscles of her legs, runner's legs. She could run if she had to.

And soon she will dress. "Dress for success," Stem would say.

And yet the sadness in his face so late at night, just last night—with his word "courage"—that word comes up.

Stem is a person whose words you take to heart.

Not to mention those sounds coming from his room, those people.

What she wondered was whether he was conducting a séance in there.

She wondered but couldn't bring herself to ask.

It seemed preposterous—a serious musician and telepathy, or whatever it was when you contacted the dead.

Preposterous, but she had her own experiences.

These dreams, the worlds of books, Werther's world, for instance, or the world of Jane Eyre that she'd lived in, or the world of Mary Shelley's *Frankenstein,* or the world of *Hamlet* or *Lear* or *The*

Tempest—whether performance of the reader or the bodily performance of acting, one enters. One lives there. She lives so much in other worlds. And other dreams she'd lived in before this one.

The very first to recall she had as a child. She feared going to sleep, called in her father. He would sing to her, substitute her name for the names in the songs, *For it was Gracie…plain as any name can be….* But soon as he left, soon as the darkness took her under, she was there, with her mission. Nazi Germany. She had to save her grandmother. They lived with their dog on a small island surrounded by a moat. The grandmother held a rifle and remained on the island. She, the child, night after night, she had her assignment: there was a candy shop, there were languages to learn, a special instrument; a sickle, it turned out was necessary to cut through a wall to get to the other side. A progression, a series of events by which they'd forded the moat, crawled through a spiraling hole in a wall, finally securing themselves—only to find they had to keep going, here and there, until it stopped. With a revelation that there was no escape, the dream ended; they were surrounded by rows of barbed wire.

She'd been entrusted with saving them. It was only many years afterwards, remembering, realizing that she'd failed. At the time, she was simply grateful for the end of it.

Too young to think of it as a metaphor.

Did not know the word.

And now a metaphorical worm. A metaphorical child. After all, wasn't everyone carrying a kind of child! Did Stem know this? Remember when he'd called her 'child'? Before this she'd had another series of men about to kill her. A series of chases. Someone had killed her in this very room and then started after others—children. And that's when she found herself going after the killer. That's when she realized she herself could kill.

Stem has séances—has filled his room with the voices of dead men and women, inviting in a world of people who long to hear their

96

dead again—how could she judge? Who is she who lives in her dreams, who lives in novels, who is living for this dream of a man because in the life of the body, there is no such man and there hasn't been since Andrew. The Andrew who ate a worm. The Andrew she let go of because he wouldn't follow her on her circuitous path, who probably still lives in Jersey, perhaps in the house next door to the one he was born in, with a wife and the twelve kids she once wished to have.

And now—she returns to this insidious world with government secrets, in the wake of the uncertain cosmos of her dream, more preposterous and sinister than anything a séance could muster up, for sure.

She requires no séance.

She is currently enjoying the order she has created. Gratitude—appreciation for the highboy or bureau, all oak, with its alabaster knobs, and the oak shelving. Her clothes, a combination of gifts, close-out sales, and thrift-store finds, neatly folded or hanging, and the few dresses stationed in her closet. The three tiny chambers—bath, closet, kitchen—all set on one side of the foyer that opens with an arch into her main room. She had—in a rare stroke of decorating—hoisted a flimsy, lacy hanging on a few hooks, woven a gold brocade around it to keep from striking her head. She thinks of it as something like a promontory, or clouds. The bed itself, brass poles and all, was a gift from Angelo, who preferred springs to the unfriendly, non-reciprocity of a futon on a hard wood floor, so a box spring under the futon mattress became the compromise. Now, she removes the food from this gift, piling the remains on the aluminum tray and returning the collection to the refrigerator, even though she suspects the nutritional value is by this time negligible.

Well, no need to torture yourself. After all, the word of the day is "courage".

This vision of order pleases her, the oyster goddess who is just looking out, oblivious of who or what might be looking in.

And now action feels available.

She reconnects herself with the wondrous world of lurid phone calls, praying for peace, however, from this very world—at least for the moment—and she is granted her wish. She follows her regimen for dressing, examining coats, hats, rainwear, skirts, jackets, dresses, and determines to waltz naked as a needle, that is, nude from both thighs and elbows down. She dons some new undies, happily possessing their sheer nothingness, puts on some musical earrings, a ring to adorn her middle finger and a trestle to brace her wrist.

She jingles into short green shorts and a skimpy blue top and salutes the portable terminal quacking in the air under her all-purpose table.

She places her telephone receiver into the cradle.

By now the clandestine code has become familiar as butter.

As the terminal spits out its percussive banter, Grace dances. At the end of Cornflaker's tut-tut-tut, Grace curtsies, then bows, anything to put off the inevitable confrontation of woman and machine. "I wonder," she says, her voice trailing off, and then, at long last, she sits down. Upon the first glimpse of the printout, she becomes one with it, having but a dim sense of what she might gain, and no sense at all of what she is about to lose.

And then Grace begins to type in commands.

The sun is setting, but Grace is riveted to letters that form words.

Innocence comes in many shapes and sizes, although it's not generally affiliated with any other species trotting about this planet. Humans are said to have lost it with an apple, but somehow each generation has the opportunity to surrender it again, endlessly. Most only realize it after the fact. Awareness itself is only the beginning. Not being responsible for what one has suddenly become aware of creates a certain complicity in most humans, certainly those above the age of reason, which sadly, cannot be given a number.

Shrouded in this moment, which she herself has created, Grace now enters the world of an alien system, having signed no affidavits, given no oaths of obedience, uttered not one promise of fidelity. She peers into the tunnel of a barely two-dimensional reality of paper, not to mention its virtual source. She starts punching keys to get into the jewel box of the U.S. government.

Namely, their intelligence, or so she likes to think of, the CIA, that is, as the Cavern of Inspired Articulations, under which is listed what she presumes is its "Taxonomy of Treasures." Grace allows herself to be taken into this world, which is very black and white and gray, and bleak, too, lacking eye-pleasers or ear-pleasers, or anything to entice the nose. Yet how greedy for information she has suddenly become, scanning the list. "But, where to begin? Why not at the beginning? See where it takes me."

Would that she could hear her father sigh. He would send in a fly to eat the worm.

He would send in Starlinsky, himself, wouldn't he?

By then, it would be too late.

Her father, the technician who engineered her world, who kept giving her assignments but died before the dissertation itself was finished.

He was more powerful on earth than he is in heaven.

For all the clarity that his box seat will allow.

And yes, they had their disagreements: about Richard Nixon, for a long time, about nuclear power, forever. Even about the bomb.

The final word for the latter two was an agreement about disagreement—'the final', meaning what Grace remembered being their last conversation before he was murdered by his bad driving.

Grace, herself, had never been good behind the wheel.

Now, she touches the paper, her right hand and her left hand, both holding the scroll as it slides, her fingers directing her down the list. She watches, mesmerized, as the keys move quickly to prepare a

99

coating, then covering, then coating again—as if little drumsticks—making quite a racket. Racket, a word often used in her house, only because her mother liked crossword puzzles and needed a double-reed instrument, curious how it could start with an "r" and not an "o" or a "b," or even an "F," upon which her father betrayed his musical vocabulary: "It's either racket or ranket depending upon how many letters."

"Yes," Grace now says. "Quite a ranket, Daddy."

She, nevertheless, stands before the machine transfixed, trying to penetrate the code, her eyes steeled for the chance to read through the camouflage, the racketing.

What she sees? The back and forth, the scrambling of the carriage to cover up its goods.

What she hears, the racket, a sound like pounding, like mashing and gnashing, like iron crags at odds.

What she imagines—starting with "A", under which are categories such as "Abortions," next to which the researcher is advised to "see also, 'illegitimate infants'," and under which is an alphabetized list including the following: "…of baby boomers," "…of Democrats," "…of the famous and rich," "…of nuns," and of course "practitioners". That list rambles on for pages, and the next category, oddly enough, reads, "Abraham, Foreskin Of," followed by "Aliens"—next to which are in parentheses, "See also, Space Populations," and under which are just three subcategories, namely "Allies" and "Axis of Evil," and "Pre-Human Influences" namely: evolution, Darwin, problematic nature thereof—". Grace directs herself to the list of categories under "B", which include "Banks" and "Bordellos" and "Bribery"—methods of, and for "C", Grace spots, among other categories, "Civil rights, Color Studies, Control of…," directing viewers to negotiate further, specifying populations Indian, Latin, Negro, Oriental, and under Oriental are listed Middle-East, Near-East, Far-East. Following "Color Studies, Control of," there are pages and pages on "Communism," followed by pages for "Confessions," and twice as many for "Dangerous people"—the section she had previously inspected—and a rather copious entry on "Einstein," with subcategories ranging from "Brain of," and "Civil rights," to "Socialism, Tendencies toward." Grace hops around, noting "Frankenstein," with its hundreds of subcategories, and "Gandhi," inspirations for, as well, along with "Jesus, Robe of," and "Peter Pan, Shadow of".

What seems most puzzling are those not listed. Nothing under "technology;" nothing under "weaponry;" nothing, even, under "guns".

She returns to the category "Frankenstein," amused.

How could the CIA possibly guess that the book, *Frankenstein*, was undoubtedly her very most favorite novel of all time, indeed the source she most quoted in her thesis, having done the traditional amounts of research on the subject of man's hubris, that is, documenting the over-civilization of the human race, using literature as a testament. Literature and philosophy. Of course, she'd covered many of the actual inventions, but more than the ideas themselves, her thesis had been about invention in a theoretical sense, its very idea and the accompanying arrogance, therein, the notions of alchemy and the mixture of spirituality with science, how spirituality infused both art and science.

Yes, to be titled, "Salvation of Man in His Technology Suit."

The philosophy difficult for not having the German. What she said—but it was infinitely more complicated. So numerous, so irreconcilable. A paralysis overcame her for the ability to observe, to see, to analyze, to report, to contextualize it—and to be utterly powerless.

Heidegger, especially.

101

Nothing good could come from Heidegger, her mother had said. The fact of his politics. A Nazi—how could you read anything by a Nazi.

Irrelevant that his lover was a Jew.

Her mother who dismissed anything German. As if Germany was the only villain. As if Germany had to forever pay for its wrong turn in history.

And how many wrong turns had the U.S. taken. Hiroshima, Nagasaki, the desecration and genocide of the indigenous, slavery.

Not to mention the species, humans, our love of money, our innate urge for destruction.

Arguments she sustained with her nuclear and extended families. Arguments for which she could hold her own.

For what good it did her.

Heidegger did her in. She never finished her dissertation. A sore, sore topic.

And now, was she headed right for the thing she was trying to avoid?

Frankenstein, the subject of choice.

Could it be that "Frankenstein" was code for all that she has missed? Cornflaker begins crackling out goods under this category, including endless lists from cloning to renewable resources and everything in the way of nuclear energy that she could ever want to know—or remain ignorant of.

A list of sorts, but a Landovitz List this is not.

Grace looks up. Up and away she looks.

Up and away from the worst anyone could imagine.

Up and away from what she herself is creating.

Or perhaps not.

Noting that the more she looks the more clearly she sees.

It's then that a disparity strikes her, and she finds herself gazing back at the outpouring, containing more information than a person can take in, much less stomach. It is poison, is it not? What has she done? What is she doing? What is this thing called government? Isn't it just the very grandest institution of hubris there is? CIA in particular. Does she really want to know? And now, at this juncture she feels herself becoming instantly aware of the slightest shift of her energies.

"Once I take this in," she says aloud, her eyes shut tight but her fingertips quivering at the edges of the thermal paper, as it inches out slowly, inevitably, moving from its cylinder onto the plane created by her two hands. "I will be part of it."

It is a shuddering revelation.

And so with eyes open and but a modicum of choice, Grace enters the deep cavern of an organization whose origins might precede those of the human race. Or so she imagines. This thought occurs to her, begins to overcome her, how problematic a thing is the concept of killing for reasons that do not remotely concern the primal hunger for food. How far away power is from food, how far away the idea of tomorrow is from today, and do animals kill for tomorrow? Grace ponders the perfectly horrible decision to brand that file with the label of Frankenstein, that it should hold everything most to be feared, namely war and the instruments of war, the theory of war, the possibilities for Armageddon, all so cleverly arranged that Grace figures a novelist might have been consulted. "Or a frustrated novelist," she says aloud, "someone who oughtta be writing. Just as Hitler was a frustrated artist." She wonders if they are all in a kind of reincarnational cahoots, the frustrated artists of the millennia and the governments of all time, and maybe there are aliens in on it to boot? But with luck, there is not a worm. At least not *her* worm.

"You did precede the humans," she says, knowing he must be listening.

The worm, she knows, but her father, she knows not.

Of the worm, she says, "I know you are here somewhere. I know you are always here somewhere. You always are, and you always were. And things must change. The world must change, and I must be a part of it. Just as you are a part of it."

With an involuntary twitch, she greets the CIA in a bit of a delirium, finding the system of nuclear reactions, their homes, their castles, their lords and manors, and their great gripping galleries of weapons. She greets the subsystems, arsenal after arsenal, a fully outfitted underground world of missiles.

"Fuck the fucks," she cries, horrorstruck but still plying, punching, pummeling to get a command to probe at least one of the lovely potential energies of war to end all wars. She makes ground, finding reactors in her own hometown, in addition to a list of addresses and names of persons with such knowledge as to blow up and pop the balloons of a world. She probes possible sights of reactors, multifarious and brand-spanking new. She discovers armies all over and plenty of guns on the moon. It begins to resemble that song about greasy grimy gopher meat, mutilated monkey's feet—grisly as can be. She finds worms used for testing the possible damage of waste, leakage, storage, potential routes for invasion. Prices there are next to these possibilities. And how, she wonders, will they gather such a wondrous world of money? Ah ha, she laughs, realizing that all they need do is to print it. Credit that to the Cornflakers of the world.

She catches herself laughing, but at what? How can she laugh? Is she losing her marbles? Is this going crazy? Not a healthy kind of laughter, oh no, though she is still without any inkling, without any solid notion of how far away from reality this little endeavor is leading her, until she catches sight of a letter she had written to her mama a week before. It sits there, this letter, on the desk occupying space and this moment of her time. She glances at the letter typed in a sloppy manner. It reads: "Dear Mama - How's Florida? Hope the heat has not rotted your looks of fine wrinkles, your groups of group picnics, your giant garden of growing gourds. Your slapdash daughter is sleeping soundly, eating heartily, dressing smartly, meeting fine young handsome doctors everywhere. And what more can you ask? Love and kisses, Gracie Pie."

No, she would not send it. She'd written it for herself. To amuse herself. It would never stand, especially now.

"Oh, to be there again," she says. In that carefree state. A state before knowing. The truly insidious knowledge. Like Eve, she was no virgin.

Yet she thinks of her mother. The one who did not accept, the one with whom she could not come to that understanding. Yet the one who in the end was right. Right about Heidegger but for the wrong reason. Although she never took this on, never tried to defend herself or her standing, Grace was the one her mother actually blamed for her husband's death. As if, were he not worried about her, he would have driven better. You'd think with all his mechanical intelligence, he'd be better with a wheel. Such things her mother said—but Grace was not a fan of fact nor logic—especially with respect to love or death. How happy her mama was when he'd finally given up the sales job, had managed to find himself in an office, had finished the degree, should have taken buses and trains, always, and of course her mother would never find such a man again, good as gold he was—how well loved he was, how well he loved—love itself was never the problem in her family. Of money, yes, of health, yes, but love? There was never a dearth of it.

She'd heard her parents argue.

"This one." Whenever her mother said, "this one," it was always Grace, the one she could not place, the one who almost died but fought to live—the one preceded by miscarriages, and her husband, the reader extraordinaire, the man holding too much knowledge to ever share it all—he was the one questioning the Thalidomide, the only reason Mama did not take it, he the one who did not care enough for money to beg for raises; he, who survived the war only to die in a car accident, he whom they thought the older took after, but was actually the one with the gene likely responsible for the anomaly of Grace. Of "this one," the child who did not follow either side of the family. The others had provided progeny. The older sister, Hope, had gone into engineering—they thought, like the father, so obviously brilliant, teeming with the innate understanding of mechanics and numbers—and who quit when the first child came—a nephew, the first; the younger, June, had become a teacher, all nurturing like Mama—but Grace was the loner, the outsider, the one who blossomed in the arts, especially the art of make-believe, the theatre, namely, as they discovered when Mama had enrolled her in a regional theatre, if only to open her up, if only to give her imagination stability.

Despite her preemie status, Grace was the first to walk and to speak, and she was the tallest of the three.

The older sister had gone to school, then settled in California; the younger in New England. They'd grown up in Jersey—but when their father died and Mama moved to Florida to live near her own sisters—the other girls gradually brought their families south.

And instead of marriage and children, and having given up theatre, Grace had prepared herself for and gotten herself into graduate school in Boston—where her life was all about Heidegger. The rise and fall of Grace—what she could now barely talk about—the supreme failure of her attempt to legitimize herself.

A subject no one would broach, the darkest time of her life.

Came scuttling back to New York, where for a while she lived with Em and Bruce, then wrested herself from them but kept them close, her dubious replacement family.

Then the job with Breanda to stabilize her.

Then the apartment.

Then Stem.

And now…

Grace, when writing to Mama, generally prepared a letter for the public, for the family at large, those who followed the preferred progression: boyfriend, husband, child—one of each gender, preferably.

The letter she'd written, the one she'd never send, the façade she was creating, she recalls the feeling she was trying to cover up when she wrote that letter. "Oh," she had wondered. "When will Mom be happy with me? God knows, I could find myself the perfect husband, and she'd still be on my case until I had a kid, and then I'd have to have another and then another, and then what? What would make her stop worrying? Death. It's the only thing she wouldn't have to worry about. Thank goodness for the others." Shall she ever bring a child into this? Her Nobel Child, notwithstanding, her dreamchild—but aren't all children dreamchildren? And doesn't she love her nieces and nephews, two of each she has, sweetest things, and Breanda will have a sweet one, as well. But, knowing this, will she? She is grateful her sisters have provided her mom with husbands and grandchildren, that kind of distraction. She wonders if she ever will, and on the other hand, she is relieved that she doesn't have to worry about such things for herself. At least, not now. Not now when she was thinking about this information. Love, of course, love she wants. A husband? That she doesn't know. Children? In truth, the world is not the proper place for children. She had wanted to change the world. That was what she had wanted, and that is what her mother worries about, and she does not like to face this thing. Not to mention the world that she now wants to change.

Nevertheless, she can spot the degree of innocence there, in that letter—that feeling now vanished, barely recognizable, yet a week has not even passed since she'd written it. Well, that is the way of New York City. Transform or die. New Yorkers oughtta have it engraved on their foreheads. Maybe it's there in invisible ink. New Hampshire's "Live Free or Die" right there on their license plates. Driving cross country with Andrew, seeing that sign on the bridge over the Mississippi, crossing from Illinois into Iowa, plain as day, posted there, high up, for everyone to see: "The Place to Grow." As if halfway across that large suspension, you would suddenly sprout new brain cells. Clearly New York City has its own, separate from its large namesake whose constituents spurn the great Apple, kick it around without thinking, the way a kid will punt and keep punting a rock down the street. But they also take pride in it, love it even as they hate it because it doesn't die. The place to shed your skins, the place to do nine lives in one, the place to be, that is New York. If you want to stay the way you are, you don't stay here. Yet, she still feels queasy looking at that letter. Ah, she sighs, it was a skin ago.

Speaking of which, Indian Point all over the printout, and the dead fish, the government asking for $10 a dead fish.

Indian Point, more or less, only twenty-four miles from her studio, itself located on a fault line that has a name, the Ramapo earthquake fault line. And leaking the strontium 90…so not just the fish.

And she wonders how much they will give her mother for a dead daughter?

Meanwhile Cornflaker maintains its racket. If only she could massage the data.

Arranged both by date and by alphabet.

Timelines galore for her, country by country, and one long integrating timeline, namely the documentation that begins with the woman Shigeko Sasamori who survives the *Enola Gay*, unlike the 80,000, and chronicles her life until 1955 when Norman Cousins arranges for her and others, called so tragically the Hiroshima Maidens, to come to the US to have reconstructive surgery. And a year before that, *Lucky Dragon*, a Japanese sailboat full of fishermen contaminated from the testing. And there's Linus Pauling, too—collecting and then handing over all those thousands of signatures of scientists demanding an end to the testing. As if the contamination from Operation Crossroads wasn't enough to stop it dead in its tracks. And those Brits, in homage of Gandhi, the peaceful resistance, Aldermaston Easter marches in the early fifties that caught on in NYC. But it's not until 1963 that Kennedy and Khrushchev agree to stop the testing. And so sobering this is, for JFK did not have long to live after that, and how she and everyone were endlessly sobbing for hours and days, and there was never ever anyone like him and there never would ever be again, how sad sad sad for us all. And yet the smaller print of course allowing the testing to continue underground.

Now would be a good time for her father to remind her about the Periodic Table and those runaway electrons.

All of it so neatly dated and arranged chronologically, these thousands of listings. A naming of names follows each entry, and following each name are three sets of numbers. She reads but cannot keep up as more incidents pour forth from the mouth of the barking Cornflaker harmlessly doing his chores.

Like children, giving them names, names for the bombs, explosions, what they called "tests," as if the repercussions could be harmless. Oh, little Adam in Eden naming the animals: "Able, Baker, Charlie, Gilda...." How could they need to test after it was, after all, successful? After all ending the war? After contaminating all that it did not initially kill? And how could they invite guests, thousands all dressed up there in the Pacific and in New Mexico, too, a little later...watching, waiting for the destruction.

Atolls: as if they exist to be destroyed; Bikini Island now uninhabitable for the testing.

Will she ever wear her bathing suit without thinking of plutonium!

Bock's Car, named for the man who would have otherwise piloted the plane, but not that day.

Operations Crossroads, as if a corner had not already been turned. Thousands there watching, yes, like the biblical Jonah, to see the destruction—and unlike Jonah, getting to see it.

To think that Madam Curie, born in the 1800s, died from exposure to the very same thing they cannot get themselves to stop fussing with—all that uranium in the US west, and the indigenous smart enough to leave it the hell alone

Enola Gay, the name of the pilot's mother.

As if God said, "let there be atolls," and a second later said, "let there be contamination." But look at all those resistors in New Zealand and Australia and France and Germany, how they come in individuals, or masses, and a list of names of course, from the identities of the dissenting scientists to the lone Acoma Indian with his one sign protesting the uranium.

How they stopped or prevented or stalled it all—and yet, if stalled, how did Three Mile Island happen? Is there such a thing as a peaceful or safe way to use this power? The hazardous waste, notwithstanding? The greed and desire of the human being, notwithstanding?

Are we simply here to orchestrate our own downfall? Surely the earth will survive us!

Oh! Such thoughts she has, these thoughts that nearly extinguished her in graduate school when she blamed Heidegger but really it was Rosinbloom, not to mention guilt over her father's sudden death—guilt, he said, a useless emotion.

Refusing a reprisal of all this.

Smiling, now, all these thoughts coalescing, and now breathing, breathing in and out, letting them go, but for another thought.

Another "and yet."

Namely, the outrage, how it was they felt the need for more testing not a year after the *Enola Gay* dropped *Little Boy*, after *Bockscar* dropped *Fat Man.*

As if naming could lighten the load.

The euphemisms making the actions swallowable.

Bock's car. Bock Scar.

A forever scar.

Clearly, not a night for the bars, compelled as she is by some veritable cliché of a higher power to witness the updating of the plutonium world. The paradox strikes her—creation is long; destruction short. And the clean-up, longer yet. Not so simple to remove nuclear waste. Sober now, she cries out to that old lord of all love. She imagines God's tears which sends her running to the fridge. As she grabs an apple of the sour green variety that retains its crunch, the one that comes from that part of the world that is so far west it's east, she thinks about the reptile and his fruity knowledge.

Cornflaker keeps popping his kernels of truth. As if it were suddenly too much information, Grace withdraws. Is there a serpent in this machine? Is she doomed? Should she turn it off? Should she just—?

She stubs her toe in the rising action of her semi-epiphany, and her fall jostles the terminal's wire. More like a familiar than a machine, Cornflaker roars himself to a finishing thud. Without a second second-thought, Grace tightens the organ's prongs, re-inserts the plug into the outlet, re-sets the telephone, and re-runs the commands. Before long Cornflaker is back in the lovely business of stockpiling bad goods. Grace waits for such military secrets, as the Vatican dilly-dallying (Nero fiddle-faddling) while Rome burns—as Paris rusting the Eiffel Tower, or London growing a row of flowers under the bridge, or Athens pricing ruins, or Warsaw raging at rejoicing Moscow. "What about we the people! Scapegoats of the world unite!" Grace—in the throes of multiple revelations now, her voice in full throttle—is perhaps oblivious to the others in this apartment complex, this microcosm of Manhattan, who feel the splashing of molecules colliding with their auras. The others, all others but Stem—Stem and his minions. Grace

111

mistakes the wall-taps and ceiling blasts and the bits and pieces of voices for a poltergeist of divine ilk. This ghost of a snake she imagines roaming about her room as the sharp cogs of Cornflaker's wheels urge themselves toward each other in a rather gnashing motion. Once again, the machine pauses, and then, with a deep, dark gasp, Cornflaker begins his assault upon the weepingly weaponous world.

Grace returns her gaze to the mountain of information spinning off the runway of Cornflaker's flat tummy. Pondering the army and navy, their new toys and the fun, she soon grows weary, and nearly seasick thinking: about the future of the ocean rocking with giant torpedoes, drone and man within; about the onslaught of helicopters and ships alike (as there are airships and sea ships); about sonar and radar; about cluster bombs, bomblets and land mines, gunpowder and atomic power whirring from off the coast of Jersey to the hills of North Viet Nam.

Grace, a goodly spirit, but divinely mortal, pushes the interrupt button, suddenly inspired to raise some hellkite, herself.

For a short moment, she sits on a yellow stool, incapable of reflecting upon anything at all.

She reinstates the telephone, runs a comb through her hair, grabs a book for Em (namely *The Tempest*), and slips on those sandals, heading east once out the door. She walks until she can walk no longer and arrives at the far eastside of just-lower-than-mid-Manhattan Island where the oldest public hospital of the country can still be found. Once a farm, a Belle Vue, and before that an almshouse, a home for the homeless, and treating those suffering from yellow fever, with a doctor trained there who held President Lincoln in his arms until he died. And now it's a home away from home for dear Em, to whom Grace is headed, as she struts and frets and strolls down corridors, up elevators, around rooms on the left bank of the reception area, headed to the temporary housing of Muriel Lyons.

"Hi, Em-Gem," Grace sings in her best contralto, whereupon Em turns her head from the whiteness of moonlight to the darkness of the door. Grace trembles at the lackluster of her friend's great eyes, a fact which disturbs her more than the small patch of gauze on the back of her head. Through the wall of silent, invisible sirens, her own, no less—Em smiles.

"Grace! Grace!" Em's voice resplendent now, a true singer she is, vibrato of brass with range of piccolo. Musk of low shadows and the springing of a coloratura. Such is Em's range. Such is not Grace's— only the lower, the very lower.

"Em, girl. We've gotta get you outta here!" Grace wraps up the belongings of Em, such fine fun rags of many colors, delivered by Em's Rorschocked parents in the morning, afternoon, and evening.

"Stop for your life. I'm staying. It's my wish."

"But Em, they, we, you, I—"

"At least for just another day."

A feeling of paranoia. This is Grace—not wishing to spread what she's learned beyond her own domain.

Grace regains her thread of thought, while tossing the clothes back into their former heap. A knowledge haunts her, namely the fact of limits. Just how many times can you negotiate your comings and goings. As if she could somehow impart this by saying "Em" with a tone. As if a tone could remind her friend how it feels when you relinquish altogether the power of self-determination. "What if the doctor said you were too sick to ever leave?"

"We think we might for once have a doctor who was worth his salt."

"What if this doctor salts you right out of space for once and for all!"

"We are very happy here."

"Em," Grace says. "I want you to be happier."

"All night we slept so soundly we remember nothing at all."

"How do you know you were sleeping at all?"

"What in the world else could I be doing? Oh Grace, I'm so sick of sorrow!" She weeps, and Grace sets down her most favorite comedic, romantic, un-tragic, little drama upon the metal and formica eating table and embraces Em. Within her arms, Em.

Grace coos to Em. "It's okay Emmi, my Em-Gem, what sorrow is in your heart that's breaking you up to bits? What is it that makes such a place as this unbearably empty room seem like immeasurable bliss? What is it that allows you no rest?"

"Grace, we are just sad bunnies that seek refuge from the top hat and rat."

"What can I do for you, my friend?" Grace says. "Shall we read together?" She opens the book.

"I'll play Miranda."

"I'll play Prospero."

"And we shall have my doctor play Ferdinand?"

"Lovely idea," Grace says. This possibility that Bruce may be on the outs.

"Starlinsky—"

"What did you say?"

"My doctor."

"Your doctor?"

"My very own and nobody else's. My sweet heel."

"Oh, Em." Grace, can it be said, is torn. Between her beloved friend whose short blue hair she caresses, whose bruised head is in her arms. And the sparking of her closeted thoughts. "You can't stay in this room for love of your doctor. Where is he now, this heal—". She stops mid-sentence, mid-word, mid-body, heart, soul, mid-mind over matter.

Standing before them is none other than the man in white himself, Dr. Daniel Starlinsky, of average height, weight, hair color, eye color. No—she is not seeing details. Perhaps a painter to find his

114

complexion would mix yellow with red, and dot with white and even a bit of blue, to conceivably suggest sleep deprivation. This is not Stephan von Stemeroff, no. But it is not *not* Stephan von Stemeroff either. Hard to place, except for the feeling. Probably Caucasian, with perhaps a little Mongol and certainly African in his distant genes that are otherwise saturated with Eastern European DNA, in part, some would say tainted, by the monolithic threads of Judaic heritage.

That last bit, regarding the ancestry, is something they all have in common, from Breanda to Bruce, and including Grace and Em. Were they in prewar Europe, they'd all be wearing stars. But here in America, Starlinsky, below and to the left of his quizzical smile, sports his simple name tag, surname preceded by an initial and title, all in non-serif type, underneath a somewhat-dulled rectangular plastic plane— which Grace had indeed spotted the night before. Nor can anyone fail to notice the moment of silence observed as Grace and Starlinsky lock eyes.

"Hello, girls," says the very party in question, as Grace releases her crestfallen charge to the rescuer in white.

"She is okay." Starlinsky, with both femmes fatally nestled in his rainbow-hued eyes.

"I'm glad to hear it." Grace, her body language saying, "preparing to leave."

"What's your friend's name, Muriel?"

"Grace, just Grace." Em's is a voice void of all feeling. "Rosinbloom she is they say."

"Oh." Sitting at her bedside, the man of the hour. "They do, do they?"

"Yes." Answering for herself is Grace, situated by the window where an East River tinged with moonlight can be seen. "We do." She follows her body's impulse, making her way to the door. She smiles both for Em and the great doctor, when the latter suddenly stands up blocking her passage.

115

"You know," Starlinsky says, halting, then speaking, then faltering again, "visiting hours are, have been, uh, were over, finished, slightly, just a few minutes, some seconds, ago, and we have, must, to remind, all visitors, to leave, because why—I don't know."

Grace sprints at the first syllable of his admonishment.

Em's voice is piercing. "Why, Dr. Starlinsky, your stutter is without precedent!"

But Grace, halfway down the hall by now, is missing his blush, though she herself is shivering. She blows a kiss to Em and waves farewells to all who live in the ward Em has known so well. A mashup of thoughts in her brain. She tries to sort them, even as they sprout fresh. Obviously chaos. Obviously love. Obviously, she must depart. And Em—stranger than ever.

Is it possible they both love Starlinsky?

If Em wants him, Grace must put a halt to her dreaming, now. Let Em have him and give up Bruce. Finally. Can you live with that? As if you have a choice?

Grace stops suddenly at the open door of a room of a very young child, whose large tearful eyes have turned toward her. She walks forward, her own large mud eyes filling with tears, and she freezes, without the heart to move. It is then she hears a soft male voice gently murmuring, an uncanny replica of the nasal high-soprano, the honeyed tone, the sing-song manner of Em: "Rosinbloom she is they say. Grace, just Grace."

Grace turns to see Starlinsky behind the door, as if coming out of hiding. With one hand, he grabs Grace, and with the other, he comforts the child, and then he is off, dragging Grace behind him.

"There's a room," he says, leading her down the hallway. "We can be very much alone. If you'd like."

"I'd like."

Reaching his destination, he lets go of her hand.

"We don't have much time," he says, sitting across from her at a small card-like table in the windowless room with a handful of cots for staff to fall asleep upon or otherwise relax while on call.

"Do you think she'll be all right?"

"Who—Em?" he says incredulously.

"The poor child—?" She watches him shake his beautiful head. "Me?"

"Yes, you."

"I'm fine, really."

"I know." He picks up her hand. "Cold hands."

"I'm just—" Grace finds herself unable to form another word.

"I know."

She would like to ask him how he knows and what he knows. Is there some way he could know? Has she told anyone? She doesn't remember telling anyone. A feeling—what is it, euphoria?—steams up her arm from the spot on her palm where his fingers have brushed. Is she dreaming? Maybe Breanda is correct. Maybe she is crazier than she thinks? Crazier than Em? Finally, the words come through. "My hand is warm."

"I know."

She asks him: "What do you know?"

"Just what I feel," he says.

He knows just what he feels. Oh, how his logic resembles the foolishness of her dreams! Yet, how can she bring herself to ask him what it is that he feels, hearing the unmistakable answer coming from her own heart.

Grace smiles. Behind that smile—many unspeakable things. She is about to give it all up for what she sees looking deeply into his eyes, knowing without a doubt she has seen these eyes before.

She says, "Might I ask you a question?"

"You can ask me anything."

"Is this something to do with—Em, uh, Em or anything?"

117

"No."

"Can you just explain something?"

"I hope so."

"I mean, is this the kind of seduction you practice every day?"

"You mean, am I a serial lover—is that what you are asking?"

"Yes, I think that's precisely what I mean. Are you a serial lover?"

"I suppose I could be, for all you know. But no, I'm not, although I can certainly understand a question like that, under the circumstances. And certainly, you might still believe it's true, because that could be true no matter what I say..."

"Yes, that's just it," Grace says, suddenly feeling the unlocking. "We're not swearing on stacks of bibles."

"And even if we swore on stacks of bibles, we could be perjuring ourselves or simply be atheists."

"You could, but somehow I know you're not, because you see, I had this, uh, dream."

"You dreamed I was a serial lover?"

"No. Oh no. Not at all."

"An atheist of love?"

"Oh, no. Not that I know of, at least."

"Did I perhaps perjure myself?"

"Nor that, Dr. Starlinsky."

"You may if you wish call me Daniel."

"Oh, but I love Starlinsky!"

"I'm certainly glad of that. So, you did dream about someone like me."

"Yes," she says. "Someone who looks, um, like you."

"Precisely?" he says.

"Yes, but it's not about the physical. It's about emanations," she would like to say, but instead just observes the otherness. The light, the spark, the liquid in his eyes, the sounds of his laughter, as he is laughing, laughing each time she says something, breaking up his laughter with words.

"That's very interesting," he says.

"And now," she says, "if you're going to say that you dreamed about me? Is that what you're going to say?"

"Oh, Grace," he says, suddenly for the reason that they are inching closer, both are, and now they are kissing. Hot kisses they are, as if the kiss itself were a small torch.

Taking a breath, she asks, "But, is this some newfangled method of psychiatry?" This, despite the sudden dance of electrons. Little glass beads of cold flames marching up and down her spine, about to make their way to the interior.

"No," he says, pulling back from her. "Although, it's extremely unprofessional of me, Grace. Extremely so."

"Yes," she whispers. "That would make sense."

"I don't like to play with words, Grace," he says. "Your place or mine?"

"When?"

"Whenever. The sooner the better."

"You're kidding—"

"You don't know me."

"We sure do," she is thinking, "know each other more than we think." But no words come out of her mouth. It is her eyes again producing a watery commentary that falls in little puddles on the card table. She makes the childlike attempt to wipe them up with her fingers. "Please don't misinterpret these things," she tries to say as the two become so spatially close that the things to which she refers are the only things between them.

"Please, let me." Starlinsky manages to speak and dry her tears—with his tongue—at the same time. "I'm addicted to the stuff."

Grace responds to Starlinsky's hot tongue with a tongue of her own, and after a while they are walking, she trailing him, as he introduces her to a padded room for the severely disordered, whose door he takes care to lock. What they do in that room is probably best described by fantasists and pornographers. A tasteful attempt follows, but it is interesting to note what they do not do. They do not discuss propriety, sanitary matters, or their respective histories of love—the who, what, where, and when of it. No precautions other than the practice of so-called rhythm are deemed necessary. Oh so quietly the giant's footsteps are heard. So hush-hush it is, this sickness-unto-death haunting the community of lovers, this time before the naming, before the baptism, just one of the many mysteries underfoot, in the Eden that is New York. A paradise, sexual and otherwise, so fleeting that even its bitter end becomes obvious only when it is too late to appreciate that fact.

May it be said that Grace opens all stops and gives herself completely over to him, the man of her dreams? She crawls over and above and under his fair moist mortal self with her own real reddening form, and were her russet bush a rose patch, Starlinsky might be said to be pricked. Who can count how many times, how many arrangements, and configurations before they finally lie in silence both knowing the world will now go on with them.

"We must see each other again soon," Starlinsky says.

"Tomorrow?" Grace snuggles and spoons against the lulled red body beside her, both of them dancing with sweat and imagined moonlight.

"Tonight? You can stay here. I'm on till late morning."

"I must go, though." She tries to tell him about the machine to which she must return.

"That sounds reasonable," he says as they touch extremities like puppies.

"Well, it's a long, true, oh it's a terrible story. Maybe I'll tell you someday."

"When you do, it will be a day I will be very happy to listen."

"Starlinsky." She loves his name on her lips.

"Grace. Grace," is all.

And so they say their first goodbyes, trying to make light of a moment whose magnetism is fading. Something subtle as the smell of a lemon lingers in the air, and then it dissipates, is gone altogether, leaving Grace wondering if it might have all been a dream. She finds herself sitting absently in a cab, as she had done the night before, but she is quite alone, now. Her soul flutters with the memory of union. Once again, she is awake, aloose in those wee hours before the sun will declare itself.

In the cab, looking outside now as she passes the beloved buildings standing there, innocently enough, the brick, the limestone, the concrete, the marble, the wood, the vessels of sleeping bodies, themselves the very souls of buildings. She is, of course, thinking of Starlinsky—and, thinking of Starlinsky, her mind shifts to Stem, and shifting to Stem, she sees him, there crossing the seas of Sixth Avenue.

"Stop," she says to the cab driver. Opening the window, she cries out to Stem, who turns while running, almost falling.

Paying twice her fare for the tip—and profusely thanking the driver, she joins Stem as they walk home.

"Can you slow down," she says. "I—"

"What?"

"I want to ask you something."

He leads her not to the building but to *Sandolino's*. And they sit. And eat eggs. And try to determine what's real.

Omelets with cheese. Drinking coffee. Both of them with much ado on the morrow.

Forks and knives, pulling the strands of cheese, then the cut, and then devouring—both of them eating with the foreknowledge of insufficient sleep.

"You know things, Stem," she says.

"It's true," he says, his knife in the same hand, like the Brits. Very delicate, no eggs on his face. He has more grace than a dancer. And he's told her that he has had dancers accompany him with the music. She should come to see real grace. He will let her know when the next performance is.

And yes, she will come, she's nodding.

But there is more, he suggests. He wants to help her.

"Grace," he says. His words come slowly but pungently. At this dark hour, there are nonetheless others about, so he sees, as he focuses on her, those eyes, up and down—not on the waiter, except when he comes to pour more coffee, to say "thanks."

"You understand our connection," he says. It's a beginning. "Or don't you?"

"I don't understand many things," Grace says. "But I'm getting this feeling that you were sent to me."

"You were sent to me, as I was sent to you," he says. "We are signals for each other. Do you understand that? I know you are on a path, a path that you do not exactly recognize. Partly I want to warn you away from it, but—number one, I know you won't listen, and number two—it's your path. Even though you don't know where it's leading, I do. I do know where it's leading, just as I know where my own path is leading, and even though I know my path is leading to disaster, I know I must walk it."

She is aghast. She whispers, "Both of us. Disaster."

"Absolutely." He says this with a grand smile, showing his perfect teeth, those perfectly sculpted lips.

"Yours?"

"Yours," he says.

"Both of ours," she says.

"Both," he says. "Not what you think. Never what you think!"

"No?"

"And in the end, not disaster," he says.

"You are cryptic," she says.

"Not for you. And not for me. Which we must remember when it begins, when it reveals itself."

"Stem—such words, such words!"

"Come upstairs Friday night," he says. "Every third Friday, I go into a trance."

"I'll be there," she says.

"I don't think so," he says. "But of course, I could be wrong."

"You frighten me when you say this," she says.

"Live it up, girl," he says. "They are just words, and you are in love."

Smiles. As if she weren't before.

He looks at her, reflects that smile. "I see that you've found love, Grace."

"You see that?"

"It's lighting up the entire town tonight."

She wants to say, no—it's the sunrise, darling. And then she says it softly. "The sunrise." And they leave the café and walk, and Stem's looking at the corners of the curb, on the street.

"What are you doing?"

"It's an obsession," he says. "I can't help myself."

"What?"

"I am looking for the pieces of my piano that fell years ago, my first one ever, my lost Steinway."

"But you have your piano."

"Yes," Stem says, smiling. "I do. One always wants what one cannot have. This is the way of love." He tells the story of the Steinway—how years ago, when it happened, which was before she'd arrived, he hadn't thought about picking up the pieces. He stayed inside. He mourned. He had thought perhaps he would move, would leave the neighborhood, would go back uptown. But he stayed, and he went looking. He looked for a new piano, thinking there would never

123

be one as perfect as the other had seemed—but he did find a new one. Never the same but always anew. But now, still, on occasion, he finds himself looking for this lost piece, a remnant, something to hold onto a broken past.

"It's foolish of me, but when I feel the urge, I simply look. I do not deprive myself. I find nothing but it pleases me," he says. "There's a lesson here somewhere!"

They part ways. And no, he's found nothing, not a sliver. She's walking on the landing and thinking about this, about how he still looks. "I think it's because I am an orphan," he said.

And this thought, as well. How it is that this beautiful man is alone. His brilliance, his knowledge, his wild world of entrances, where he can look and see the future and the great past, and the two of them walking up the stairs together, until she arrives first at the third-floor landing, and then at her own door, when it hits her—a spinning feeling.

The coffee, and then the thought like a wave—the desire to look back, she is always doing it. How Stem's words are enveloped now by Starlinsky's kisses. Like an undertow, the past. The paste of a thousand kisses on her lips. The burn, her body burning. Of course—the fire that lit the town. Stem noticed. And he told her to come upstairs on Friday night for a séance. An invitation.

"I'm asking you," he said, "even though I know you won't come."

"I'll be there," she'd said.

"No, you won't," he'd said.

And then she moves her mind entirely from Stem to Starlinsky.

Starlinsky. Turning the key. Starlinsky, walking through the door. Starlinsky, twisting the locks. Starlinsky. Lying down. Starlinsky, rising up. Must reconnect the portable, let it ruminate, let it steam up the room.

Having managed to rise, she returns to Cornflaker, reconnects him to the world, sets him up to pour out the knowledge, to print out all the secrets of hell—let it be.

Coffee or not, she's exhausted. She will sleep, so she thinks, and she falls back upon her bed into the deep, deep, deep.

Chapter 5

"**G**race, Grace, Grace," whispers a proud, repentant worm from a small roadway in the sky.

"Be what you are," Grace says to the freak fellow. "A worm with a paramecium for a father and a human being as a son."

"Grace," says the magical gentle beast that he is. "Grace, wrest from me my ancestry and heir and see me for what I really am—a worm with an advanced case of prototypitis. That's it for me."

"Please, see yourself as you wish to be seen."

"Grace," he says, "that worked for all the other girls, but somehow when one discovers one's truest love, it rebecomes—Grace, Grace, Grace. How difficult to be when you want to have, Grace."

"But you have grace."

"Grace is all I want." The worm gloats, inflates his ganglia as if it were the pharyngocele of a trumpeter or the vocal sac of an aroused frog.

"Oh, dear worm. We have a baby to grow you know."

"Grace, you have really lost something down below."

"Are you speaking of my cherry, sir?"

"Presumably, it would have been so, were it not already several times removed."

"Yes, it's true. The pit remains."

"Please, Grace, be mine."

"Upon my honor, sir."

"My own sweet maid."

"Maid, my ass. Take a look at this, if you will." Grace reveals the slight swell of her lower abdomen.

"Well done, I must admit."

"You know the father."

"It is so."

"Now then. Let's talk about matters consequential."

"Fine."

"How will the world react to one more child?"

"Grace, so well as we know, we can hardly predict the future of the species. The world is special for all concerned, but we are not permitted to disclose such things as mortals are not ready to hear. They might take the wrong matters into their right hands. We must wait until they have proven themselves worthy."

Had she forgotten? Had she left the knowledge upon her pillow? Regarding human greed, how easy to overlook, Grace reacts without thinking: "Withholding again, dearest worm, and why suddenly this business of wrong and right and all in the middle of the night?" Her anger sends the worm off in a huff of disgrace.

She dreams of Starlinsky in the padded cell, such stuff that is better imagined than spelled out.

*

Just in time for the imagined song of the lark, the alarm bursts with Handel's *Messiah*, and the unlikely trills of "Hallelujah" fill the air.

Grace alights upon her earthly bed feeling as if her head might split.

As for Cornflaker, he has suffered the night, but not in silence. He has his own little nightmare and does not take his punishment without sounding off.

"A pile of shite," Grace says, nakedly leafing through the roll of Cornflaker's uproar. She hunts for familiar names and places—just a quick peek—and then enters the hot shower to waken Rosinbloom from her multi-level stupor.

Ruminating on the Plume—a word ruined for eternity.

Three Mile Island, yes, last year. Yes, keep telling us not to worry. Two million people exposed to radiation. Low levels. Keep telling us you get more from sunlight, from x-rays, from sex, from chewing gum, from the soap, from the steam all around that we breathe in—from all the directions.

To the north: Indian Point, once an amusement park, bought by ConEd in 1954; uranium dioxide fuel, leaking into the groundwater strontium-90 and cesium-137 and cobalt-60 and nickel-63 and tritium and hydrogen but not exceeding regulatory limits, so they say. To the east, foiling a plan for a facility in Ravenswood, Queens: "No Hiroshima here." Further east: Shoreham—biggest mass protest in Long Island history.

Resistance: in 1955, Bertrand Russell: Russell-Einstein Manifesto; in 1957, Pugwash (Nova Scotia) conferences on science and World Affairs; in 1959, Bulletin of the Atomic Scientists (letter) regarding dumping of atomic waste (Boston); in 1961, women's peace movement.

"Mirror, mirror on the plaster," she says to her own reflection as the mirror clears. "What I really want to know is—who asked ya?"

Determined to feel positively gleeful despite her preoccupation with what Cornflaker has to say—until she opens the door, and the steam vaporizes, revealing the great confusion standing before her.

Namely, what to do about what she knows.

The machine sits quietly. It is innocent, an infinitely docile matter of weight in the process of decomposing at its own pace. Like that garbage can in Bruce's film, Grace thinks, Cornflaker resembles a trashed young hunk of metal littering the way, but little do we know what its past might have been, or what its future holds in store. She takes a second glance at motionless Cornflaker and sighs, drawing her shades up to let in the morning sun.

She packs her bicycle pouch full of the fruit that has remained uneaten in the deluge of the night before, and she puts on a light pale-yellow dress and assorted undies. For the sake of the bicycle ride, she puts on a pair of running shorts. She tries on a shawl, but tosses it off, deciding that the weather does not exactly call for shawls. She rides out a tad wet-headed but clear as the day is not.

Upon arrival at the work in question, the dubious workhorse colliding with the nettled elevator operator who seems to have swallowed a thistle.

"How many times we gotta tell you not to bring your bicycle in Schlang's elevator?"

Rather than speak, she raises the bike and walks to the stairs. At the second-floor landing, she calls for the elevator. She waits until only a partially-filled elevator opens its door, carrying the one and only Breanda Liberfried and the all-possibility that resides in her kangaroo pouch.

"Hey, you all," Grace says.

"Hello, Grace," Breanda says, but her eyes say much more.

The topic is weather as they make their way to their cubicle-like room.

"Hot as blazes, humid as my nose, my brain feels like toilet tissue, my poor wasted soul is tired of one body, no less two bodies in one."

"I guess it's tough," Grace says, parking her bike with a sigh and slipping off her shorts, folding them into a neat pattern and stuffing them into her pouch. "I guess I have no idea, but my guess is you'll get over it by the end of—"

"My life," Breanda says. The amusement she reads on Grace's face gives her the temerity to keep on going. "We are such nuts. You're great for sticking by me. I don't know why you do it. Maybe it's because I'm the only one who listens to your dreams."

Shame—for dreaming—and humiliation—for telling— overcomes Grace who lowers her head. "Gee, Breanda, I never would have expected you to hound me about this."

"Gracie, girl, cool down. I was only joking. You take these things so personally."

"Breanda, tell me, what could be more personal than a dream?"

It is upon the end of Breanda's giant exhale that the womangirls of New York City Housing's Terminal Room resume their work. Grace tracks rent receipts, and Breanda lists demolition candidates. Everything proceeds without further incident until a cry comes out of Grace: "Oh, let me look at that sheet," and Breanda reaches over to hand her the list. Seeing to it that Starlinsky's home has remained unscathed, she is about to return the document until another familiar name catches her eye. It is the very Angelo Palermo in Brooklyn whose building has been chosen for demolition. A reaction worms its way up her spine.

"Not this one," she says.

"Why not? I spent a few hours last night picking out the selections. It's a horrid building. The wonder of it is that it hasn't fallen down on its own accord."

"Probably you're right." Grace is overwhelmed by the gross coincidence, by the twisting of people's lives, the gatherings—an orchestra it is, or a dance. And didn't Angelo call her yesterday, or was that, too, a dream? She prays that the generations of Angelo Palermo will somehow survive, and if she were meant to be the appointed savior of that clan, she will be forgiven. She lets this balloon go.

Today, in this little room, it is a full house of work. Grace reaches for the key to the storage closet. She removes a box of paper for the terminal with the wide, wide mouth. She proceeds to get on this high-speed machine that is nailed to the bedrock, and she traces all the houses or apartments that have energy leaks, then tests them.

Grace whistles as the hushed duck quacks away. It is a loud, attention-seeking sound Breanda's terminal makes, a serious sound, not casual and cheery like Cornflaker's. As Breanda lists and tackles her items, the printout soars, reeling its way up from the floor into its little collection box. Grace finally turns to Breanda and smiles.

"You haven't asked me any questions for at least two hours. Is there something the matter?"

"I'm just keeping my distance, because you seem to be keeping yours." Breanda looks back at her printout that is temporarily halted.

"Looks like it's thinking about something," Grace says.

"Grace," Breanda says, patting her belly. "Will we ever be free?"

"Poor mama! Your day is not far off, that is certain. What day is it again?"

"Any day, Grace."

"Any day?"

"Yes. It could be today?"

"Today?"

"Primigravidas, they say, are generally late."

"So, you could have a solstice baby?"

"A cool thought, except that...I'm not ready."

"You're ready."

"I'll know when I drop."

"Drop?"

Breanda stands up, her hands around the wide girth of her belly. "When this," she says, her fingertips barely meeting, "becomes this!" She signals the lowering with her arms and hands, and then waddles a bit.

"You're going to be a great mama," Grace says, "and I'm going to watch to see this dropping, because I can't wait to spoil the little wonder."

"You and everyone else. Both sides of the family—Richard's parents and my parents and the aunts and uncles and great-grandparents-to-be. Both sides can hardly keep from reminding us how long it's been since there's been a baby in the family. Can you imagine how spoiled this kid is going to be?"

It is clear to Grace that Breanda feels something akin to pride, or perhaps it is just some healthy premonition of satisfaction, and it seems to Grace that the entire room is aglow, as if a song has been sung.

Such is life in the terminal room, and Grace returns to her business of checking receipts and receiving checks from righteous tenants. She suffers away without complaining, just hum drumming right along with a short drift between spaces to the land of partial memory.

But then she is lifted out of the present, drifting into a paradisial aftermath. A smile registers upon her goldilocks-framed, fair face, which shifts the atmosphere of the windowless room.

Breanda licks, then raises her finger as if to feel the changing winds. "I detect a minor modification in the room," she says. "Grace? You, Grace. Grace there. Hey. Grace, remember me?"

"Partially—"

"Anything you want to talk about?"

"Not really."

"Yes, really."

"I shouldn't."

"No, you should."

"Sure?"

"Never been surer in my life."

"So—you know?"

"No—not until you tell me."

"Really, I shouldn't, but it's true that it really doesn't matter whether I talk about it at all. But here it is. The love of my life appeared last night, and I'm not sure whether it was real or unreal."

"Please tell me all." Breanda, it would seem, believes there is a line to be drawn and crossed and even erased at times, only to be elsewhere drawn again. "And I mean all."

"Well, I can't really say too much yet, because there are so many complications that you would not know where to go from here."

Breanda accepts the gobbledygook in silence, debating to be or not to be questioned.

Submitting to her friend's unspoken plea, Grace relents. "Okay. His name is Daniel, and he's about six-foot-two, eyes of... hmmm, hazel, better say, and he has this smooth skin and probably somewhat thinning hair. He's not thin or fat or whatever. Some muscle, some wonderful smell. He's very beautiful...I can barely believe it." Her voice trails, and some salted watery drops there are.

Moved beyond speech, Breanda gives Grace a squeeze of the hand.

"I found out that I'm not a candidate for sainthood, after all. Please annul my application, return my credentials. Please rescind all prizes." She begins to tear up, due as much to a lack of sleep as to a preponderance of thoughts. She rushes off to the ladies' room with its suffocating stench of amorphous waste.

Sobbing a new wave of tears, she closes the green, metallic door to her own little booth and perches her bottom on the edges of the open bowl with her bare feet flat upon the bowl as well. She leans her back against the white oval lid, and in this unlikely but secure position, she falls asleep.

Time passes for the world outside Grace's, and at some point, Breanda comes in, asking if she is all right, and Grace manages to indicate she will be fine but wishes to be alone.

As Breanda exits, Grace enters her strange but true land.

Albeit in a smelly old bathroom in New York, Grace receives the calling of an unlikely protozoan.

"Hi there," she says. The worm is afloat in a commonwealth whose color is more teal than the android apple green of the latrine. He is a miniscule yogi experimenting with his body, performing feats of shapes, his own golden color taking on the sheen of silver, then emerald, then crimson.

"I was in the neighborhood being selected for some bait. I decided to split in my best manner of escape." The worm shifts into a pose that looks rather like someone lying down with a bent elbow and palm under his head.

"This sounds familiar," Grace says. "When I dream, what are you doing?" Now the worm has himself in the shape of a question mark.

"Fine first question," the worm says. "What do you think?" This shape is a worm in shrug, where he looks rather like the letter "M."

"I hardly know what I'm doing when I dream; how could I presume to know what the dream does?"

"Such things, my dear human being, that only live under the sun."

"Be serious, worm. That which cannot thrive under the sun dies. What else can be said?"

"Plenty. Just think, what if we lived forever?"

"Life would be a dream."

"There you have it," the worm says.

"Worm, I have a big problem if you want to know the truth."

"Always. It's my thing." The worm smiles with a jerk to his tail. And then his mouth widens in such a way as to take over his entire body.

"I think I have something to be done, and I'm frightened. Reason number one is—if you'll be so kind to wait until I'm finished…"

"My pleasure, only no unkind thoughts directed to where they should not stay."

"Number one: what if I tamper with some secret records of the national interest, well, I mean *in* the national interest. Number two: what if they catch me? Will they shoot me or hang me or dump me in some well? Number three: will they listen if I do it in the legal way—write a letter of simple true facts of reason? Number four: is there some subtle art to catch the eye of the tiger? And, number five: if you have a suggestion I have not intuited, please do tell."

"What things have you found lurking in the monster's brain, might I ask?" The worm is now vertical, a bit of an "S" shape, as if he were positioned in the pose of Rodin's thinker.

"Such things, oh worm, as not even you could imagine. Horror and war and even peace treaties and some awful inventions. We will barely survive if we stub our toe and get a reaction."

"Well, do you think possibly you are over-reacting a tad?"

"Not on your life."

"In that case," he says. "I might want to introduce you to my girlfriend."

"You have—oh, of course. Oh worm, please excuse my surprise, but I would be honored to, love to meet her—what is she called—or rather, what is she? Like you, a worm?"

"There are some who call me serpent," the worm says.

A swirl of greenness that was until now just a bit of a raft for the sake of the worm's flotation device begins to be available to Grace. Feathers of colors, from chartreuse to cadmium, begin to approach Grace from a point on the perimeter of her vision, and with it, a fugue-like orchestral chorus. Whether it is human or insect, Grace cannot discern, only that the sound is percussive and melodic at once, deeply comforting. From this swirling verdure, it becomes obvious that it is a woman emerging. She is dark and pleasing to behold. Lights like the aurora borealis surround her. While she is the only human, she's certainly not the only being in the emergence. The verdure around her deconstructs itself, distinguishing the ivy vine from the trumpet vine, and the grape vine from the wisteria vine. Several members of the hummingbird nation fly out, along with the great blue heron and a multiplicity of winged beasts, from the fly to the loon, that are all shrouded in this green swirl. A thousand eyes—moving and alternatingly opening, then hooded—surround Grace.

An ordinary fly distinguishes himself from the others and cycles about her, and then the others follow. A terrific organization becomes apparent in this motion, and Grace is transfixed by the beauty. The woman seems to be walking toward Grace, but never arriving, enveloped in the vines and flowers and clinging animals, until she makes one fluid motion, dancelike, which is the signal to release. She shakes them off, her focus on Grace all this time.

"How familiar you look," Grace tries to say but is unable, having been made utterly senseless by the sheer spectacle.

The woman opens her hand, a palm with lines, and a golden worm, *her* worm.

The worm performs his introductions, simply: "Grace, meet Zeldele. You can call her Zelda."

"I am in awe," Grace finally manages. Then she adds, "The pleasure is mine," as she puts out her other hand, and they shake, the two womanly hands, the contrast is there, in black and white. They are both in western clothes, but Zeldele's wearing a pink bikini, and her hair wildly curls out two feet from a face that is as if lavished with make-up and cream.

"Yes, you can call me Zelda," Zeldele says, her voice a mixture of breeze and moan. "I can call you Gracie, right? So, Gracie, the proto has told me some pretty funny things about you. Are they true?"

"Perhaps. Not necessarily. But surely he doesn't lie to you."

"No, we have one of those rare relationships. All I have to do is think it, and it's all over or begun."

136

"I guess that has its good and bad points." Grace smiles at Zelda, who dances for her, or for the world, her hair like the vines, and her body, too like the vines, with absolute abandon but slow-moving, with the poise of a fish under water. Grace determines they become instant friends. "Is it possible we have met before?"

"Who, you and me? Why not? We are happy to meet each other. That should be sign enough. My advice to you, if you were to ask it, is to invest yourself in the eternal."

"Why yes, of course," Grace says.

"All that nonsense about the self, my dear girl—is just that, nonsense."

As if brought on by a master stagehand who remains unseen, a set, or a large prop, appears—once again moving from the horizon to center stage. It is a selection of potted roses that are in various stages of blossoming, so hues of yellow and orange and pinks appear with a spray of bees and dragonflies, one in particular, with black stripes on its lace-like wings. Grace stares, loses her focus for that moment, watches a fly rub its short antenna buds. But then she is jarred back, that very action catapulting her back to her concern at hand.

"So you see," Zelda says.

"Yes, I see, but…"

"But what? What but?" Laughter and music—that anthem of insects, which Grace takes as insult, suddenly.

"Zelda, please tell me whether the worm has filled you in about my most real and unreal problem to date."

"You mean saving the world. You wish to save the world? So, save the world if you can find anything worth saving, although you can be sure that anything worth saving will surely be saved." Again, there is that sound, gorgeous but mocking.

"That sounds meaningful," Grace says. "Are you in favor of apathy and absurdity, then?"

137

"You completely missed the drift, and you must be snowed under, madam. What we are asking is this: what is your true motive?" The first part of this is voiced by someone other than Zeldele. It would seem to come from the stagehand himself, but it is a woman's voice, low and guttural, with an inflection.

"What should it be?" Grace asks.

"Just love is all there is, we say." Zelda and the worm, together now, and he snuggles his tail around her pinkie fingernail. But then it becomes song, and theirs is a duo. Behind them, a world chorus gathered from indigenous populations, the voice of nature, and then it's just a dream of voices, a matter of voices in her head, and all visuals fading as if releasing themselves back into the ethers, leaving just their soundwaves.

"You do say that a lot, don't you, and I guess it's true, but where is the love in a nuclear reaction is my question?"

There is at first a silence, and Grace says, "You are still there, aren't you?"

"Good question," the worm says. "Don't you agree, doll?"

"Yes, are we still here—this is a good question."

"And the next?" This is said by the worm.

"The question is," this is Zel, "what shall Gracie do with the love in question."

"That's another thing I want to know," Grace says.

"Well, it's a matter of judging opinion over fact, and once you know that—"

"I know for a fact that—"

"A fact—"

"My opinion of fact—"

"The fact of your opinion—"

"Makes no difference—," Grace says.

"Why not, dear?"

"Because, I believe—"

138

"Ah, now we have a horse of many colors. So, what makes you believe?"

"Why are you teasing, plaguing, tricking me? I just want to help, so please be straight with me. Oh worm, this is sheer torment."

Grace opens her eyes to the room and booth she presently inhabits, finds herself still seated, with grooves marked on her thighs and behind. She rises, pulls up her sundries, opens the booth door, washes her face, waters her fingers, soaps and scrubs her hands, looks unforgivingly, then forgivingly into the mirror and departs.

*

"Sorry, Charlie," says a voice with the lilt and cadence and gruffness of Breanda's.

"Breanda?" Grace is walking down the hall, a tired woman in a yellow dress, girlishly confused. She looks to her side and even behind her, while walking forward in a hall with many doors opened, each with its own collection of people sitting at desks saddled with telephones and hungry machines, in colors ranging from off-white to shades of gray—all of them hungry for blood.

Returning to her very own cubicle, she finds a note from Breanda, saying, "Dear Grace—What is going on with you? I went to lunch, and I will return soon. Bye, B."

Grace sits at the terminal, lights off, elbows resting on the lacquered wood. She questions how has she gotten herself in such a stew with dream-men, babies, and worms with girlfriends talking nonsense, and printouts of disgust, not to mention mad girlfriends with madder boyfriends. But was there ever a time she didn't have crazy friends and crazy dreams?

Not in a yogic pose of meditation, but rather engrossed in the flood of thoughts between her hands, she considers in that crude but still contemplative manner what the worm's girlfriend had to say

139

regarding the love motive. How can she question the stubbornness of her own unreasoned belief that the news on the printout is not very good, and how can she run away from this opportunity to take some steps to make a change? Meanwhile, as the terminal room is dark, she determines to turn on a few switches. "This will put some mediocre light on the world," she murmurs and begins working at the grumbling quacker.

She writes up commands to release the information she had recently put in, namely rent checks, and she absently examines and re-examines her work, wondering why these rents are even collected if radiation is going to pollute the waters, and how it will destroy the animals and plants along with the rest of us.

Or if the whole world is just going to blow up.

Aloud she says, "Shut up or else you deserve to blow up. Or maybe it's the other way around. Maybe it's 'Shut up *and* blow up'. You silent voices are the reason we shall be no more." She struggles back and forth. What should she do? To whom can she turn for advice? No proper supervisor for such work, she laments. Whatever happened to the idea of proper rule? The sun by day, and the moon by night, when the stars shine their light—as if to keep the moon company, whereas, who keeps the sun? Grace's wonderings bring her to the version of the golden rule that she was taught: do not do to others, what you would not have them do to you.

"Such good advice, no?" This is that voice again, that sounds almost like Breanda.

Breanda just then arrives with the excess part of a tuna fish salad, an unburnt offering for Grace, as if to apologize for the guilt of being a catalyst. All this, Grace brushes aside, and she accepts the food.

"Oh, thank you sweet Breanda." Graces takes the plastic fork and chomps immediately. Then she remembers the fruit she'd stored in her pouch and offers some to Breanda, who uncharacteristically refuses.

140

"Breanda—whatever is wrong?"

"Funny, I was just about to ask you the very same question. Grace—what is going on with you?" Breanda flops down on the chair of her choice.

"I'm having a spiritual crisis," Grace says. "What else is new?"

"Anything I can do or undo?"

"Breanda, this is no problem for you to worry about. Be happy. I am just a lunatic with a good imagination."

"Putty is what you think of me."

"No, no. Actually, I was thinking angelic thoughts about you. What advice you give."

"Advice?"

"The best, Breanda. Just say 'you're welcome, Grace,' because Breanda, I'm thanking you. Don't be angry with me. You react as though I specifically projected my right to speak into your ears."

"Well, didn't you?"

"No, I just said the most perfect collection of words I could think of to match the torment in my heart."

"My heart blushes for insult," Breanda says.

"No, it doesn't," Grace says. "Your heart might pity me, and you might want to express your pity, but then you might feel unable to help me, so you might project your helplessness onto me and turn my comments into reflections."

"I get it. We are one mess of a species."

"You got it."

"You can have it."

"You can take it."

"No—you! You had it first."

Breanda wincing, Grace smiles at her friend and gives her shoulders a squeeze. "I think you are the greatest. Don't worry about me so much. My mother worries enough for ten gods and goddesses."

"All mothers worry."

"Do you find yourself growing worry-muscles?"

"I think I was born with them," Breanda says.

"The divine mother," Grace says. "The divine worrier—who would have thought of the deities as worriers. More like generals."

"Well, such esoteric thoughts don't work terminals," Breanda says, as she prepares to barge in on a machine doing its thing. "You going out?"

"Nah. I'll just stay here forever."

They return to their work—rent checks and demolition selections—in solid silence that is suddenly broken by Walph and his cheerful twittering counterpart.

Grace says, "Watch out for the tan pair of geese."

"Good afternoon, folks," they say in unison. "Have you any news to break?"

"Nothing yet."

"Just a list."

"You've got it then all done?"

"No, almost. We'll let you know."

"Well, do let us know soon." This is Tina.

"Great," Walpho says. "Now where's the other stuff?"

"Peachy," Grace says. "The City is only losing one half of its rent these days. Maybe they ought to reconsider the process of redemption, and charge the landlords future rents instead of back taxes."

"Grace, you are always peeking into the affairs of this city. You retain the most impossible trivia. Working for the CIA, are you? Such strange things you say!" They walk out, but Grace feels as if the blues of Tina's eyes have a new edge into her shoulder blades.

"Ewwww," Grace says. "That hurts."

"What CIA on the moon?" Breanda says. "What unkind words from the furnace face. What strange looks she gave you. Maybe she's got her period."

142

"Oh, Breanda. What should I do to that poor woman wonder of a window washer, mind and soul? Just smudge, smudge, smudge it? Or do I try to reason her out of her suspicions, or do I quit on the spot, thereby putting stock in her soup?"

"She was just teasing you—and look how far she got?"

"What if I said she was right?"

"I'd be fearless, well almost. Certainly less paranoid about the CIA and a lot of things. Oh, come on, Grace. What's with you? Do you have your period, too?"

"We are all in the flow," Grace says, "even when we aren't." She and Breanda turn away from each other to return to the meaningless machine that sits before them, waiting to be fed.

They work until the day's whistle sounds, resembling the sneeze of an enormous beast, whereby the city releases its captives, and the elevator is like the big fish that delivers up a hapless Jonah. If you had x-ray vision, you would see the tall brown-to-golden-haired girl in the pale-yellow dress beside her bike, and just in front of her, huddled in the elevator, the shorter pregnant girl with her flaring, blue-patterned bodice. And if you screwed your eyes a bit with that supersonic sight, you might see a baby slowly swimming itself into position. Simultaneously, the door slides open, and they venture out the double doors of the building into the dispersed yellow light of the utterly endless day. For a moment their eyes meet, and then they separate—the shorter one hugging her pocketbook, high under arm, a little tighter, as she waits for her husband, and the girl with the bike is saddled. Off goes Grace, into a modern-day Nineveh.

She barely keeps her balance for riding so slowly down Maiden Lane. Her eyes alert for pedestrians slipping onto roadways, her wheels squeezed between the curb and the civilian tanks beside her, Grace makes the silent observation that nobody missed Cornflake. And then up the hills and down the streets she sails, returning to her own one-room castle with its runes and satyrs, receivers and transmitters, and

143

her beloved bed. Having dumped the mail, parked the bike, grabbed a glass of New York's singularly delicious free drink, she busies herself beside the terminal, seeking better hold of its spilled-forth contents.

She tears off a sheet-sized section to read, and how it wants to roll its waxy self up again, like a little Torah scroll. She carries it a choice ten steps, sinful girl that she is, into that most private of chambers, where young Jewish males are forbidden to pray or even permit themselves to ponder the wholly energetic One, blessed be S/He. But, lacking circumspection or circumcision or even verbal warning, Grace, it might be remembered, has in fact dreamed and pondered on that throne. Her mind presently meanders upon her dearest father, Moses Rosinbloom, who did, indeed, as her dream-self told her dream-interlocutor, descend from Russian and Polish Jews, a perhaps simplified way of referring to Vilnius, once a thriving Babylon of cities, torn to shreds by more than one demagogue, and now claimed as the capital city of Lithuania. But, even for Moses, the old country was twice removed. He knew it by the stories his father told him, who knew it by the stories of his father, who was on the boat, who survived the crossing with a brother who doffed his religion into the Atlantic. It took a few generations for the doffing to come to Grace. Moses Rosinbloom was raised with *tallis* and *tzitsis*, and given not to mix *fleshic* and *milkic* and presumably to resist the crustaceans and uncloven, non-cud-chewing beasts as *traife*—but these are laws by which Grace does not abide. Nor does Marnie, her mother, continue the laws of *kashrut*. And only God knows whatever her father was thinking when he, the only male in a house of women, took his thick fold of newsprint into the bathroom with him on Sundays, and the little house in the Jersey prairie vibrated with great feminine storms for what seemed like hours.

How she loved her dad. An engineer, he was more concerned about the greenhouse effect than the disasters of nuclear power. Nor did they see eye to eye about such things as the dropping of the atom bomb, which he insisted she ought to be grateful for. According to

144

him, it was the sole reason she was alive. He'd been stationed in Europe in 1945, due to be sent to Japan, where he would have surely died, and what would she have been without his noble contribution?

And all those of her generation, all of them with the blood of innocent Japanese civilians on their sleeves. Ironic it is that when she was a tot, she played war-games, with sticks for guns, and of course nobody wanted to be the villains, namely the Japanese, along with the Germans. And now who is the villain? Could it be that it was us all along, she thinks again? Yes, this is the initial trigger of the thought, as she reads, but how quickly she looks up, requiring immediate distraction, which she spies beyond the window, framed with peeling white lead paint, where a trapezoidal blue sky shines, interrupted by thick, geometric patterns of gritty steel and brick.

Grace thinks upon her dear departed father with bittersweet thoughts that soon lose all sweetness and become much more than bitter, as she reads down a list of atrocities where poisonous weapons lurk and leak into fields and homes and communities of the uninformed. She seeks the list of chemicals ready to spring into action upon the great agricultural fields of this earth. She considers the root of the system—contamination by fear and greed—and she studies some concoctions of war machines, delineating underground routes that are patterned after the ant colony, on-the-ground routes plotted by the tiger where trees are worn to stumps. There are others, routed after the hawk and crow in the air, after the shark and platypus in the water, and after the grace of God goes Grace, taking care of her derriere and environs. She retrieves the now-wrinkled but still curling scroll, a soft cylinder, whose circled end she'd placed for a moment on the bathroom floor before her, and she returns to the main room prepared to snuggle up with some cool pillows, and to work her way to sleep, always ready and willing, if able to enter the land of dream.

So, what starts out with lists of moneys ends with a torrent of weapons, her last conscious thought that she will nevertheless forget.

Grace breathes in sweet rhythms, resting easily before an abstract presentation of colors and shapes, when Zelda, in her electric blue brassiere and emerald-tinted panties, comes tiptoeing in on her, breaking the spell of darkness. Grace says, "Oh, it's you again."

"Oh, it's you, you, you," Zelda says. "Welcome, my dearest angel. Where have you been? To see the Queen?"

"What queen?"

"The queen bee, of course. There's no queen on earth her peer."

"Really?"

"Yes—take a look for yourself."

Zeldele has not abandoned her verdant swirl. If the past instance is any example, it's there, wherever she is, there at her calling—and vice-versa. "Come see the bee in what your scientists like to claim as her natural habitat, with a horde of drones buzzing at her every whim, and some of those buzzing, my dear girl, are women."

Adorned with black and golden velvet bands, the queen is bejeweled with jaws of amber, eyes of sapphire, and a darkly glowing crown with black opal beaded up her antennae. At her posterior swings her tail of hot ruby—a real stinging work of wonder.

"What can we do for you?" the queen bee, whose name is Beatrice, asks. That voice, so familiar, the not-Breanda voice, but so reminiscent as to surely be a compatriot, a member of the extended family.

"Nothing I know of," Grace says. "But perhaps we'll see what it is soon as it comes to be."

"Sounds reasonable." The bee gives a kick to one of her stick-like legs for some drones to lick.

"So, Bea. Tell me what do you think."

"Looks bright and short," the bee says to all her fans, and the drones buzz their delight, while mumbling to each other their own secret wishes to be fulfilled.

146

"What does?" Grace, confused, ignores the masses for a moment.

"The solution."

"Ah, you mean to the problem of—"

"The world, of course."

"Short? "

"Bright…"

"But how short?"

"Short, as you know is relative to long, so lanolin is for example long, whereas a sheep is short. But what is the matter that you look so glum?"

"How can you reduce a thing to its by-product?"

"Easy," the queen says. "Remember who you're talking to—"

"Yeah, a buzzer loved only for its honey—otherwise scorned."

"You do forget our other function."

"Oh yes, how could I forget? You are the fecundators of the world. Forgive me."

"Precisely," says the bee. "So what is important remains."

"Such wisdom! Do you think this way all the time, or just upon the hour I happen to ask about my dilemma?" Grace starts pacing, walking without destination, in a large meadow. She is going on and on, imagining the bee is following her, expounding in some detail and gesticulating. Finally, she turns and finds herself facing a brick wall. "I have been talking to myself all this time," she says, about to slam her own head into the wall.

"I wouldn't if I were you," she hears, that voice again, but now she knows, even if she doesn't see her. Grace watches as the brick wall undergoes massive shape shifting, metamorphosing into a black cloud and then a swirling miasma of brick. The large swarm of honeybees—sixty thousand, no less—becomes a mass of buzzing that envelops Grace, silencing her, finally.

"Turn around, dahling," says the bee. "I'm in front of you!"

147

"You have many followers," Grace says.

"So will you, my precious," the bee says. "I must tell you that a problem like yours is for the ears of my greatest admirer."

"So, you are passing the buck, Beatrice?"

"It would seem so, wouldn't it?" she says. "There is a water lily who is quite anonymous, but she will try her hardest to tell you what you need to know."

"She can speak?" Poor, incredulous Grace begins to feel the sense of being badly tricked.

"We are just fooling you? Isn't that what you're thinking?"

"Unless I'm capable of fooling myself, but—"

"Yes, well, of course that is the only way."

"The way of the fool."

"Yes, that is the way…Down the road to the brook, and follow it to the pond, where one flower will shout, 'Hey, Grace!'"

It is a perfect loveliness Grace finds herself in, and she follows the lush greenery and the silvery blue of a thick and thinning brook to said mud-pond with its lap of floating pods and lilting petals. The lilies are closed for the evening, all but one—to which Grace wades. Once again, Grace tries to speak very carefully of her life—how this strangest of circumstance came to be, and with exquisite precision, she tells of the disease that has overcome the little world she grew up to be thirty years old in, and how now it feels like being in the sandbox with machines instead of a thumb-sucking friend.

With the fragrance of clear expression, the flower responds: "Now listen, and listen well, because this is not going to happen twice. The problem you have is so serious, and yet at the same time, it is very light. What you must do, you must know, and before you know, you must think, and before you think, you must believe. Otherwise, all is reaction to reaction to reaction. The difference between reaction and action is monumental. Imagine the worst, and that will always be reaction. No questions, please." The waterlily, easily one thousand steps ahead of Grace's impulses.

"Let me say that reaction is not instinctive, unless the species is in a hurry to be extinct. Why is the fecundating bee not a reactor to the pollen in the tree, when perhaps it lacks choice of the human kind? Precisely because of its predilection for the blossom, it mates it to its other with no strings intended. Nature is its own law, and you humans must learn to obey."

Once again Grace is about to interrupt, with a question, but the water lily raises her voice just enough to curtail the thirty-year-old child. "Grace, please be free, and you will drift to the perfect decision. Please love all, because there is no creation unworthy of creation."

"Not even the nuke...?"

"Not even the nuke. What is the problem is *man* and not the nuclear reaction. If man did not tamper, in his ignorance, perhaps you and I would be in Eden this day. Perhaps if man had waited until he knew, we would not have to re-new the knowledge today."

Grace says, "What are we going to do?"

"There is always something and nothing to be done. Just try whatever comes to you and see how it goes."

"But we have gotten into this very fix in that very manner!" Grace finds herself arguing in the middle of her reveling, splashing water on her face, and sniffing in the earthen odor of swamp and blossom.

A mass of trembling, the graceful flower, in her outermost ripple, braces against the rustling breeze. "Perhaps what you say is true for you for the instant that you say it." She pulls in her slender petals, closing up. "Farewell, my little one."

"Fare well," Grace says.

More like, oh well. Grace walks to the edge of the pond and positions herself on a boulder meditating on beauty—its simplicity, its complexity, its vastness. Her gaze is drawn outward, extended far, her soul absorbed yet taking over like the breeze having its way with the pond and trees.

Chapter 6

Grace angles out of her bed and performs multiple rites to prepare both mind and body for earthly night fantastic, greeting a ringing phone with the gratitude of one granted the right to arise of one's own volition.

"Hello," she whispers with husk in her not-yet-jaded voice.

"Guess whom?"

"Without asking, I must depart, Bruce. Be well, but distant." She returns the phone to its receiver.

Regarding the subject of her obsession, Grace begins to feel the advent of an idea, as if it were marching from the very back of her mind to the place right before her eyes, namely the tip of her nose. It is as if it just fell from the third eye, dropped there, an egg falling out of a nest. A baby crow. An omen, a sign, a gift. The common crow. Common but smart, dangerously smart, uncommonly smart. A *Corvus brachyrhynchos* flopping down on the ground while still a nestling— dangerous on any account, the kind of thing that forbids you from re-tracing your steps or second guessing or even begging the question.

This idea. Stunning and clear and precise as a hired assassin. Would that she could do this like a god—in actuality—than accomplish this theoretically.

And yet—it is gesture that sings louder than a dissertation rehashing a few ominous truths that have been disregarded for coming from a dubious source.

It's an act, actually, isn't it? An act of will. An action. More than a statement, less than a solution.

Presto, and all the weapons disappear.

Presto, and the penchant for hurting is gone.

Presto—and peace on earth.

151

She's thinking of "Delete." A function. Different from death. Erasure. Is there really such a thing? God creates. Humans erase. It feels strangely deadly, strangely powerful.

"Yes," she says. "What if I just erase it all? What harm could that be, and then—well, we can figure out the next step when we get to it. How sublime, how easy!" She is still cheerleading for herself when the phone reissues its ring.

Less fragmented, Grace now holds onto her reserve and says, "Hello caller. Please indicate your name, age, and serial number, or else be so kind as to hang up."

"Starlinsky, aged somewhere between birth and senility. My cereal is Total, and its number is Infinity, which would be the name of my car—if I had one."

Grace greets this caller without a peep.

"Grace, if, as I think, you are Grace, is this some exotic method of weeding out suitors?"

"Are you wearing a suit or suing for peace?"

"A piece. What say you?"

"What else but when—when when when when when?"

"Say *now* as many times as you said *when*, and you will be really close," he says with a click, and within the time it takes to walk one-half block, approximately seventy seconds if the clip were fast, Starlinsky can be seen buzzing the buzzer to Gracie's mansion.

Wearing nothing underneath a flimsy robe she'd quickly grabbed off a hook in the bathroom, Grace manages to answer her door without revealing herself. It would appear to the one entering that the door were self-opening.

"Well, well?"

With her foot, she sends the door back where it came from and then wraps that foot, along with her ankle, calf, and thigh around him.

Starlinsky moves quickly upon her face with his lips and tongue, and receives an identical welcoming. They remain awkwardly

152

kissing at the door until the action behind Starlinsky's zipper moves into play, and in slow motion, they fall upon the hallway floor where they sink organs into orgasms. Their breathing sets off a hundred stereos, radios, and televisions within a radius of a few thousand feet.

"Would you like to stay for dinner? I'll give you a tour of the house?" An understatement, as they sample each room in the bustle of moving from hallway to bathroom, against wall, on kitchen floor and to bed, where they lie like one long snake.

"Might, although I had a great meal about a minute ago."

"You're making me blush, you know."

"Well, if you're calling that a blush, rather than a flush," Starlinsky says, "then you're making me blush, as well."

"I'm afraid I've got some very rotten things swimming in my mind, remember? Are you still willing to listen when I'm ready to tell?"

"Yes, but prepare for the end of my flush-blush, my darling."

Starlinsky rises suddenly, sits upon her desk chair naked as a defrocked and defeathered goose, but his face is upon her. "I'm all ears and eyes, although I will permit my fingers the freedom to roam."

"To tell the truth—" is all she can say for a few minutes. She feels herself fumbling but follows the impulse to gaze into his eyes and speak. A backstory, hers, the least she can tell without collapsing, namely that she had a little trouble in academia, in the world of theory—but that she had taken an interest in the incompatibility of humanity, art, and technology, especially the machines of weaponry.

Seeking only to frame this specific issue, with the intent to avoid the more serious revelations, she makes a point *not* to tell him that this coincided with her father's untimely death.

She launches into the story of the password, how it appeared before her eyes, almost like magic, and then disappeared, but she had remembered it. The chaos that followed, and how now she is dreaming of worms and lilies offering geometrical equations of advice, and of her very latest idea—the process of eliminating on paper what cannot be eliminated so easily in reality.

"What do you think?" Grace finds her way upon Starlinsky's soft, furry lap, where she apologizes to him for burdening him with this information that he must hold in his mind and never tell.

"I'm a professional secret keeper," he says. But then his eyes turn away. He senses the deletions within the backstory, as concerned about them as those proposed. "It's not very pretty," he says at last. "Not pretty in the least, and we will certainly not find any lies on tape."

"Oh, would that we could," she says, marveling that he had heard, that she had not put him to sleep, that he had not stopped listening, nor did he appear to be analyzing or judging her.

His eyes look far, far off to a place she can't find, although she sits there staring as if a god lurks there.

"Oh, you see it perfectly, Dr. Starlinsky. Now tell me what exactly should be done? I will surely try anything."

Certain that action is not the preferred remedy, Starlinsky says nothing, just rises with a stretch and a screech, and Grace, too, rises to go and brush her teeth. He wraps his legs in the whites he'd entered with and had scattered, and he bundles up his underwear with the question of where to put the dirty clothes?

"Everywhere," Grace says. "Be creative."

"I'm the type that likes to bump up against a structure."

"Put them up your anus!"

"So rich a place would only spoil them," he says, having joined her in the powder room, where he gives a serious pinch to her right cheek.

"Ouch, you creep. Stick them here," she says, pointing between her legs to a menagerie below the sink.

"Thanks, my darling dumpling."

The pair of storybook lovers retires to the bed once again, until the hunger bird crows, and they rise once again, this time certain of

154

parting, yet pretending nothing unusual exists in their post-coital blues. Grace reaches for her flimsy robe, as Starlinsky for the second time in less than an hour pulls up his pants, as they try to resist touching each other, both sensing the tug of goodbye in the air. Suddenly, Grace says, "You have no underwear. Do you want to stay for dinner?"

"Why, I thought you'd never ask!"

"I had asked already."

"That was an hour before my hunger returned."

"Please, how would you like carrot juice cocktails, soy cakes, and rice ice cream?"

"I'm sure I could survive it," he says.

"Such nice manners, to be willing to risk death for my honor."

"I'm allergic to health food, starry eye. Roach legs, pocked apple pie, roast hamster, bristle of oxtail, and squirrel tongue are good enough for me."

"Surely you write yourself short by saying 'good enough', when in fact you are talking of the esoteric gourmet." Grace tears into her bureau, quickly slapping on some blue jeans and a faded pink top, and makes for the door, with the thought to run to the nearest supermarket. "Stay right here, Daniel, dear. I shall return in less than the time it takes you to holler."

"Do not move," he says, anchoring her forearm with his hand. "I want to take you out to the Waldorf or Plaza, or never eat again."

"Well, since I am a humanist at heart, I should give in."

"Gracie Rosinbloom, who are you, where were you, tell me all you ever wanted to do in your life and why have I missed you all these forty-five years of my living dying wonderful terrible existence?"

It is as close to a formal proposition that Grace has ever had. She feels his gaze upon her, that feeling, as he stands before her, holding both her hands—they stand about a foot apart—as she watches him watching her, taking in the full frame of her—the woman who he believes is his counterpart. He looks down at her face. It is a

45-degree angle, as he stands about one-half foot above her. She looks up, both of them oblivious to the light reflecting from their eyes that has accelerated to an immeasurable speed.

"Starlinsky, I have been here always, dreaming dreams of you."

"How do you know? How do you know it was me?"

"From the way that I feel," she says.

"Just that?"

"That's a lot," she says, "but no, not just that. And you?"

Starlinsky, his eyes intent on her, says, "There was a series of dreams. Some were daydreams, some not. When I saw you the very first time, when you were leaving the hospital at some ungodly hour, after delivering Muriel, I'm guessing—I knew I'd seen you before. I knew, and then when it happened again that I saw you, with Muriel, I couldn't let you go—well, I could, but, no, I couldn't. I could not."

"How did you know it was me?" she asks—the very question he'd asked her.

"How will we ever know whether you conjured me, or I bewitched you?"

A stinging, piercing sound comes from Starlinsky's shoe. So small a sound, yet terrifying it is, a signal that he must leave immediately. He curses, leaps to grab his sneakers and to shut off the beeper. Leather, they are, and large as toy canoes, painted a designer shade of white. He runs to the bathroom to grab the undies, and Grace follows behind, grabbing ahold of his undershirt.

"Mine," she says. But he won't let go.

"Mine," he says. Nor will she let go.

"Leave me something to sleep with," she says.

"No," he says, releasing his hold but catching her before she hits the floor. He then lifts her up and flops her on the bed and embraces her.

"Take it," he says, and covers her up with it and a million kisses. Within no time at all, he's gathered the remainder of his belongings—shirt, tie, jacket, the boxers— laced up the sneakers, and once again, he stands before her, this time fully clothed. "Oh," he says. "By the way, will you be mine forever?"

"You don't know what you're getting yourself into." Her warning between kisses.

"Naturally, how else would I know you were perfect for me, and so, quickly, what say you, Yay or Nay to my declaration of dependence?"

"I do," Grace says.

"More…come on, say 'love,'…"

"You say it," she says.

"I implied it."

"I showed it." Now this is theatre.

"I felt it."

"I knew it." More theatre.

"We've done it."

"So believe it," Grace says. She's talking to herself. Maybe she's created this man. Or maybe Stem created him. Maybe Stem—no, she cannot really conjure up any other human right now, no, not thinking of Stem. She is so totally enveloped in this being before her.

In that singular voice of which there are only musicians but no writers, no words to describe its very earthy but still celestial sound, Starlinsky says: "I do love you, Grace."

"I, too, love you, Daniel."

"Goodbye."

"Goodbye."

"Bye."

"Bye."

So goes Starlinsky sans undershirt and dinner to his hospital, and so goes Grace, wearing said undershirt to her refrigerator door to edibly ponder a myriad of things.

Grace looks around, her eyes settling on the jam and butter rack, both for the apricot jam and because how different her studio feels, as if she could love it more! This man who was here, she wonders, was he ever really there? Signs of him. She is walking around sniffing, but suddenly it occurs to her that she didn't say hello to Em. What should she do? Call her at this hour, but yes, of course.

To the phone she goes, bringing a three-part invention: food—namely, carrots and jam and rice cakes; thought—namely her excessive joy, paired with her excessive anxiety regarding the printout; and now action—namely the plan to intercept, or to perform an intervention for Em, to help her move toward the door of Bellevue and out scot free.

"Em, is it you—too late to talk? How are you?"

"I'm jealous of you, Gracie-Pie. What should I do? Wait it out till one of us dies naturally, or send Brucie to do the job on you?"

Em's drugged voice, so slow, so gravelly, so granular—making Grace's husk sound like high strings.

"God, Em—what is it, now? What have I done to make you so sad? Maybe it's time to get you released. Your register has lowered to that of a didgeridoo."

"Oh Grace, if you haven't done anything, then why does it seem as though you've stolen all the love I ever needed. That's why I feel so bad now."

"Stolen love? Oh, my Emmi. What's happened to you? We've gotta get you out of there—now!"

"No! Nooo. Not now—here he is. Here he comes. Here is Starlinsky…" And she hangs up the phone.

And there is Grace, with a phone and carrots and her rice cake with its jam dripping on a bed where love has spent itself, where Starlinsky is not. She licks the sweetened, cooked & cooled apricot off the flowered sheet, and decides love over matter.

And where is Bruce in the equation?

He's been strained out of her own life for good. Return to a professional relationship. But why any return at all. From the start, Bruce was Em's. From the start, she never wanted him. It happened by mistake. With regret always. Bruce was always Em's and always wanting. And Em, too, always wanting. But she, Grace. A weakness, when Bruce fogged up her mind. She shouldn't blame. But yes, she blames him. Not entirely. She did not fight him off. Should have but did not. Convinced herself, drugged herself. Fooled herself.

And then stopped.

Walked away. Ran away. Hung up the phone.

And now, her womanhood. A man who reminds her of her personhood. A desire fulfilled. Her person has arrived. This, not exactly because she waited. This because of luck or destiny. And now, too late, for her heart is his as none has ever been, a thing one knows: one knows that love is coming and recognizes the arrival. Love preceded by bells. Love preceded by dreams. Love arrives with kisses. Kisses the beginning. No rush for an end. And why does she hear nocturnal piano arpeggios? Is Stem channeling Chopin? She played Chopin. But this is starker, almost more beautiful? Russian. And then after a minute, it's Bach. Or Bach-like. She played the two-part inventions. But the beauty here feels drenched in something sinister, a quality none could associate with Bach or Chopin or Mozart.

Grateful for the distraction in this post-coital loneliness. Her ears have a mind of their own. Would it were Friday, she would attend. Tomorrow, she shall. Today, still Thursday, the third this month. Tomorrow, she will ascend the two flights. Tomorrow, she will take part in Stem's party. He has asked her, and she has said yes.

But, music filters in. Like sunshine coated in night flowers, shivering sounds permeating the ceilings, coming through the pipes. There for her ears. Unless Stem's window is open. Surely, his window is open, as are hers. A tiny but powerful fan that is off. The sounds of night chatter, of horns, of humans in their various emergences. Many asleep by now. Others perhaps listening to the television but not her—never. No, she has dreams for a screen, except when trailing Em to see Bruce's latest. Are these more of the preludes? Or have we graduated to sonatas? Or toccatas? Or just dances, although these seem more for the mind than the body, these sounds.

Now that the rice cakes and apricot jam and the carrots are no longer in her fingers, her lips, or the blue floral dish, but instead transformed into energy, she decides to adorn in something for success and knock on the door of the one who is tinkling the keys. Not nearly tinkling but more like tolling them, pressing, finessing, the Bach bells, the riveting, transforming and piercing and gonglike. From Em to Stem. No, she cannot take a shower. She cannot remove the traces of Starlinsky. She will sleep with his aura glazed upon her skin, the sheen of Starlinsky. She places the yellow dress over the undershirt and slips on an under-covering, as well as sandals. And that music seems to stop, then rise up again, the closer she comes to his door, more muffled than when it was coming from the window.

She is knocking loudly at his door.

"Door's open, Grace," he says, still at the keys. At the keys in his triangular room. He is wearing only a ribbed tank top—an undershirt, along with light gray linen pants.

She who is dressed though bra-less has let herself in. She falls upon a small loveseat with its brightly-colored print, her hands fingering a pillow that was an animal pelt.

"Yes," he says. "You have a good sense of what I'm playing. The great Russian music of Shostakovich—these are like grafts from Bach and Chopin and many others," he says, while playing. "Deep and light, but sometimes they are like wails, like cries, howls from Siberia, I imagine," he says. "A great poet labeled one of the pianists who played this work as 'Beethoven in a petticoat'," Stem says. "So once, in Juilliard, I put on a wig, dressed up as Beethoven in a petticoat, and I made my professors guess! When I play this music," Stem says, "I feel the world is swirling before me—a big green swirl of nature and all of those who gave their lives to make art."

Grace is mesmerized by him, by the music, by the room that has so quickly become invested with an energy, as if the very objects in his room are at attention, just as she is at attention.

Stem's walls are white, but the light is dim, and almost everything is in shadow. He has a double arch, where Grace's flat has just one, the entrance to her studio proper. Where she has rectangles, he has triangles—two: one for the piano, one for his bed. Everywhere, the walls reveal texture where the white is not, and where the white is appears to be strips and stripes, rectangular shapes of white. Mainly there is not white. Mainly there are paintings, large and small, along with fabric hangings, shelving of various sizes, blossoming with statues and books and fossils and stones and other relics. The light sources are two: street and the spot from the ceiling illuminating both keys and notation splashed across the pages.

Stem's fingers pressing, prodding, groping, grazing. His arms totally exposed. Like the features of his face, his body seems chiseled. His eyes closed or on the keys, but his arms occasionally raised, for his fingers to pluck and flip the pages. A moving sculpture, his narrow chest like a dancer's, the muscles in his upper arms she can't help comparing with Starlinsky's—but they are not at all similar. Stem's biceps and triceps sculpted like eggs, whereas Starlinsky's arms conceal their strength, yet the underside of the upper arms like silk to her fingertips, currently alternately brushing the sides of the small couch and making little circles on the fur of the pillow.

The sound makes her feel the silk. Feel the silk and miss the man. And she closes her eyes.

"Keep your eyes closed," Stem suddenly, surprisingly says.

A feeling of vertigo comes on. The tonality of the music awakens her the way a sensation of light has on occasion pricked her, delivered into her bloodstream, and she finds herself hearing words, as

161

well, and yes, she is doing as told. Her eyes closed, although now it matters not whether open, whether closed. She is not sensing the actual room. Outdoors, with trees, their leaves rustling, their branches trembling, the waters rippling, and words coming to her as if from outside of her, as if they are marching from books on his shelves.

"You have drugged me," she says, now lying down, her head on the pillow, her legs draped over the edge of the couch. "I know I am here, Stem, in your room, but I am traveling. Your music and your words are like a drug."

"Where are you?" Stem says. "I'm probably there with you. Fear not. Courage, girl."

"I am frightened, Stem."

"You are alive, my dear," he says, and still the music plays, the piano of Shostakovich, his preludes and fugues, and Stephan von Stemeroff is traveling through them, one after the other, preparing for a recital. He uses the pedal on the left, and the one in the middle. He stops moving so much. His back still, he finds his reserve, allows the music to speak among the silences.

"I hear words in Italian and also Russian and also French and now it seems Greek, among words like *marcatissimo* and *tenuto* and 'Shakespeare' the way a Russian person would pronounce it. I hear someone say that the only thing we own is a grave, that the rest is a mirage. And I'm hearing someone telling me about suffering, about the more 'ardent' your 'gift,' the more you will suffer. I see Joan of Arc, and I see concentration camps. I see the World Trade Center in flames, and I see a woman running for president, along with a man who is Black. I see you, Stem, and you are quite thin...."

"Ah," he says. "I should lose weight?" And now the music takes on the chords and arpeggios, and he presses the pedal on the right.

"I don't understand how you can speak and play this beautiful, trenchant music at the same time."

162

"The same way you can speak and see a world that if you were to open your eyes would vanish," Stem says. "Now gently breathe. And tell yourself it's time to emerge, time to come back to the present."

"The present," she says.

And now he stops playing. The silence itself as profound as the music. Now beside her, sitting, her eyes are still closed. He takes her hand, and if she were watching, she would see him moving his own hand slightly above her wrist. His eyes also are closed, and his voice has changed. Even his accent has changed. He is whispering, and she hears him but says little.

"Yes," Stem says. "I see we have met many times before, my dear little one. You remember that all that's good in the world is at odds with authority. Many lives have told you this, have told me this, as well. It is a rule, life's rule. It can be no other. You understand this. Here is why you need this dose of courage, my little Joan of Arc, my little Greek oracle, my little whale who sings under the water. You have heard me singing, as well. Under the water, under the radar, but one of us is bound to rise. One of us is bound to grow. One before the other. Where you go, I will follow, and many others will follow, as well. You know how to do this. You've done it before."

A large silence, as Grace has fallen asleep. His words have taken her into a place of no words.

"Time to rise, Gracie-Pie," he says, back in Texas drawl and gently kissing her hand. "You've gotten your kiss! And I am about ready for a cheeseburger with fries!"

The word, or the "kiss" itself, singing her awake, a lovely hissing in her ears, and she is laughing.

"Oh," she says, with a yawn. "Oh, Stem. So much more than kisses!"

But he is already back at the piano, practicing, as she imagines that she has stood up. But realizes only a few moments later, when her eyes open, that she has in fact not stood up. Like pools and fish

163

swimming in her thoughts, a self like a flame and then a bird and watching Stem anchored to a rock, climbing like Sisyphus, a self like a prophetic voice in a mountain—and Stem like the fallen Achilles, a self like Mary that is carrying a poor Stephan-like Christ, and then she sees herself burning at the stake, and a Stem-like character jumping in with her.

"We go back," he says suddenly.

"Is this what happens in your séances?" she asks. "You scare the world to death—and they go to the bars and drink it off?"

And then her mind produces an image of many of those she has seen walking out of his apartment in hospital clothes, their bodies like those skeletons in concentration camps, their faces distorted in pain.

"What I see in my séances," he says, "I barely remember. I'm told that I speak in voices, and sometimes I wake myself up with a huge craving for a cheeseburger and fries—which, as I've said, I am currently suffering."

"That sounds great," she says.

"Be grateful it's not exactly alcohol," he says, laughing, and she is hearing the music again, displacing the image of an army of men in blankets sweating and crying, reminiscent of civil war movies, making her think of Whitman and Louisa May Alcott and mercury poisoning.

"But I'm sure we've met many times before, where I swallowed you up, in Pythia, you little Oracle, you, and dragon that I was, and you were the mother goddess. Oh god, do I miss my mother," he says. "You are so the closest thing to her!"

And Grace feels herself swimming now and again, ready to rise up and leave but once again unable to.

"I'm so thirsty," she says.

"Yes," Stem says, stopping suddenly, the music giving way to this abrupt silence, and then there is a stemmed glass of sparkling water

164

that she drinks, and he is once again sitting next to her. "I should have thought of this," and he takes a sip of her glass.

"Your next days you must be strong—you know this."

"I feel as if I'm swimming," she says. "And why do I feel as if New York City is slipping from me?"

"So much of what happens here in this life," Stem says, "is behind closed doors, and you never know, you just never know when you will end up in one big bathtub and you look at yourself and you've transformed into a whale, and all you can see is water and whales swimming, and the Sargasso Sea is flipping you about, and one day the sky will be so thick with trails that no one will see the stars any more than they can see the virus that is plaguing this town, and whales will make their way to earth until the only thing you can see are stars, and we will be the stars...and one by one they will fall into the ocean, and the light will be more majestic than—"

"The atom bomb?" she interrupts.

"Stop," he says. "No more fear."

She thinks, "If you saw what I saw, you would understand." But stays mum.

"Wherever you go," Stem says, "I'll be there if you wait for me."

"Where I go," she says. "You will follow. That gives me more courage than you know. Except..." she says.

"Except what, dear?"

She cannot bring herself to tell him what she has seen.

"But you must tell me," he says, reading her thoughts.

"As you have seen me," she says. "I have seen you."

He stops playing for a moment, and there is an exchange in their eyes.

"You are free to tell me," he says.

"Am I free as well to desist?"

"Absolutely," he says. "Of course, I must practice—and you must sleep."

"I'll be here tomorrow," she says, standing up again.

Stands up and walks out.

Walks out and closes the door behind her.

"Let me know," she hears him say, "if you want a cheeseburger. I'm famished!"

Her laughter in the stairwell.

Walking down the steps, she takes note of the iron quality of the railing, the fact that someone painted it green, and she thinks of all the people who touched that railing, and suddenly she wants desperately to touch one of the fallen keys, the broken parts of Stem's lost piano.

How interesting it was that Stem alluded to the information on the printout without mentioning it any more than he had invoked Starlinsky by mentioning the kiss.

The broken key—how she wished to touch, to feel her fingers against Stem's beloved keys.

But first—must return to Cornflaker, to her own home.

No, no desire for a cheeseburger. A funny man. How she loves him. And Starlinsky. A great feeling she is carrying.

She makes a note to look for that piano key, some fragment of his loss. And then opens her own door, returning to the local, the contemporary problem of Em, and the entire mess of her beloved apartment.

And in none of her readings by Stem were there mentions of Starlinsky, or even of Em. And how suddenly the idea of derangement, of a world one might not recognize.

But not in her lifetime, nor in his.

No, not exactly a relief.

Everyone on drugs to stay sane.

Everyone with their own private shrink.

166

But then again, she has her own private shrink—and her own private medium.

"But Em is now." Grace, now thinking aloud. "And now is all there is. Oh, you doctors, I hope you know what you're doing.

"That includes you, dear Starlinsky—"

Grace now making a prayer proper over peanut butter: "Oh God, you strange commander of energy matters, please keep Em in the pink, and Bruce out of the black and blue, and keep Starlinsky true, Breanda happy, along with you, Mom and all your clan, and keep me here, please, oh you heaven dream.

"And, by the way, please tell me what to do about this…our… my…world. Amenandwomen."

So on to the work of sleep goes Grace, after nibbling a bit of the dinner she'd offered to Starlinsky, and with a nightcap of vitamins, she toasts herself to sleep. But it is insomnia that greets her, and her eyes stiffly remain open and dry and non-blinking. She considers her many-layered problem of how to save the world without losing her skin.

"I'll just think about it tomorrow," she snickers in the manner of the oft-quoted hero of fallen women, but this wishful resolution does not dissipate the insomnia in the slightest. Whether she lacks the southern etiquette or possesses just the necessary amount of the western work ethic, the illusion that what *is* is, *is* does, she is forced to come to a more active conclusion, in order to be in the ultimate pastime of passivity.

"I'll just delete all the horror and that's that," she says suddenly, and she is up, pacing like a general contemplating the battle that he (she) will be remembered by but that might kill all his (her) soldiers and perhaps himself (herself), as well.

Using technology to defeat technology. Initiating salvation by way of technology.

"Just let them try to document their weapons, consult their absent information booth, receive no worthy updates of this weeping and weaponed planet worth dating.

*

Grace grows up to a bulbous belly blossom in her dream. She sits like a bodhisattva beside muddy waters.

"Beatrice," Grace says. "You around?"

A bustle—definitely not a bissel—of bees hovering above her head.

"Oh, you silly old men, where is Beatrice?"

"Here I am," Beatrice says, appearing upon a carriage of the two ushering heads.

"Welcome, Beatrice."

"Such a nice way you say my name," the Queen says, noting the three syllables. "Such a ring."

"Speaking of rings," Grace says. "Do you think I may be a bit too late for one?" Like a toddler, she extends her waist out for all to see.

"Well, what do you know," Beatrice, with a buzz of her own. "You need a man, for the way you look is impossible without one."

Grace says, "No wonder you were crowned. You have a way with the obvious."

"Thanks dear, but keep your cracks for the worm. You don't want us to use our tail for advice."

"Beatrice! I'm sensitive about this issue, like all new mothers. You can understand."

"Be quiet and just let it happen. So what if it takes a few months, or whatever you call it when you want it to come and you wait. Patience and diligence don't always come in the same package, but when they do—when they do—when they do? Watch out world."

168

"Bea, will you tell me what my mother would say?"

"Don't ask."

"The worm says it is going to be great."

"So, worms have their share of knowledge, just like the rest of us." While speaking, she manages a twist of her neck and a thrust of tail into the folds of a yellow rose.

"I never knew…"

"We queens do it, too." Beatrice returns to light on Grace's belly button.

"That's what I mean!"

"Now you know. What shall you do?"

"Something that I thought of on my very own. What do you think of this?"

"What I know is you might have a baby by the time you go."

Grace says, "I will do what little I can when the world comes to call on me, but really, Beatrice, shall I tell you my plan?"

Beatrice buzzes up to Grace's ear. "My dear, you needn't say anything, for this is no news to me."

"You mean you heard me tell myself when I did this morning, afternoon, and evening? And were you listening as I pondered mercilessly the whole livelong day?"

"We never say how we happen to know the things we know."

"That is probably the only way, but it is extremely unscientific, you know."

"Science, schmience," Beatrice's words in departing.

Grace, meanwhile, sees her tummy growing fast as a mountain would seem to grow if there were a speedometer next to its side. She wonders whether she might also be graying and bluing up the back of her legs and blushing up her cheeks and sallowing below the eyes and lightening in the brain and darkening in the eyes and loosening a tooth, but then she floats to the world of a laboratory, where she has come for examination.

"Hello," says Geology, a man who so worships the earth that he's part of it, his hands and face grounded to Grace's body like that of a cow or sheep or pig to the land, munching, munching. His feet themselves are boulders.

"Hello, Geo. What can I do for you? Some pulse? A temp? You want some blood? Private measurements? Take my clothes off or what? Can you imagine the fetus inside, or must you pull it out to see if it's growing?"

"Sure. We can pull it out and put it right back in, these days."

"Please leave it the hell alone, doctor." Her clothes are off, folded so neatly on a wooden chair, and she lies there, as present and docile and vulnerable as a grassy knoll in the mid-day sun. Meanwhile, his hands are gripping pelvis, his monitors are impressed upon fundus, his face so close to her nether parts that she considers to let fly a fart but desists.

"You must eat," the man manages to say.

"Something I never would have thought of myself."

"You must get off your feet!"

"My pleasure," she says, rising up, dressing. She feels a kind of reversal taking place, as she moves from woman-as-victim to the great and terrible mother-to-be. While hooting in the poor man's face, she suddenly stops and asks to speak with the expert on bearing the blues of the postpartum kind.

"The blues man—uh no, now wouldn't this be premature?"

"Please," she says. "Will you send in Prehistory?"

Geology, at this juncture, succeeds in leaving, slowly, pulled down by his weighty feet.

Prehistory enters, an impeccably dressed, short, squat man, with mackintosh and vest, a passel of old, worn books on the shelf of his belly, and lenses on chains attached to a pocket. He opens a book with a myriad of illustrations, pen and ink, extraordinarily detailed, of extinct animals. He lets go of the latest lens and speaks slowly and

170

softly, a man of much thought, much perspicacity, and little tolerance for even the slightest of falsification. His lips are thin, and it seems as if they do not enjoy moving. And no, he will not look her in the eye. "Just stuff in retrospect is all I'm basically good for. You will have been lucky, for example, not to have given birth to a Gila monster, a saber tooth tiger, a woolly mammoth, or many kinds of apes. They will say you nearly came from the planet Mars. But what do they know? It will take them thousands of years to discover that the Earth was once flatter than a planaria in retrospective, respective, relative fact."

"This makes some of the best sense I've ever had to swallow," Grace says. "Where did you find that—not in a pre-history book."

"Never in a medium that came after the message. Why, if we started believing in pre-history books, we might have to accept diplodocus as a scribe, or tyrannosaurus a pope and the brontosaur a lay-dinosaur, so we make no bones about our guesses, but many guesses about our bones."

"I will make sure to remember that. Goodbye, Sir." Grace calls after him as he twaddles down a hall, but it appears as though he cannot hear, so she waits. Soon enough, she is back down, prone and naked as a jaybird, again, for the mass of experts. A barrage of interns arrives, including nascent geniuses in Sociology, Physiology, Anatomy, Psychology, Graphology, Ontology, Logarithms, Biorhythms, Curiology, and more of the latest of scientific fields that have yet to be invented. Fingernailology, Wartology, Loveology are waiting in the wings in order to be nearby in the event of an emergency.

Inside, Grace can barely see, what with the white cloud of analysis hovering overhead. "Please go away. We need no more of this. Please remove your stethoscope from my underwear. Try that speculum on your wives. Get out, you beasts. I'm getting up." She rises to a sitting position on the table, and thinks if she were a man she could pee all over them, but because she is a woman, she will have to use her mouth. She curses them out with the curses of many tongues, many colors, and one by one—because, after all, this is her dream—they disperse.

She next finds herself on a hill, a faithful witness to the sunrise. Then, she looks to the western sky for a falling morning star.

In its fall, the star releases a fly that cycles in series of negative swirls, then drops upon Grace's nose, creating a slight knot of buzzing that bids her hands to move.

*

Rubbing her eyes, Grace yawns catlike, extending those lanky limbs of hers. She stands up slowly, walking toward some very gritty windowpanes, her fingers upon them, with their odd ribbony treatments, her face jutting out like a masthead into the city air. She imagines herself a sailing ship, with a morning prayer to that effect, rather than a plank aloft a stormy sea. The fly moves on its appointed rounds, as Grace gratefully sucks at the grimy stream of oxygen and marvels at the gush of pastels flooding the eastern morning sky.

She is pumping up her adrenaline while fingering her make-up case, figuring to adorn her face in sunrise, her routine at a fast gait, when suddenly the phone startles her, and she leaps to the ring, with a few twigs of make-up applicators in her mouth.

She wonders if "Hello" is too naïve a thing to say.

"Well? Well?"

"Oh, hi Ma," Grace says, removing the instruments from her mouth, placing them in the finger webs of her left hand as she drags phone to mirror. Listening, she paints, powders, brushes, coats, punches earrings through lobes—a full Friday face of embellishments, ornaments, grace notes. So many things she wants to say, but her mother on the other end is chock full of questions and comments, not really requiring the answers. Just bursts of consoling sound, Grace offers, which range from a second soprano's "yes" to a tenor's "no"

172

and including a few staccatos of "sometimes" and triplets of "oh really" and "you're kidding" and "are you sure?" It's the stuff of lamb to sheep or roe to flounder, Grace disengaging the fine probes of a mother's words.

"Grace, will you please talk, or do you have cotton in your head?"

"Oh Mama, what's new with me is just a bunch of new, same old different stuff. The job is boring, Em is sick with a head-cold, and I am dating a middle-age..."

"Middle-age!"

"Ma, I'm nearly middle-age."

"Don't remind me."

"Doctor."

"A docta?"

"A physician."

"Very nice—so what's his name?"

"Like I said, it's hot up here."

"Same down here—what do you expect. It's summer north of the equator, I hear. Give it another month; it will be fall. So, this physician, has he got a name?"

Grace groans. "Mama. I love you. How are you?"

"I just told you—weren't you listening? Gracie, Gracie, Grace, your head is full of space, but your mother loves you. Now get up and go to work like a good girl. Goodbye."

"Bye."

And, donning a red dress, off she goes, this good girl, making sure to leave the portable home for the work she plans to finish up on the weekend.

Fridays are the worst for your average bicyclist, so on this day, she decides to treat herself to a sixty-cent ride on New York's luxury underground. She passes through the few dozen thresholds and lands before her terminal room door, deciding at just that very moment to

173

take a U-turn, to start the day with a joyful smile. She writes and deposits on the terminal a short note to Breanda: "Meet me, you-know-where, for today is tea-day. Love, Grace." Her plan is to go back out the doors she has just entered, when halfway down, in the elevator, she realizes that today might be Breanda's day to go to the doctor. Ah, she is stuck in an elevator that is unable to accommodate her fickle mind until it reaches the top, or in this case, the bottom.

Chapter 7

On the landing of the first floor of the infamous building, the great marble and limestone cave run by the Klang brothers, but owned by the City of New York, Grace encounters Walpho and Tina. Having no hat to tip, she bows her head, wishing to pass in nonplussed silence. But Tina can no more allow the young woman to pass without speaking than the heavens can part the earth without breaking.

It rather looks like a bad case of gout in the area, Grace thinks, what with the bulge of the lid and brow of her superior, and there seem to be eyelashes unleashed, as well.

"Hi Walpho, Tina—what can I do for you?"

"It's what you have done that I want to know!" Tina's face turns a bright shade of pale. "What am I going to do with you, girl? Where have you gone with that lousy stinking portable? Have you ditched it somewhere or unloaded it on some mafia chief, and what's the idea of taking it home without asking, when we never knew where you were taking it, and how—"

This is all too straightforward for Walford's sensibilities, and he asks Tina to "...hush, for Christ's sake."

"Relax, Walpho," Grace says. "The thing is home doing homework overtime." What else did you think, you brute, slob, stinking, CIA narc creep, jeepface, is the unsaid thought.

"Good to know. I was terrified someone might have stolen it from you, poor dear, on the subway, or even—oh well...Let's go, Walpho."

As they waltz out together, Grace follows the old familiar linoleum hallway, whose morning echoes ring sinister in her ears. She keeps step, then veers off as they head directly to their offices. In her demeanor there is no change, as Grace directs herself at that same controlled pace, but heading straight like a rat from a sinking ship to the stairwell and down, down, down. Upon closing the door, she dances down ten floors of steps, so claustrophobic yet prism-like it seems, zigzagging down. She feels herself a skier, and with the opening of the door to the lobby, a feeling of destiny strikes her as she breezes out of the double doors, grateful to be on her feet. She is a woman all made up, a woman on the run from the brothers Klang.

With propelling speed, not just any walker in the city, Grace finds herself making split-second decisions about where to place this foot, that, the sandals themselves, more lace than shoe, the cement and the earth, the bedrock below it laden with at least a few thousand years of feet, human and horse, dog and rat…maybe woolly mammoth and bugs of all sorts, birds, a dodo perhaps.

A feeling that is both akin to a fuse being lit and of feeling outside time, definitely a Precambrian moment.

As if all the lands had rejoined.

A moment outside of time.

The pressure and the anti-pressure, both.

Her heart is aflutter with epinephrine making a course through her tiny capillaries, arteries, and veins, roadways of sorts, begun a few hours before, the release of adrenaline swelling her vessels so she can skitter and perambulate.

Now, she can percolate thoughts, can think clearly. Her sense of being, of a self both inside and outside time, is profound. She feels herself evolving, making her way forward, one would hope, although that kind of quality crucial in defining direction is often something best determined in retrospect.

She is currently sprinting in those dicey, lacy, sweaty sandals with toes burning, hot breaths and gasps, not to mention sweat elsewhere where skin rubs against skin itching for hairs; she elects to cater her tea party for one at home, instead of having it at the nameless luncheonette. Home is where she is headed. Her pace now slackened, she watches other walkers whose strategies have them taking the bus up Sixth, the street wide as God's smile, this Avenue of the Americas, more cars and trucks than not, this Friday morn.

This is a bus that stops near enough to her domain on the hill of the island on the Atlantic inlet off the coast of Jersey situated in the U. S. of A. on top of the sinking, spinning earthen planet, the watery egg of God and His heavenwench—or the Goddess and Her stud—in the one universe with its myriad of galaxies and whatever else the discoveries of the future will tell.

Feeling so small, so terribly insignificant, if terribly vulnerable, Grace is thinking big. She's trying to create a frame of reference for location, as she seems to be failing to do so for life. And now, for reasons unknown (but time will tell), it's the subway she heads to.

Grace, on her short (relative to a universe) way, happens by sheer accident—however coincidental it might appear, and if one were to question such an event, the answer would be simply because it could not be otherwise, which, of course, would not hold up in a court of law, or even a house of justice—to meet up with Starlinsky, it is true, at a candy store entrance of the Chamber Street subway, where the latter is buying a *Post* for the morning.

Grace is about to chide him, thinking she is the one who has experienced the first recognition. Instead, she gives him a pinch on the behind and a more inconspicuous tickle somewhere else.

"I saw you a few blocks ago—in your berry-red dress—bursting out of that cave on Maiden Lane.

"Well," Grace says. "See you in court."

"Court? What court? The court that I am courting?" Starlinsky is following. He's screaming, "Of course I'm courting you. Yes, I will make it legal. A court of law, no need. A justice of the peace, oh yes."

She runs like a criminal at large. Words loud and accusatory coming from her questioning him, his reason for not saying hello, how he must despise her—such things.

She flees like a woman disgraced.

He follows like a man in love.

She dives down the stairs into whatever subway station, she doesn't care, and on her face, the colors flow in greens and blues, the powder coagulates, softens, liquefies, and the mascara, too. All that was flaked and matted, pressed and patted, rolled and glossed is now in streams, stripes, and puddles. She doesn't care that all the hot, spicy tears of the god she pondered two nights ago are now in her eyes and dripping onto the subway floor next to a spot of urine with its rising heat.

"I'm guilty," he says, upon catching up with her. "Yes. But not for the crime you've accused—"

"You hate me."

"Never."

"Yes."

"Yes, guilty of loving you."

"But you couldn't even say hello? I don't understand…" The word 'understand' is echoing underground. "What you have is contempt for me."

"Never."

"Always."

"I always love you. I will always love."

"Always?" she says, in a moment between paroxysms.

There is the sound of applause. The eavesdroppers are happy, they who are watching, waiting, there to make sure all is well in the world of the sobbing woman in the red dress, as the train roars in, and Starlinsky is whispering words for just Grace to hear.

"Yes," he says into her ears. "I was stalking you. I am guilty of that."

"And no," he says to her silence, "I did not need a beeper to know.

"Yes," he says to the mountain of her tears. "I am here.

178

"With only love," he says, to the volcanic-like breathing, the heaving, the accusations and recriminations, the words that she will take back in less than a second, but that the full car of passengers must overhear—must overhear and will likely recall when a little more than a day has passed, when her face, a little changed, they might happen to see again.

She is a polluted reservoir of anger and fear melting into pure sorrow, and because, if nothing else, he is a good sniffer of suffering, Starlinsky, there, having heard what he'd heard just a handful of hours ago—he had his suspicions. You could call them fears. He lifts her and carries her to the uptown side, and in his specially trained subway bedside manner, he comforts her.

They travel in this manner to her home on the planet. And soon recriminations give way to apologies. He is sorry, and she is sorry, too. Their fashion of forgiveness is not much different from their mode of celebration last night or the preliminaries the night before. A distinguishing feature now is the phone, its ring. Grace reaches for it.

"Hello," she says, trying to control her breath.

"What has happened," Breanda says, neglecting to identify herself. "You aren't at tea, then, are you? You get food poisoned?"

"Close," Grace says. "May I call you right back?"

"Bye," Breanda says. There is a double click.

"Who was that?" Starlinsky says.

"Work."

"I never did ask you why you came running out of there like a bird on a live wire."

"I'm afraid it's a long story, and I might have to go back, but I have a lot of work to do here. I'm apathetic."

"Apathetic? You are as apathetic as an infant sitting in—"

"I'm actually just a little anxious."

"You must tell me."

179

"No need," she says. "Please, just love me, and don't test me anymore."

"Testing, testing," she hears, then sees PreHistory shaking his head. PreHistory has tiptoed into a new dimension, and he is looking around, fascinated. Or, he is looking for the fly, whom he'd thought might serve as his traveling companion.

"No more of that," she says to them both.

"No need? Please, you just love me and don't test *me*," Starlinsky says.

"Oh, so that's what p—"

"Tell me quickly. We've both gotta go." They both begin to dress, listening to the phone deliver its one song.

"Hello."

"Grace, you must get back here."

"I know."

"Bring the portable."

"It's been stolen."

"Why?"

"Why? Ask the robbers."

"I am."

"Breanda, I have not stolen."

Starlinsky watches Grace return the receiver to the phone and then quickly reaches for it. "Please hand me the phone, Gracie."

Grace marks the resonance in Starlinsky's voice. She remembers hearing that tone of his in Em's room. There is both danger and safety in his cadence, which she finds simultaneously ticklish and frightening. Absolutely, she is frightened. She stands back, after handing him the phone, the both of them only partially clothed.

PreHistory is still standing there, his hands upon his books, his books upon his belly. Lenses hanging from the mackintosh pocket. He nods at a fly that has come in from the open window. "Hello," PreHistory says to the fly. "Regarding yourself and the worm," he says

180

to the fly, "if you could, what would you place your money on? This is a decent question. I know you hail from Cenozoic, a little older than the Cretacean, a little younger than the Triassic." He then turns to Grace, but his eyes are focused on the other two creatures, although the worm is not in attendance.

Neither Grace nor the fly provides an answer, but the fly makes himself scarce.

"Hello," Starlinsky says after dialing. "Starlinsky here. Will not be in today. Why, yes. My mother-in-law has just been robbed. Yes…yesterday, as a matter of fact. Justice of the Peace, yes. A very precious jewel."

Meanwhile, Grace reminds herself of her favorite watch, once her grandmother's, that Grace never wore but always set. She always set it, and it always stopped a few minutes after she set it. It is ticking on the highboy, and time with it. The word "escape" comes to her. The way the word "run" had come to her a few hours before. Starts to plan it, her escape with Cornflaker. "Where shall we go," she says to the machine, which now sits tucked away in its box. "And what is the best way to travel incognito?"

"Traveling incognito—not an original idea," Prehistory says. "Yes, some of us here have been traveling incognito for years. Years and years, and no one the wiser. And what have we gained? That is another good question. Raising questions, my dear Grace, represents the beginning of the answer." With that sound piece of advice, he imitates the fly, leaving his books to scatter but holding onto his lenses.

"OK, Grace Rosinbloom," Starlinsky says. "You had better tell me everything, from the beginning."

"Starlinsky," she says, her hands and face upon him, hugging and caressing his scratchy neck and face, hairs of salt and pepper and all shades of brown reaching to hatch into wool. "I will, I promise, but first please help me pack up some things, and we should get out of here very quickly okay, love, love, love?"

With Grace taking grand charge, they unsnap the metal fasteners of a small, worn leather suitcase, and quickly toss in or otherwise place the aforementioned watch, scissors, some make-up, all her money (seventy-five dollars and thirty-nine cents), a pair of sunglasses, one large cowboy hat, a scarf, a belt, and two days' worth of clothes.

She gives Starlinsky the suitcase and sends him on ahead of her.

With the desire to at least let Stem know, Grace runs up the two flights but, hearing nothing—no music, no sound—she cannot bring herself to even knock.

She is locking her own door now, with a kiss and whispering a goodbye.

"Who knows how long it will be until we see each other again." Those with hearts on sleeves and ears for such things might hear a slight heave of brick, a still softer crack.

With Starlinsky ahead of her, his plan to hail a cab, and now again on the stairs, what Grace hears are bells, the Prelude of Messiaen, unmistakable. No more the nightmare but the impalpable dream. Stem's music filling the stairwell as she rushes down, her feet like his fingers. The steps like the keys.

No, there's no time to go back up. No time to say goodbye, to ask for a prayer.

She feels his absence at the mailboxes, at the door, across the street.

"My incongruous beauty," she says, another whisper, almost a prayer. "Be well, Stem. Who knows if I'll see you again!"

And walks out that door.

Looking down on the ground before her, vertical against the inner curb, she spots a rectangular piece of ivory, which she picks up and pockets.

*

As there are no cabs in sight, Grace and Starlinsky are off to a loft on the Lower East Side by way of the underground. Their words are few. It is just a host of touch and go, as if they are relying on the radiance of fire to light their way and a cloud of smoke to cover their tracks. Upon arrival at Starlinsky's ale-house-like space, Grace barely holds in her excitement. "This loft is so lofty. I can almost hear my own echo."

"And is its beauty beautiful?" Starlinsky stands there, looking at his space with the eyes of his beloved in mind. What does she see here, he wonders and then asks.

"Light," she says. "Lots of it."

"I'm a spare kind of guy," he says.

"Whatever you are, that is my kind," she says.

But there is no time for a discussion about his taste in furniture, or the story of his gathering of this piece and that one, or even of the others who may have sampled its goods. Those stories exist, of course, but Grace expresses little hunger for them, little hunger for the past, having a sprawling present and a dwindling future in her thoughts, and a pocket full of a piano key. Nor does Starlinsky wish to fill up her mind with more accessories, so the stories of a loft remain untold—at least for now—and to be honest, all that he sees when he looks out over the unified field of his loft is really its newfound queen.

What she sees is space.

A disinterested onlooker would perhaps note the antithesis of coziness, the newly-sanded oak floor with a light stain, an array of brown couches and small unpainted wood tables, a few standing lamps, a sprinkling of Turkish rugs.

There is more light than stuff here, which is what Grace says as she sets up the small valise on a wooden table and opens it up next

183

to Cornflaker, rummaging through her things and looking around to see just how to make herself, and Cornflaker especially, comfortable.

She says, "Do you mind me?"

"No, but now tell me. Sit down and begin with the end."

"I stole this portable terminal, and now you are my accomplice."

"Okay, that's not so bad."

"I have access to CIA files, remember? I plan to erase all I can. But if I don't do it quickly, I may lose access, or they might catch me, and it will be a complete failure for which I would suffer needlessly."

"Oy," Starlinsky says, reverting to the Yiddish.

PreHistory, zipping up his fly, has also arrived. "You can say that again," he says and then does.

"You speak it like a pro," Grace says to PreHistory.

"I am a pro," Starlinsky says, "you little *meshugannuh*. So, what kind of a nut are you?" Starlinsky's tongue happens to actually be close enough to her tongue to find out.

"I'm only half of this nut, sweet love." She fishes for the scissors in her bag with her free hand, and then she hands them over to Starlinsky.

"You want me to ease your burden?" He places the closed utensil at her throat.

"No, jerk-off. Cut off my hair like a star surgeon."

"No."

"Then cut my throat. It will be academic, if you don't cut my hair."

"Okay," he says. "But only if I can cut your toenails while I'm at it. They require it, if I may be so indiscreet."

Starlinsky leaves about two inches of the two-and-twenty, giving Grace a surgical do, though not so short as to arouse the attention of onlookers. She sweats as he takes the scissors to her toes, sprawled out on his wood floor and thinking of nothing but hunger.

"I am starved," she says, suddenly with a smile, conjuring Stem, for the reason of a craving. "Whatcha got in your fridge—any chance of a cheeseburger and fries?"

"Toenails galore," he says. "Stay right here," and he walks quickly to the distant area of the kitchen with its utensils and appliances and what-have-you. He presents her with a carrot that is about as large and brown as an oak branch, as well as a freezer-burned-smelling container of tomato sauce. "Here, sink your teeth into this," he says, referring to the root. "You can use your tongue on the ice cream."

"Mercy, mercy," she says, laughing. "What, no knife?"

He returns, carrying a fork and spoon.

Grace tries her hand at the ice cream but realizes that it's frozen spaghetti sauce.

"How very wise thou art. It's all the food I've got," he says with a bite on the bottom of her foot. "I'm hungry too, Toots."

"Well, thanks anyway for the two-ton carrot. Or is it a gourd?"

PreHistory is there to supply an answer to such a question, but it's the fly who sees where this is going. In conference they are, he and the fly; the fly who is actually even less prone than the scholar to use his voice, speaks: "It's nuh nuh nuh-not for nothing that my longevity is sealed, man. I'm not a voyoyoyoy-yeur, nor am I very greedy, but I'll be ba-ba-baback for the spoils. Define yourself, Gra-a-a-acie, and know that when you need us mo-mo-most, we will not desert you."

"What is it really, Sir Lancelot?"

"I thought there was a fly on your buttocks."

"Do not kill it," Grace says.

"Wait for me," says the squat and persnickety old soul to the fly. "We'll be waiting in the wings of history, Grace," he cries as he runs off stage, his mackintosh rising up almost to the tip of his tweed trousers that have fallen for the loss of a belt, showing the beginnings of his own cracked behind.

"I don't have the mettle for killing," says Sir Lancelot, who finds himself with a conquest on his hands, and Grace rolls the carrot away from them, speaking no more of hunger.

Only after the very air is saturated with their sounds and words and waters of love, do they rest, albeit on the floor itself, pretending to sleep in each other's arms. So complete is the stillness of their union that someone watching might think they have both somehow expired, but now, at the same time, they breathe, bound together like one large sacrificial beast. Their breaths are the only sounds that can be heard within the large, sparsely furnished loft. On the other side of Starlinsky's walls, however, the Lower East Side carries on its incessant noon hour dance.

It is not only the twitterings of the outside world that find their way into Grace's ears, but the buzzing of a fly, and she jostles, ever so slightly, whereupon Starlinsky withdraws from her, and the two make motions to rise and put on some clothes. Unable to resist, Grace begins gnawing at the carrot, making sure not to ingest the fly, and Starlinsky begs her to let him take her out.

"Remember, I promised. The Plaza. Really, we deserve it," he says, roughing up her two-inch coiffe.

"Why must we go outside at all? I'm reluctant to leave until nighttime unless it's to cross the state line. But I'm not sure if I have to be exactly that paranoid. I mean, I wonder how far shall I take this thing?"

"Grace, we should eat before we decide anything. We are safe in a city of seven million. This is a place where they really leave you alone. I'll take the responsibility—okay?"

"No," she says, with the same finality in her voice that she had when she'd refused Breanda.

"How about instead of cheeseburgers, I go get some bagels and lox and herring and all the stuff of celebration. Pretend someone got bar mitzvah-ed."

186

"*Bat* mitzvah, if you don't mind," she says, "and I already did."

"But I didn't."

"Okay, go get yourself one," she says, then adds, "Someday I'd love to go to the Plaza for the bar mitzvah of Starlinsky."

He heads out to the Jewish markets, taking no notice of PreHistory, who is absent-mindedly pulling up his trousers as he walks down the street, tickled by the changes upon that part of the Island, namely the sprouting of art galleries and fine dining where there were once warehouses, where people who'd just arrived on boats en masse, once released from Ellis, would find their way to sweat shops. PreHistory imagines the fields of daisies that preceded the fields planted by the Dutch and English. He remembers the foraging and harmony—much of it unrecorded, this kind of harmony. "Perhaps the best," he says to the fly at his side, "is when there is no record."

The fly, notably sparing of his words, nevertheless responds: "The be-be-be-best, PreHistory—and the worst, I'm a-a-a-a-fraid."

"Me, too," Grace says. "I'm afraid. But I take a deep breath, and I do what I must, right?"

"Right," PreHistory says. "Right."

Determined to do what she must, Grace snoops only insomuch as to investigate the outlets for Cornflaker, and a phone for his coupler, the cradle that will hold the handset. She finds one near a tabletop, with a window view of three bridges and a bright blue sea, and the tips and middles and some bases of buildings, and a sidewalk with walkers standing in the way of the world.

And most important, proximity to the phone, stationed on a side table.

PreHistory has returned to where Grace putters about, where she is prepping but also taking stock, looking around at her things mixed within the very spare domain of Starlinsky. In a moment of weakness, she looks at her grandmother's watch, fingers it, feeling the bumps where the marcasite is, looking at the time stilled on it, 1:31

exactly, wondering whether it's the true time, the past time, what exactly happened at that exact time and what exactly transpired when its time-keeping ceased, then places it in her closed fists, one hand around the other.

She looks at her fingers, brings them to her eyes for a moment, rubs away some tears with the double fist. How frightened she is. She closes her eyes just for another moment, with her hands still around the watch, and asks her grandmother for strength, for direction, for courage. The fly has found entrance through the window facing Cornflaker that is not entirely sealed. He is carefully smoothing his wings past the coat of paint upon the otherwise rotting windowsill. PreHistory, on the other hand, walks right through the brick and plaster, situating himself against the wall next to that very window, as though pressed up against it into barely what would be defined as the first dimension, when, in fact, he exists in such an elevated dimension that it has yet to have been assigned a number.

"I don't know how you deal with this," PreHistory says to the fly that has managed to fly up to the ten-foot-high ceiling and is there, just hanging. "They don't see me, they do see me—it doesn't matter. I don't have much they seem to need. Their lives are so manic. They are without a center. They are without grounding. All their knowledge, all that they unearthed, all their fabulous civilizations doomed for their frenetic forging ahead, their unwillingness to examine what they've done. Their lives are a conveyor belt, a screen of motion, an event, a dispersed focus—all that Grace must turn away from to do her part."

"You duh duh duh-don't want to know how I see it," the fly says. "I tell you, you duh duh duh-don't want to know."

"Excuse me guys," says Grace, as she sets down the watch and sets up shop, and soon Cornflaker is humdoodling away. She begins the deletions just as Starlinsky lands at the palace door, making knick-knock sounds of five locks snapping. Finally, the door kicks open revealing a veritable carriage horse unburdening itself of its bounty, handing one bitten-into garlic bagel to Grace.

"Or take one that hasn't been tampered with," he says, with his stuffed and masticating mouth. In his arms, three large brown paper bags filled to the brim, leaning Towers of Pisa.

"Thanks, dearest. I love tampered-with things. Have you forgotten so soon?" She takes a big bite, then says, "The deletions are going to work. Then we can really celebrate with lobster Thermidor, filet mignon. More appropriately, we should just have garbanzo beans or potatoes, some mutton and humble pie."

"What have you deleted, honey?" Starlinsky says from the kitchen. "Have you gotten rid of Indian Point? Oh, maybe they've closed that down already, but for how long—and what about Seabrook?"

"Give me time. I'm getting rid of obsolete weapons, first of all."

"You mean submarines."

"Some."

"Torpedoes?"

"There are ten million kinds of torpedoes. I got rid of the ones in helicopters run by men."

"Drones?"

"Newfangled drones, the Predator with hellfire missiles."

"Great. Those things have killed more seaweed and whales than the enemy."

"The enemy is their creator."

"Now why do you say that, sweet thing?"

"Gee Willickers, I don't know. Somebody must have programmed me wrong."

"That's an understatement. What is your mama like?"

189

"Marnie is just a Marnie of a mama. Thank goodness she called me today. She would have called the cops, my own mother, if she had tried a few more times without an answer."

"Your mother's a worrier?"

"Yours is not?"

"You wouldn't believe my mother," Starlinsky says. He feels Grace's thin arms coming from behind.

"This talking of mothers," she says. "How can I resist?"

"I don't see her very often," Starlinsky says, his face softening with tenderness. "She's the type of person who's always got herself tied up, always helping people she barely knows, always marching for causes, writing letters. I can't wait for you two to meet. She's a very strong woman. There's nothing she couldn't do."

Grace leans on him, holds him tight.

"We're the only ones left in our family," Starlinsky says, still chopping, still gathering, proving himself quite the man in the kitchen.

"What happened to the others?"

Starlinsky pauses while slicing some onions, and looks at the sun in the window; his eyes read the skyline like a line in a book, and he slowly tells her what he says must, for the moment, be just the shortest of stories about how the two of them came from Russia when he was an infant. There were letters that stopped coming, and he grew up in Pennsylvania with a secret life, until he came to New York for college, medical school. "And now you," he says.

Grace looks to his hazel eyes that really are oceans she can and will be and is just now diving into.

"Russia," she says. "Russia." The music of Shostakovich comes into her mind, the last of his preludes and fugues. Number 24.

"My mother's name is Sonia," Starlinsky says. "She will adore you. Soon you will meet her."

"In Pennsylvania?"

"We'll visit someday."

190

"Maybe sooner than you think?"

"Why not now?"

"Now," she says to him, "I am swimming in your eyes." She kisses him but releases him, realizing how madly she'd been studying him, allowing herself until this very minute to be taking a break before her return. "Swimming in Starlinsky's eyes," she says to him. "But now, if you don't mind, I must work to save the world."

"Please be a little more humble, Gracie-kiwi. We have yet to see the might of the pen over the sword."

"Ah, Starlinsky. You are my pen and sword." She returns to her thwirpping, cheeping portable, and she watches the deletions of weapons of all colors and sizes.

"Food's on, so get your bottom off."

Grace leaves her misanthropic business for the salty delights of Starlinsky's platter. They munch on foot-long sandwiches, the stuff of liquids and solids of all hues splattering out the sides. Their laughter makes a trio of the great loud Bach mass playing, gratis of WNYC, also his station of choice. It is among the most glorious of times when the phone rings, and both sets of eyes glitter with fright.

"I'll get it. I must."

"Oh."

"Hello. Yah. Oh. Hi. No. Oh. Okay. When? Okay. Bye."

Grace is certain that so short and insubstantial a conversation means she may forgo the fear.

"It's nothing," Starlinsky says, reading her eyes wherein a tinge still lingers. "But we'd better get to bed fast. I've got to get to work in an hour at the latest, or we might lose Em."

"Lose Em?" Grace says. "I'm stunned. It's all my fault! I missed this—I didn't take this as seriously as I should have. Please let me come with you. I've known her for centuries. I can help!" She is frantic—in both tone and cadence, her heart racing with more knowledge than a heart can handle, in vain the brain forewarning. "But

191

how can this be? I had thought that all we needed to save Em from was herself? Why do you keep her there?"

"How do I tell you this, Grace?" Starlinsky sits down again, extending his hand to hers, then releasing it upon feeling her pull to withdraw. "She's more dangerous now than ever, and not only to herself. She says you molested her and tried to kill her. She says that her parents want to marry her off to some fruit, and that her producer tries to make her sleep with every act in town. But now she's swallowed a ton of other patients' medication. Apparently, everything is under control. She's sleeping, but if I'm not there when she awakens, it will not be so good."

Yes, it's too much to take in the possibility that Em has fallen ill because of her own betrayal. "Are you sure you don't need to leave this very minute?" Grace says, putting down the impossible sandwich.

"I won't leave you until I must," he says, taking her hand again, leading her to his big waterbed, which rules the vast room. "We're both so tired. We rarely sleep when we're together. Come fall asleep with me." When she does, and when he sees that she is deep into sleep, he rises up very quietly and dresses, preparing himself for a few intense hours with Muriel Lyons.

PreHistory, with his flying companion, slips in as Starlinsky flies out the door. PreHistory shakes himself out of sleep mode. "As you were saying," he says. "I remember you were about to open up to me, so I want to let you know I'm listening."

"Yes, as I was say-say-say-ying, you didn't want to see how I see, and that's because I see many multiple poi-poi-poi-points of view simultaneously," says the fly. "This leaves me to anti-ti-ti-ticipate the future by way of anima-a-a-a-ating the past. I am neither a sa-sa-sa-savage nor-nor-nor-nor a sa-sa-sa-sa-sa-savory character."

"But," says PreHistory. "You are a survivor."

"Because I sub-subsist on fi-fi-filth, and humans are monument-men-mental deliverers of what I need to sur-sur-survive?

We are symbi-uh-uh-uh-otic partners. Cast your vuh-uh-uh-vote for me and not the proto." He's speaking not only to PreHistory but to Zelda, whom his antennae has picked up. This is the reason for the slight lifting of his stutter, his response to the filaments of the lime green swirl coming from a far place that only he can see. But soon it becomes clearly apparent that Zeldele, with her full entourage, are in the finishing stages of their dramatic entrance. A fine green mist begins to envelop the entire apartment. From all corners of all the rooms, and from the ceiling and floors, as well, the green dream of Zelda's world arrives.

"What have we here?" PreHistory addresses the fly, who has made himself scarce. "The opposition? The enemy?"

"The enemy is you, I'm afraid," Zelda herself says. "Not 'us'— let's get that straight." She's looking at the fly, who, of course, has split. "As if I don't know where you are, my tiny renegade," she says, more than a little flirtatiously. She can barely be seen in the mass of greenness, but her voice is unmistakable. "As if you are not part of us, little darling." Emerging from her green fold, she approaches PreHistory, who pulls out his lens, backing up from her, step by step, as she begins to make moves onto him. Just a hug or a kiss, a short embrace will do. She is absolutely naked now, and PreHistory is floored—that is, on the floor. "And even you, Mr. Mackintosh, are part of us." She stands there, her eyes fixed, light pouring out, the female gaze—an expression more of pity than disdain.

Eventually, PreHistory gets his act together, stands up and bows to her. "Much obliged," he says. "Well, what are we to do?"

"We're growing a baby," she says. "And we obviously need your help."

"Obviously. I'm here, Madam, at your service." He salutes as his pants fall, and he is grateful that Grace has been ignoring him all this time.

While Starlinsky contends with the wilds of a New York afternoon, Grace dreams of her friend and protozoan, a most highly developed, humble being.

"Oh, hi, worm. What's new?"

"Worlds, since we last spoke, Grace. Animals and insects and birds and fish, and all with the seed within, that grows and blossoms, and suddenly, one day, the fruit appears with its share of the seed within. Amazing wonder, perpetual motion—an idea for which no man has received the prize. What a great invention."

"What's that," says pregnant (lest we forget to mention) Grace.

"The seed within."

"That is for sure. I'm working on this notion that probably I told you about."

"Oh yeah, the salvation bit. We didn't really, no offense, of course, take you seriously, so have no fear. Now, what about Starlinsky...?"

"Worm, I've done it—well, almost, I'm—"

"Stop. It's not important. What you must remember is that we will continue no matter what. We have the seed within, and can't you just see it grow!"

"Great joke, worm. I feel it, and you simply have no idea. But worm, are you telling me I'm wasting my time with this life? Please!"

"Grace, Grace. You are doing what you are doing. This is fine with us."

"What's this 'us'—you and Zelda engaged or something?"

"Yes, how did you guess?"

"I saw you wrapped like a ring around her finger—it didn't take much."

"Well, you've a good eye, we'll say that much for you. My only warning, as a former reactor, is to keep free of all reactions to your work—or you might find a reaction when it's least expected."

"Oh worm—who—what—where? Tell me!"

"We can only say that you should be careful with Starlinsky."

"Worm, you give me horrible words to ponder. We are as one."

"Not yet, my dear Grace. Where is he now?"

"With poor Em."

"Precisely."

"Worm, I shall not react to you!" Grace is screaming as he vanishes, but when her eyes open, she finds she is no longer screaming. Her mouth is comfortably at rest, and even Cornflaker is quiet. When she tries to plug in the phone, she sees a note slipped into the dial. She takes the crisp paper—from his pad of prescriptions it is—the note reads: "To Gracie. Starlinsky will never, never leave you. He is here in his heart, and his body will be back soon. Marry me."

Elsewhere, a fly is smiling, inasmuch as a fly can smile, his black tongue moving almost imperceptibly upon some dishes of herring and lox left in the sink. But also elsewhere, a short, plump, well-attired gentleman—albeit beltless—is shaking his head. His study offers him little hope for a future. He is pondering the separate rooms of this planet, where tasers are being readied for a market so dark, rooms where computations are being made in silence, rooms where coal mines have been hollowed out, where gas lines amid water lines and even nuclear plants are investigated, and were it for love, or even the common good, perhaps he could exact hope.

"Look there," Zelda says to him. "Look there." She, not yet accessible to Grace, can find the love anywhere, and where there is love, there is hope, she would say if asked.

Grace, in her glory, smiling broadly, her fingers on the small prescription. How small he writes, yet elegant is his script, balanced, in

195

the vertical—a European sensibility, then? Oh, who is this man? She cannot resist reading:

The Grace Poem

She moans with the grater
They spit on her shoes
She lends pitterpatter to the neighborhood meows.
They sup till dawn
And she is up for the man in the moon

Where are the many she freed from the ground?
Why, they were the worthiest suitors the world had known.
So proper a maiden she searched for a home
Never a woman born had proven so bold
And bolder as older she grows
Till one day there shows
A bundle all of her own.

Grace reads with some blush of embarrassment, and the quizzical expression of glee on her cheeks and brow, as she takes in the last verse of what she thinks of as a perverse thing:

She guides by no star but her stars bring truth
Who wounds her must wound himself, too
But 'round where you are she rounds up the light
Of glorious love from morning till end of night.

As Grace reads the last few lines, little rivulets spill from the rims of her eyes:

Grace is the word but no word is in place

Till the graces of the world take up the law of Grace.

Grace responds to his poem with a poem of her own. It too is spilling from her. She finds the pen and the very pad he used, Dr. Daniel F. Starlinsky, MD, with his special number, his room number, his association with Bellevue, more initials there—and what they signify remains beyond her. Just before she is about to put pen to the pad, she hears a moan. She looks around, almost fails to notice the ever-so-slight green light settled in the corners of the room—was it there before?

The moaning, a lovely moan—she imagines lovers in the not-too-distant horizons. But there are words coming through that moan. Zelda's? "Write small, my angel," and "think big, but write small!" Looking up, she sees the green recede, registers the moan gone, and as she writes, she herself intones. Words sing out into the air to be held there in that space. And anyone who sets foot with ears to hear will hear. The words, the manifestation, the inspiration filtering, weaving itself like antennae hairs, like the foot hairs of the fly, impossible to see but not to feel. Her poem like his, a prescription.

"Listen!" Zelda's voice is a command directed at PreHistory, who doesn't answer. "Does the man have ears?" she asks.

"Good que-que-question," says the voice of the fly in the kitchen still, his tongue hard at work.

"It is once again, my runt, a rhetorical question. What he lacks in ears, he must grow in heart."

"Listen," Zelda says, as Grace writes, keeps writing, keeps speaking, her poem:

A Star in the Sky

Starlinsky rock of my grace
Which star in the sky does he replace?

197

Starlinsky broke the wishbone of my breast.
He brought my pulse to the moon and my blood to the sun.
He befriended the rest of my parts just for some fun.

Daniel will you be mine?

There might only be the end of time
For me to be in your arms once more.
My gravest wish will be the wonderful wond'rous wonder of
them all.

"OK," Zelda says to all of them. "You watch her now, my girl.
Watch her now."

"My girl, too," says the worm.

"Aw-aw-aw-all of ours," the fly says.

PreHistory is quiet, but he's listening.

And then, Grace takes a deep breath, closing her eyes, the best
of all possible worlds in her mind, as she re-dials, beds down the
handset, connects—as if she might command the technology at her
fingertips to disrupt the technology that is beyond her imagination. A
gesture it is, to remove words, but words, too, are things.

And there goes Grace to quacking Cornflaker like a troop of
sheriffs from the cow pasture, and sooner than later, the reactors begin,
at least on paper, to vanish into atmospheric pressure, to rise
innocuously like tactful atoms. She can nearly see them disappear, all
of them, from the redwood forests to the gulf-stream waters, of the
land that is made for you and me. She removes them from Russia, too,
and from all of Europe and Asia, and places in between and to the
south, but she can only infiltrate those places that are publicly secret,
and not those barred from even this partially confidential tape, which
cannot tell what it does not know. But wherever they exist, it is where

they depart from, and "Wherefore ever do they exist," she cries, "Oh lord of lords. Wherefore are thou, God?"

"Now this," PreHistory whispers, so as not to disturb. "Now this is a rhetorical question, as well."

"Not exactly, PreH," Zelda moans. "Not exactly at all. There is an answer to that last one, and you won't find it in a book."

"What is in a man," Grace further thinks, as she watches one, then another and another, twaddle in his breezy colors and stone-clenched face down the avenue before her sight in the window. "That he can build and build and hire and fire and stick it in the middle of a patch of greeny sunned pasture? For the sake of his children, he thinks. And for the sake of his children, he buys stocks in Canberra, in Sperry Rand, in Bergdama, in Navy and Army, in General Electric and Consolidated Electric and the greater industrial power." She is thinking out loud, now. "And the fool's gold sun that cannot bring forth its refinery falls down for the sake of their children. They kill wildlife for the sake of their children. They poison the underground, overground, on-the-ground streams. For the sake of their children, they fill up the atmosphere with Ozone, Carbon, Uric and Sulfuric Acid, Iodine, Fluorine for the sake of their children. They build bombs to protect their children from the other children."

In her fury to delete the masses of information, Grace establishes her own ritual, call it methodology, and a calm surrounds her. Much the way a rower propels the boat ahead, by means of simple repetitive gestures, Grace types commands, finds files, lists data and eliminates items, or partial items. Onward she traffics, through the satin and lace files of the Central Intelligence Agency of the U.S. of A., or, as she will have it, the Copious Intrusions of Assault, discovering so much to distract, if not blind the eye. How little there is for a heart to comprehend, even less for the soul to stomach. She deletes strangely systematic ratings of such things as suspicious television programs, films, art objects, books, records, scientific and practical inventions,

199

wonder and non-wonderful drugs, their true side-effects, their false beneficence. She witnesses the disparaging of great academic giants of all fields, their suspect philosophies contracted down to a phrase and given absurd ratings that reflect the degree of danger posed by their ideas.

"You can't even *believe* in peace and not be considered a threat."

It isn't as if she is deciding to take a break, but in the middle of deletions, the terminal suddenly goes dead. Thinking nothing of it, she figures to take advantage of the situation and give Starlinsky a call, but in the process of trying to engage the receiver and obtain a dial tone, she discovers that the phone is inoperable. Very quickly it occurs to her that danger might be near, a revelation that is made more intense when she spots a patrol car just outside the window.

"Now," Grace says. "It begins now. And now there's no time to think but act."

Nevertheless, she takes a moment to collect her thoughts, which is to say, she freezes for a second or two, blank as the stump of a tree. Then she snaps-to, dons a cowboy hat and some shades, breathes in deeply, and pulls on some tight jeans—aware of the scratching of an ivory piano key in her pocket that nonetheless makes her smile—as she reddens her cheeks and lips to cover her pale, pale face, tears off the printout, grabs a bagel, and prepares to walk out the door.

But there is a touch of Lot's wife in all those classified as "XX," and she turns back, hoping to see what it is that she failed to remember. She is not looking at the presence of green filaments, but they are there, nonetheless, and the fact that she is not looking, doesn't exactly mean that she does not see, does not feel the presence of Zelda and company. It is her little note to Starlinsky that catches her eye, which she swiftly removes from the top of the table and folds into the heart of the telephone, right behind the dial.

200

Then she kisses Cornflaker, salutes the cop car that remains in the window, and looks for a window that might open into the fire escape. But a patrol car is visible from that view as well. The only remaining window leads to a very narrow airshaft, but this window faces the window of the neighboring building, and what's more, this other window happens to be ajar. Grace looks down—one storey steep—were she to fall, she would not be in good shape. She makes it a point not to fall by the method of simply *not* looking down when she takes her leap.

Quickly, she situates herself in the open window, looking only at the corresponding window in the building less than a meter away. She sits there in that frame, checking on her hat, squeezing the handle of her bag with its precious cargo.

And, in a matter of seconds, Grace takes a whiff of the unguent smell issuing from the window of interest and negotiates the leap into that frame, traversing the two-foot-across, storey-deep cliff, and landing in a small kitchen with its dour but sweet and almost comforting odor of rancid oil. Oblivious of PreHistory's soothing explanations, a frightened and shrieking partially-dressed elderly woman emerges with two kitchen pots understandably flying in all directions.

"Thanks, but no thanks," Grace says to PreHistory who stands there helplessly, his words falling on deaf ears, which is nothing new to him. Grace tries to calm the woman down, crying, "I love you. I won't hurt you," but the woman disappears with small, fast steps into another room, and quickly she reappears with a printed cotton robe covering her, and tossing to Grace an old, disheveled wallet, still with smell of leather in its body.

"Out, out, junkie," the woman cries, then saunters back to the other room.

"I don't want your money!" Grace follows the woman in search of the exit. Meanwhile, PreHistory is fascinated by the building

201

itself. Grace, seeing the woman grappling on the floor to secure herself under the bed, whispers, "I love you," and sends the wallet skidding back.

PreHistory gives it an extra push, but then runs to help Grace with the door. She presses about forty years of locks, walks down several short flights, and opens the door to a hot, muggy, humid world. Grace smiles with a newfound feeling of satisfaction when she spies a handful of officially-dressed fellows first politely, then brutishly, tackling the door to Starlinsky's building.

"Fools," PreHistory mutters, walking by her side.

Minutes later, she hears bullets grinding into steel. Walking away, she thinks, "Ah, if only there were time, I would take my hat off to you, young men. I would catch the bullets in my hands. I would turn them into butterflies. I would turn them into flowers. I would turn them into rings and bells and buttons and bows. I would render them invisible. I would take the words for them right out of the world. Their very names would not exist."

"You would, would you?" PreHistory says.

"Yes, sir," Grace says, "I would, and I have. So there."

"I for-for-for-for one," says the fly, "am im-im-impressed."

"Oh, there you are," says PreHistory. "Still licking your chops on the herring and the lox?"

"Riot squa-squa-squa-squads," says the fly, "are not my cuppa tuh-tuh-tuh-tea."

Remembering Starlinsky's prophecy not even an hour ago, Grace decides she is safe in a city of seven million.

"I'm limited," PreHistory says, "which is to say that I accept my limitations, but I'll do what I can."

There is a roar of applause from the universe, and PreHistory takes his bows.

Grace is not exactly oblivious of her companions, at least no more so than she is of the other sights that greet her in this infinite universe. She walks for an extended stretch in a kind of mourning for a terminal left behind to fend for itself. In her hands, she is clutching the stash of deleted outpour that she has yet to destroy. A feeling of blankness comes and goes. It's a palpable sensation accompanied by the color green. Years ago, months ago—even yesterday—she might have spent some moments questioning the propriety of each action she has taken, but now such an occupation is beyond her.

The ivory in her pocket grounds her. She fingers the piece with one hand. How smooth. How long ago was she touching Stem's furry pillow and looking at his biceps and imagining touching Starlinsky's. How multi-layered this life. How many histories, how many parallel lives, and at this minute, Starlinsky is saving Em. And Bruce? And is Breanda having her baby?

The sun is yet present in the sky. Behind her it is, the feeling of protection. She walks but slowly, the Bleecker Street of yesterday studiously *not* calling to her—*Sound City, Heartbreaks, Riverrun, Fruitstand, Meows,* are but icons of the past. They are so distant as to be in Odesa or Paris or Budapest, or Johannesburg, or Lake Titicaca. Grace is drawn to a park, as if there were filaments of green doing its work, the slow beginnings of a cocoon being built around her.

A buoyancy there, that she enters, people talking, sitting on benches, or standing, throwing a ball, a Frisbee, offering a little weedhashpills. She smiles at the ruddy, soiled, numb, and ageless ones with their lived-in clothing. Their eyes take her in as one of them, in spite of or because of her hat, which is seen as sun protection. Her dearth of hair—the bulk of it in Starlinsky's possession—gives her an androgynous look. She escapes no one's gaze, not the males, not the females, not the young, not the old. So nondescript she is, all the world can relate. It is what is called "Alphabet City," this turf, and she is new to them, but they have a place for her, the homeless, as one of their own. So many smiles, ah such wonderful society, Grace thinks, and laughing, she takes part in the back and forth, and she rummages into her bag and hands over whatever—save the ivory—falls into her fingers. And when there is nothing left but a brush, a non-ticking watch, a much-diminished cache of quarters, and the printout, she carefully rips the computer paper into swatches, with promises that they will someday be worth something.

"Thanks, lady," and "thank you, miss," and "kindest person" are the comments she receives, which thrill her. She reaches up to scratch her head and realizes that somewhere she has surrendered her cowboy hat. She yawns, with that feeling of lightness brought on by utter exhaustion and insufficient food, and she sits down on a bench near a phone booth on Broadway, figuring to give her love the possibility of a second chance, fingering the stash of quarters in her sturdy pocket. Many times she dials up the hospital and asks for Starlinsky. Although he is paged countless times, he never comes to take the call, so Grace phones Em, who for whatever reason, does not pick up the phone.

Grace leaves a still-ringing phone when she hears sirens that she knows are for her, and she goes running down a small side street where an alleyway proves most cozy. She lifts her head to the beacon of the barely blue sky that is not dark enough for a star, not even on the easternmost horizon, but knowing that it's there, she makes the only wish she feels she has left.

Chapter 8

Sabbath it almost is; sundown it's not yet; summer solstice will commence in the middle of the night. If Grace had eggs to set on their apexes, they would surely salute her before sunrise. Little does she know how much more easily the world turns, how much brighter the sun shines, how much longer it holds on because of her, because of what she has done. And yet, another day goes by without the release of the hostages. Does she know that it's just a matter of time for another to replace the Ayatollah, just a matter of time for the nuclear stockpiles to grow—this she does know. But who can hold all that is promised, whether it is eschatology or entelechy, whether it's destiny or knowledge, whether it's being or self or nothingness—when there is horde of police on your trail?

Another luminary is up, and its lone inhabitant has returned from his waxy crescent more than once today. The stars of course refrain from revealing themselves, but they are there, just as many things unseen, some of which sport filaments of green. And where did she leave that hat, Grace wonders. The brick she leans against creates a smarting sensation on the back of her head—and where is that bee now? Grace looks up at the sky, its color shifting, more periwinkle than cyan, now slate, bordering on a smokey gray, those wisps of clouds, the particles reflecting or dispersing the trillions of rays of city light.

Friday night, then, time to reflect—time it was and what a week it was.

Not exactly hungry, but that sky is a feast of clouds.

Currently, no sirens to break the cadence of the early nightlife. Just voices, shouts, cars breaking, subways shuttling, horns blasting, the friction of one thing against another—all of it a music unto itself.

Seeking another place for sudden exhaustion, the buoyancy depleted in an instant. The earth turning. The sun setting—the onset of the longest day of the year. Whatever the explanation, the light recedes, and Grace, like a flower, bends in the direction where there seems to be more of it. Now out in the open on Fifth, now in the Mews, standing there on cobbled stone.

She walks further in, supposes herself in some European town, a stranger at home. She could be Beethoven in a petticoat, and looks down, finds a place for Stem's ivory key among the stones. Belgian blocks. Touches the stones there, a kiss before burying it among nubs of grass between old, grey, mottled beings of stone. For this whole wide world is hers—she tells herself this, or someone reminds her. The voice comes to her, and it feels like her own. Her hands among the grounded stones, and feeling the coolness, she lowers herself.

Again, her back against brick, a less ancient brick. Still prickly on the back of her head. Gentrified, this street is, with its flowers cascading down window boxes, its gaslights. Sirens now. They might as well be harbored in the pit of her stomach, in the core of her middle ear—that's how they rouse her. It isn't as if she has told herself she is done with running. She is not giving up. But she is tired.

Her eyes flutter. She tries to keep them open. How horrid it is, this homelessness, the spiral of loss, what a conceit this idea of home, and now she has resorted to speaking to herself, and are her eyes closing or what? Is it a place or a state of mind?

Does the idea of home exist only in retrospect?

Is home only to be had when lost or remembered?

Surely, no place can be home to someone on the run. But if she could just remind herself that here is her planet. Here is her home, unless this is a brainwashing, unless it is false. Unless she is a fool, but not so foolish as Em to slam her head into the brick.

In the defamiliarity, a voice that drawls then morphs—moving from Stem to Breanda.

"Poppycock! Preposterous! Balls! Absurd!" There is a bee in front of her, and the brick wall behind her suddenly crumbles, and she falls backward. What was once a wall is now a mass of dancing bees.

"I'm falling, falling," Grace cries. There she is, flat on her back, with Beatrice spinning around her, trying to revive her, and there is the voice of Zelda as well. They are a chorus, and as they sing, the brick wall undergoes transubstantiation of sorts. It's a shattering, a smattering, a clattering that turns into metamorphosing, a buzzing and hissing and sneezing and spinning throng of swirling bees. This block of bees that has been called a black cloud manages to wall out the sirens that have, it seems, managed to minimize their circle, to follow their lead, to narrow down the search to a certain square footage within the central village, where east meets west—namely Fifth Avenue.

For the moment, the sirens now are stalled, as no one will contest the territorial rights of the bees, and they know as the sun sets that the bees will slow down to a near halt, their cold-blooded selves needing the warmth to keep them moving. Rather like the hummingbird, such thoroughbreds they are. But for now, there is a show taking place in the vicinity of Washington Square Park. It is under the Arch that Grace travels, to watch the singing duo around the stinging mass. Although for some, the swarm is also a song, high-pitched notes they are, and they are singing for their lives, for Grace, for you, and me. "For your ears only," Zelda says to her.

Grace can barely speak.

"I shall speak for you, Gracie. You have without a doubt fallen. The falling is undeniable. You feel it, and Beatrice has affirmed. The bees themselves have certified it, have surrounded you and hidden you. This is, in fact, in spite of the darkening hour, and my dearest, it is your darkest hour."

Beatrice takes center stage. "In the world of your reality," she says. "There are many opportunities to fall down."

207

This falling sensation reminds her of the grand piano. Reminds her of the key she left among the stones. She is now among the fallen. Yes.

And of the key—may it call out to Stem, who tried to warn her.

Zelda takes up her cue from Beatrice, about the opportunities, the vagaries of falling. "Why one may slip up, smack into, stumble upon, or just plain collide—with person, place, thing."

PreHistory decides to be a cameo: "There are steps, ladders, slides."

"There are cliffs, ditches, wells," says Beatrice.

"There's folly," says PreHistory, "and melancholy."

"There's duh-duh-drowning and ca-ca-ca-crashing," says the fly.

"There's falling in the eyes of someone else," Zelda says.

"And," says the worm, who's nestled there around Zelda's finger, "there's falling in love."

PreHistory steps up again, puts his lens on and almost mimes this: "They say the higher you go, the lower you can fall."

"But," says Beatrice. "If you've not falling asleep or turned into falling stone, what a thrill it is, before you fall."

Beatrice snaps a little, and the swarm creates a protective barrier resembling a golden igloo around Grace.

"Unheard of," PreHistory says.

"They caw-caw-caw-call it a swarm," says the fly. "I'd steer clear of them."

The cops are steering clear of them as well, at least for the moment; that slow motion receding of the last light of the sun is certainly a saving grace. Grace herself is in that state that renders a human utterly helpless, that takes the air from the self and leaves the body at the door. The sensation of an uncontrollable setting causes the beasts of her own private Bardo to loom up right into her face and then back off, and these are none other than Walpho, with his glasses

208

and his desk and his hands shaking papers. Standing beside him is Tina, who has situated herself on a large gold cross, blood trickling down from her hands and feet, and Walpho is saying, "Look what you've done, what you've done, what you've done!"

Grace sees the bees circling them and swarming onto the cross, making themselves at home, and lifting the cross back into the skies, allowing Tina to drop from it, drying up her blood, and Grace sees Walpho catching her in his arms, and he's holding her pieta-like, crossing a desert.

"You are next," Walpho says to Grace, his words echoing as if under a marble dome. The cross is spiraling up to the heavens back into the moon, and Grace is waving goodbye, goodbye, goodbye. Or perhaps it's she that is falling, whereas it appears that the cross is rising. And that little rectangular piano key is rising. And the piano itself is rising, and Stem with all those who have come to the séance are rising, and all the sprites and fairies and shades are rising as well. The bees return in one gorgeous line that curls into a script, spelling out "Love is all there is" in the sky. They then surround her in that one line, then cycle, building a cone around her which is penetrated by the green filaments heralding Zelda and then Zelda herself.

"You've done nothing wrong, Grace, but everything right."

"And I've a baby to grow," she sobs.

"We haven't forgotten about that baby," Zelda says. "Your baby is my baby. It cannot be otherwise.

"You realize," the worm says, "you were summoned."

A few bees fly off, leaving room for the entrance of the fly. "Yes," he says. "You you you," his body, its flight indicating first Grace, then the worm, and then Zelda—accusingly. "You three three three asked for this."

"None of this matters, guys," Zelda says. "What matters is what Grace knows—we have a baby to grow."

"About the baby," PreHistory says, taking advantage of what he presumes to be the breaking up of the hive.

"What about the baby?" Zelda says. Zelda herself is growing. She can make anything grow, and she can grow herself, as well. Soon, she is bigger than a bear, and even though the sheer largeness of her form has completely dispersed the bees, the police car that has been circling the block keeps its distance. "If we are to have a stand-off," she says to PreHistory, "you realize I will win. You are nothing without me—on every level there is—"

"OK," Grace says. "Wait. Let's get this straight, folks. This is about me, now."

And now, they, too are, for the most part, dispersed, as a cloud of tear gas mushrooms from one end of the park to the other.

A trail of words in Grace's ears that seem to have the ring of the worm: "I think she's got it. By god, I think she's got it."

And then, are they gone? The skies now dark, and that star there, the one she was waiting for, and she once again makes a wish, and a thought bubbles up during this wishing, namely that Starlinsky is indeed on his way, and she is waiting for Starlinsky. The sirens sound again, and now, she knows it is just a matter of time. Either they are here now, or they will come for her. But so will Starlinsky. She merely responds to a compunction to wait, and soon her eyes clear up for a smattering of sight, having been blinded by a swirl of tear gas that found its way to her, and she looks out to the large street, the ocean that is Fifth Avenue, from her little stream that is Washington Mews.

She can plainly see that there are some men in uniform approaching. With those men sailing in the hazy, wavy wake of her eyes, she remains seated. It is as if they are ripping pages out of a storybook, entering such a pristine scene. She listens to the sounds of their dark heavy shoes upon the stone. She watches them, their fingers, their hands, the glistening silver on their uniforms. They do not raise guns to her, although they slap some great handcuffs around her

210

elegant wrists. Though saddened by the weight of the shackles, she does not put up any kind of fight.

"The Federal Government will take you from the precinct," says a pasty-cheeked, large-faced cop, whose tone is almost apologetic. He has a dimple that appears in the middle of his left cheek when he says certain vowels.

"I don't know," the second cop says—a smaller, grayer fellow, who is doing the driving. "They might actually do the questioning right there."

"How's that?" the first says, dimple-less.

"Friday night late, you know. She might stay over till early morning."

"True," the first says. "At any rate [dimple], we'll [dimple] probably have [dimple] you all night, so don't worry. We'll [dimple] treat [dimple] you like a lady [dimple]." His smile more than advertises, actually broadcasts, his dimple.

Grace smiles back. "I'm most grateful for that."

The cops stop their innocuous bickering when they arrive at the precinct where Grace will indeed stay for the night. A woman introducing herself as Sarah Thower escorts Grace to her cell.

"Where will they question me?"

"In a small room in the precinct that we use for conference with prisoners." Though not more than ten years Grace's senior, Sarah Thower displays a distinctly maternal manner. Grace spots it sitting there in her golden eyes and in the indelible cut of her strong, cleanly-set jaw.

"Shall I be safe until then, here in my own little cell?"

"Yes, honey." Sarah Thower gently rifles through Grace's things, leaving her with Starlinsky's poem and the half-eaten bagel, in addition to her housekey, her hairbrush, and her watch, and whatever else she has somehow neglected to give away. The watch, in particular, Grace holds like an amulet, although she—in her adult life—has always

211

expressed contempt for the idea of a watch, the idea of time and surveillance, for the watch itself is a thing of surveillance, abstract in theory, concrete in actuality. A thing with strings. Even without its tick, it makes a statement. She looks at its slender pointers saddled on Roman numerals—the day, the time, the moment of now. What is it saying to her now? But cannot she have a say? Let it sit with its share of history, but let the future be in her hands. She places the watch that feels rather like the shell of a sea urchin into the pocket of her jeans and takes the poem Starlinsky wrote to her, first flattening the tiny document in the two palms of her hands. Someone watching would see her lips moving almost soundlessly, like a zealot reciting the prayer after meals.

Likewise, if the star Grace has wished upon were itself outfitted with eyes, and were Regulus not only all-seeing, but also an all-knowing thing, a super-quadruple-Cyclops, if you will, with the ability to see past prison cells and through layers of ozone and the brick of a city-owned building, he would see both Starlinsky and Grace reading poetry. Following this, the bright star of the Leo constellation would see Grace mesmerized unto sleep—or at least it would appear that way to the star, brilliant as it is and with the ability to shed enormous light around a soul. Regulus can shine a light on Starlinsky on the run. Regulus can even peer inside the window and catch a glimpse of Starlinsky, upon his return to the loft, aghast at the condition of his home, groaning, and at the same time shrieking for Grace. But even Regulus cannot, what with all his brilliance—no, he can't get inside a soul, not without that soul's permission—at least not in this world.

Such a one who can is the one who, as she reads his poem to herself, finds herself lifted into Starlinsky's life, merging with him in a very different manner than ever before. Seeing what she sees, hearing what she hears. It is as if she is back in his space, his loft that has been torn, unrecognizably so. The fly, along with some renegade bees—both with their miraculous eyes—have also made it their business to

212

be there upon Starlinsky's arrival, thinking they'd take turns keeping track of what is happening—and then reporting back to Grace, in whose cell PreHistory has decided to remain. Now, even if the star itself could not penetrate the interior of Starlinsky's household, and even if Grace were not somehow witnessing the terror of her beloved, we can count on the fly and a few bees for reportage.

So, what they saw, and what she is seeing now is a frantic Starlinsky, having found no sign of her, except for the little suitcase he helped her pack, which contained her choicest possessions; Starlinsky was about to leave almost immediately, which was just a moment after arriving. It was with the suitcase in his hands that Starlinsky looked back, another Lot's wife, and remembered he'd wanted to make a phone call. In that way, he discovered the poem harbored in the telephone itself, where it could not be seen except by one for whom the deadness of a phone might signal the immediate local problem of the instrument itself.

It is then that he stopped to read the poem, but he was too harried, too distraught to take in the sentiment. This is the moment Grace wishes to still.

A stilled moment. A moment to breathe, to remember not simply Starlinsky but the world in which she herself has been cocooned. The series of cocoons in which she has lived, from which she has metamorphosed. Her life a series of pupae. The apartment key in her fingers, she considers her most recent flight, from her building, her room, her beloved Stemeroff, whose music is going from prelude to fugue and from fugue to prelude.

Such a thought encourages her, a post-metamorphic recall— the way a prelude evolves into a fugue—whereby numbers of scenarios simultaneously exist, whereby the parallel universe may find actuality, say, perhaps in a black hole. Whereby Bach becomes Chopin becomes Debussy becomes Shostakovich. Becomes Stem. Becomes Starlinsky. And will she ever see him again?

And how, just when the world seems to end, it does not.

No, not at all, because she finds herself in torpor; in that stilled moment, she is a witness—whether it is memory or imagination or a traveling back in place and forward in time, she sees the piano of Stem. She does not see herself, but the hordes that have entered his apartment, how they've scattered on his throw rugs—the weavings themselves from Persia and Katmandu. Patches of material, swatches, the way they come together. The hordes are sitting in their shorts and skirts, their sandals at the door—a number of people sitting on his couch, huddled together on the little couch that she'd practically slept on.

The Himalayas right here in New York, she is thinking as her lips widen.

"We are signals for each other," Stem is saying. He is saying this at the same time his hands are outstretched and the notes are ringing out, the waves of sound rippling out of his windows into everlasting time, everlasting space. She remembers his saying that to her.

"Signals," she hears them, some of them whisper back.

And among what she remembers is the moment he said that to her. And signals, like stars, like sounds, like movement, like the sudden odor. And more, the wave itself, the thought.

And then her attention shifts—and they are gone. She is returned to the astonishingly real confinement, along with the abstract, the idea of signals again, what that means, the attempt at communication, that perhaps something is being communicated even though it might not exactly seem to be communicated.

Seems. She is thinking about "seems," about perception, and this perception she thinks about leads her to the desire to manifest. All this to say that she is not only seeing and feeling Starlinsky, but she is trying to exert some control, which, of course, is forbidden.

214

"Stop," Grace cries. "I'm here, I'm here. I'm here. Can you feel me, Starlinsky, darling? Why can't you see me?"

Understandably, she sees that Starlinsky, likewise, is seized by the need to make something happen. Starlinsky, there in her mind's eye, with that poem stuffed in the pants pocket of his whites. Grace watches as the fair, grey-eyed man takes to the streets. Galloping from one hotspot to the next but finding no trace of Grace, he takes out the poem again.

"Yes," Grace says, the notes—they are now the first octaves and the occasional chords, the occasional stillness and silences of Shostakovich's 23rd prelude that strike her like an avalanche in slow motion, like a string of church bells tolling, their echoes steadying her, and then the silence—and in that stillness, she whispers: "Focus on me, and I will bring you to me!"

But he cannot focus on the words—she sees this. She can even see the image of her he has in his mind—outdated, to say the least.

"I'm not wearing the cowboy hat, darling," she says. "Come to me," she says in her mind. "Here I am, I'm on a small cot in a room with a window and lots of bars. Think police, my dearest one. It's where the opening is—my window of dark blue night, imagined stars—only imagined, though. If I strain my eyes, I can see the moon. Perhaps it will shine through. Depends on its journey. Perhaps it's on its way to me, to my window. I'd like you to follow it, Starlinsky. Picture bars. Cinderblock. Picture me in jeans and a pale yellow shirt. See my eyes, gather yourself into their wake, their trail of tears. I'm waiting for you. I smell of desire, Starlinsky. Desire and growing power, for I am going to grow a baby, they say. And if I'm going to grow a baby, Starlinsky, it's *your* baby." She says all this in her current locale—the cell, namely—and so softly, almost under her breath, as she is surrounded, not only by others, but others like herself, if in different rooms. Still, she is as if lifted from her place, as if a fraction of an inch off the ground.

215

There is a fly returned to her, giving her a bit of a debriefing, telling her "Ca-ca-ca-ca-close your eyes. What a guh-gift eyelids really are, you-you-you know?"

"No closing eyes for you, fly?"

"No," he says.

"But you must sometimes get tired."

"Yeh-yes," he says.

"Well, I personally give you permission to take a break."

"Ri-ri-ri-right," the fly says, having some foreknowledge of what awaits them. "You, tuh-tuh-too, now, Grace."

Grateful for her eyelids, that she can close, but still see, and contemplating the paradox of the fly who, without the gift of eyelids, may still turn off the world and sleep, she closes her eyes. There she goes, into a place where she might be able to have Starlinsky in her sight again. Grace will simply watch him, and she will visualize, praying as she watches. Projecting, trying to project, with what energy she has, and there is PreHistory—whom she is desperate to tune out—pacing, pacing, back and forth like an expectant father.

"Don't worry so much," she says to him.

"Right," PreHistory says. "But if you knew the past like I know the past."

"There is a future to build, PreHistory, and it's in my hands. I'm meant to remember that," she says, her eyes closed, speaking really both to him and to herself. "Help me project good things, PreHistory, please help me! Your worries are getting in my way."

"Okay," he says, scrunching his face, shrugging his shoulders, and now lying down on the floor next to her cot, after using his hand to move out some of the dust. "He's trying to find you, you know."

"I know that, PreHistory," Grace says, her words slurring, as she descends deeper into meditation and sees her beloved.

As if onto her scent, Starlinsky places a coin in the rusty, disgusting old slot of the very telephone Grace had used trying to contact him.

"This is one of a number of coincidences that will seem to go unnoticed by the collectors and detectors and trackers of facts," PreHistory says.

"Yes, that would be you, PreHistory," she says, as he decides to lie next to her, remain close to her, of course platonic as ever.

PreHistory indicates to anyone who will listen that very little escapes the fact trackers. It just gets to them a little late.

"Oh, hush, PreH," she says. "Listen."

"What I hear," PreHistory says, "are the night sounds, just part of a distant orchestra, something percussive with occasional strings. Lots of sporadic brass—a little wind coming through. It was a warm day, and it's a warmer night, the heat settling into all the old flat tar roofs of Manhattan Island."

"You do not hear preludes?" she asks.

"No."

"No?" she says. "Nor fugues?"

"E minor," says PreHistory. "But it's not Bach."

"If you hear Stem," she says, "you should be able to hear Starlinsky."

The vibration is too low for PreHistory.

"Hush," Grace says. "I'm listening, and I can hear his voice."

"Starlinsky—any calls for me?" he says to the receptionist in Bellevue in charge of the page.

"Dr. Starlinsky, to be honest, we have no record of your pages. We must have misplaced them, but I do remember calling your name sometime around the hour of ten."

Grace not only hears but *feels* the edge in Starlinsky's voice which cuts into his throat—and her throat, too. "Please tell me who— do you know? Please, what did she say?"

217

"I said 'come to me'," Grace whispers.

"Pardon?" This is the voice of a distracted receptionist that Grace can hear, but luckily not feel as well. "She? Why, I can't even say that it was—hold on, please, I have—"

Grace smiles, witness to a barrage of curses slipping from the mouth of her beloved forty-five-year-old brainy specialist in depression and fear, who fears he might himself, and for good reason, despair into thin air. Instead, he asks to speak with Muriel Lyons.

"Oh, Em," Grace says. "Em, my trusty old friend?"

"Don't get me started on her," PreHistory says.

The receptionist is clearly annoyed—that much Grace hears in the voice: "Muriel Lyons has checked out. I believe she was here just few minutes ago with her parents and..."

"Oh," Grace says. "Em is free?"

She sees Starlinsky dropping the telephone, which to this day might still be seen hanging on Broadway.

"Oh Grace," he cries. "Where are you?"

"How is it that I hear him?" Grace says. "How is it that I see him?" She extends her arms, and says, "If only my arms were long enough to grab you!"

Bereft of father and lover, Starlinsky calls up his mother from a different phone on a different side street, yet that can now also be known as the phone that still hangs. Grace hears the wail.

"Grace, Grace, Grace!"

"I'm here, I'm here, I'm here," she cries back.

PreHistory tries to calm her down, but she has turned him off, can no longer hear the music, and can barely see her familiar plump and Mackintoshed shade.

What she does see is her beloved standing under a streetlamp. She cannot help but to survey him, scan him, top to bottom, and in the middle of trying to see if she can penetrate his whites, she spies a

218

police car driving up to him, its window open and a crackled voice pouring out. Grace cheers, but then sees it's all for naught.

"Buddy," says the cop. "You got a dumb look on your face. What a sweet little overnight bag you have. Wonder where you found that? Get in."

Starlinsky offers the cop a peek at his license.

"Sorry, Doc. We thought you were a bum on our beat. Be happy you're not, and, uh, try keeping your voice down."

Grace cries now, unbearable for PreHistory. Even the fly starts buzzing around again, and takes it upon himself, after some prayers, some cleaning, his tiny legs brushing against each other, to go on a seek-and-find mission.

"Pain in the ass," Starlinsky says, losing himself in a mass of slaps.

"Just you tra-tra-try and swat me," says the fly, making himself such a pest that keeps Starlinsky running in the direction of the precinct nearest his home. By the murmuring of his heart, he knows this is where she will be.

"You, fly," he says. "Thanks!"

The fly spirals up to a waxing moon that sits there hanging on its own threads, more in darkness than in light.

*

Grace, too, drawn to the moonlight, rises up out of her incessant envisioning to look out the window where it does seem the moonlight is heading. Through the bars, she sees the fly, watching him cruise upward into the vast, steamy sky. Through clouds that part for the passing whim of a breeze.

"Now," she says to herself. "There's a journey. I wonder," she says, drifting on the thought of a soul—that journey—one that leaves a body, one that enters a body, where she comes from, what kind of a flight or sail, or is she taking an out-and-out journey? How long, how arduous, what hurdles? The journeying soul, does she peek inside windows of houses? Does she hear clocks ticking and see people sleeping? Does she take one last look? Does she retrace every step she ever took? Does she hover just above the foreheads of her beloveds? A must to ask permission. Otherwise, voyeurism, even for a soul. Is a soul free from passion and retribution and obedience? Does she grow viciously smart in the absence of a body? Does a soul relinquish desire? Desire—this is what it's come to, she thinks. My desire. The passion of a soul in a body.

Grace looks out, makes an executive decision to let go, and she watches as if her worries could wave goodbye with their little hands, as they sail out of her harbor. Or maybe they are sputtering out, flitting about, a balloon losing its air or floating off to another galaxy, one that feeds on human pain. All of it, everything from the fear of her punishment to the desire for Starlinsky. She leaves it in the hands of the moon—the darkness of the moon, that part of the moon that will soon be covered in reflective light.

"Courage," Stem said, she remembers. "Fearless."

"I appeal to you, darkness," she says aloud. "There is a world peppered in darkness. A breeding world. A world that prepares for light—a world that germinates seeds. Once again, I appeal to you."

Having done with that, she flops again onto the cot, ready to sleep, with a plan to pull open the white sheet and pale blue cotton blanket upon which she had lain down. She stands, then sits on the bed and slips off her pants, folds them neatly at the foot of the little bed. It's just the moonlight shining through, casting a soft glimmer onto her legs. She takes a long look at her legs, marveling at the sheer existence of them, the heft and fact of texture, both smooth and soft, a little fuzzy, yet imperially strong—that paradox, and the fact that it's hers. She pats her right thigh as she would the flank of a horse, grateful for a body, her body. She pulls the sheet back, the little envelope and the letter, and slips herself in, with a sigh.

Almost as if that sigh is a signal for its emergence, the tentacles begin swaying. Green they are, filaments and vestments and garments and embellishments of the green swirling mass, unseen, unnoticed, except by the nocturnal beast, the one gifted with a dearth of eyelids, but instead sports a compoundedness of eye or eyes in multiples or no eyes at all, but sight—that swirl with cilia-like follicles, each split into a sea of hair, furry meadow grasses that have been in abeyance for a time that is unclockable at best. It arrives, building its cathedral of light, and within the simple groundswell envelops the entire building, like the ultraviolet, there but undetected. That the swirl remains unmentioned in the annals of history is among its enigmata. Surrendering its name, it shall, nevertheless, linger. Nameless, it shall outlast the human catastrophe.

Into the rectangular vessel that is the legacy of penitentiary experts, both Zeldele and her minions are slated to arrive, but first a profound silence envelops Grace, a little death. So full of emptiness is this moment. It resembles the preambling sunshine and clarity before hurricanes, or the room where a thousand people sit awaiting the inhale of a conductor before the baton rises at the premier of a symphony. And not just any symphony, but the one that plays to an outraged audience, scandalous reviews, the one that provokes the emperor to kill the composer. It not only survives audience, reviewer, conductor, emperor, and composer, but sits eternally on the lips and ears of a billion people, who take it with them wherever they go—into their parlors, their bedrooms, and into the forests and mountains and seas where they will drown themselves with this melody on their lips.

Terrified, Grace is. No sword of peace to slice up the terror like Errol Flynn, like Zorro, or Bruce Lee. No Lone Ranger or Tonto deflecting the enemies and fools alike. She sits there just waiting as the terrifying moment expands until it encounters resistance in the sprouts of green that pierce through the nothingness of the terror. Grace imagines a wave or two of the Atlantic variety, not fifty miles to the southeast of her.

"If I could hear the sea," she says to herself, "which I cannot, but knowing that it's there, perhaps I can coax my mind into imagining it." Soon enough, the swirl envelops her, and Grace finds her rotund self enmeshed in as pastoral a setting as one can imagine. A world, more like rainforest than city, superimposes itself upon stone edifice, blacking it out, exposing it as artifice, displacing it. Grace watches as the walls of brick and cinderblock and steel melt under Zelda's green swirl, and now Grace steps into conference with the full cast of characters she has met by virtue of the worm. It is the operation of childbirth that presently consumes her. Starlinsky himself is in the neighborhood, as is the fly, who, like Starlinsky, feels himself summoned and is trying to give Grace a heads-up, but he cannot find his entrance where the worm, blind as he is, is center stage.

If Grace has pulled herself inward to the laboring chamber, PreHistory has strayed, pushing himself to the periphery of the swirl. He catches a glimpse of another fringe member, namely Starlinsky.

"Starlinsky is the great father." Grace issues this announcement to Zelda, whose ruby-painted lips one must imagine shimmering.

"Who does not know that is unworthy of knowing anything."

"Just thought I'd mention it in case he doesn't show."

"Fancy meeting you here," PreHistory says to the fly who, like himself, has easily made it past the guards and warden. The same thing cannot be said of Starlinsky.

"Stuh-stuh-stuh-still another hoo-hoo-hoo-hoop to jump thuh-thuh-thuh-through," says the fly. "I saw-saw-saw it coming."

"I think I can talk to this guy," PreHistory says, referring to the fellow seated behind a desk, whose face betrays nothing of his thought, listening to Starlinsky, who is doing the equivalent of a filibuster.

222

Starlinsky has managed, with his impressive talk and handy documents, to learn what he suspected is true, but further than that, he has not yet gone. The person in question, dressed more simply, is a man who in his body-type and his predilections resembles PreHistory—an old fellow at a slightly younger desk upon which is placed a metal sign that identifies him as Roger Warren. It is to Mr. Warren that Starlinsky has so far unsuccessfully appealed, using rhetoric gathered from his field. The doctor intended to continue speaking until he got his way, although he has now reached the limit of his command of the language: "Sir, we cannot but have you put under treatment for your dependency on the hypodermic syndrome of the polio-politico. Your progress is impeded by waiting for a precedent. Please, open the door before my young hoodlum sleeps herself to death."

It would not take an experienced face-reader to surmise the thoughts of Roger Warren.

Grace herself is adrift in a bit of a paradise, even as her body sports the ungainly position of a crouch, with her feet on water lily pads, her hands holding the branches of a hanging myrtle stem, steering the way to delivery.

"Starlinsky, I must say, O ye goddesses of Nature, that, that, that—" Having managed her breathing quite well until now, Grace gasps upon seeing—or shall we say, detecting—in the distance the very one whose name she has uttered, present before her, in the thick, awkward body of a father-in-waiting.

There he stands, Starlinsky, stilled in the process of becoming. Try as he might, it isn't until his reasoning becomes informed by the ventriloquism of PreHistory that a shift occurs in his status. A few degrees outside of where precedents fall is he. This, because of the very precedents he began coming up with that suddenly filled his brain, gaining the interest of Roger Warren, which sent his already-arched eyebrows further up his forehead so that they almost touched what was once his hairline. Having heard many pleas from his location behind the desk, Roger Warren is the kind of man who adheres to his own methodology, namely the doctrine of silence. His is a fine face that exudes patience and impenetrability. PreHistory had sized him up at once as a man who listened to reason, with the sensibilities of such as one as himself. The seeming immutability of his silence, however, did not suggest anything remotely resembling a block to PreHistory. How similar they are, PreHistory realizes. It was just that Roger Warren has heard it all. Or, at least, he thinks he has.

And so now, that shift begins to show itself, having begun somewhere in the darkness, sending its blood into a series of muscles, first in his large seemingly at-rest body, and secondly, in the shudder that seems to awaken his fingers and hand, and then a quivering of his cheeks and chin, as well as a few blinks of what now seem to be much softer than reptilian eyes. Sound emerges from his opening lips. "Doctor, please do not repeat what you just said, or you will lose what you have already gained. I can see by your eyes what is in your heart. And, as I have a son and a daughter as well as a wife that I love, no matter what terrible trick she has up her sleeve, I shall let you in for the moment. Please, do not say another thing, until I ask you to leave, when I shall expect a word with you." Mr. Warren rises, and takes from Starlinsky the little suitcase that he will hand over to Sarah Thower in the morning.

Starlinsky's mouth opens in amazement, but not a word comes forth.

Thus is Starlinsky led into the cell of his sleeping heart, and he cannot help but wonder at her short-haired unmade-up face of beauty. Beast that he is, nor can he help but touch. So it is that she awakes, the look on her face inexpressible. She showers him with kisses, and moans of love break through the iron bars of the precinct, but the old man at the desk has fallen deaf to such sounds.

It must be said that Grace's angels—namely PreHistory and the fly, stutter and all—talk a very good game.

224

Great moments exist when a person who is but a witness is called upon to ponder an event in which he has no part or purpose, but which nevertheless promises to disturb him just the same. It is just this kind of moment with Grace and Starlinsky at love in the jail that seems to catch Roger Warren off guard. Even though he is kind enough to leave them in peace, he finds himself troubled. He is not a newcomer to this business. Nor is this a first. He's seen mothers and children, children and fathers, and lovers of all persuasions. No, he is not an idealist, but cynical is perhaps too harsh a term to describe his stance. Such a man is he that he believes the renegade a parasite, a perpetually hungry thing that feeds off the state. So why should he tremble at such a time as this. Has he ever seen such a pair of geese? Certain, he is, that the good doctor belongs *within* the ward, rather than without, head resident or not. Does that likewise mean that he, himself, would be better off in jail, and the small, thin womanchild set free? These are the ponderings of Roger Warren, as he strolls over to the cell where lovers lay in chains of the freest country of the freest land.

Starlinsky opens his eyes and wrests himself from Grace Rosinbloom with a soft kiss on her lips, forehead, each cheek, and upon the whiteness of her breast. Sensing the presence of the officer, Starlinsky covers himself, making sure Grace is cosseted under the sheets, then he pulls on his whites, having utterly forgotten that he'd removed them. He walks to the men's room, and then, because the old man has bargained for a word or two, Starlinsky leaves him with some: "Grace be to you." And then Starlinsky keeps walking home to his empty loft, having left a bit of his soul, his immortality—the part of it that weighs less than an ounce—and kisses, whose mass and weight not even Einstein could calculate.

"Grace be to me?" Roger Warren locks up, as he is alone for the night, having sent away the others before Starlinsky had arrived. The old officer of the law returns to his desk to think on his wrinkled life of time and love some more.

"Grace," he says to himself, the name again, the vision of her in his very core, stuck there, as if she bestowed upon him a piece of herself. Somewhere in his body, he'd swallowed it, could not rid himself of it, the image, as if it were a masterpiece of a painting, her breast, the repentant Madonna. Nor could Roger Warren resist looking. No, not a painting, a pulsing breast of a woman, just the barest glimpse, no sheet and blanket could conceal. Once seen, it would stay with him, as would her voice, the whisper that he heard, "…love you."

*

"Grace!" Her body in that very cold, wet, wrinkled state of histogenic paralysis, she appears dead or deeply sleeping, her soul claimed by dream. She hears her name as if ringing from the rafters of a sky that can only be seen by those standing in the Prado in front of one of those hundreds of paintings that depicts the verticality of sky, its chaotic assemblage of illuminated bodies. How full of people and angels is Gracie's sky! The world is up there for Grace. Through those bars, after all, is sky, and where sky is, there's flight. Just as Roger Warren cannot dispel this image of Grace, nor can Grace dispel this world of hers, its green light drawing lines, stems to a common ground, and a blue light as well, anchoring itself to the heavens. A thousand people in flight.

"Grace," she hears her name again. It is surely Starlinsky, materializing from the small fraction of the DNA that he left behind, rising from the few drops he left on her and within her, both doctor and father, the dream of a man, Starlinsky, the deliverer of the most noble peace child, who stands equipped for nothing but love. His hands, gloved in gardenia petals, upon her belly, his eyes that are now gray, now hazel, on hers that are brown, and his shoeless feet wading in the waters. His baffled heart is ready to spring, but it is his business to manufacture calm, so he does. "Grace. We are all ready, so let's have a baby."

She feels herself gaining strength from him by just looking into his eyes, while around this group, trees are trembling, their lush limbs aquiver in rainbow trim, and the pond ripples, crests silver with light. The insects and dragonflies, arachnids, and bees of all castes are abuzz, and birds whistling, whirring, aroused in their nests. Gardens of hipatica, bluebells, bloodroot, and lavender open as if waiting, and the roots of every lovely blossom with a pulse. There is trillium, sweet william, a thousand lilies, their petals spread in anticipation, while a worm snuggles in the earth, feeling happier than a lark but proud as a cock.

The world is a giant bathtub. And you and I are whales.
This comes back to her in the lilting drawl of Stem.
I would like a cheeseburger and fries.
But this is not a time for eating, no, but a time for birthing, for delivery, for the child.

Grace, a whale herself, is presently in the round belly of a whale. How like a placenta the very green swirl of Zelda. How very like a whale, the room wherein she begins the journey of miraculous birthing. How like an ocean, her sky. Accompanying her on the lily pond birthing chair is none other than her dream man, Starlinsky. Secondhand childbirth is not without its enthusiasts, and surely every mother-to-be would stand in line for forty days and forty nights if it were possible to have pain-free childbirth without strings attached. Some would call it a virtual childbirth that Grace begins to experience, the marvel sans the suffering. Without a clock's run of rhythmically irregular spasms, without the mathematics of a few sets of intervals closing in on seeming regularity, without cramps, without jabs, without any sensation of contraction and expansion, without a hair or quark or lepton or even a string of the electronic torture monitors, without even a trail of crimson, Grace senses a swimmer in her birth canal, but oh,

227

she's doing the back stroke, slipping into breach position. Without the assistance of well-positioned mirrors, Grace senses her infant's bottom appearing and then disappearing at the opening of her own body, her earth body at its finest hour. So it seems to Grace that the pond itself without her is also within, and she is at one with that great sopping gush of a gulf stream, as the baby pushes herself out, out, out, brief candle. An essential element highly underestimated in the pecking order of collectibles, namely the uterus, makes quick work of dispelling her, and like a tadpole, she wiggles slipperish, and swimmingly parts the waters of the very pond itself.

Starlinsky lurches tenderly for a wet flipping limb or two. Not one false move do either of them, father or mother, and now child, make, first one foot and then other at womb's end. The little wonder stops kicking, and from her grand leap into her father's hands and forearms, she—such a dream baby—is placed by the dreamy doctor into the hands and on the breast of the dreaming mother. And then Starlinsky snaps the pulsing red and white and flesh-tone cord. Grace nurses the baby, calling for some help from the birds to gather the wisteria vines for a mat. She calls the bees for some honey, and she seeks flowers for the canopy, and she whispers to Starlinsky of her desires for food and comfort. The dream father then steps back to give Grace some privacy with her baby. She coos in the face of this impossible dream of peace as the infant nurses greedily, knowing somehow just what to do, when suddenly from out of nowhere a nurse appears with an injection to dry up the mother's milk, and a bottle to stick into the mouth of the child.

"Hellkite, you hellkite. Get out of here!" Grace protests wildly. "Please give me what is mine. You thief, you horror, you traitor, you, you, you."

In an attempt to calm her down, a nurse plunges a syringe into Grace's breast, ironically making a rattling sound.

Exasperated, the nurse cries out, "Grace Rosinbloom, Ms. Rosinbloom. You? Grace? Rosinbloom?"

Grace is jarred out of the swirling phantoms of green, the beautiful blue ball of her swirling planet into the stilled stone drama of a prison cell, and she tries to remember what she cannot forget, namely that there is no baby in her arms, on her breast, of her flesh; its eyes not opened, not closed—no baby in her body, no baby at all.

"You cannot deny," says PreHistory.

"Nah-nah-no you can not-not-not," says the fly, both of them there, a salute to past and future, and permitting the worm and Zelda's hordes to be present.

"What cannot I deny?" Grace says, her eyes still closed, full of tears, sniffling.

"You cannot deny," PreHistory says, feeling a little righteous, because he too is learning, he too would have never noticed this thing he's about to report. "What you cannot deny is—"

"Suh-suh-suh-spit it out, PreH," says the fly.

"A stirring, Madam. This you cannot deny. One cannot call what you have stirring a baby, but—"

"He's emb-emb-barrass-assed," says the fly.

"But what?"

"May I be the first to tell you that there is a zygote now stirring, oh, so desperate to cleave to you, a little world growing into mulberry, or rather a potential morula, blastula, and embryonic masterpiece— indisputable, if I can be so indelicate to suggest, on the order of seventy-three hours, twenty-seven minutes, and fourteen seconds of age."

"The worm told me not to trust him," she says.

"Forgive the buh-buh-blind one," says the fly. "Suh-suh-suh-sometimes you need to cuh-cuh-cuh-close, buh-buht, now yuh-yuh-yuh-you need to oh-oh-open your eyes to suh-suh-suh-see what I see."

229

The sunlight, flaxen, the color of sand, rectangular behind the barred window, casts its slant upon the cinderblocks rather than upon her cot. It has barely called to her, just a breath of light, and then her own big breath, a sigh, and several stretches later, Grace opens her eyes, only to see the older woman smiling down upon her. "Good, what is it…morning, Sarah?"

"Very much so, Miss Rosinbloom. Has your watch stopped?" Sarah Thower is visibly scanning Grace's almost insect-like thin, sallow body for the watch, which she spots on the floor in the heap of shed clothes. "Will you come with me, after you put on your clothes?"

Grace feels a slight feeling of shame, for having shown the jail her person, place, and thing. She puts on her jeans from the day before, which are not nearly so tight, and the pale pink shell. It's not hard to stuff her watch into the right front pocket, as she brushes what is left of her hair, slaps her face with some water, and then joins Sarah Thower walking down the gray-green cinderblock corridor. It is a small room she is led to, with a large, rectangular table, around which several men in gray and blue uniforms and some plainclothesmen are seated.

"Hello, Grace," one of the plainclothesmen says. "Please sit down and make yourself comfortable. We shall try to make this as pleasant as possible."

And so she does. Holding onto the table, she lowers herself into the only available seat, a folding chair that is wooden, slabs of oak tarnished, and her fingers find each other again at the table, the one hand folded into the other, and her toes flexing in sandals that occasionally tap the linoleum. She glances at Sarah Thower, who stands just outside the closed door. Trooper that she is, Grace does nothing but smile in the face of these pulseless poles of flesh. Her eyes are drawn to the light between her and the men. The particles, like those she once saw as a child. Hallucinations, her mother called them, that were impossibly more than she could handle, dozens of imaginary friends that came in both animal and human form. But her grandmother, who had found them charming, kept them going longer than they otherwise would have—setting the table for them, asking questions, creating tales, repeating them. Grace lost the charm in the way that children do, but she remembers enough to recognize what is happening to her now.

"Grace Rosinbloom..." This is the first man, the plainclothesman who has seated himself directly across from her. "We have come to ask you—er, some questions about—er, your supposed criminal act, which we define as treason of the highest count against the Government of the United States, as well as the relatively minor—er, but still criminally inexcusable act of robbery. Are you aware of these crimes that you have allegedly committed? Or have you been unmindful of the severity of the punishment that accompanies these crimes against the state and local and especially the Federal Government of your own legal and moral and beautiful—er, of your own country of the red, white and blue? Or are you yet protesting the Vietnam War, silly girl? Please try to explain your alleged criminal acts, or if you choose to—er, lie or deny what you have been hereby accused to have done."

Grace observes that he has stopped speaking, but she has lost track of what he was saying in the middle of his speech. She wishes he might repeat all that double talk, or is it triple and quadruple? And mightn't she at least have a lawyer present? Instead, she tries to state her own impossible case. "My dear sirs—and why are there no ladies? To be sure, not a public matter of the state when mixed company is excluded from meetings of such fine purpose and intent." She stops for a moment, stung that she has lost all their attention. Not a one has remained alert enough to actually listen. She raises her voice: "Gentlemen, please be attentive. Our lives are at stake!" The men appear to rouse themselves, as she continues. "Please lend me your ears. We shall soon come to burial, if you do not listen to my well-chosen words—"

Grace stops to summon her wits, as if her entire life were a runway for this particular flight. "Gentlemen, what we have before us is a case of very foolish thinking. It is a cancer on our lives. In order to live, we must fight the cancer, or we shall lose the body to an ugly rotten, stinking, smelly place of death. How do we fight death?"

Grace stops and plucks her watch from her jean pocket, the watch whose hands have not moved since the last time she had looked.

The others also glance at their watches.

"Well," she says. "Is there still time?"

"Go on, miss. We will stop when we stop."

Rather than a display of temper, she is overcome by a feeling of formality that is as surreal but sweet as a blackberry blossom. "I want to have an idea of my time, please."

"We have as long as it takes, so please continue and try to stick to the facts."

"Now, sirs, we cannot fight death in the manner we fight an ordinary opponent. For death is the one and only one predestined for winning. We obliquely concern ourselves with death, when we should only concern ourselves with life, friends and—"

"Madam—er Miss Rosenberg—"

"Bloom," she says, "Like the flower. That is Bee, Ell, Oh, Oh, Em."

At the mention of "M," the letter "M," and its coincidental homonym, namely Em, the name of her best friend, Grace finds herself refocusing, seeing past the particles, through the male bodies, through the stone, and through time—this very same Em. She is watching her in the street.

"Em," Grace shouts. Grace sees her there, the tall, elegant Muriel Lyons, her hair electric blue, her fingers twirling it up in a bun, the book in her hand—Shakespeare's *The Tempest*. "Em," Grace shouts. Em is not terribly far from where Grace is, walking down the avenue, picking up pieces of paper, inserting them into the book, and walking on. "Em," Grace says, once more.

"I see you, Gracie," Em says. "I know you're here with me somewhere. I see you, and I feel you, and I'm angry as hell with you."

Grace sees Em turning about, looking around, looking up at a sky that is more lapis than ice, more the color of her hair than not, more condemning than serene, and Em is now looking for a place to sit, having almost twenty swatches of paper, computer paper, in her hands, stuffed into the book with a distressed ship on the cover. A wind overcomes Em, and she is suddenly out of Grace's focus. "Em," she cries again.

"Yes, we understand. Rosin*bloom*, it is," says a new Fed, shifting Grace back to a room where instead of bullets, they are words, and she is the target. "Okay, Miss Rosin*bloom*," he repeats, with a voice that is crass and gruff, just as is his body, otherwise void of distinguishing features, except for the discoloration of his shirt around his neck. "We must remind you to engage yourself on the specific issue of your criminal—" He stops just short of the word "perpetration."

With his pause, Grace looks down, for having seen Em back up to a building, brick, to steady her, and then seeing her bend down to pick up a piece of paper, another piece. She watches Em reading, moving her mouth, and then Grace looks up, feeling something like a breeze in the room she is sitting in. She hears the sound of wings flapping and looks up, catching sight of the eagle that is perched atop the head of this new Fed. She tries to refrain from reacting to these things, realizing that this fellow must be suffering from the rooting of those large talons, those claws so sharp, the spectacular color of the tearing of the man's flesh. She sees blood trickling down his shoulders, joining the sweat gathered at his neck.

Grace looks at this, a disturbing sight, and then shifts her focus to the window, thinking to catch a better glimpse of Em, but she feels her own energy waning and looks down again, fumbles with her fingers. She takes a breath in, a whiff of mold and bodily oils, a trace of tobacco smoke, and a million metals that PreHistory begins to name, but she is blotting him out, ignoring the buzzing fly and the slow gathering of Zelda's menagerie, tendrils of green edging in from the windows and the corners of the ceiling and from the linoleum.

"So," Grace says, finally, feeling also the encroaching wall of anticipation hungrily escaping her interlocutors, about to attack her. "You want to know what I have done to jeopardize this home of the brave yes-men? So, what I have done, you will perhaps never learn until you understand why I was forced by the highest government in the land to do what I did. What prompted me, as you may gather from my previous statements, is loyalty and conscientiousness for the sake of this government. What inspired me was the love of my people and of my God, and the only crime I plead guilty of is this. I committed the crime of the borrower. I took a peaceful instrument that I was free to borrow, so long as I returned it, which I had planned to do. Gentlemen, we have come to celebrate the murder of our future children, and which one of you would not raise a finger to save a child, even though it might mean having to listen to and possibly even having to obey the harsh words of a harsher boss?"

"Ms. Rosinbloom, please tell us how exactly—" The young plainclothesman speaking, suddenly stops. It's a little swallow flying over this particular fellow, who has a gleam of truth in his deep chestnut eyes. "How do, did, would, could, will, uh er—please." The young man is coughing, groping for words that will disguise what he actually feels. "Please excuse me," he says, standing up, for to leave would not do. So he sits back down and tries once again. "How shall you save us, Grace?" His face is awash with wonder.

Grace looks at him directly. "I shall not save you, sir, but you shall save me if we manage to stop this way of killing with our thoughts. It begins with our thoughts, Gentlemen. It begins with determining what the word 'enemy' means, and if there is such a thing as an enemy,

234

how we should deal with it, and once we determine the correct manner of determining what it is that qualifies as enemy, only then can we begin our dialogue. Yes, that is the beginning—before we even attempt to have dialogue, we must examine our thoughts."

Another Fed—the one Grace sees as both burdened and suspended by an eagle—makes an attempt to quickly stand as his blood pressure rises. "Now you must be more grounded, or we cannot even talk." He lets himself back down, shaking his head, but there is more than one man here who feels it his own personal misfortune for having begun this confrontation.

"You shall see, Sir. I shall explain!" Grace says, suddenly seeing the worm curled in the palms of her hands, with a smile wide as that of the Cheshire cat. The worm has words for Grace, as do the others of his ilk.

"So here we are again, Grace. Where have we been, but here all along? Now we can really make use of our silent speaking mechanism, known by your mortals as thinking. Sock it to them, Gracie. You are a real pro, by now. You can be the princess of my heart."

"Oh, worm," she responds in her thought. "No one wants to be your princess. Keep your heart on Zelda. Starlinsky and I are one, and anyway, where is Zelda?" Grace winks at the worm, but the chestnut-eyed officer takes it as a sign for him, and he watches anxiously to see the reactions of the non-observant others.

"Worm—hold off one moment, but stay with me as long as you can."

The worm smiles and curls up tight, into a golden ball, as Grace begins to speak again. "So what can be more grounded than a nuclear reactor?" She is watching eyes that can only pierce but cannot be penetrated, the feeling of loss upon her, a minimal drain, as by the entrance of an IV drip, but she senses it just the same. Still, she marches on in her mind. "And what can be less grounded than its reaction?"

235

"Yes," the man with the gruff voice, says. "Continue."

"And with that I rest my case." Grace finds the energy to give a wink this time, ostensibly for the chestnut-eyed fellow, which the worm this time mistakes.

The leading officer of the Federal Government calls for a break, and Grace is escorted by Sarah Thower to the ladies room, and then to the cell, where she is given some victuals of sour coffee and some fried burnt crisps of bacon bits scattered about a plate of eggs over easy, with white toast where butter never melts, but a plastic container of purple jam stands by its side. Grace returns to the bathroom directly, releasing whatever it is she might have taken.

She is stunned looking at herself. It's the first time it registers, the years of hair cut off, gone. "Oh hellkite!" She ruffles up the fur with her fingers, smoothing down. "And I'm so hungry I could die! My cheeks are a sunken ship. My eyes look jaundiced. Mirror, mirror on the plaster—" She turns away from her own pale frame of a face with no solution of its own.

Grace returns to the woman cop with the news of her sick stomach, and Ms. Thower tries to keep a look of pity from decorating her own face as she thinks, "If only you had thought before you acted," but says, "What food can I bring you?"

"Something alive," she says. Before her eyes, she sees orchards of fruit, vines hanging as if in the Italian hills, olive groves—even the teal color of the Adriatic comes up before her as if in supplication, as if to say, "Help" and "Thank you" at once.

"Help," says Grace. "Thank you?"

"Take our energy," Grace hears these words. "We owe everything to you."

"OK," says Grace. "I will tell you what I love to eat, and you can tell me what you think. So, what I would eat right this minute would be fruit—say, cherries, grapes, peaches, plums, and cheeses of all kinds, and a glass of wine, and maybe some pumpernickel bread.

236

Oh, olives! What do you think of that? Please don't go out of your way, but I would feel like a prisoner of a million if you could buy any of those things for me. But, ah, it suddenly occurs to me, Ms. Thower, that I don't know when I can pay you back." Grace turns away, her eyes having filled with more tears than they can hold.

Sarah Thower's eyes are reddening now. "Consider it done, honey. I'll send my granddaughter to the store, and we will collect you when you are finished. Now, doesn't that look like something to be happy about?" They are walking down the corridor again, almost at the door, when Ms. Thower speaks in a hushed tone. "Now, don't be fresh to them sonsabitches, because someone told me they can bite worse than they bark. And their bark is bad. Sends shivers up my spine, it does. Be good, Gracie girl, and we'll see you when they're through." With that, the door is closed to the public, Sarah Thower included.

Seated, as before, Grace takes in the view, intent on picking up the thoughts of the only blood and guts and soulful human being in the room, namely the young African American man with his glistening chestnut eyes, and she gazes at this fellow, digging into his eyes until he smiles at her, upon which she smiles, too. Of course, the worm has been waiting there for her, and she returns to him and his wormy way of worming himself into this most intimate of meetings where a barrage of questions will be aimed and fired and shot and still miss the point of Grace's heart, one of those lovely encounters that will have to be seen to be believed.

"Just sit tight, Gracie," Zel says.

"This part makes me sick," the worm says, hissing.

"Well, keep your thoughts to yourself," Zel says. "And we will let Grace show us her stuff of silence."

"Be silent yourself, woman," the worm says.

"Shhhh. No more bickering, you guys." Grace is concentrating on the flower sitting center stage, whose species is wisdom, whose genus is poverty and whose phylum is God, whose kingdom is come.

"What made you think you could mess with confidential files—?"

"Who told you there were reactors that—?"

"How many written names of the dangerous people did you see and del—?"

"Who gave you the right—?"

"Why did you lie to your bosses, who wanted to give you work for overtime, with extra—?"

"Why must you sleep on the john—?"

"Who is that communist—and why was he here last night?"

"Why do you like to eat tomato paste?"

"What is the nature of your companionship with Muriel Lyons, alias 'Em', and when was the last time you saw her undress—?"

"What caused your father's death in—?"

"What is the origin of the name Breanda—?"

"Grace. What Jew is named Grace?"

"She is not answering. Why do we keep asking these terrible questions?" This is the only question coming from the chestnut-eyed fellow, whose beautiful face is practically disfigured by anguish.

"Shut up," the gruff one grumbles. "We must have answers," he says to Grace. "Please try to stick with the facts."

Grace finds herself looking up. "Facts," she thinks, allowing the word to form, to fly out like a bubble. Only that word, though. The rest of it, she considers, whether they are for consumption or for self; she settles on the latter and decides to contain herself. Facts are outside this room, she thinks. Those eyes, those brown opals settling on a window that is open, bars dividing up the facts, she thinks. A slice of sky like blue pie out there, but cut up so thin, this sky, this slice. A sun out there. All the light that's not in here. Em's about, Bruce, too, no doubt. A silence creeps upon her. Exhaustion, its cause, and now, she cannot will herself to speak. Has she had a stroke? Has she died? She is wondering whether these might be facts. Unable, she is, to summon words, to form sentences, no words to exit her lips.

No, I'm quite alive, she decides. She smiles. At least she thinks she is smiling. Is the smile on her lips? She can barely lift her hands to touch those lips. I'm tired, she says this thought to herself. I see men moving their mouths in here. Whether or not there's a piano outside this building, I hear music, as always. That's a fact. There's a silliness, a disparity between us. That's a fact. I hear words coming at me. I see my dolls—my queen, my worm, his earth. They're here, flitting about. And where they are, I am okay. I see myself looking out the window. Somewhere, the city people are doing everything imaginable, and most of them, she's thinking, are sleeping.

It's important to breathe, Grace says to herself, and takes a breath. That's a fact. She imagines one of those apartments, not like her own, which is only five stories high, but one that is thirty stories or more. She imagines the structure gone, vanished suddenly, all gone except for the people. Thirty stories of people. She puts wings on them, imagines them fluttering like butterflies—no, not really butterflies, but fairies or angelic things. Thirty stories of people with wings. Wings curled up over them, if they are supine, she thinks. Wings surrounding those making love or cast in dreams; they are afloat. Nothing to be frightened of, she thinks. This isn't exactly a crazy thing to think, she reminds herself. Michelangelo painted people with wings. Lots of painters did. Just because we don't see them, doesn't mean they aren't there. Where is the fact in that?

A persistent vision, it keeps growing on her. Those thirty stories become one hundred stories. All the skyscrapers around—every building that she sees and doesn't see suddenly disappears, and what comes upon her is this image of people, like the bees that comprised the brick wall. "It's people who are holding this city together," she says suddenly. "It's not the walls. That's a fact." Did she just say that? She thinks she did. Has she become deaf, suddenly? Has she fallen asleep?

Perhaps, she thinks. Perhaps this is a dream. But nevertheless, she says to herself now, her energy returning, it's my dream. It's my vision. I will honor it. This is a good thing, because the vision is not ready to disintegrate until it blossoms, and these angelic people that Grace sees are also under the ground, which is to say, in the bedrock. For her, the whole globe is an anthill of people, people coming and going, flying upward, going in circles. They are laughing together, on the telephone together, making love together, making babies, having babies, feeding babies, and people are robbing, killing each other, and they are all lifted with wings into the air.

She stands up for a moment, and she feels herself rising. Uncanny it is. An inch off the ground she is.

"Gentlemen," she says, or she thinks she says. "There is more to life than facts." Grace motions to the vision that she had seen outside the windows, first cut into slices—that vision. She invites them in, the ten thousand—or are they ten billion angelic humans with wings—ghostly visions, even there on a Saturday morning when many New Yorkers are still asleep, but they come in, those New Yorkers, joggers with wings, heart attack victims with tubes coming from every orifice in their body are floating, their wings intact; there are lovers with their wings violently fluttering, and there are babies, with little nubs for wings. Hordes of people, flying up from the floor now in shrouds, and wings on them, as well, that are veiny and moldering. And for a moment, it's as if there are no walls at all, just one vast amphitheatre, with the Feds in the ring.

"Stop this," says the Fed with the eagle, although the eagle is now large and looming, his wings flapping, the sound deafening. That eagle is chasing out the others. "This silence will not help you, young lady." As the eagle flies off him, he is up and on Grace.

He tries to shake her into responding to them, and he asks to put manacles on her wrists, which Sarah Thower must do. But the chestnut-eyed officer comes to her rescue. "Please, sir. You must keep your hands off her."

"She must spank."

"Spank?"

"Speak, I mean. Speak."

The two men are at each other's throats, and the others are also up, pulling them off each other.

"Order. Order." There is commotion about, that's a fact.

Grace looks down at her feet, those sandals, her toes, the nails so short, and she remembers Starlinsky.

Order manages to be restored in the room, and the questioning resumes.

"The fact is," Grace says, sitting down. These are words that come out of her mouth as she is holding herself down, her hands under the table, the manacles against the wood tabletop. That is how it feels to her. "I am very tired."

Grace returns to her silence, as if in conference with her worm and his earth and its queen and their king. She keeps her dream world intact as they examine her with terms that to her seem more fleeting than dreams, a world that for her seems like a ticking clock, and what time is it, she wonders.

"No matter the time, Grace," Queen Beatrice says. "You are now outside of time, but such a situation makes a mother sick. So just tell them to stick it. Better you should just be healthy and let them fight among themselves."

Grace sees Beatrice flying in spirit above the speaker, who feels a sudden buzzing in his ear. Next she travels to the gruff one, into his great region of the lower stomach, and gives him a buzzing in his belly. Finally, she turns herself into a three-dimensional, living, stinging wonder, and she flies in, makes her entrance by way of a soda can in the garbage of the street, above which is the open window of the conference room. She gives the sting of a lifetime to the generally silent

241

fellow, who had earlier undertaken to question the grounds upon which Grace had stood.

"Ooooooh. Help." The fellow, with his hands covering his crotch over his pants, howls and charges out the door.

"Close the goddam window," the speaker says to chestnut eyes. "We shall not stop for a bee-sting."

Grace, in her oblique manner, thanks Beatrice upon her return, and Beatrice curtsies. "The pleasure was mine."

Grace begins to wish the questioning would end in the way that night falls or flowers open or trees dismiss their leaves, or the way that the moon's light waxes and wanes according to the movements of clouds and planet, as if nature's actors know how to take turns, when to bow, where to exit. But, like the automobile or a wretched tenement, the interrogators began to crumble and rage and fall madly to pieces. It is most unfortunate, she would like to say. She would like to remain impassive.

When the wounded man re-enters, she finds she can no longer hold in her tears.

"Why are you crying?" the speaker asks.

"She feels guilty."

"She's sorry."

"What a silly, horrid thing this is," Grace cries to the water lily, who has, for the duration, greeted no one as she sits spiritually harbored in the ashtray in the center of the oblong wood table.

"Why Gracie, you have just lifted the shadow. Be happy. The world may long note, but little will it remember what you say here. But you will never forget what you learned here. So be ready. We must now leave you, but you shall see us again." With that, she slips away with the air.

"Grace Rosinbloom," the speaker announces, rising, and the others slowly follow. "We shall meet you in the district court in some moments, where you shall be arraigned and charged with, we are sorry to say, the charge of high treason and a lower count of theft." These are the final words of the speaker, but it's the word "high" that resounds in Grace's mind.

Echoes of "high" transport her to a place of height. She finds herself rather high and looking down. Again, she wonders about the state of her body. She is quite aware that her body is locked, as it were, in a room where a bee—single handedly, as it were—has managed to upset a roomful of government officials, there to serve an elusive order of correction. She is well aware that there are penalties for the deletions—but even as she looks down (oh, even with those heavy handcuffs on her wrists, her mind is now ten thousand feet above the city and looking down)—even as she sees a very well-ordered people-colony whirling themselves about a well-ordered maze, she—monstrous as she is, and truly she feels monstrous at the moment—has done nothing wrong.

"High," she manages to say.

"Hi," Chestnut Eyes says back to her, smiling. He cannot take his eyes off her. Grace notices this, and she has also taken note that he's caught on to the other matter of her concern, besides the penalties, that is—namely, her difficulty staying grounded, literally grounded. She looks at him, brings her hands to her mouth, a forefinger attempting to touch her lips. How heavy those manacles are! With that finger approaching her terribly dry lips, she hopes to suggest the idea of "shhh" and then a wink to secure it, and then with one last glance, she tries to stand up, but this time gravity wins.

"Goodbye, gentlemen," she says, falling, falling, a feeling of dizziness, and proceeds to collapse into the arms of Sarah Thower, who along with the keys to remove the handcuffs, has a surprise in store for Grace.

Starlinsky, namely.

Chapter 9

Starlinsky has indeed arrived with such a stock of frolic and condiments that Grace's cell has virtually become a marketplace, extravagantly dressed in the décor of the summer palette. The light behind the barred window shines a hot white, almost pink with heat, and the music of summer, the children's screams, the metal drums, the swish of kites in the air, distant fog horns and certainly sailboats, skiffs in the Atlantic. Revived by all this, mixed with the foodstuffs, smells of mango and Limburger, Grace imagines wending her way through young apple orchards and hills with vineyards where flocks of sheep and stray cows graze, and country kitchens where biscuits are baking, and then to the park, standing there, watching the water, like the elegant gentry in Seurat's "Sunday Morning," even though it's Saturday, the day of rest for her ancestors. Between Sarah Thower and Daniel Starlinsky, the veritable world has been transported to her little cell, and together the lovers sift through sumptuous dishes of lobster and mignon and rack of lamb. Ms. Thower, standing just outside, is munching as well.

"You are prince, king, god, oh, a worm of a man," Grace says—thinking, more than anything else, that this food will sustain her, give her weight, keep her grounded.

"Worm?" Starlinsky is taken by surprise, startled. "For what reason do you procure for me that label of worm?"

"Oh Starlinsky! I am in love with a worm, and you are he. Be not offended. My worm is the most magical wonder of them all. Be happy, someday you will see. So, let's eat this meal fit for a water lily."

"A water lily, as I recall from my semester in Botany, chews sunlight, digests our hazardous air waste. And, perhaps a little nitrogen, along with anything else she can glean from the water."

"You don't know the water lily I'm referring to, sweet love. But she is going to be the next God of the world. Wait and you will see what I mean."

"Grace, Grace." Starlinsky's arms carefully gather her up almost as if she's in pieces, as if she could break into parts. "You are my heart." He whispers this, as if his breath could make her whole.

"Starlinsky, what we will do for our love of you is not to be believed."

"Oh Grace!" Starlinsky is trying to hide the dismay of one who prides himself in being able to recognize a delusion when he hears one, and who does not at all like to hear from the royal we when not in Bellevue. "I can only—" Then he stops, his voice breaking, his own eyes filling and filming with the stuff of his addiction.

Grace attempts to lick up a tear or two, and as he turns his head to wipe them, she says, "Please, let me. I'm addicted to the stuff."

Piteously, he turns back to her, crying helplessly. They embrace, almost melding into one, while the gorgeous food waits and the little cot crinkles, and they creak their bones to just short of breaking.

They speak again in great whispers, and the wonder of it was they are never alone. Watching them are the guards and the cops, and Ms. Thower and the Feds, and the sun in the window that faces a building that is plastered with windows, where there are necks outstretched, and the entire sky stands above them, and more than can be imagined is watching.

"You think I'm crazy."

"No," he says, having paused too long.

"I know you think I'm crazy," she says. "I'm deeply stressed. I'm incredibly tired. I'm hungrier than I've ever been in my life. I knew this might happen, Daniel. You know, I told you, but I think I had to do this. As if there were no choice. But there was choice. And I chose. Unable to not do what I did and to live without having done it. What

I'm trying to say is I could not have lived with myself. Otherwise. You understand? Do you? I'm guessing not, but maybe. All I can tell you is this. It feels just exactly like the thing I thought I'd have to do. But I'm scared, remember that. Although I'm going to put up the best front I know."

"I love you. You know I'll never leave you." He says this between sobs. "But must you—"

"Pretend I'm a cow," she says. "Give me a big pasture. You'll see what I mean, if you're meant to." She is pulling these words from somewhere so deep in her mind, she doesn't even know how they came. "Someday you'll understand. That, I know." Her own eyes are arcs of light in his eyes. She stares into them, seeing the blue light behind the gray light, and the green light behind the blue. His eyes are glowing like the celestials. She wipes his eyes with her lips. "We shall have such a great life, a great life. Won't you stop crying now?"

In a distant place, perhaps in her mind, Grace sees a pianist. In her mind, she hears the bells of the Messiaen prelude, that impalpable dream. And before her, Grace sees the water lily above Starlinsky's head opening like a crown.

Music of another prelude follows, Messiaen's number six, bells of anguish, tears of farewell, and also encroaching upon them, as if in a layer below, are sounds that form into words, passages, certificates of sound. A crowd forming outside, and the piano, its notes implacably playing while the other, also there, dark and unstoppable, like the River Styx, like roots all gnarly and full of thorns, the words themselves begin to grow into things like stones, like pitchforks, like knives, little cluster bombs that permeate their space like fumes.

"Well, do they live together?"

"Maybe they are secretly married."

"No, they are just off the street, can't you tell by their—"

"Wonder if she even has a mother, who—"

In her half-clothed state of undress and her equally fractionated state of being, Grace rises and speaks. "My mother is actually the most beautiful soul in the world, and you had not better say another word about her."

And there is no more piano. At least she cannot hear the notes. Nor was it there for her to see. The music overwhelmed by this other sound. Nor can she see them, the people with claims on her outside, their voices like ropes. Like chains.

She drapes the blue cotton blanket around her to hide, not only body parts, but the fraction of an inch between her feet and the linoleum. Starlinsky joins her under the blanket, and then both of them, covered, almost. Enough that they cannot see those who are looking at them. Enough that they cannot hear what others are saying.

Starlinsky and she, embracing under the blanket.

"Ti ami, Je t'adore, Ya tebya liubliu, Te amo, Ich liebe Dich, Ikh hob dikh lieb. Ani ohave at, Iyay ovelay uyay."

All Starlinsky can do is repeatedly declare his love for her, and that is what he does again and again in every language he has ever been taught, including pig Latin.

"Ti ami, Je t'adore, Ya tebya liubliu, Te amo, Ich liebe Dich, Ikh hob dikh lieb. Ani ohave at, Iyay ovelay uyay."

And before them still, the cameramen and journalists and the curious.

And so, on the radio, on the television, what people are hearing is muffled: *"Ti ami, Je t'adore, Ya tebya liubliu, Te amo, Ich liebe Dich, Ikh hob dikh lieb. Ani ohave at, Iyay ovelay uyay."*

And then the blanket falls off, both of them opening their eyes.

And the television screens, the newspapers will show this, the two of them, the doctor and the dissident, a blanket around them, falling, their faces streaked, a mournful beauty. And the granular photograph will find its way around the world, while they both try to ignore the picture-takers and question-askers and catastrophe-addicts-anonymous, along with those who care, those who are playing their instruments or bringing foodstuffs in baskets, that are lining up just outside the jail, all of those who seem to need the up-to-the-minute information of their doings and undoing.

And sunlight, large and looming, every morsel and intimation of light escaping, as it must, on the day of the summer solstice.

But directly blocking everything, obstructing sunlight, the dark representatives of the Federal Government, with a document, their own slip of black and white. Starlinsky and Grace both rise, seeing them approach. Her cell door has been opened, and she has taken a few sliding steps outside of her domain. Her focus drawn to the few windows, the few open doors, where she can see out, where her eyes detect light, she deduces that the crowd that has formed is not exclusively a crowd of heckling and hectoring.

Wherever there is an opening to the outside, Grace detects people. But right before her, not two feet away, are guns, glisteningly silver, flanking the thighs of three men standing there in uniform, who are waiting for her signature to the affidavit which accuses her of willingly, unlawfully, and knowingly creating the disturbance of high treason in addition to the piss-stain of a troublesome theft.

What Grace feels like signing is the affidavit of her love for Starlinsky, as she reads the indictment of her crime against the law of the government of her land. She reads aloud: "Starlinsky, I, Grace Rosinbloom, by power of the virtue vested in me, do hereby declare that I love you unlawfully, but knowingly, and most willingly."

She holds the paper tightly in her fingers as the uneasy Fed watches her twist its contents. The crowd that is gathered has hushed, and he decides to wait and see if she will sign it anyway He coughs to get her attention, then hands her the pen.

"Starlinsky," she says, slipping the pen above her ear. "Will you be mine till life does us part, till death joins us forever, till life gives us unto death, till death, which grants us life? Starlinsky, I am yours as the

248

two become one. When we part, we part nothing but strings. Our bond shall steel you to me, and likewise, shall it arm me, for you are my man, and I am all your Grace."

There are not a few tears in her presence, although her own face is dry and radiant. She signs her name on the record of accusation and delivers a plea of "Not guilty."

Having signed, she looks up, sensing the solidarity. Beyond the officials, she feels the sympathy of those who have surrounded the building, people who are listening to radios and television sets broadcasting the news. What is happening to her is news.

Grace recites her plea to the people standing there, who seem stilled, practically to paralysis. What she doesn't realize is that part of that stillness is coming from her, from the light of her own eyes.

"It's their wings," Grace whispers to Starlinsky. "They are frozen."

Starlinsky remains silent, barely a tic in response, as the notion of wings rather eludes him. He does take note of the peculiar stillness, however, which he attributes to their desire to hear every word, every breath. The light is unmistakable. It's coming from her—that much he can see.

Grace is looking around for its source, figuring the luminescence to be something that comes when the filters are present and well-placed, when the atmosphere contains the perfect balance and degree of vapor allowing transmission, with properties like those of a prism which permit clarity and definition, thereby distinguishing the various waves, the invisibles.

She perceives a light coming in not only from the window in her cell, but from all of the windows of the precinct, as if each leaf on each tree, now in its penultimate growth, is turning to her. In this part of the world, the leaves in question hail from ginkgo and acanthus, maples and some old oaks, white and red—their jagged leaves floating.

In gratitude, she thanks them, an exaltation of leaves. Not to mention the convocation of people who have gathered. A solidarity confirmed by the light, her signal. The warmth, as well, palpable as a magnetic charge. And if their wings can catch the air, why then, they will be able to fly—how she explains her newfound ability to rise.

She cannot see them, but she feels them, those wings—her wings. The proof is in the fraction of an inch between her and the linoleum. It's a matter of control, right now, she thinks—control to both conceal and to master. A silent prayer she makes for time to explore.

She recalls in the insane, unstoppable series of visions she'd had earlier—how taken she was by the beauty. They are no longer in flight. She cannot take her eyes from the windows, where she might catch a glance of her people.

Starlinsky also sees them—she deduces by the way he looks at her.

"Your people are carrying signs—can you see?" Softly, he reads them out to her: *"We love you, Grace Rose in Bloom—Saving Grace."*

More people seem to be walking from the side streets. A blue fence made from saw-horses is in the process of being constructed. And there's a piano that's being carried in by someone on a bicycle. Moving on the street. Someone who looks a lot like Stem sitting on the bicycle. It is true? More police, sirens, and yet there's that incredible sunlight. It shines down on all of them, slivers of light making little wing folds on their shoulders. Folded up they are, maybe sewn tight. She can see that, not the threads, but the crease, the sign of wings that haven't been used. She knows hers are growing. She feels a tightness in her back that she attributes to wings. That it's insane, she knows, too. She mustn't speak of it. But her people, they seem so terribly grounded. She takes pity on them. And at the same time, she is so grateful for them. They are there for her. She feels that. She'd like to speak to them, but the time is not right.

It takes a few moments for the Fed to gain both their and Grace's attention. Finally, he informs the world that Grace Rosinbloom still has the opportunity to change this plea in several hours, at the hour of her arraignment, just down the road apiece. At that time, he adds, she will have a lawyer by her side.

It is almost without expression, the kind of glance the Fed gives Dr. Starlinsky before he marches off with his fellow officers. One can say what it is not—it is not glaringly happy, nor dour, but it is not a complimentary look.

He also has some words for the crowd along with the press, whom he hopes will have the decency to disband after the Federal gentlemen make their exit. Once the reporters leave, the patrolmen of the precinct will have no trouble dispersing the crowd. Obviously, others will reappear at the arraignment a few hours hence.

*

Starlinsky and Grace, meanwhile, have fallen asleep in each other's arms.

Grace pulls herself back from Starlinsky, an image of themselves suddenly appearing to her in black and white, photograph-like, very still, with a caption below and above in big block letters. Looking around in the distance outside of her cell, she sees that a new batch of newspapers has been delivered.

"I believe we are famous, my dearest," she says, "but I wonder whether that's going to be something we might regret."

"I remember when you were just—," Starlinsky says, then stops, closes his eyes, his arms, his body cradling her.

"I believe I see us on the front page of *The Post*," she says, pointing at a pile of newspapers on Sarah Thower's desk. "In black and white. How many copies of the two of us can you imagine? We will be

251

a story, Starlinsky. Mothers will read our story to their children. 'Once upon a time,' they will say."

"Once upon a time," Starlinsky says, "there was a girl named Grace."

"And that is all she was, because Grace was she," Grace says.

"The first time Gracie ever became my love was the first time I saw Grace—and how wonderful she was—"

"Was?" Grace says. "Was?"

"Is," says Starlinsky.

"Once upon a time was the world."

"And then what happened was the rest of it," Starlinsky says. "But how did it really begin?"

"It began with light," Grace says.

"And with this light came much that would later be brought to light," Starlinsky says.

"Once upon a time," Grace says, "there was a worm."

"And that was me," says Starlinsky. "And a worm is all I am next to Grace."

"Not *all*," she says. "Not as if there's not more to you. Not as if there's nothing to being a worm," she says. "Worms have their share of knowledge, too."

Starlinsky is not without his own, albeit repellent, associations when it comes to worms, and also cockroaches and raspberries, his own childhood stories there, of dissidents, of musicians and artists and writers, of Mandelstam himself—and of the son of Akhmatova—and the silences, the end of his culture when he came with his mother to this country.

And now, his beloved.

This knowledge she speaks of terrifies him.

As it happens, the worm Starlinsky dreams of is not the Socratic interlocutor of the Library of Congress, but instead Stalin himself—and the cockroaches of his upper lip, and the fat worms of his fingers and the raspberry of the underground mob.

*

They are both asleep and intertwined with just their heads visible when Grace chances to open her eyes, only to see Bruce Steen looming like a pirate ship on her great horizon, his entrance accompanied by a gust of something cold, as if he's found an air conditioner, as if the cold air latched onto him.

"Oh hellkite," she says, quietly. She pretends to ignore him but for the corners of her eyes, which keep tabs on the very tall, thin fellow standing in front of Sarah Thower's desk with his head down, his foot tapping, his fingers rapping soundlessly against his blue jeans. He's there in her mind, eyes open or eyes closed, rapping and tapping and zapping. She watches him speak, his lips moving, his hands gesticulating, long arms, they are. He's all limbs, a small trunk, with something moving on his shoulders. Starlinsky jerks awake, jarred by Grace's sudden change of position. Grace looks at creases on the two sides of Starlinsky's already sunken cheeks, and he becomes aware that she's looking at him, and he pulls her completely under the covers for a kiss. Escorted by Sarah Thower, Bruce adds a throat-clearing sound to the tapping and rapping to make his presence known, although the sensation she had already experienced as a "zapping" is enough to quicken her, and Gracie pulls herself out of the bed into standing position. Starlinsky, too, rises up out of the bed.

"Well, well," Bruce says.

Grace puts out her hand for him to shake, but Bruce tugs at her hand and kisses the back of her hand first, and then each finger. Even his lips are cold, and she shudders.

253

Grace makes a faint-hearted attempt to retrieve her hand but too late. She looks at him, shakes her head, produces a chirp that is more like a giggle than a cry.

"Meh," he says. "This poor thumb for my flawed attempt to win your heart. Forefinger—for the way you pointed me to your best friend Em. This one, the long one, the one I kiss for your release, and the ring finger, for betrothal, my pet. The pinky—for the communist doctor, of course."

Grace pulls her hand back, while Starlinsky's smile indicates nothing of the ire he experiences as he wonders what law there is that allows this maniac audience with Grace.

"How nice to see you, Dr. Starlin-*sky*," Bruce begins, stressing the last syllable of the name and deliberately mispronouncing it. "Yes, I've gotten to know you quite well in my recent travels, as you are holding my Em hostage."

Now it is Starlinsky's opportunity to clear his throat, so unpleasant is the term. "I believe she's turned the key and found her exit, Mr. Steen."

"Bruce, Doctor."

"Bruce," Starlinsky says.

"Yes, yes," Bruce says. "I have actually come to speak with Grace, and Grace alone, if that might be arranged."

No one actually responds to this, but Grace steps back toward the bed where Starlinsky is. She feels the sudden presence of PreHistory, who says, "Past events compel me to speak. Take care here, Grace. This fellow is of dubious character—I believe you've noted this, as well."

The fly, too, is making a pest of himself as Bruce battles him, raving about the stink and filth of the jail. Then Bruce moves from trying and failing to swat the fly to inserting his arms into the cell proper to see if he can break the trance-like quality of Grace's staring. This, of course, is in violation of the rules, and within seconds Sarah

254

Thower is beside him, and then in front of him, threatening him with immediate expulsion. He asks, rather than demands, to see Grace in private.

"I hope I have made it perfectly clear," Sarah Thower says, her chin jutting out so far as to practically touch Bruce's face, which is completely veiled by an expressionless mouth, his lips thin and half inside his mouth, and his eyes hidden by dark glasses. "No one but the doctor is permitted in the cell with the prisoner, but you may speak with her in private, if the doctor and Grace both agree to it."

Grace nods, but her eyes follow Starlinsky as he walks through the cell door that Sarah Thower has unlocked. He avoids glancing at Bruce, and simply heads to where the desk is, sits in a dark wooden chair and picks up the newspaper.

Bruce bows when Starlinsky passes.

On closer inspection, Grace sees a jungle cat atop the face of Bruce, its claws like a comb secured in his scalp, with dark hair on either side of the cut. There are teeth sinking into Bruce's neck, a muscled neck curled up, like the body of a snake but thicker, if shorter. The cat was what she'd seen on his shoulders, but it's now staring at her, its yellow eyes more curious than ensnaring. It's not until Starlinsky is out of the vicinity—and Sarah Thower, as well, that Bruce begins to speak. He flips his head back and forth, almost comically. "What the hell are you looking at like that, Gracie sweetie?"

"I should think you'd be with Em. What brings you to my side, and not hers?"

"Grace, if just once you would understand. I could do such things!" Bruce's gestures are subtle, what with his exceedingly long arms, long fingers, and when he removes his sunglasses, Grace can see both the electricity and trouble in his eyes, his attempt to mesmerize failing, but so clear to her is his intent to trap. "I've come to serve you, to save you. Can't you see how much I love you, still love you, have always loved you? Would do and have always done and will still do

255

anything for you. Come closer. I need to tell you something that is for your ears alone, darling."

It is a menacing plea, and she rests her head upon the bars in such a way that the only place his sound can travel is into her right ear. Bruce whispers, with distinctly sour breath, and narrowness of focus such that it could fit into a buttercup, but with threat of venom, the promise of sting: "I have all the ammunition we need to blow this place to kingdom come." He nods, then dramatically returns his glasses to his face.

Grace moves quickly away from the edge, as if a bomb has been dropped there. "No ammunition. All that I've done, my life would I give for the eradication of weaponry."

"Even for your own salvation?"

"My salvation is never to be gained by way of a weapon," Grace says.

"Good God, Grace!" Bruce removes the glasses again, looks at her, his eyes wild, frenzied, his hands flailing with the glasses, but luckily for him, the fly is in a more dormant state of being. "What has gone wrong with you? Your head is so loo loo, where spunk and sass and scorn did dwell. And why do you look so frail?"

"It's just the best of me you see. I've thrown off my skin."

"You are not kidding—"

"Bruce, why aren't you with Em? Please go find her. I think she's walking the streets. She needs you dearly. Oh, spot that love on your face. Bruce, go to her. You know we shall always be friends. And where? Oh, there is Starlinsky." She sees him speaking to Ms. Thower in the distance. "Be well, Brucie, my friend. Say hi to Em. Tell her I've got a new idea up my sleeve."

"A new one?"

"Yes. Instead of spellweaving or praises about falling, it's about rising."

"Rising?"

256

"Tell her to think about rising. Imagine all of us rising up out of this mess? Instead of World War III, tell her. Imagine we grow wings. All the antennae in the world are useless without wings—tell her that. We ascend!"

"A little Rapture in the midst of all this."

"It's about world changing. It can be done, Bruce."

"Don't I know it, Gracie baby," he says, trying to get to her lips between the bars, but she turns her cheek to him. "Be good yourself, Gracie."

That voice, such a smooth tenor quality, Grace thinks. And yes, she further thinks, there is a stink here, namely the one he brought with him. It's got a smell, she is thinking—something almost smoky and challenging her. His words and the tone of his voice hang in the air. A stale air it is, still holding the smells of food and oils, and this hint of smoke, too, despite the window open to the west. A window open into sky and a park, but Grace is not looking or thinking out the window. Her focus still on Bruce, his back, where the yellow-spotted cat has slithered down and curled up as if embedded into him.

In leaving, Bruce passes the doctor with words very pointed and for Starlinsky's ears only, although there are significant others who also have access to the information. "You blew it royally with the last one," Bruce says, "but you'd better be fucking good to my girl, or I'll fucking kill you."

PreHistory takes this moment to signal to Grace, a quick wave of his short hands. "See me, see me?" His voice is small but distinct. He stands in a corner. What PreHistory has seen—does he tell? He just stands there, holding his knowledge, weighing it—knowledge, not a heavy commodity, less dense than diamonds or gold, but massive it is, not literally, of course, and he says as much to Grace, imparts that knowledge. The knowledge about the stats, facts, and limits of knowledge.

But Grace is missing both the information and the concepts of the parameters of knowledge, at least the parameters of preference. Currently, she is more focused on "sound" than fact. For instance, how would she describe the sound of PreHistory's voice? It isn't that she isn't hearing him. Or is this hearing a feeling, nothing to do with ears at all? Is it rather more like the way the hairs on her body are feeling? Has she adopted the policy of her insect friend? As she had been bombarded by visions, it is now sound that overcomes her. Sounds of the scurrying of people in the jail, the sounds of traffic and horns and sirens. To her, it seems that the sounds of the seven million are flooding her ears. How to shut them out! A dissonant and hurtful sound, a sound of skyscrapers scraping the sky. And against this column of sound, the golden string waving its long peaceful notes— that is, PreHistory's voice.

"The worm speaks in thoughts," she says to PreHistory, "but your sound and the sound of the fly—a different dimension altogether. I am at a loss to describe."

"Interesting," PreHistory says, "that you are talking about sound at a time like this—when I have knowledge to discuss."

"Yes," Grace says, her eyes on the corner of the room where he stands, as if backed up against the painted cinderblock. "I'm still thinking about sound," she says. "It is like knowledge, you know."

"This is information that I might want to share with you," PreHistory says. "It might be valuable."

"I'm guessing it came by way of a sound or an image or—" and she stops with a shudder. "Or, if you were your newly found friend, the fly, it could come by way of a taste or a smell."

"This knowledge," he says to her. "It came by way of a sound."

"Feeling," she says, that feeling of foreboding again, this time much stronger. "Knowledge for me, but not for you, PreHistory, may also come by way of feeling—of sensation, of touch, of physical suffering, say, for example, by way of a bullet, or by way of a kiss."

"Grace," PreHistory says to her. "I want to tell you how much I despise your friend Bruce."

Grace nods, but she is still unable to leave this concept of instrumentation, this sound of massive orchestration doggedly upon her, the sounds of a city there before her, juxtaposed against the serene sound of PreHistory's voice, her remembrance of the jagged sound of the fly, his stuttering, a woody essence there. And she is thinking about the infinite world of sound, how it exists, how it has come to be that the receptors are the ones granted the power to discern. How the speakers themselves could talk endlessly, but without a receptor, without a receiver—it's as if nonexistent.

"But oh, PreHistory," she says. "This is about knowledge. It is! Because if I see you—you must see me! Or else it is pointless, like voyeurism—you said that, right? And yet I could talk until I'm blue in the face, and my message could still remain unheard."

"I'm listening, Grace," PreHistory says, as he welcomes Starlinsky, who is pondering Bruce's threat, the very thing PreHistory has been referring to, this knowledge that came to him by way of a sound—which is a knowledge he decides, finally, to spare Grace.

Grace also welcomes Starlinsky, the only welcome Starlinsky has acknowledged.

"My darling," she says. "May I speak with you?"

"Always," he says.

"Things are happening to me," she says.

"I'll say," he says. "That's an understatement."

"No," she says. "Other things. Things you perhaps can't see."

"It's only natural, dearest," he says.

"Yes," she says. They are as close as can be, even with PreHistory there, although PreHistory, nothing if not sensitive to their need for privacy, has once again made himself scarce.

"Yes, we are so close, aren't we?" She says this knowing that she cannot speak, cannot share it, these sensations, these ideas. But, she thinks, one more try. One more try. She says, "Starlinsky. I feel as if I'm a radio antenna."

"Radio antenna?"

"I'm being bombarded by signals," she says.

"Signals?"

"We are signals to each other, Starlinsky."

"Yes," he says.

"I hear things," she says. "And I see things."

Starlinsky, a man of words, ponders her words and Bruce's words.

Some hint of Starlinsky's agony reaches Grace as she sits on her cot in a kind of repose—statuesque, her pose bears resemblance to that of an Egyptian cat, languorous but focused. "I see Em," she says. Those words cutting into a silence that is thick, if warm, and sad, if very localized. Which is to say, the inhabitants of the precinct are generally scurrying about, newspapers in their hands, while they converse with each other, albeit in hushed tones, of the drama of the day on either side of the present—more there is to come, and they move like people who know it. In the space defined by bars and cinderblock, however, the silence is screaming. Grace breaks it once again.

"I do see her, Starlinsky. She's walking around, retracing my steps. She is like some kind of proselyte or some kind of spy. I can't figure which god she's serving."

"What an unusual way of putting that," he says, standing beside her, his hands on her face, his eyes thick into hers. Although he's well aware of how frail, how thin she seems to be, Starlinsky does not think to question her sudden resistance to gravity, her floatability. The slackness of her jeans hides the fraction of an inch between Grace's body and the bed. "She told me many things that I, of course, am not at liberty to share—"

260

"Then don't, Starlinsky," Grace says, leaning into him. "The last thing you need is to jeopardize her trust."

"Her trust," he says. He's sitting down now, his hands unable to resist her body, so close, so redolent of pollen, so ever-ready, ever responsive to him. He can feel it. She is on fire.

"Yes," she says. They are face to face now, side by side, and no longer sitting. "You were saying…"

"I was. Saying," he says. "That's true. I was saying."

"Her trust is questionable, and she says she's allergic to life."

"Yes—how did you know?" he says. It is a moan.

"I heard you say it. I heard her say it to you."

"When? When did you hear this?"

"Just now," Grace says. Her lips are resting against his, their breaths close, hot and sweet, two grapes on a vine. "If I focus on specific voices," she says, "then I am not bombarded by the most horribly huge of sounds. Starlinsky, it's like the entire city is screaming in my ears!"

Starlinsky is silent. "Surely my lips were otherwise engaged," he says, then.

"Surely I heard it, my darling. She has the book I gave her."

"My favorite," he says.

"Who's your favorite character?"

"The much-maligned Caliban," he says.

"First I loved Ferdinand. Second I loved Prospero. Finally, I loved the missing one, the character of Sycorax," she says. "She was also Em's favorite, as well. We put together a prequel to *The Tempest* in college. It was a monologue spoken by Sycorax, where she essentially predicted the coming of Prospero. She thought Prospero would fall in love with her, but—"

"So, it was a tragedy?"

"How could it not be? It was a monologue, kind of like a voice-over. I read it, and Em mimed it."

261

"Sorry I missed that one," he says. "Next time you do it, hire me to play Prospero, on the condition you do the miming."

"Em's amazing. Her illness is partly genius, partly false—and then there's the genuine sorrow, the sorrow I believe that gives her the ability, which she translates, to make fantastic art. The trick is to know which."

"I don't think there was a minute she wasn't performing for me. Except for when she took the pills—and later I found out that she'd never swallowed them. Thank god."

"And now she's finding my printout—all over the city. She's collecting. Reading what I've managed to delete. I hear it, as if it were an announcement at a sporting event."

But he's fallen asleep now, and she stops talking for a moment, watching his face, the scruff face, providing it with kisses, little baby kisses. He is otherwise not awake. His slight smile, more a trembling than a widening of lips. It is all there is. Exhausted man that he is, he makes no other move to suggest consciousness. His eyelids so still, so too those brownish, blondish, grayish lashes. She kisses them. She holds him, her body fastening itself to his at the edges, as if she were a parachute, her fingertips under his back, thinking it will hold her down. Against his chest, the rhythmic breathing and the warmth, she rests her head. But she hears what she hears just the same—whether it is Stem's piano or Em's conversations—and she sees what she sees whether her eyes are opened or closed.

A large piano, a man playing there. A man building a piano from parts. A piano mosaic.

"What does Stem play when he comes to the end of the preludes and fugues?" she wonders.

"He goes back and practices," Stem says. She hears him say it. But where is he? And where is this large piano?

"Where are you?"

"I'm with you," he says. "I will join you."

"Have you seen the newspaper?"

"I am the newspaper," he says, while echoes of the soft, dark chords from number #4 in E flat minor, Scriabin, play over and over and over again.

*

A fly has joined them, and PreHistory, too, has returned.

"Buh-buh-buh-been a luh-luh-luh long ttttttime."

"I'd say," Grace says to the fly. "You missed all the action. I'm kinda dead meat."

"Thuh-thuh-that's wa-wa-why I'm huh-huh-here."

"Great, great," she says. "I guess you're not the one to go to for hope."

"On the contrary," says PreHistory, "if I may be so rude as to intrude. From what we have managed to find, in terms of research—I have not done this alone, mind you. My future-oriented wise fly—has helped me. We have even consulted with your, uh, worm. It looks as if you will have some options with respect to bail."

"Gi-gi-gi-normous," says the fly.

"It's not going to be cheap," PreHistory says.

"Would be nice," Grace says, "if I could get my body to do what my mind is doing."

"Some transformation is in order," says PreHistory.

"You-you-you've g-g-g-got the choice," says the fly.

"Right," says Grace, snickering. "Between being a bug and being—hmmm, I don't even know what to call you guys."

"What do you mean," PreHistory says. "I, my dear, am one of a kind. And he's rather an unusual sort, as well. Besides, we belong to you."

"I remember Breanda telling me I could be the patron saint of Space about a week ago. Who'da thought?" But then her face clouds over. "Wait," she says. "You belong to me? Does that mean you don't exist outside of me?"

"The-the-the-that's," says the fly. "Ah v-v-v-v-very gggood question."

"We are classified information," PreH says.

"The-the-the-that's uh-uh-uh-a fact," the fly says.

"Right," Grace says, thinking the matter might best be let be, at least for now. "Well, right now, I'm glad you're in my world, because if the Feds saw you guys, they'd probably nail you for testing, isolate you in some underground window-less pressure cooker, and attach electrodes and wires and tubes to you, and, and, and, they'd probably kill you—" It's a thought that sends her bawling her fool head off, waking up Starlinsky, just for a moment, and how he cuddles her, and she recovers, tearfully and hiccupping, but still talking, still with the intense desire to know where she stands, to make sense of what's happening.

"Without you guys, and Starlinsky—wow, I'd really lose my mind, but anyway, I'm really curious about Em. She's gathering the other bits of classified information. I am not sure I want to know everything she's doing. I'm not sure I want to know any of this at all, frankly, guys."

She forgets to ask about this 'rising' thing—that feeling of weightlessness.

As it is, what Grace sees is rather more than she wishes to see. "I mean, it's not on television, is it—all that I deleted? She's not selling me out, is she? I mean what would possess her? Why would she do a thing like that?"

"Tuh-tuh-tuh time for a li-li-li-tuh-tuh-tuhle reconnai-nai-naissance," the fly says.

PreHistory stands there literally twiddling his thumbs. The fly takes off to where Em is walking, getting first-hand knowledge,

264

although Grace's antennae, invisible as they are, are nonetheless profound.

"Well, lookie here," Em says to no one in particular. She picks up a rather large piece of printout. "DANGEROUS PEOPLE DELETE: BRUCE STEEN, FIREARMS, HOLD ARST. UNTIL CASE OF UND. FILM. GIRLFRIEND MURIEL LYONS GOES TO CT."

Not thickly rooted in Em's memory is the event referred to in the printout, but it happens that Muriel Lyons is already past her case in court, having sued the inquiring folly of a gossip column for libel. This is not the first time scandal proved lucrative for Bruce Steen, and possibly for the powers that be, since they never came to collect Bruce.

"Now they see fit to delete him," Em thinks. "Wonder what he's got on them, now, my Brucie," she smiles. She carefully places this piece in her little book and proceeds on her way.

"You see that?" Grace says to PreHistory.

"I know it," he says. The two of them are sitting on the cot, and his hands are flat on his belly, the tweed suit riding up where his oxford shoes rest solidly on the linoleum, which is more than one can say of Gracie—not her sandals, but her bare feet, an inch or so, dangling.

PreHistory's head is on his hands. He is resting.

"Well, there's more, PreHistory," Grace says. "A lot more where that came from."

"They will not make it to television," PreHistory says. "Don't worry your head over that."

"How can you be sure?"

"And yet another," Em says to herself. "Will you get a load of that: 'DELETED: PEOPLE PROTESTING V. N. WAR: MURIEL LYONS, GRACE ROSINBLOOM, BRUCE STEEN, BREANDA LIBERFRIED NEE FREEMAN, RICHARD LIBERFRIED, MARNIE ROSINBLOOM' (and a whole kit and caboodle of

265

additional Rosinblooms) 'DANIEL STARLINSKY, SONIA STARLINSKY…'

"There are many more, a great many more names of people," Grace says. "There are names of musicians, and artists—dancers and writers—of bisexuals and homosexuals and transexuals—who are in grave danger—and they don't even know it!"

PreHistory says, "Your friend doesn't consider them significant. But, my foolish charm, don't fool yourself: they always knew it."

"My, my, my!" Em shakes her head, groping for a word to match the surprise so well mimed on her face, anyone could read it. In another time and place, she could be arrested for such a look alone. "Grace and Bruce and Starlinsky and Em all deleted together," she says in the most childlike of voices. "We wonder where will she be, that Grace of my heart. Well, we're not on the dangerous list anymore, now are we?" She finds an unoccupied space in her book for this swatch and continues merrily and prettily along.

"There he is," Grace says, "Bruce."

"Yes," PreHistory says. "That well-dressed fellow in a limo. He's spotted her."

"Greetings, fair pink and blue disaster," Bruce says.

Grace recognizes these are words of love to Muriel Lyons. "I'm turning it off," Grace says. "I'm not sure exactly what's going on with her, but I'm looking the other way. Please let me know—you and the fly—please tell me if there's anything I need to know. Right now, I'm beginning to feel like a voyeur. Not my thing, PreHistory."

"Voyeurism, it is, when what you see doesn't see you," he says.

"Right," Grace says. "So you've said, so I've memorized."

"I do what I must to recover what must be magnified and glorified for the purposes of deciphering, for the sake of the appendix or some such vestigial item. Purposeless, my existence. Voyeurism it is, at best, my dear. But, do not fear—between the fly and me, we've got your back."

"Not to mention the worm and Zelda."

PreHistory follows, as does the fly, who winces at the singing.

"Somebody loves you/I wonder who it can be…" It's Bruce, his tenor, which, by the way, is on key, coming from the limo, blasting the tympanal membrane of the fly's ear—not his music, not the song of a cricket, that's for sure.

"Who me?" Em says this looking around, and she is also dancing, making herself ready for the lap dance that will follow.

"Hop in and don't say no to me."

"No" is the last thing Muriel Lyons would ever say to Bruce Steen, a.k.a. Frederick Wurre, a.k.a. Lucien Sorrell, a.k.a. Dave Gwemble, a.k.a. Zeek Flounder.

As is his penchant, PreHistory, if not the fly, gives them some privacy for their meeting and mating in the lounging back seat of the large car with its velvety blue interior, where Em will have the best black and blue time of her life. So sorry she is to have been so long away from him, during her four-day-long hospital stay. She clings like a mosquito to him as he tries to unhinge. Finally, he succeeds in removing her.

"All I want is to be held," she says. "I wonder, will it ever happen?"

In response, he is offering her a line of cocaine already prepared, ready for the both of them. They take turns, the little mirror shaking in each of their hands. With a push and pull, he teases, and she sulks. It's all in fun, until it isn't, but there's a barrier between the driver and them. Afterwards, Bruce happens to spot some familiar words on one of the masses of bookmarks he's poring through in Em's book. "What's this book? Oh yes, I remember this sissy play." Bruce opens the velvet curtains for some light in the back of the limo, his portable home, which in this case has opened from a living room to a bedroom,

267

when the inhaling moved into lap dancing that metamorphosed into cloud dancing, and then morphed into claw-dancing before the lovers re-aligned themselves and their clothing, a mass of black and white, if a little stained, and the bodies themselves reddened with finger prints and nail sketches. The imprint of Bruce's piece, that he leaves strapped onto his calf, can be seen on Em's thigh, and the prongs of her wristlet on his.

"Nothing sissy about it in my version of it, baby."

"You have a version of it?"

"Yes, darling, I am the star. I am Sycorax with the power to destroy Prospero."

"Must not be the same play," Bruce says. "Prospero is my man."

"He destroys her. She loves him. He kills her. In our version, she's a prophet. She's a sage, and he's an imperialist."

"Our?"

"Grace and mine."

"I like it. Let's do it, after we do Grace's rising?"

"Rising?"

"She says she's got a new idea in the works."

"What she has is a new Prospero in the works," Em says.

"He'd better watch his step," Bruce says. "What the fuck are these?" He is pulling at the filthy, waxy bookmarks, and then quickly scanning them and surmising the rest. "Lordy, will you look at that!" Bruce's is a devilishly high laugh. "Some angel has deleted our bad records. We can give it all up and be like new—whaddaya think of that, Emmie?"

"Do you think? Do you think we can start all over again?" Em says, pushing her face up to his, her fingers on his face, manipulating it into masks that she first creates on her own face—without thumbs or fingers, and then tries to mimic on his. "Such a sweet face," she says, inching up the edges of his lips and eyes. "Oh, danger here," she says, with a tug.

"Stop it," he says. "You scare me with those faces."

"No such thing possible," she says.

"Nice idea to start over, though," he says.

"Where would you begin?" she says.

"Interesting thought," he says, "to start all over again. I'd probably play most of it the same way."

"Most?" Em says.

"Most," he says, imagining himself cloud dancing with Grace.

"To begin again," Em says. "I'd have to die first. You'd have to kill me, darling."

"Not as if I haven't thought about it," he says.

"Would be good for your films," she says. "You could film it, Bruce, my immortality right there. I don't see the point of life. I've never seen the point."

"Right," he says. "I'm almost there with you on that one." The salient word is "almost," and the vision of immortality is not Em but Grace; a vision of Grace rising, he sees, her face an angelic countenance, a renaissance painting with a halo. "A Joan of Arc, our Grace of Jersey."

"What grim thoughts are you thinking?" Em asks.

"No more," he says, pushing her away. "But I do have some real sad weird fucking nuts news to give you. Gracie is in large trouble. I don't know what will happen to her."

"These are too many feelings to sort," Em says, pulling up her thong, trying to see if he's still watching, which he isn't, and cursing the fly, who is. "Hey, fuck you," she says to the fly, who finds a way out through the curtains to the driver's seat, and out the window to get a breath of fresh air.

"Grace is being charged on two counts of treason," he says, pulling on his slacks, buttoning up his shirt, grabbing a beer from the small refrigerator.

"What, our Gracie?"

"What exactly she has done is known only to Grace. Apparently, she has not told a soul. But she is strangely happy. I've never seen her so happy. But what with that crazy doctor of yours—"

"You mean Starlinsky—Daniel Starlinsky—that doctor?"

"Yeah. Starlinsky."

"Oh, no wonder."

PreHistory now makes himself comfortable sitting next to the driver, inspecting him, a man happy to keep track of what's happening out the window, read the newspaper, look at his watch, and listen to the Yankees on the radio, all at the same time—and to hoot when Spencer opens the game with a homerun in the first inning. PreHistory assumes he's got strict orders not to listen to the news and is probably happy with those instructions, by the way he figures it.

PreHistory hears Bruce feed Em a few bites of what's happened to Grace, avoiding mention of the *Post*'s front-page spread.

"Incidentally, how did you hear about this, Brucie, baby?"

Self-educated in the school of lies, Bruce carries on, makes light, but slowly dishes out a few crumbs. "Streets. Word of mouth."

The lack of spine-tingling detail moves from disbelief to incredulity. "Arrested? You sure? But not sure of what can we do for Gracie?"

"Nothing until she's arraigned, because she is being as passive as a worm."

"Oh." Em pulls the murdering savior back down to be with her again.

PreHistory has seen enough. Even the curious fly desists, his eyes so full of flashes, the photons becoming fewer as daylight recedes.

Nor does Grace require their reportage. They are free to wine and dine and define themselves in the diminishing light until their presence makes itself known to the one whose world has called them into being. If they have spun themselves from the orbiting planet that is Grace, it will be the planet itself that signals their return, the world she has generated, the world that generated her. To the extent that they are the same, that is the extent to which they are dissimilar. Em, as such, is a character in Grace's world, and Grace is a character in Em's world. PreHistory and the fly, as well as the species that rides among the green swirl of Zelda, have emerged onto a playing field like that of Yankee Stadium, and the worm is up at bat. We can only hope that he, like Jim Spencer, can hit a homerun early on and bring PreHistory and the fly home.

As for the two couples—their distance is about that between two large city trees, from which a small bird might fly back and forth in the space of a few minutes. One of the differences between the two couples is that a crowd is still gathering about the duo behind bars. The other couple has the privacy offered by opaque windows. Another difference is the matter of their chosen nets. One of the couples has been caught in something legal. The other couple is in a less tangible net. Both will come to the same end, although one will reach that end slightly earlier than the other, thanks in part to the entrapment felt by the other couple, whose net is not made of steel, or even nylon, or anything the unassisted eye can see.

Both couples have come to that impasse where words will no longer do. There are perhaps different reasons for this impasse, although there are perhaps some similarities. It becomes increasingly difficult to put both the terribly ineffable and ineffably terrible into words.

Time is running out for the couple behind bars, as they try to find a way to negotiate such an impasse. Starlinsky sees a muddled look darken Gracie's face, and he asks her if there is anything he can say to lighten her mind.

"Oh, Starlinsky. Tell me that my mother shall have no fear, and that I can explain it all to her."

"When did you last speak with her?"

"Yesterday—seems like a lifetime ago."

Starlinsky suggests that she might consider trying to call her now.

Nodding in agreement, she sees the anguish in his face. "You, Daniel, are being torn apart here. I hereby invite you to take a vacation. Why don't you go home and freshen up, and I'll call my mother, then take a nap until…" Neither of them likes to use the word "arraignment." Starlinsky agrees to leave, and both keep the promise of no tearful goodbyes. Sarah Thower responds quickly to their request. She unlocks the door, and Starlinsky walks out. When he turns back, he sees Grace looking away.

Her eyes are, in fact, cast upon a worm sitting on the small windowsill, smiling with an ace of spades in his mouth. It is at this point she wishes she could rescind the invitation.

But PreHistory and the fly are already on the case.

Each step Starlinsky takes away from Grace's cell feels to him like a step closer to freedom. A feeling of anger rises up from his footsteps, although when he reaches his loft and opens the door and falls heavily onto his bed, he is able to be more precise; rather than anger, it's an amalgam of self-contempt and utter helplessness that he feels. And with those lovely energies ensnaring his soul, Starlinsky falls asleep.

Grace, on the other hand, has broken her promise. She, who has plenty to sob about, has been unable to prevent the inevitable. What she is sobbing over has nothing to do, however, with the thought of her mother, or even about the unspeakable "arraignment."

272

It's a mix of longing and the fear. The self-reproach, the bitterness for having practically commanded him to leave. Why did she do it? Is she crazy? In her hysteria, she sees Zelda sitting beside her. What is Zel saying to her? Maybe she should stop listening to these voices. Turning her back on Zelda and the hordes at the part of her cell which borders the door, Grace wonders, is it possible to control one's thought? Is it possible to deny entrance to what exists as a presence within one? Where should she go? Where is there to go when agony plants itself all around one? Grace feels herself searching for comfort, but there is no source, no inkling of delight. She stands on the cot looking out, fearful to close her eyes, to look inward, for fear of the uncontrollable sound, the enveloping world of imagery that seems to attend her.

Her bare feet upon a bed that is already losing the smell of her lover. Perhaps he will never return. Looking down at her feet that are not exactly touching the covers. How strange, how passing strange. And how alone, how utterly separate from this world. The abundance of sound now gone, a relief it should be, but it's not. Even looking out so distant from sky, from the cricket sounds, from the sliding of tires down streets, the wheezes of the buses as if they were headed down a runway, and the trickling steps of walkers. The breeze comes through, warm it is, and if she had to give it a color, it would be pale green, the color of sea water, and of a pale green dress she remembers buying with her mother when she was not even ten years old. She was going to take a sewing class, and she needed material to make a dress. How very long it took to select the right material—that she remembers. But there is no memory of wearing the dress—only of the material itself, and her battle with it and with the sewing machine. What she's thinking about is the touch of that fabric still in her fingers, as well as the great hope she had in her mind for that color.

Such a child she was—the inner world extending far beyond the reach of eyes. Not even a world of art, not even a sandcastle, but a world of dreams, for the idle brain.

Yes, Mercutio was her man for that play—and Edgar in *Lear*.

But Starlinsky was neither Romeo nor Mercutio. More Henry V than Prospero, although he'd teased her, saying he was from the tribe of Caliban. He was more Levi than Hemingway, more Bakhtin than Derrida, but perhaps Keats. Yes, not the characters but the writers themselves. Nabokov's Adam Krug—she would marry him, but of them all, she would prefer Keats. Starlinsky was most like Keats. Krug was too damaged, too wounded. Was there another? No one on earth or in literature like her Starlinsky. If she survived, she'd write his biography—his, and Stem's. They must meet. She would have to arrange for that! And soon!

But where was Starlinsky. Should he not return? And Stem is not even a thoughtform—just a fleeting idea. Oh, having run out of thoughts, she is on the verge of bereft.

Zelda has patience. She begins her sentence between the spaces of Gracie's thoughts. She starts from the beginning each time. So, for Zelda, it goes something like this: "Men...Men have the...Men have the problem...Men have the problem that women...Men have the problem that women haven't, which is just...Men have the problem that women haven't, which is just the problem...Men have the problem that women haven't, which is just the problem of breaking when the heart...Men have the problem that women haven't, which is just the problem of breaking, when the heart is only aching."

"Zelda?" A sudden enlightenment strikes Grace. "You are something else. How can I thank you? Where did you get so much patience and understanding?"

"I've been around. A long time," she says, with a grand smile. "And, you don't get understanding without patience, do you? Now listen to me, and don't worry, Gracie. Starlinsky and the worm are one, so we know he will learn."

"I bet you taught that worm everything he knows."

"Can you keep a secret?"

"I think so," Grace says.

"That worm, that bee, and even that water lily would not exist without me."

"You're kidding?"

"Just keep it to yourself," Zelda says. "I do what I have to do. I let them take the titles, but I'd be a fool if I didn't stand my ground. Now, remember that, lady."

Grace smiles, and with that smile, Zelda takes her leave. She just walks through the wall back into the bedrock of this earth, but leaves her swirl, that abundance of green.

Grace is left with the words "stand my ground," and looking down, she realizes that she is not, no, not at all, feeling the coolness of the linoleum on her feet, and for good reason.

Grace signals to Sarah Thower, and the guard approaches with the little suitcase Starlinsky carried to the precinct. "Look," Sarah says. "We have your wardrobe here. I think I could arrange a shower for you—would you like that?"

Grace nods, then asks permission to make a phone call to her mother. "Is such a thing permitted?"

"And if it weren't, I'd call her myself and sneak you in, being a mother and a mother of mothers myself."

Grace steps into the shower.

She keeps her eyes averted, but Sarah Thower need not look to know the change of energy in her charge. How she would like to fatten her up, as if she were one of her own. How that wan face stays in her mind, how she cannot dispel it.

Grace climbs into a white cotton sundress that looks more angelic than sexy, but most important for the mothers of this world, it is clean and neat. She also puts her grandmother's watch around her wrist. "You would be pleased, Marnie Rosinbloom," Grace says, half to herself, "if only you could see me now." Sure—by the sheer number of concerned reporters—that the news is out, Grace finds herself thinking how grateful she is that her mother lives in Florida and not in New York.

"Hi, Ma," Grace says into the telephone, while the world of the precinct listens in.

"What's the matter?" her mother says in recognizably lilting tones. "I had a funny feeling you were in some trouble. Do you need money? Do you need food, a doctor—no, that you have. So, why are you calling? Have you lost your head? Are you going out of your mind? Drugs, Grace? What is wrong with my girl?"

"Oh, not so much, Mom. What's new is just the sad reality of my arrest."

"Your *what*?"

"I have been arrested on account of doing my duty to my country."

"What duty did you do?"

"Treason I did, they say."

"Treason? Gracie?"

"Mom! Not treason by my standards. You taught me to always to do what was right, right?"

"Always. And did you do what you thought was right?"

"Oh, yes." Grace tries to give her mother a vague idea of what had happened.

"So, you tampered with the status quo, my darling, and now you must pay the price. Was this the reason you called?"

"Yes, but Starlinsky—"

"What is Starlinsky?"

"My love and my new husband-to-be."

"Wonderful—you, you are not tampering with the law of childbirth, I hope."

"Not that I know about, Mom."

"When is the wedding?"

"We haven't set a date, yet."

"What can I do for you, my darling? Shall I fly up to visit you now, or should I wait until you have been—"

"I've been indicted, and in a few minutes, they will take me to the arraignment, so it looks like there's no rush."

"You are my bravest one, and you will be found innocent, for you are innocent."

"Bye, Mom. I love you."

"Be a good girl, my Grace."

After speaking with her mother, Grace asks and receives permission to make one last phone call. Then the criminal is escorted once again to the bathroom, where she might be able to throw some fairy dust upon her face.

Water is what it is, splashing upon her face, mixing with tears, with that liquid essence of eye that gives her sight, access into the material world, and into the mirror she swims, seeing the other fish in that sea, namely Sarah Thower and others watching her from the other side.

It isn't that she means to be a voyeur. In fact, neither she nor Sarah Thower mean to be spying, but both are, one for the reason of her job requirement, and the other for no reason at all. No reason under the sun would explain Grace's newfound ability to see what she sees in the bathroom mirror.

Was this here all along, she wonders? Has she been moving toward a point of invisibility or indivisibility? Or is she just cracking?

"Am I cracking?" she asks herself this. Presumably to herself, Sarah Thower is thinking. It is Ms. Thower's paid duty to look, to watch, to ensure the safety of Grace. It's no wonder that Sarah Thower is haunted by the ever-present face of Grace Rosinbloom, a face that seems to be growing more and more pale, and her eyes more and more luminous, the browns separating in yellows and golds and grays and silvers.

"I see you, Sarah Thower," Grace says. "I don't know why you need to look at me in this tawdry manner!"

Still, neither of them can take their eyes away from the mirror. What Sarah Thower takes in is really a bombardment by the very face she is having a hard time erasing from her mind. It began moments before Grace arrived the night before. It was as if she manifested the woman. Or was it the phenomenon of déjà vu, Sarah Thower wonders, that which only *seems* to have been seen before, because the mind apprehends the sight seconds before the consciousness of it happens. Perhaps the repeated glance creates a feeling of familiarity. And isn't that face watching her? That look of innocence yet accusation, something ethereal about it, something light-filled, those eyes that are so brown turning a dark liquid gold.

What Grace sees in the mirror is a world outside of the prison cell. She sees into Sarah Thower and out of Sarah Thower. It's perhaps why her face takes a different cast, the fact that she is being given a series of visions. Or she is moving through them, leaving her body as if ushered by a light, as if riding on a light, as if the light itself were a stallion out of control, and Grace were upon its back. Galloping. Where to gallop, she asks herself. Where do I wish to gallop? Why, of course, into the world of my beloved, into his dreams, if I might, and there she goes, not as a voyeur but as an actor, one who acts, one capable of motion, given to life or at least the performance of life.

And so, she slips in. It feels a bit like a cartwheel, and there they are, he in a pale blue and gray striped summer suit, and there she is, all dressed in white. They stand under the heavenly canopy. They travel—a honeymoon?—into the sun, with a world of children following. Up there, as in one of those Renaissance paintings filling up the impossibly high halls in the Prado, a series of lightning bolts and thunderous clouds create a flashing, pulsating light, and all but Grace survive. She sees him alone in a field, and Starlinsky cries in his sleep, "Please stay with me, Grace. I cannot live without you," and he wakes up.

"But I am with you," she says. It's a whisper that Sarah Thower thinks is for her, and with reddened face, she looks away.

"She is there with me," Sarah Thower says. She says it over and over, as she leaves the spying room and begins to knock on the bathroom door.

"Momentarily," Grace says. She is trying to force the recognition upon Starlinsky as she watches him shower and dress. "How handsome thou art," she says, somehow not feeling any pangs of guilt as she spies on him jaybird naked, pulling up shorts and a three-piece affair that is blue and gray striped. A summer suit it is with a white shirt, and now he snaps on a black bowtie. Ah, clothed, he loses her interest, and there is the pounding on the door.

*

Life is a dance with many partners, Grace decides, arm in arm with Sarah Thower.

"No," the guard says. "I will let no one hurt you."

And there are hundreds of people, it seems to Grace. There are placards held up with her picture and her face, the short hair, the words "Free Grace" on many of them. "She has freed us, now we must free her," she sees that. Outside she walks now, and then into a car with Sarah Thower.

"Is this a parade day?" Grace asks. The police car takes her to New York City's version of the Parthenon, its version of Athens, the buildings limestone, marble, brick, copper, bronze, a gilded-gold, and good old concrete, with centuries of justice steaming from its crusted sands. Still hot it is, and sunny, as well. Grace's attention is on the people who have gathered. It's as if they descended from the sky—that vision of floating humanity. They've landed there, Grace is thinking. She asks, "Is it a holiday?"

"No," Sarah Thower says. "Honey—this is for you. They're all there for you."

"Where are we going now?"

"Foley Square. We're about there."

As the door opens for her, and she's following Sarah Thower, Grace's eyes naturally roam to where Starlinsky, too, is stepping out of a car, this one a taxi. She sees him exchanging money with the cabbie, their hands in that God birthing Adam position, and Starlinsky is wearing the striped suit.

"You are the guest of honor here," Sarah Thower says, as she hands her off to a Fed, and to Richard Liberfried, whom Grace notified prior to leaving, the recipient of her phone call. This, of course, is the one and only Richard Liberfried, who had been expecting such a call by the sounds coming from Breanda all night. Of course, those sounds became increasingly louder, volcano-like, and lava and more came erupting out of Breanda, namely the now few-hours-old girlchild they have not yet named, but this is another story indeed, one that he is withholding from her, namely that he's now legitimately a father, although he's hoping this little red-faced bellower, drinker, shitter, and weeper won't follow in her namesake's footsteps. Breanda wants to name her Grace, of course Grace, if not Gracia. And now, he's looking at her, the lawyer, his eyes burning, the sunglasses over them, and he is waiting for the right moment, the desperately right moment, as they climb cement steps, and Grace is counting them, looking down at her feet, at those sandals, at her toes, and then they are walking into the large room. Walking forward now, going from cement to marble, to something soft, carpet, Grace asks to stop, for a minute, and she looks back. Starlinsky walks in just as Grace turns to see what sudden worm is buzzing like a bee, but smelling like a lily, with its feet on the ground.

"Oh," she says, with a swoon, and instinctively, Starlinsky rushes to work his craft, that he knows well, and she revives, which is essential if she is to be sworn in.

The silver-haired, friendly-eyed Judge Dupente smiles, for he, too, knows his craft well, and the presence of someone swooning is nothing new to him. When Grace, Richard, and the indispensable Fed arrive at the bench, Judge Dupente speaks: "Ms. Grace Rosinbloom, please step up to the bar and swear upon your honor to tell the truth, the whole truth and nothing but the truth, so help you God."

And with these words, Grace swears, and with her swears, she once again swoons, and with her swoons comes Starlinsky to the rescue. Once again, she is to swear, so the Feds can read off their accusations and she may register her plea of not guilty to the counts of treason under the law of the government of the United States of America.

Starlinsky is instructed to remain near with his invisible bag of tricks.

"Sirs," Grace says, suddenly. "I have nothing to say at this time."

"We will ask only that you say a word or two, Ms. Rosinbloom," the Judge says, who cannot help but feel the exhaustion in her eyes, and pity the thirty-year-old aging child, as he pities almost every person he sees standing in her position.

"There are two words that I have to say, your Honor. Not guilty. So, there is no more to be said, but will you set me a date and grant me a bail?"

Still smiling, the Judge says, "Wait, my friend, till we have sworn in your friends."

"Friends?" Grace says. "My friends have nothing to swear but swear itself. Please don't involve my friends. I acted alone, and this isn't even the time—and what time is it?" This is a question for her wrist, which informs her that of course her watch is broken. "Well, it looks like the time of rest is approaching. What is the next step, oh judge of my heart," she asks the Judge of the land.

"Please calm down, Grace, or you shall faint again and again," her trusty lawyer says, who then goes to her side and speaks to his client at length, his voice so soft that even she finds it difficult to hear.

"Grace Rosinbloom," the Judge says. "We have, you will be glad, of a sort, to know, set bail at five hundred, that is five hundred thousand dollars. You understand the first would be for the theft alone, but the second, well, the act of high treason is a hard act to follow." He speaks in the voice of a decree, mentioning a date that does not find its way to Grace's ears, although she does manage to hear what follows, namely: "That is when you shall next appear before the United States court, under an impartial jury with your standing council."

"Thank you, Judge Dupente," Richard says, and then Gracie turns to Richard and says, "See ya in the can," as she promptly falls upon the floor. Richard carries her to a small room off the side at whose door stands Sarah Thower. On the other side of the door are two Feds, but it is Starlinsky who ministers to her, wishing he had some tools at his disposal. To him, her signs do not look very fine. Standing outside, but well beyond where the Feds are hovering, are the so-called friends of Grace and the counsel, who has just been dismissed by the very judicious judge, who feels more than a twinge of grief in his own heart.

Only the one dream-man show can help Grace now, and he is, under the circumstances, doing his best. "Gracie," Starlinsky whispers. "You must listen to me and look at me. You will have no chance to escape." He grasps her face, locking her eyes onto his own. "You are going to be strong, and that is that. Think of your fiery blood, how it flows to and from your heart, which I touch, that I am yours and you are mine. You must breathe all that sweet, good air into your good soul. Or else you will be giving me a breach of promise. Let's see you do that."

Within moments, her face gains color, and she stands, albeit silently.

Their small group walks toward the first door, outside of which a large crowd has gathered and is not very silently waiting.

Soon as the door opens, the questions come like spears:

"Gracie, will you please say what kind of terminal you—"

"Ms. Rosinbloom, what is your education? Did you ever finish your dissertation on—?"

"Were you a crook by choice?"

"Are your theories based on Marx or Lenin?"

"Heidegger or Hannah Arendt?"

"Sartre or Simone de Beauvoir?"

"The real reason for your ABD?"

"What did you—?"

"How are you—?"

"Why were you—?"

"Who told you—?"

"Will you get the crap out of her way," Richard shouts, as they walk down the corridor to the stairs for a private exit through the revolving door, and then into the air of the outside world. Upon the steps a throng, a collage, a chamber orchestra backed by a horde of participants whose business it is to look. Familiar some of them would be to Grace, had she eyes for them; Breanda's face not among them, but Bruce's and Em's there are. Stem is there, dressed as a flag, his entourage, as well, all very patriotic. The man with the red beard is also there. She looks past them, through them. Faces, too, of those who know hers from handouts she's given, or from the news coverage on screen and paper; or they know that husky voice from what the radio has managed to proclaim, even WNYC; even Steve Post has dropped her name in between his jokes and his classical offerings. Those who have seen her atop or beside her bicycle in Klang's palace are there, as well as those whose buildings have been set for demolition. She, the notorious woman in white, the focus of so many eyes, sees only a worm in his glory, standing in the distance like an Empire State and with a light that glows heavily in his heart.

"Worm," Gracie thinks, "I want to die because I hate this place, and they hate me. Whoever thought they would do this to me? I used to work in this neighborhood just yesterday. And where are those clouts who did me in—those freaks of a feather, those butts of asses, those horrors of humanity. Why am I going to jail? Worm, I have done only good!"

"Gracie, we can only say we sympathize," the worm says. "We cannot say we understand…"

"Oh my God," Starlinsky murmurs.

"What," Grace says. "What?"

"Worm," Starlinsky says.

"Worm," she repeats.

"I mean gigantic, iridescent worm-like blob right there," he says, pointing high to the needle-like structure at the tip of the Empire State Building, its shine a little pink for the reason of a setting sun.

"And you," Gracie continues. "You worm, you tease, you crackpot. What makes you so smart—you frigging hermaphrodite?"

"Oh, Gracie," cries the worm in thought. "We feel so sad for you. Please try to see the other side of the—"

Gracie's attention to the worm is interrupted by a reporter holding the dull silver microphone like a popsicle to his lips, forcibly instigating a reply from Richard, "for the sake of the viewers at home."

"Okay, now," Richard says, the boy born and bred in Brooklyn, his "r's" and "g's" buried in the caverns of his mouth, not a drop of drama school, not a drop of attention-seeking in between the lines. "We are walking to the Women's Correctional Center, where Gracie will wait until the bail is raised or until the trial is tried."

The sound of instruments can be heard, strident and in unison. The music stops them, stops everyone. Somehow a piano has planted itself, with three others—all with music stands—a cello, violin, and clarinet. It is no other than Stem at the piano—a piano that is attached to a bicycle—not a grand or even a baby grand, but a small console. For the most part, Stem is not playing—the others are, that sound like trumpets—and then a silence, followed by a cello with soft chords that Stem is playing on the piano.

There is a moment of silence—in the beginning of the movement, which Grace takes for a sign, implacable with something to say to the television crew, and no matter how powerfully Richard protests, she manages to hold the microphone in her hands: "I have some words to say before they take my mouth away…You people of this land will die faster than a swatted fly, if you don't trust your heart and start believing in peace."

Almost at the same time, the worm in her mind harps with ideas of his own. "How can you expect them to listen to you when you are not listening to you? You probably thought you'd never have to listen to me again, poor girl. I'm yours till the end of time. How about I talk, and then you repeat after me. Okay?"

"Okay," she says. "But no tricks."

Her entire demeanor changes as she listens to the worm. She is listening, and the quartet resumes playing, but more softly. At least for the moment. As if to help her take in the moment. She does not repeat all that the worm says, but she listens, and that word "listen" seems to take command of her. As if the word illumines her.

"Listen, all who have come to listen," he says. "And listen, you who know only that you wish to live forever, because this one is going to die for you, and she is going to live for you, and you are going to die for no reason at all, but just for the hell of it. All of you must listen if you can listen." He has words to give her. His thoughts are coming in words. And the music grows in a chaotic manner, both rhythmic and difficult. The violin is playing on the wooden part of the bow. And still Grace is hearing the thoughts, the words, and some are slipping through her. Although Richard has done and is doing all he can to prevent it, the press is in its glory as she speaks, gathering her words like money, shifting the cameras to catch nuance and glance, admonitions and sighs—capturing the musicians who are playing Messiaen's *Quatour pour la Fin du Temps*. Grace sprouts words as she walks, the pronouns changing as she catches sight of the crowd, individuals melding for her into one large beast of wit with a vacuum in its hands, journalists and photographers and onlookers. They are bedecked in a coat of many colors, she thinks. She listens as the worm—majestic as the king of kings he is, was, and will forever be…continues at his own game. To be caught in the midst of the throng is his only fear. She is watching the trees in their weighty summer coats like a canopy over their heads, and she can feel the unmistakable feeling of Starlinsky nearby her handcuffed sides.

Pity it is she cannot exactly look into or even see his eyes that move from sheer horror, when he glimpses the Empire State Building in the distance, to something akin to rapture when he looks back at her, at the light that seems to emanate from her heart. The color of the light seems to be so pink he thinks it might actually be the sunset. It expands and grows more intense, the further away he is from her, and it seems to actually cover the crowd, like the firmament.

The more Gracie listens to the worm, the calmer she becomes. As she speaks, her voice intones a sound that provokes balance, and a serenity that seems to descend from the sky. Her voice, now devoid of anger, has become clear, almost as exultant as the voice of a water lily might be, although when Grace hears the words, they have morphed in their deliverance from something that originated as thought-forms of a most extraordinary worm.

Profoundly moved but stumbling in the attempt to pass along such a message, Grace finds herself choked. But the sight of so many people, the swaying of trees and a feeling for the life forms that came before, that are still present in metamorphic places…she simply brings a voice right up from the bell of her throat and sings out the words she hopes will adequately render the thought.

"Be brave, you girls and boys, and be true, you fathers and sons, and be strong, you mothers and daughters, and be happy, young and old, lovers and friends, and be free, all."

There is applause and cheering coming up from the crowd. It is as if they are waiting for an encore, or at least another word from Grace. And perhaps because they wish for a word, she feels obliged to give them one. But first, they give her leave to embrace Starlinsky, and they applaud after that, as well. But then, he steps back, and as she enters the prison doorway, leaving behind everyone but Sarah Thower, she turns to the crowd that stills itself. A word of farewell she wants to leave them with, and with this word of her own making, she will part the chaff of the wheat and the wheat of its seed and the seed of its egg and the egg of its youth and the youth of its age and the age of its death—and of death, its parting.

As the music ends with the violin, Stem is free to focus, to smile, to pronounce the word "courage" more than once. Like the worm, Stem is glowing. He winks at her.

"Bye," she says with a smile.

"Not really," he says under his breath. "Not yet."

A man with sparkling blue eyes, sporting a red beard, who has suddenly appeared, sitting not too far from the bicycle with the portable piano, says, "Not ever."

Chapter 10

Inside the Women's Correctional Center—a tall, ungainly modern brick building—Grace is part of a trio waltzing through the corridors, a sculpture in the elevators, and now solo in a room of her own, with a view. She stands and pulls herself up, how easy it is, to the window, and looks out. Her feet, ballerina-like, barely touch as she walks, although there is a settling down. She notices that. Perhaps it was something about the concrete. Something about limestone or brick that must ground her. Perhaps it was the people on each side of her, the handcuffs, the darkness of windowlessness. Grace looks up at the sky and down at the city and its green spaces.

Outside the Women's Correctional Center, where Grace is not, but where her shadow still lingers, how large it is, and how full of greenery. At least, this is what concerns the man in the blue and gray striped summer suit. Of course, Starlinsky's not the only one in a three-piece suit, as PreHistory is there as well—along with the fly, all three of them rather despondent.

"Not what I had in mind," PreHistory says.

"Cer-cer-cer-certainly it is," the fly says.

"No," he says. "I knew what would happen, but I didn't know that I would feel so bad."

"It's not-not-not oh-oh-over," the fly says.

A bench. A waterfall. Masses of beautiful people with their lovers, with their children, with their signs. A gorgeous day, in terms of weather, sunlight. They could just stay there and bathe in the sunlight. Lie down and bask in the setting sun. It's that long of a day.

The longest of the year. Some are already doing it, basking, that is; lying down, that is.

But not Grace.

Grace is sitting on a bed. Through the window, a view of the golden woman, her hand raised. A clock tower. Grace does not see the sun setting, just its effects. Decides she'll see the rising sun, makes a point to either stay up all night or get up very early and greet it. Now, it's well after six. Her mind is dancing through ideas. Do I look at the time? Do I ignore the time? My life? What is to become of me, the essential me? What is it that I boil down to? What are my lasting ingredients, besides bones? Why am I thinking about my bones?

The lost and found ivory key, an elephant's bone.

She now speaks her thoughts. Not all of her thoughts, just some that feel speakable. Is she waiting for an answer? There is none.

"I've been abandoned by all," she says. "Well, then. That's why I'm thinking about my bones." It's true she starts decomposing herself. Deconstruction She starts thinking about what she is. What she is made of. Composition. How to unpack herself. As if she were an idea, a performance, an art. An inescapable dream. Impalpable. And where is Stem? She remembers seeing him, that awful vision, but in fact, this dissipating body she'd seen in a vision resembles hers. Stem is glowing somewhere, while she's a pile of bones.

"Bones," she says.

For what purpose?

"For courage," she hears.

"Not a purpose, Stem," she says. "It's a word. A rather dumb word, at that."

"More than a word," she hears. "A vibration."

"Poppycock."

"Poppycock's just a word."

"It stands for a thing."

"Where are you, Stem? I don't see you."

"I'm in your mind. I'm holding you together right now. It's taking a lot out of me, I'll have you know, Miss."

"You are in my apartment building on Bleecker Street. You are home, where I want to be, and you have managed to make me think I'm talking to you when actually I am talking to myself. Anyone listening would think I was losing my mind, Stem," Grace says.

"You're gaining," he says—or so she hears.

She is burdened by a thought that she cannot put into words. About his ivory piano key. He must know.

I found a piece of your heart. Do you know? I can't tell if it is for me to tell, if it is for me to say, if it is for you to hear, if I have to let this go, this gift of a knowledge, this piece of your sorrow that came to me.

"I'm bones and a beating heart," she says—as if interrupting him, unable to give or even to enlist his support, well-meaning or not. "But when this heart beats no more, I will leave bones." It is not a startling fact, she thinks. But it is a fact. Ah, this is what a fact is, then, she thinks. Bones are facts. Facts are bones. What I am is more, or less than bones, she thinks. "Bones I am" is not a fact, she decides, but still she is thinking about them. Ideas are something that I am, she thinks. My ideas, she thinks. Can they exist without me? Now, that's a question. If they can exist without me, then "Ideas I am" is not a fact. Unless "I" am not a fact. This is a line of thinking, she thinks, that started a long time ago. Bones again comes up. Her mother's bones, her grandmother's bones. She has had dreams about her grandmother's bones. Dreams where she is actually in their presence, down in some vault. It was dark. It was underground, and there were people there in robes, skirts down to their feet. They didn't wear shoes. There were voices—echoes. Other languages, they spoke, the caretakers of the bones. It was distressing when she awoke from those dreams. She had them more than once. Well, who will dream of her bones, she wonders. Eventually bones decompose, she thinks. But they last a long time before they do that. Unless, of course, one is cremated.

290

And then, gosh, you'd better have a lot of ideas, or a lot of children. You'd better know your grandchildren. I am having dire thoughts, she thinks. Where will this end? Will she stop thinking in this manner? She wonders about that. She wonders why she cannot steer her mind off the subject of her demise, even though she suspects it's because of this immense confinement, a confinement that might never end.

"I'll put off thinking about it, then," she says this aloud. "I'll have lots of time to contend with this line of thinking."

But then, what do I think about? She sits on the bed and looks out and thinks about what to think about.

As for Stem, his meditation has stopped. He returns to the piano but cannot bear to play a thing. Time for a cheeseburger, time for fries.

That much, Grace hears. "Go have one for me, too, Stem," she says. "Put some meat on my bones.

"And go to Washington Mews."

"Washington Mews?"

"You will find a bone."

*

As for Starlinsky, he begins to see great fireworks coming from the north, in the direction of the Empire State Building around which a great worm appears to be coiled and all aglow.

"What are you so happy about?" Starlinsky says to himself, or so he supposes.

*

No, Grace hears none of this. She is putting on the striped pajamas that have been neatly folded, sealed in a plastic bag. She wonders who might have worn these last, and whether she might retain

291

her very own undies. She will need more, as for a vacation. No, no more tears. She says this to herself. No more. Else she would flood the place like Eloise flooded the Plaza. It would be Alice in Prisonland. No. Just dress. Dress and breathe, and then lie down. Relax. Try, because exhausted. Should, could, would, as in shouldcouldwould she write? She could finish her dissertation? A letter? A love letter? A love letter to Starlinsky? To New York City? Is there a pad somewhere?

Lying there, she rummages in her mind to construct a list of her things. Her suitcase. What remains in her suitcase. What she has placed into the bureau. What sits with her on the cot. In addition to all these are a carpet, few hooks, a window. She becomes distracted by the window. So high up, she feels like Queen of New York, like that gilded statue upon the limestone trove of offices. It must be so pleasant, she thinks, to be living in a building that is all in white, all stone. Limestone is metamorphic. She remembers that. Stone that comes from sea animals. Ancient. What will come of her? Different from what will be-come of her. The limestone building is not the one she is in, as the one she is in is made of brick, which is made of sand, which perhaps has the detritus of once living, breathing beings. But now she's looking at the limestone, the white one, the building that is like a galaxy itself, the one she has a view of, that and the sky, and with its gold lady up there. And why is there a sudden peaceful feeling? No, she is not fretting any longer. It is a feeling that has come over her. Yes, there are bars, and yes, she will gladly wear these disgustingly ugly striped pajamas. No, they're not pajamas? Pajamas for a long sleep, no, they're not? No, Grace does not feel like talking. She feels like sleeping. Pajamas are perfect—but will Starlinsky come to visit? Surely, she knows he will. Ah, what more can she ask for? Starlinsky and sleep. She has done only good. Sleep will be a wonderful thing. She thinks these things. Steps, she thinks. I'm still taking steps.

*

"Will you get a load of that?" Now, that is distinctly a woman's voice Starlinsky hears, but there is no woman to be seen. In fact, that crowd has instantly dispersed, and it is just Starlinsky—alone now, sitting on the blood-red stone steps with his head in his hands, gravely sad, his eyes thick with tears.

However, even in the midst of the greatest tragedies humankind has known, the kind that resist articulation—even in these, there has always been a place for distraction. Maybe it's to point the way of survival, but perhaps not. Maybe the mind is a snake, coiling and uncoiling, taking its time to swallow the burden of an impossible truth. Strangle the truth first, then take it in.

Which is just to say that Starlinsky looks up for only one reason: he wants to see if that worm is still straddling the Empire State Building.

"Yup, he is," Zelda says, introducing herself to the fellow who has just beheld the sexiest version of the Empire State Building known to man.

Starlinsky turns himself around so he is now facing the door of the Correctional Center, but then, like a frightened child, he cannot resist taking one more look at the very thing he wants to deny. He notices the vision is fading, but he hears that same unmistakable sexy voice, "Don't worry, honey. He'll come 'round."

He turns back to his viciously painful thoughts. Why hadn't he married her first; that thought, for example. If he were her husband, maybe he could visit more often. Well, that would be one of the first things he'd arrange, but what is wrong with him? What has happened to his sense of responsibility? Why didn't he think? He tortures himself, imagining her signing her address and name. Those should have been his. He feels as if he's abandoned her, and he hates himself for this. It is this last thought that has made itself into words sitting like a crowbar in his throat, when he is approached, tapped on the back by some more democratic entities.

"Hi there, Doctor Daniel, my savior," Em says, wearing her shades and bonnet and her skort of all red, and her bodice in black with some beads hanging down from her neck, her pasty face dry of all color. "Thanks for setting me free."

"You, as I heard from my secretary," Starlinsky says, "have found your own freedom, by which you shall be free to be yourself, Muriel. Congratulations."

"Hello, Starlinsky," Bruce says, offering his nail-bitten, ever-so-clean hand.

"My regards to you, Bruce." Starlinsky agrees to shake.

"What do you think?" Bruce says.

"Not much to say," Starlinsky says. "When there's that kind of a bail, you wonder whether we have a case of treason in the robbery of the people by the state." Starlinsky buries his head, trying to bury all thoughts of grand larceny, while hundreds of banks stand nakedly before him.

"Oh," Bruce is off-handed. "Bail's no problem. You don't think they really intend to let her be bailed out, do you?"

"Bail's no problem?" Starlinsky laughs. "Tell me another one."

"The question is, how do we go in there with half a million, and worry when it looks like she just wants to go back? I mean, do you get the picture, Starlinsky? We got the solution, but what is the real problem with Gracie? We don't really know. But when you give us the—uh, okay, that she's uh…ready—"

"Stop, already!" Starlinsky's voice is a command. "Why didn't you say so back in that court? But the banks are closed now, anyway."

"Hey, man." Bruce puts his arm around the smartly-dressed doctor. "Cool down. We got it, get it?"

Like a child who has witnessed enough violence to recognize its introductory dance steps, Em senses where this is leading, and very slowly, she begins to slink into the shadows. Instinctively, Bruce catches her by the arm. "Where you going, honey? Don't want to be around for some action?"

*

In the bed now, propped up against the wall, gratis of a pillow with an antiseptic smell, with a pad and pencil in her hands, Grace is trying to find something worthy of being written. "There's not much profundity available to me currently," she writes on this pad, which has a line drawing of her new home with its name and address on top. She peers out the bars of the window, her eyes widening at the sky. She is a tenth of a mile up. The sky is cerulean, an eastern sky. Her last window, the tiny jailhouse window, also with bars, of course, faced the west, and the window on Bleecker Street faced south. North—the windows of her childhood bedroom in Jersey, where she'd see Saturn and stars, falling stars. "Remember stars," she writes. She remembers seeing the rings of Saturn once, too, when she was in college taking an astronomy class, and how excited the Grad Assistant became when he knew they'd all see the rings. Rings, palpable. Not just an idea. "Palpable as Saturn's rings," she writes. "Not just an idea." Her body in a deep state of relaxation, she notes that: "Very, very sleepy," she writes. "My body relaxed as if I were in a cocoon of light." PreHistory climbs through the window, followed by the fly, who squeezes though a small break in one of the squares produced by the weaving of the screen, one little wire cut off from the rest. The fly rather gingerly steers himself away from the rogue metal thread.

"Trouble," PreHistory says. "I knew it."

"Who-hoo-hoo didn't?" says the fly, zooming around now.

PreHistory says, "You did nothing."

"Sometimes truh-truh-trouble is uh-uh-uhnavoy-voy-voydable."

295

"Unavoidable? Unavoidable? Unavoidable?" PreHistory exclaims. PreHistory is as close as he's ever come to a splitting atom, in danger of exploding. "You don't want me to explode," he says. "I'm pretty messy when I am all fired up. Because at this point, even I can predict the future, and my prediction is not very pleasant."

*

"You mean you *have* the money?" Starlinsky says. "God, I hope it's not too late."

"You are not kidding," Bruce says. "Gracie seems nuttier than an Em-cake." He stops, suddenly, as his eyes catch sight of Em about a block away. He screams loudly, "No offence, sugar pie."

"Not too late to get her out tonight, you lout," Starlinsky says, raising his own voice, not thinking that perhaps crossing Bruce is not the wisest thing to do in the world. So, Starlinsky is not exactly prepared for the fist that makes sudden impact upon his face. Nor do either of them see Em run for it.

"Hey, you punk rock idiot," Starlinsky cries, grabbing his face. "We are on the same side!" Bruce once again raises his fist to the doctor, but this time, Starlinsky is ready to prove himself quite the capable fighter. But when Bruce pulls a blade from his shoes, Starlinsky knows he cannot unhand him, and instead screams, "What the hell's the matter with you? Will you put that goddam knife away? For God's sake, aren't we on the same side?"

"We were, man," Bruce says, "before you went and called me a louse."

Not ready to relinquish his knife, Bruce tries to taunt Starlinsky, who simply backs up from him, but keeps speaking: "Listen, I'm sorry I insulted you, but I'm not your enemy. I want to get her out as much as you do. Look, don't worry, she's not crazy; she's had a bit of a trauma. She'll get over it. She's fine. I'm fine, you're fine; even old

Em is fine, but Gracie's in prison. I want to get her out, and you want to get her out. So, let's do it together. It's the only thing that makes sense, right? You need me and I need you, right? I know I can't do it without you, and I get the impression you think you can't do it without me. Am I right? I'm right, no?"

Starlinsky sees the look finally change in the way Bruce holds his mouth. It softens as the creases on his cheeks loosen. He can't see the eyes behind the shades, but he takes his chance. He puts his hand out to Bruce, and says, "Now, doesn't that make us on the same team?"

"If we're on the same team, Doctor, I'd advise you to stop calling me names," Bruce says, folding up.

"Forgive me, Bruce." Starlinsky is still with his hand in the air. "I don't know what's got into my head. Now, please, don't make me look like a fool. Shake my hand."

Finally, Bruce does just that, but at the same time Starlinsky feels something very cold and hard, though not particularly sharp, at his back.

*

A stillness there is, like that of something immured in glass, and that something is Grace. Still lying down, the covers helping her to stay down. Still with the writing. Still hosting a couple of swells in her room. Suddenly, a small feeling of panic erupts from within her. It comes like something stinging, but localized and very tiny, and she pushes back the sheet and light blanket and stands up quickly.

PreHistory asks, "What is it?"

"I'm frightened," she says.

PreHistory says, "I hope it wasn't something I said."

"You are ab-sur-sur-surd, man," the fly says.

"It's just a feeling that I have," Grace says.

"Sometimes that's all you can ask for," the fly says.

"What is?" Grace asks.

"The fact that your antennae are working. Sometimes that's all there is."

"Your stutter is gone," PreHistory says.

"Happens," the fly says. "I came out of my shell. Like that. I feel as if I'm on my way. Can't explain it and not gonna try." He sits on the sill and watches.

*

Were someone watching all this from on high, say from the Empire State Building, or from the spot of space that once shared itself with the flat apex of the World Trade Center, or from a cloud in the sky, or from the highest point of a rogue planet, or much lower down, or from the position of a medium or even, say, from a windowsill of the Women's Correctional Center, this someone might see a few guys traipsing toward a black limousine. One of them, the darker-haired guy with the shades, would be opening the trunk and handing one of the suitcases to the other guy, the one with the fair hair and blue and gray suit. But except for the medium, that someone, unless he or she were terribly far-sighted, might not see the gun in the hand of the guy with the shades pointed in the back of the more formally-dressed guy. Nor would that someone hear the one-sided conversation that begins with, "This is one thing we're going to do *my* way, doctor."

Indeed, it might well appear to someone looking from a distance that the doctor willingly takes a seat next to the driver, in front, while the filmmaker sits in the back. And it might also appear that he willingly takes a pistol into his healing hands. It would be hard to estimate how much the doctor is noticing as they drive around Chinatown, so Bruce, or as he is now called, "Gwemble," can see what is happening. They make a few stops, and the driver, who is also wearing shaded glasses, steps out, and within a few moments he is back again. Starlinsky does not say much; nor, in truth, are his thoughts in great quantity. He merely holds the gun that was placed in his hand and stares at it.

The medium, who might see it, might be unable to do anything about it, might not even remember it after he'd stopped playing the piano, there as he is still doing, with the occasional musicians stopping by, but Stem is in no position to do anything but play his heart out, and his minions—not really a horde, but stragglers who have come with their various instruments—are also looking at this longest day of the year as a moment to play their hearts out as well.

As Starlinsky is not really aware of the music, and as he finds himself unable to do much of this activity we call 'thinking,' for him this moment is rather like a re-playing—speaking of playing—in his mind of the last little bit of conversation he just overheard:

"Will they take the bail at all?" Bruce had said over the CB radio.

"Not a chance, Gwemble," the voice had answered back. "Not tonight, not tomorrow, not ever. She's lucky if she gets out of there alive."

"Thanks. We'll be there pronto. All hands on deck. Gwemble, over and out." Bruce had clicked the CB to its off position, and under his breath, he'd said, "Ah, what the hell do you know anyway?"

That's the part—the "what-the-hell-do-you-know-anyway"—that Starlinsky keeps thinking about, playing again and again in his mind, even as the limousine pulls around the back entrance of the Women's Correctional Center and stops.

Now, supposing there exists some God or alien, some omniscient being with the apparatus to both see and evaluate every last little action. And supposing this god-like one or thing were gazing down at the spectacle of nighttime in New York City, after the sun had set and all the shining ornaments glowed electric, endless waves spiraling from never-never-never-never-never-land. Supposing the one or thing with its (his, her) inestimable powers of insight, happened to spot this group, with its fair share of guns and money and drugs and high hopes. And supposing the one who planned only to use his high hopes looked up—and saw the one looking down. If all that had actually happened, as the one with high hopes had imagined, it would, in a way, change nothing; but it would, in a way, change everything.

For Starlinsky, the one riding on high hopes, everything changes when he steps out of the front seat of the limo, looks up at the sky, and happens to see first one, then a second, then all—the full cast of Gracie's dream characters hovering like Macy's Thanksgiving Day balloons over the massive building. For that moment, he forgets that he has a suitcase of a couple of hundred thousand dollars in one hand and a gun in the other.

As he closes the car door, Gwemble sees the smile on Starlinsky's face. "So you decided not to be so morose, after all," he says to Starlinsky, patting his back. "Good for you, Starlinsky. You know, you're pretty smart for a doctor."

"You think so?" Starlinsky says, still looking up.

"You'd better hope so, Starlinsky," Bruce says. "You'd better hope so."

"I guess I'm meant to see what you mean," Starlinsky says, still smiling.

"I guess you are," Bruce says.

But Starlinsky is referring to Grace, and this time he is indeed smart enough to let Bruce remain in the dark about what he might have meant.

*

Meanwhile, except for one moment of panic, Grace has carried the unshakeable faith of a zealot about her. But something convinced her that, so long as her antennae were working, all would be well. It's the best you can hope for, to be able to feel your way forward and to go there. What was she fighting for, anyway, but to learn what it was she had to do and then do it? Or be it, or sing it, or just see it, and go there. In a way, that's all there is, and she is grateful she's got it, and so be it. Both the guards who escorted her to and fro, and even the other inmates, have taken note of the radiance upon this newcomer's cheeks. And how could they have known how stark white those cheeks had been, as pale as a shroud, Sarah Thower had said to herself.

But if she has visions, the joy of which is evident on her face, her lips are sealed. Grace has nothing to say to anyone. And here, there are both male and female, for these are federal offenders, and here is where they will stay until their trials. If it were just the offense of the theft, Grace would have been off to Riker's, and housed dormitory-style with a houseful of other women, and there were nurseries, too. But this alleged act of treason makes her dangerous, and here, she is given a room of her own, which she takes for just another reason to be joyful.

Now her ecstasy is not exactly religious in nature, unless love itself were the religion and Starlinsky the god. She knows, somehow, that Starlinsky will come to be with her, with the full flower of belief that the rest is in God's hands, in whom she does trust, as it is written in so many government rooms.

So when the two of them arrive, namely Bruce Steen, although in his alias Gwemble, and her Starlinsk, alias Starlinsky, Grace is only partially honored, but she is more than startled by the fact that with them she may now leave.

"You have raised the bail?" Grace says, with the ultraviolet ray of blue coming out of her eyes and the beginnings of a halo about the crown of her head, although this can only be detected by the one recently indoctrinated into a new wave world or two. Grace hugs first Bruce, and then her Starlinsk, where she lingers a bit too long, in the eyes of Bruce, who then requests a second hug, which Grace refuses.

They walk down the hall, an awkward trio, as Bruce drops off the keys to a guard, who looks the other way, trying to forget the same thing that Starlinsky is trying to forget, although they were inspired differently.

For it is one thing to have the bail, and it is another thing to have it accepted. The latter proved to be as costly as the former, and when the bribes did not properly circumvent whatever reservations an officer might have had about accepting the bail, a friendly clobbering became the preferred method of persuasion. At least one guard, who Starlinsky happened to observe, was the recipient of that formula. Starlinsky quashed any temptation he might have had to protest when he saw the friends of Bruce—at least five thugs, there were—dragging the guard away, without a word from anyone.

In the elevator, more corridors, and there are still no words coming from any member of the unlikely trio; these are people with three very different sets of thoughts, yet a momentary feeling of wellbeing might be said to have existed in each one.

Once outside, they walk slowly, aimlessly, even with the sounds of sirens beginning to fill up the air. This is a sound that makes Gwemble uneasy. He is thinking of himself in alias, now, but he is concerned that a certain Muriel Lyons is out on her own—not worried, but concerned. The sirens sound again, although it is relatively empty of people on a Saturday night in that part of town. Rather than streets and sidewalks, Bruce leads them to the park where there the remnants of the crowd gathered to protest Grace's incarceration, some cleaning up picnics, others walking away, signs lowered in their hands, some with children.

"I'll catch up with you two later," Bruce says, as he falls behind, with the urge to empty his bladder and fill up his nose, not particularly in that order.

As for Grace and Starlinsky, they are down on the ground as soon as they can find a sweet nesting spot. Between kisses, they whisper about such things as worms and water lilies and children and wedding dates and how to fix up the loft.

Then Grace looks with up her great starry eyes and asks Starlinsky how long he is willing to wait for her. He says softly that he's given it all a great deal of thought, and perhaps the cleverest thing she can do is to plead not guilty by reason of insanity, and on that peachy thought, all whispering and kissing and embracing and lovemaking comes to a halt.

"Not you, Starlinsky," she cries. "Not you, too!"

"What do you mean, me too?"

"You think I did something wrong."

"No," he whispers. "I think you did nothing wrong."

"Then how can you expect me to lie like that?"

"We'll talk about it later," he says. "Just kiss me. I love you. I love you so much," he says. "Too much."

"I love you too," she says. "Enough to lie if you really want me to. It's just that I wasn't expect—"

"I'm so scared, darling, of losing you," he says. "I've never been so scared in my life."

"And I've never been so calm in all my life," Grace says. "Not a worry in the world."

And then there are no words, but there are sounds that could be terribly misinterpreted.

"Wait," Grace cries, more than a whisper, less than a shout, but audible enough to rouse someone in a stupor, someone already irritated with Starlinsky, someone suspicious of his intentions, and most significant, someone with a gun who is not afraid to pull the trigger.

A bullet comes out of nowhere, grazing Starlinsky's finger, and instinctively he throws himself over Grace to shield her, when he hears Bruce growl, "Can't wait, can you, big boy?"

303

Starlinsky freezes, but Bruce continues, "Get up, pig, and get out of here. I haven't shot you to death, but I will if you aren't gone by the count of five." And Bruce begins to count, while Grace, thinking only of his life, gives Starlinsky a rather violent kick in the groin. The doctor groans, but he will not move.

"Get off me, please, Starlinsky," she says quietly, and then continues, seeing he will not be convinced. "I'm hurt. Please do as he wishes."

Starlinsky will not budge, even as Bruce reaches the end of the countdown, and Grace and Starlinsky begin to wrestle like animals in the attempt to protect each other from the bullet that has left its nest. And as luck, or destiny, or shall we say chance, would have it, the bullet, aimed for Starlinsky's back, is delivered into the left breast of Gracie, leaving both men stunned, when Gracie cries, "Okay. Stop."

*

And for a moment, the world does just that. It stops.

It stills, rather. A slowly moving atmosphere collides with it, the atmosphere of a consciousness that has been circling, that has invested itself in this organism, this Grace. It resembles a sudden darkness, occasioned by a meteor or comet or falling particle or the bending of a gravitational wave, that a scientist one day will receive a Nobel Prize for—but here it is, happening on Earth, in New York City, on a day like any other, at a time when night begins to fall—a moment of peace, as before a theatrical event or symphony, when the sound of silence must make itself known, that sound that both precedes and follows a great momentous event, like the passing of the cortege of a president or the one you happen to love.

Even Stem's musicians are for the moment stunned into silence.

This is the nature of the profound stillness that enters the consciousness of Grace, and she looks around. She takes this moment to focus on what is outside of her so that she can just understand where she fits in. There they are, the masses of points, fuzzy though they are, the stars that have always been there, but are just now making themselves known, and then, she looks into the crowd. For a moment, there is a hush. It's as if New York City has seen the conductor of the world lift her baton, and Gracie, too, does raise her hand, just as the gilded woman does who stands at the top of the gloriously huge limestone building. Grace lowers her hand to her left breast and retrieves the bullet. It is slippery and warm. She rubs her fingers and it against the shirttails of the gray uniform that is somehow still hanging from her shoulders.

"Anybody else feel like taking a shot at me?" She speaks with the distinct tone of a small bell. Her words echo from the walls of stone, ring through the trees. She holds the bullet up. The people who are gathered there, in the fringes of the park, are those who, for some reason, could not leave, were still waiting for a glance at her, even through a window. There are many gathered, and many more are walking in, people still with their signs, people with their children, people who somehow felt pulled to the plight of Grace Rosinbloom.

"Please," she says. "I'd like to ask you to remain still. I'd like nobody to move—not even you, my dearest," she looks toward Starlinsky. "Or you," she looks at Bruce, "my would-be killer. And not you, my very best friend," she looks to Em, with whom Bruce is holding hands, both of them, their eyes bright with tears, and Richard is there too, and his shades are off, too. Tears there, too. She sees a few cigars in his pocket, and that registers. She sees the man with the red beard, and for a moment, her lips widen. Life goes on, she's thinking. Even for Stem—at least for a few more years at least. Life goes on. And oh, life must go on. But for her, this is a moment. The moment Stem's word "courage" was waiting for. As if a word could wait. But there are times for the perfect word, like a perfect note, a note in tune played at the moment it's meant to—well, she's that note, and "courage" is her word. If she had breath, she'd let him know, but she suspects Stem knows, suspects that he knew a long time ago when she was just a novice, a novitiate, a proselyte, a child. He called her "child."

"Please be still," she says to those who are in the gathering throng, "my faithful friends. Even you, all of you, my companions on this planet—my protectors, my jailers, my bosses, my executioners."

Her voice is loud, the projection of her voice great. "Ok, it's my turn. I understand. But, let's get this straight. This entire planet is a land mine. Weapons. Where are there not weapons? Is that all that's left for us to do here? To kill as many as we can? We can maim or kill ourselves with our weapons! We can destroy the planet—or at least make it unlivable, unlivable for us, that is.

"Look here," she says. "See this!" Grace extends her hand now, a small rivulet of blood falling down from her breast, inching down like a baby slug, this dark line going down her body, down to where the pants, so long, so baggy, are touching the grass. The blood from her body begins to pool where she stands, but Grace keeps speaking. "See this piece of lead. It weighs a little more than a three-month old fetus. It's got a name and a number and a history. It's got a price on it, and its price is your life." She holds her hand out to Roger Warren, who stands there in a daze. "And your life," she says to Judge Dupente, who is also in attendance. And she continues to point out individuals, and add them to the list of lives who will pay the price of the bullet.

Once again, she raises her voice, as the park fills up with more people, and her voice projects over the sirens, but there is not much else in the way of noise.

"This bullet," she says. "This particular bullet has my name on it, but the others—the others, the stepchildren of this bullet, the adopted cousins and second cousins and the fragmented nieces and grand-nephews of this bullet—have the names of posterity on them. Bombs, nuclear, thermonuclear—all the pretty names they want to bestow upon these savage, vile inventions have the names of your posterity on them. Your posterity, and even the posterity that is not yours.

"I myself have no other posterity but yours. You are my baby, and your babies are my babies—if you will have them and make the world safe for them.

"Your posterity's inheritance, then. The placenta—the planet itself is doomed for this bullet, for the sake of power? U.S. power? Money? U.S. money?

"That's just what will be left—the money and the power.

"I erased words," she says.

"I erased words," she says it again.

"The weapons will erase the world.

"But lucky for me I won't be around to see it happen, because, if you can just leave me alone for another few minutes," she says, and she looks down to see if it's true, and it really does appear to be true.

She cannot hide it anymore, and she can see in the eyes of Starlinsky, it's been sighted. Tearing her eyes away from his eyes the most difficult thing yet, each infinitesimal fraction of turning hurts, as if she were tearing fabric, tearing the skin around each other's eyes, and those tears stream down, and she feels the pain of each small hair of attachment as it's cut, as she cuts it, and they are still staring at each other, as if each of them were on either side of a river bank.

And yet she is rising, and she sees that he sees this. She cannot get away with hiding this anymore, the fact that she is more than a fraction of an inch above the ground, that nasty puddle of her blood where the bottoms of her trousers were, just sitting in and soaked with and now are dripping from. And it's because she's rising, goddam it, more than an inch now, and now more than a foot.

It's going faster, and up she goes, and she's not alone, mind you, she sees them all up there with her, but oh‚ she's never seen the worm so quiet and smiling, and the green swirl is going just so far, and then it's returning to the earth with all its entourage, Zelda's entourage, and Zelda is waving with her beautiful hands, and the worm is waving with his golden tail, and PreHistory is there with her, and the fly is going up there just as far as he can, but maybe he, too, will turn back. She can see PreHistory fading back into thin air, and his clothes are going up, rising up with her. Maybe she should hang on to his mackintosh, or that vest? Buttons exploding off them like tiny fireworks, a light show, not falling but rising stars. Oh, she thinks, this is the stuff of celebration!

But Starlinsky is down there, and she can feel him pleading with her to come back. It goes something like this: "I love you. I don't want to live without you. Consider this, Grace. Consider life. What are you running away from?"

"I'm not running," she says to him. "I'm rising. I'm okay, Starlinsky. I'll see you. I promise."

"What about our babies?"

"They're here," she says. "All our babies are here. I have the feeling that even Breanda's baby is here by now. All babies are our babies. Don't you see? Take care of them for me, Starlinsky!"

"Alone?"

"I'm wherever you are," she says. "Just like you are wherever I am. It's always been thus." She is looking up now. Irresistible it is, this journey. It's nothing she can fight.

She is about the height of a traffic light when she decides there might be something more she must say to those below, to her flock— and she can still see the red beard, and Stem as well, with that piano that looks like it's an aperture through which a key might fit—a keyhole that might open up a world. "Who will play for me and you, when they give this virus a name?" he says. "And how many times will you hear the Barber *Adagio* when the towers fall down?"

And the music begins again, tones that sound more like water than a series of hammers striking a series of strings, and Stem cries out, "And after that? It won't be the Barber, it won't be Messiaen, it won't be this *Jeux d'eau*," he says. "It will be a hush. A hush."

And so Stem plays the Ravel that sounds like waterfalls in a city that is very still, under a sky that is watching as if it has a decision to make.

And a sobbing Em keeps whispering, "Nevermore."

In a year or two, it will be Stem's turn, but for now, it's all about Grace.

"Like I said," Grace says, "I'm hoping you won't try to shoot me down now, but just let me inch my way out, and I promise I'll watch you from above, if you can just, Starlinsky, keep out of trouble...watch out for wayward women who've been dreaming dreams of you."

She's looking down now, and rising, dancing on the tops of trees, she is—and how she loved to climb a tree just to look down at the world and sideways, too, and just breathe there, at the top of a tree in New Jersey. For God's sake, you could see the George Washington Bridge on a good day, and you could imagine whales swimming in all the gullies, which might just happen when the polar ice caps melt and the ocean takes over and delivers us from all this evil.

END

Acknowledgments

More than forty years have elapsed since the first version of this book appeared on the transoms of New York publishers. How grateful I am to DarkWinter Press and Suzanne Craig-Whytock for taking the chance with it—albeit much revised—but especially now, when those who run our country have placed both our nearest neighbors on alert. I am also grateful to my then literary agent, Charlotte Sheedy, who tried to send off this first version in 1981, but who rightly predicted that I would never be published with Ronald Reagan in the White House.

I am grateful, as well, to the members of my dissertation committee at Ohio University, chaired by none other than the powerful and prolific South African writer, Zakes Mda, who, some twelve or so years ago—muddled through a second incarnation of the manuscript that morphed into a monster saddled with more than a hundred footnotes, along with a critical introduction that I titled "Kissing the Corpse."

I should also mention CAPS (Creative Arts Public Service Program)—the grant from New York State that I received in 1982 for what was then the first two chapters of this book, that encouraged me to ask Woodie King, Jr. if I might do a reading at New Federal Theatre. I could read, he said, but I would have to go through my fiction and craft shorter passages, which led to his production, three years later, of my one woman show: 'Once upon the Present Time.' While the first two chapters of the original book were taken by *The North Atlantic Review* in 2002, some of the poems formed from those "passages" appeared in *UCity Review* in 2023 and this year in *JudithMagazine*—and are forthcoming in the children's book of poetry titled *Did You Kiss A Cat Today???*

Enormous thanks to John Irving for your generous and iconic Foreword.

Similarly, to Philip Henry Allen, for the use of your gorgeous painting, *Carmine Street*.

Also—much gratitude to my brother-in-law, Jeff Wong, for the magic of your artistry and expertise with the cover.

I wish to thank many people for their emotional, and even financial, support. In addition to the writers' residences, including Wellspring House, Sundress Academy, Writing By Writers, and Tiffany Farm Writer's Retreat, I'm grateful to a number of families who hosted me, who offered food and shelter, and so important—who read my work—and we're talking more than the forty years: Claudia Liu and David Calicchio and Robin Bourjaily and their families certainly top this list, along with my sisters, Judith Gampel and Debora Fields and their families, and my husband, Erwin Wong, who says I am his way of supporting the arts.

I'm grateful to Susanmerrie Hellerer and her willingness to read one novel after another after another, when our world was Greenwich Village, and my writing a veritable secret. I am also thankful to Kathy Robbins for reading every novel for which I queried her.

Much gratitude for dear friends and family who kept the faith— and more—among whom are Cheryl and Eric Olsen, Catherine Gammon, Diane Stevenson, Cornelia Guest, Louie Skipper, Anita Garner, Mallary Tytel, Eve Weiss, Kami Seligman, Lisa Edwards, Barbara Porceddu, Jim Berger, Janice Buckner, Thalia Greenhalgh, Julian Müller, Constance Barrett, the Zabitz family, Lisi Tribble, Dorit Netzer, Frédérique Keller, Robin Bienkowski Kreismer, Maryellen Rothberg; and especially during the last few years, the Fieldings and Pamela Salant, at Canada Lake, who have kept me sane.

Many thanks to my Athens, Ohio people: Dominica Adamova, Marlene de la Cruz-Guzman, Iver Arnegard, and Alison Stine.

My thanks to Joan Connor and Janis Butler Holm and Lucy Wang.

My thanks to Diana Colpitts, to Paris L. Simms, and to Zelda Cohen.

My thanks to Liz Posner and Roger Sheffer, my beta readers.

As for the rest, especially those who would rather not have their names in print—thank you—you know who you are.

To my children, David & Eliza—I thank you for your understanding and your inspiration, and your pure being-in-the world.

And, finally, to my parents: if only you were here to see what's become of the many seeds you've planted.

About The Author

Twice a Pushcart Prize nominee, Geri Lipschultz has published in *Terrain, World Literature Today, the Rumpus, Ms, The Toat, The New York Times, Black Warrior Review, College English, and many others.* Her *work appears in Pearson's Literature: Introduction to Reading and Writing,* and in Spuyten Duyvil's *Wreckage of Reason II.* She has an MFA from Iowa and a Ph.D. from Ohio University. She currently teaches writing at Borough of Manhattan Community College. She received a Creative Artist Public Service (C.A.P.S.) fellowship from New York State. Her one-woman show was produced in New York City by Woodie King, Jr. She is one of three writers for the children's book of poems, *Did You Kiss a Cat Today???* (which may be pre-ordered on Amazon).